FAULT LINE

www.transworldbooks.co.uk

For more information on Robert Goddard and his books, see his website at www.robertgoddardbooks.co.uk

FAULT LINE

Robert Goddard

BANTAM PRESS

LONDON · TORONTO · SYDNEY · AUCKLAND · JOHANNESBURG

TRANSWORLD PUBLISHERS
61–63 Uxbridge Road, London W5 5SA
A Random House Group Company
www.transworldbooks.co.uk

First published in Great Britain
in 2012 by Bantam Press
an imprint of Transworld Publishers

A CIP catalogue record for this book
is available from the British Library.

ISBNs 9780593065204 (cased)
9780593065211 (tpb)

Typeset in 11/14.25pt Tmes New Roman by
Falcon Oast Graphic Art Ltd.
Printed and bound in Great Britain by
Clays Ltd, Bungay, Suffolk

2 4 6 8 10 9 7 5 3 1

FAULT LINE

The Wren family in July 1968

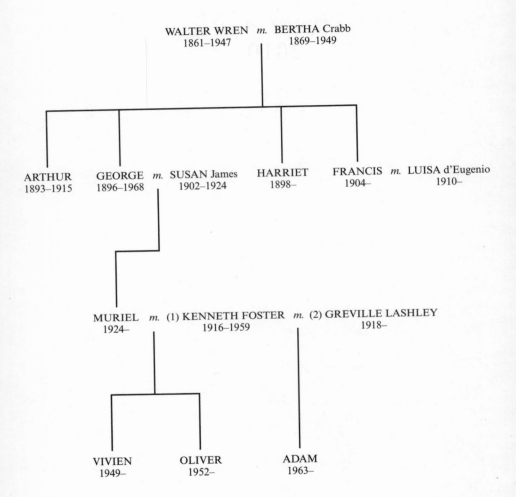

WALTER WREN *m.* BERTHA Crabb
1861–1947   1869–1949

ARTHUR   GEORGE *m.* SUSAN James   HARRIET   FRANCIS *m.* LUISA d'Eugenio
1893–1915   1896–1968   1902–1924   1898–   1904–   1910–

MURIEL   *m.* (1) KENNETH FOSTER   *m.* (2) GREVILLE LASHLEY
1924–   1916–1959   1918–

VIVIEN   OLIVER   ADAM
1949–   1952–   1963–

2010

ONE

I wasn't a frequent visitor to Presley Beaumont's office. I wasn't a frequent visitor to Intercontinental Kaolins' Augusta HQ at all. For years I'd been a field man, happy to steer clear of head office number-crunching. I remembered IK's base in Sandersville and preferred it (by a long way) to the anonymous tower of angular steel and tinted glass that was our new centre of operations.

Our new centre? *Theirs*, I'd soon be able to say. I'd handed in my notice. I was on my way out. Resigning or retiring? You could take your pick. Either way, I was leaving.

But not, apparently, as quickly and quietly as my line manager had led me to expect. He'd supposed – I'd supposed – that my three months' notice would be waived; that I'd be seen off swiftly with a back-slap and a cheque in lieu: the travelator of working life moving on, with someone else stepping on at the start just as I stepped off at the end.

Then the call had come from the HR director: Beaumont wanted to see me before anything was finalized. There were 'issues he wanted to address'. What might they be? No point asking. I knew that even as I asked.

I'd worked for Beaumont's father. A good man. I'd said a few words at his funeral that came from the heart. The son was smoother, smarter, *sleeker*. I didn't like him. I certainly didn't trust him. He probably knew that – though, naturally, neither of us was ever likely to admit as much.

He'd put on some weight since I'd last seen him. But his tailor had kept pace effortlessly. The suit was a work of art, celebrated in shimmering fibre-notes that threw crimson in among the bronze. His smile was broad, his handshake firm. The extra poundage made him look younger than ever, puffing out his babyish complexion. He clearly thought he was looking good.

'Can we get you some coffee, Jonathan?' he enquired in an amiable tone.

'Will I have time to drink it, Presley?' I countered. 'I mean, it's good of you to call me in for a parting word, but I know how busy you are.'

'There's time.' The smile stiffened fractionally. 'Sit down.'

We took our seats either side of his vast and virtually empty desk. He leant back in his ergonomically over-designed chair and extended an arm to flick an intercom switch. 'Fix us some coffee, would you, Beth? I believe Jonathan takes his black.'

'I'm impressed you remember that.'

He smiled. 'It is impressive, I agree.'

Someone once said to me he thought Presley smiled a lot just to remind you he had teeth. Expensive teeth, by the look of them.

'I was surprised to hear you were planning to leave us, Jonathan, I surely was.'

'I turned sixty last October. Time to come in out of the weather.'

'We could have fixed you up with something less physically arduous here, if that was the problem.'

'Coast down to retirement behind a desk, you mean?'

'Exactly. Not one as big as this, of course.' He chuckled.

'Naturally not.'

A pause, inching towards awkwardness. Then he said: 'I heard you'd expressed . . . reservations . . . about the Rio Tocaru project.'

Reservations? You certainly could call them that. The Amazon Basin represented the future of Intercontinental Kaolins in particular and the china clay industry in general. It was going to be a bigger source than Georgia and South Carolina. It was already bigger than Devon and Cornwall. But extraction involved deforestation – a lot of it. I'd overseen much of the geological research that had taken IK into Brazil in the first place. I couldn't deny the part I'd played. But I could end my involvement before any more rain forest was strip-mined out of existence. It was just about all I could do.

'Not going green in your old age, are you, Jonathan?'

'Late middle age at worst is how I like to think of sixty.'

'That's probably—'

He broke off as Beth entered with the coffee. There was a grinning flurry of three-way small talk as the tray was set down. Then she was gone, leaving Presley to eye me, still smiling, over the rim of his cup.

His expression planted a question in my mind. We'd locked horns a few times over the years. So, were his memories of those times the same as mine? Had he forgotten more than I had – or less? And which of us did the answer hand the advantage to?

'Any reservations I may have are irrelevant,' I said, after a cautious sip of coffee. 'I'm out of the game.'

'Not yet.'

'Surely you aren't going to insist on me working out my notice?'

'I'm not proposing to insist on anything.'

'Then . . . why the summons?'

'Summons? Is that how it came across?'

'Pretty much.'

'Well, I'm sorry. Communications glitch. You know how it is.'

I did know. That was why I didn't believe there'd been a glitch. 'Is there something I can do for you, Presley?' I matched him smile for smile. 'Before I go.'

'Not for me.' He raised his eyebrows and spread his arms expansively, disowning responsibility. 'I'm just the messenger.'

'And who's the message from?'

A beat, as he let me wait for his reply. Then: 'The old man.'

I should have known. There was only one person in Presley's world he'd be carrying a message for. The old man. Greville Lashley, former chairman, officially retired, yet still not quite out of touch. And he never would be while he lived. Everyone

5

who knew him knew that. And I, for my sins, knew him well.

'It's the damnedest thing, Jonathan. I got the word from him to call you on the same day I heard you were leaving us. Seems you'd have got a break from Rio Tocaru anyway. Without having to do anything as drastic as resigning.'

'Unfortunately, I have resigned. So—'

'You can wrap this assignment up within a few weeks, that would be my guess. Well, *his* guess, I should say. I apprised him of your . . . pending retirement. And he said, "There's time for him to do one last job for me." You should be flattered. I got the feeling there's no one else he'd trust to do it.'

Trust was hard to win from Greville Lashley. And I didn't fool myself for a minute I'd ever won it. But, then, who had? Maybe that was the point. It wasn't that there was no one else he trusted. There was just no one else at all. 'What's the job?' I asked warily.

'Has word reached you about the old man's vanity project?'

'His *what*?'

'A few months ago, he asked the board to commission a history of the company. Well, both companies until the merger. CCC *and* NAK.' Cornish China Clays and North American Kaolins were IK's forebears. I couldn't for a moment imagine why Greville should want their corporate paths documented. It would amount, in many ways, to his own professional biography, something I'd have expected him to do his level best to prevent ever seeing the light of day. But maybe, just maybe, extreme old age was chipping away at his reticence. 'So, we set it up for him. Hired a suitable historian. Fay Whitworth. *Doctor* Fay Whitworth. Bristol University. Gave her all the access she needed and let her get on with it.'

'I've heard nothing about this.'

'No. Well, no particular reason you should have, I suppose. She hasn't touched the NAK side of things yet. Or anything post-merger. To be honest, I'm not sure she ever will. *That's* the problem.'

'Meaning what, exactly?'

Presley's smile faded. 'She claims whole chunks of CCC records from the nineteen fifties and sixties have gone missing. They should be in the basement in St Austell – but they aren't. Anyhow, the perfectionist doctor says she can't make any further progress without them. She's effectively gone on strike. The old man wants you to get her back to work.'

'How?'

The smile was restored. 'Find the missing records, I suppose. Between you and me, Jonathan, I don't care whether this history ever gets written or not. But the old man cares. So, we need to look as if we care too.'

'Maybe you need to, Presley. I don't see how that applies to me.'

'Really? You disappoint me.'

'But I'm sure I don't surprise you.'

He gave a pained frown, as if baffled by my uncooperative attitude. 'I'm going to have to insist, Jonathan. It's in your contract. "Such other duties as the chairman may at his discretion ask you to perform from time to time". This is one of those times. And you wouldn't want to put yourself in breach a few months away from your pension, now would you? That would be . . . kind of stupid, don't you think?'

It would be stupid, of course. But then chasing after missing company records from forty or fifty years ago didn't sound very sensible either. Casting my mind back to my earliest involvement with Cornish China Clays, in 1968, I felt a shiver of apprehension. That period was surely a book Greville Lashley should want to keep firmly closed. What was going on inside the old man's mind? 'Maybe I ought to talk to Greville about this, Presley.'

In Presley's eyes there was a gleam of something close to pity. 'I suggested that myself. He said there was no need. You were just to . . . deal with the problem as you saw fit. We've scheduled a meeting for you with Doctor Whitworth, day after tomorrow. Beth has the details.'

'The day after tomorrow?'

'The sooner you go, the sooner you can get the job done and start planning your retirement.' Presley drained his coffee and glanced at his preposterously bulbous wristwatch. 'Now, I need

7

to move my day along, so I'm afraid we're going to have to leave it there. I can tell the old man you're on the case, can't I, Jonathan?'

There could be only one answer to Presley's question. I would be on the case. Not because of a clause in my contract. But because, like Greville Lashley, I'd have trusted no one else to find out what was really going on. I was uniquely qualified for the task, as the old man well knew. And for a host of reasons – many of which he was familiar with – I was bound to accept it. At his contriving, a mystery I thought I'd put behind me had tapped me on the shoulder. And I had no choice, as he must clearly have understood, but to turn and face it.

1968

TWO

Memories are more than recollected experiences. They're displacements of ourselves in time and space. They're events our younger self witnessed and participated in, recalled by an older self who often wonders if he's truly the same person. They're visions of people we once knew. And, bewilderingly, we are one of those people.

When I left St Austell Grammar School in July 1968, I was well aware my life was entering a new phase. A new and exciting one, if my hopes for it were to be fulfilled. The world was changing in big, mind-expanding ways. The old order was crumbling. And I liked the sound of what was reputedly replacing it – liberation in every kind of beguiling form.

But in St Austell all that was just rumour – second- or third-hand accounts of glamorous, even dangerous, events far, far away. For first-hand experience, you had to leave. And that was exactly what I was planning to do. A place at LSE awaited me in September. London was where I was confident I'd find everything – including myself.

Ironically, London was where I was actually from. But we'd moved to Cornwall when I was two, so I had no memories of my birthplace. The bank had offered my father a branch managership and west we'd gone. Managership of a bigger branch elsewhere had failed to follow. I could see in him the narrowness of vision his

11

bosses had probably seen too. If he'd ever thought of St Austell as a stepping stone to greater things, he'd stopped thinking that way by the time I was old enough to understand him.

We'd moved into a brand-new three-bedroom semi in Eastbourne Road, between the cemetery and the bypass, on the southern edge of town. Sixteen years later, we were still there, or at least Mum and Dad were. In my mind, I was already packed and ready to go. Dad had tried gently to steer me towards engineering or geology degree courses, on the grounds they would help me get a job in the china clay industry back in Cornwall after I'd graduated. I'd opted for economics because a job in the china clay industry was the last thing I aspired to. I didn't want to think about returning to Cornwall. I wanted to think about getting out and staying out.

As a child, I believed the spoil heaps on the horizon north of St Austell were natural formations. Later I understood that St Austell's hinterland was entirely man-made: a weird, out-of-scale moonscape of vast pits worked by huge machines that looked no bigger than my Dinky toys when seen from above; of conical waste mountains dwarfing the terraces of labourers' cottages; of gleaming blue-green lakes in flooded pits and drying sheds as big as cathedrals; of long, lumbering trainloads of clay trucks heading for Par Docks while Mum and Dad and I sat in the Morris Minor at the level crossing in St Blazey, watching them slowly pass. The china clay blew in storms of fine dust on dry, windy days, or flowed in milky slews of mud on wet ones. It curdled the rivers and bleached the land. It was everywhere.

It was also every other local resident's employer. St Austell wasn't just a china clay town. It was *the* china clay town. The industry was dominated by one company, Cornish China Clays, operating out of a large, newly built headquarters easily visible from the playing fields of the grammar school. While I was in the sixth form, we were taken to see the wonders of their IBM computer and tour their research laboratories. We met assorted science graduates recruited from all over the country. The message was clear: this was a modern, efficient, innovative business we should think seriously about getting involved in. Absolutely. Just a pity it was in St Austell. Where I had no intention of remaining.

A summer job with CCC sounded too much like being sucked in to me, so, to raise money for the wild time I was determined to have in London, I looked elsewhere. Walter Wren & Co. were a china clay firm right enough, but much smaller and older-fashioned than CCC. And their advert in the *Cornish Guardian* made it clear the vacancy in their office was menial *and* temporary – the perfect combination, as far as I was concerned. Two months would suit them as well as me. I started the job ten days after the end of term.

Wren's operated out of dilapidated premises in East Hill. Not only were there no research labs or computers, there was little sign that anything much had changed since before the war. Maurice Rowe, the lugubrious, chain-smoking head of accounts I was at the beck and call of, informed me before the end of my first week that the company would be swallowed by CCC sooner or later, so the directors saw no sense in investing in new equipment or procedures. 'We're not exactly what you'd call go-ahead.'

That was a serious understatement. The accounts office functioned on manual typewriters, double carbon copies and wooden filing cabinets. It was fortunate for me I didn't have to spend all day every day there choking on Rowe's cigarette smoke. There were errands to be run at the so-called shipping office, attached to the firm's drying shed near the harbour a mile away at Charlestown. I never had to be asked twice to take the van down there. The place was every bit as antiquated as East Hill, but livelier, thanks to all the loading and unloading that went on around it.

Par Docks was CCC territory, so Wren's and a few other small firms used Charlestown for their shipments. There was no rail access, the harbour was tiny and facilities hadn't been upgraded since the village was built by local landowner Charles Rashleigh at the end of the eighteenth century. But it was a pretty spot when the sun shone and the sea sparkled. I spent as much time there as I could contrive. Jim Turner, the shipping manager, cordially hated

Maurice Rowe, so took pleasure in keeping me hanging around. And I never put up much resistance.

Most of the staff were at least twenty years older than I was and behaved as if the gap was even bigger. Exceptions included Polly Hodge, the long-legged accounts typist, who tormented all the men in the office with her micro-mini-skirts but was so wonderfully brainless she never realized it, and Peter Newlove, who was exactly my age and had joined Wren's at fifteen straight from school (secondary modern, in his case). A whippety lad with a Ringo Starr moustache and an insatiable appetite for Polo mints, he viewed me with a mixture of awe and resentment. University and London were both unimaginable concepts to him. He cultivated me, I think, in the hope that I'd invite him to visit me in the big city after I'd left Wren's. Naturally, there was no chance I'd ever do that. But he was amusing company during lunchtime forays to his favourite pub, the General Wolfe, at the other end of Fore Street.

Pete pretended not to care what would become of him in a merger with CCC, but his detailed knowledge of feuds and alliances in the Wren family suggested he was pondering the future with some anxiety. George Wren, son of the original Walter, had died a few months previously. His son-in-law, Greville Lashley, was now cock of the walk and was rumoured to be cosying up to the CCC board for all he was worth. He'd married Muriel, George's daughter and only child, after the death of her first husband, Ken Foster. 'Suicide,' Pete gleefully informed me, as if he had some personal knowledge of the event, whereas under questioning he admitted it had happened when he was still at junior school.

Further rumour had it that old George had let the firm's finances deteriorate to the point where a takeover by CCC was the only way to avoid bankruptcy. Pete was all for it. So were most of the staff, according to him. 'Provided we get to keep our jobs.' There was the rub. Lashley would be negotiating to protect himself and the family, not the staff. There was no way to tell how many of them would make it to the promised land with him.

Greville Lashley struck me as a clever, quick-thinking man doing his best in difficult circumstances. Tall, slim and darkly handsome,

14

with distinguished wartime service in the RAF behind him, he always dressed immaculately and drove a mirror-polished Jag. If he was staring ruin in the face, you'd never have known it. But that, according to Pete, was just an act. 'This year's make or break – for him *and* us.'

The problem, apparently, was that the split of shareholdings in the family meant Lashley couldn't put through any deal he succeeded in negotiating without support from one of George Wren's two surviving siblings. There was a brother, Francis, who lived abroad and a sister, Harriet, who shared Nanstrassoe House, the Wren residence in Carlyon Road, with Greville and Muriel Lashley, their young son and Muriel's two children by her first marriage. Harriet was believed to be opposed to a takeover. Francis's opinion wasn't known.

None of this was of more than idle interest to me. Unlike Pete and his co-workers, I had no stake in what happened. I'd soon be on my way to a place where the fate of a small Cornish china clay company was supremely unimportant. Still, it was impossible not to be aware of the intrigue and uncertainty that lay behind the workaday routines at Walter Wren & Co. and Pete made sure I was kept informed about what was reckoned to be going on.

The consensus was that a crisis was looming. But how long it would go on merely looming was unclear. 'You'll probably have left by the time it comes to a crunch,' Pete speculated. 'But don't worry. I'll tell you all about it when you come home for Christmas.' In my own mind, I felt sure I wouldn't be the least bit interested by then. I'd forget all about Walter Wren & Co. as soon as I got on the train to London on Sunday, 22 September. Oh yes. I already knew the date when I'd be putting St Austell behind me. And it couldn't come fast enough.

The reality, of course, was that it would come when it came and no sooner. Meanwhile, there was a summer to be enjoyed and I was going to do my best to enjoy it, humdrum working days notwithstanding. And, as it turned out, the crisis Pete had predicted didn't wait until after I'd gone to break.

*

The first sign of its imminence came one damp Tuesday afternoon in the middle of August, though at the time its significance was lost on me. I'd just driven back in the van from Charlestown. As I turned into the small yard behind Wren's, I had to slam on the brakes to avoid a collision with a boy who darted out of the back door of the offices and ran straight across my path, heading for the road. He didn't even seem to notice me and was gone in a flash. All I remembered of him was jeans, a white shirt and a mop of blond hair. But that description was enough to identify him in Accounts and to elicit a frisson of unease that I found distinctly puzzling.

'Oliver Foster,' Maurice tartly informed me. Ah, of course. One of the two children of Muriel Lashley's first marriage. He'd looked about fifteen, which probably made sense. 'He's been making a nuisance of himself. Don't encourage him. He's a pain in the neck.'

Mutterings from Pete while we were at the tea urn later suggested there was more to be learnt for the price of a lager and lime (his drink of choice) at the General Wolfe at opening time. As he'd probably calculated, I was bored enough to relish any gossip. So, just a little after opening time, off we went.

Oliver and his sister, Vivien, had been sent to private boarding schools outside the county. Not much was seen of them in St Austell. They were both home for the summer and Vivien was about to go up to Cambridge. 'That outranks London, doesn't it, Jon?' Pete observed. (I'd tried to stop him calling me Jon, which no one else did, without success.) 'Her and Olly are a brainy pair, apparently.'

Exactly what Oliver might be applying his brain to at Wren's was unclear, but evidently Lashley had sent his secretary, the formidable Joan Winkworth, down to the basement, where records dating back to the company's formation in 1895 were stored, to fetch something shortly after his return from lunch. Joan had come upon young Oliver searching through the files. He'd scooted off without explanation. She'd reported back to Lashley, who'd reacted by issuing an instruction that the basement door should be kept locked in future, with the key in Joan's keeping, and emphasizing that no non-staff members were to be allowed the run of the premises. By implication, the ban applied to his stepson as much as to anyone else.

'I guess Olly came back to finish doing whatever it was Joan interrupted, only to find he was locked out,' reasoned Pete. 'He must have been leaving again when you nearly ran him over.'

'But what would he have been after in the basement?' I asked. I couldn't imagine the dusty archives of the family firm holding any sort of attraction for a teenage boy when there were girls in bikinis to be ogled all day down at the Lido swimming pool.

'Beats me,' Pete admitted. 'But some people reckon he's not right in the head on account of witnessing his father's suicide.'

'He witnessed it?'

'Well, more or less. Ken Foster drove out to Goss Moor, parked at the end of some track and gassed himself in his car. You know – tube through the window from the exhaust. That's how he topped himself. What he didn't realize, though, was that Olly had stowed away in the boot. Some kind of prank. He was only seven. Anyway, he was still in the boot when a pair of hikers came across the car. Too late for Ken. I'm not sure what state Olly was in by then. But it's bound to have affected him, isn't it?'

I conceded it might have. But that still didn't explain a clandestine visit to the basement. And why now, nine years after his father's death?

'Maybe it's something to do with the merger,' Pete suggested. 'Maybe Olly's worried about being robbed of his inheritance.'

Incredulity at the idea that anyone of our generation might want to inherit an outfit like Walter Wren & Co. must have been written on my face.

'It's all right for you,' Pete complained, scowling at me. 'Some of us need to earn a wage. Wren's isn't so bad.'

'It's had its day, Pete. And if Oliver Foster doesn't understand that, then he really isn't right in the head.'

I gave no further thought to Oliver Foster's state of mind until Thursday, when I found myself down at Charlestown again. Jim Turner had borrowed me to clear a backlog of paperwork, which involved sorting several months' worth of shipping orders into first date, and then alphabetical, order. I needed some fresh air come lunchtime, so took my sandwiches down to the harbour wall and sat in the sunshine on the bollard at the end of the eastern mole.

There were a few tourists wandering around taking snaps of the quaint old port, but it was otherwise a quiet day in Charlestown, with no loading in progress in the dock. I had the harbour wall to myself.

But it didn't stay that way. I'd just lit a cigarette when I heard a voice behind me. 'Can I buy one of those from you?' The accent was cultured, the tone casual.

I looked round to find Oliver Foster gazing vacantly at me. He was dressed as he had been the previous day, in white shirt, jeans and plimsolls, with the addition of a green sweater tied round his waist. His hands were thrust into his pockets and his face wore an expression of heavy-lidded detachment. A high forehead made him look much older than I knew him to be, despite his unruly mass of blond hair.

'Well, can I? Would thruppence do it?' He fished a threepenny bit out of his pocket.

'You can have one for nothing.' I proffered the pack.

'OK.' He took a cigarette, peering at the label as he did so. 'Ah. The international passport to smoking pleasure.' He chuckled, though whether at his own ability to recite Peter Stuyvesant's advertising motto or my pretentiousness at choosing the brand it was hard to tell.

He flourished a silver lighter. There were some initials inscribed on it that looked like *K. L. F.* I wondered if it had belonged to his father. He took a long first draw on the cigarette and gazed past me out to sea.

'I nearly drove into you the day before yesterday,' I said, reckoning that would get his attention.

It wasn't immediately obvious I'd succeeded. But after a long pause he said, 'So, you work at Wren's.'

'Yes. Just for the summer. Then I'm off to university.'

'Where?'

'London.'

'Lucky you.'

'You're Oliver Foster, aren't you?'

'Apparently.'

'Jonathan Kellaway.' I offered my hand.

He smiled, amused, apparently, by the quaintness of the gesture. But he consented to a handshake. 'How do you do, Jonathan?' He was a couple of years younger than I was, but it was hard to believe. He already seemed to be an adult – mature, self-possessed, cynical even. Pose or not, it was impressive in its own way.

'Been for a walk?'

'You could say that. Been visiting. At the Carlyon Bay.' I took him to mean the premier hotel of the neighbourhood, a mile or so along the coast. 'Fancied a stroll afterwards. Told my chauffeuse to pick me up here.'

'Your chauffeuse?'

'Sister. She'll be here soon. Very reliable, my sister.'

'How old is she?'

'Nineteen. She's off to university as well.'

'Really. Which one?' (I knew the answer, of course, thanks to Pete.)

'Not London.' Oliver grinned. 'Ah, here's the chariot.' He pointed with his cigarette towards a bright yellow Mini heading down the road on the other side of the dock. It pulled up at the landward end of the western mole, separated from us by the harbour mouth. A blonde-haired girl climbed out and started walking along the mole towards us. She was wearing a white safari-suit, dazzlingly bright in the sunshine, with several bead necklaces. Large, circular sunglasses and her long, breeze-ruffled hair gave her a glamorous, sophisticated look. Her world, I felt sure, was exactly the one I aimed to enter as soon as I left St Austell.

But the impression she made on me didn't stop at glamour and sophistication. As she neared the curved end of the mole, with just the narrow mouth of the harbour between us, she pushed her sunglasses up on to her forehead – high, like her brother's – and smiled.

She was beautiful. That was the realization that hit me almost like a blow. Not pretty or sexy or attractive, or, rather, all of those things with some other magical ingredient thrown in: the shape of her mouth, the sparkle of her blue, blue eyes, the hint of mystery as well as allure in her gaze. She was quite extraordinarily beautiful. She was the sort of girl I'd dreamt of meeting in Paris or Venice or San Francisco. And here she was, not half a world of fantasies away, but standing in front of me, on the harbour wall at Charlestown, in Cornwall.

'Coming home?' she called across to Oliver, her voice soft and slightly husky.

'Glad to see you dragged yourself away,' he replied.

'You said you'd want picking up, so here I am. Are you coming?'

'Guess so. But say hello to Jonathan here before we go. He's working at Wren's until he starts at university. Not Cambridge. But still university. This is my sister Vivien, Jonathan.'

'Hello,' I said, painfully aware of how sheepish I sounded. But great beauty, as Vivien must have been aware, is an intimidating thing.

'Hello, Jonathan,' she responded, smiling at me briefly, before returning her attention to Oliver. 'Now, can we go?'

And that was how we first met, Vivien Foster and I. I watched her walk back along the mole to her car while Oliver headed towards the bridge across the dock gate. She never once glanced round at me, though she cast several glances in her brother's direction. It was pretty clear she'd barely noticed me. But I'd noticed her. And I was already certain I'd never forget her.

How right I was.

20

THREE

I couldn't stop thinking about Vivien Foster for the rest of the day. I wanted to see her again – I longed to see her again – but I knew that wouldn't be easy. Even if I could engineer an encounter, I suspected she'd give me the brush-off if I asked her for a date. The fleeting glance I'd got from her suggested she'd judged me as barely more interesting than the bollard I'd been sitting on.

By the following morning, I'd more or less abandoned the idea. I set off for work in a glum mood, Mum's parting report of a fine weather forecast for the weekend doing nothing to lift my spirits. 'We'll probably go to the beach hut on Sunday.' Poor old Mum. I think she genuinely believed what I'd enjoyed as a twelve-year-old I'd still enjoy at eighteen.

The walk to Wren's was generally as uneventful as it was short, involving a cut through the cemetery to Alexandra Road. Not so that morning, however. As I approached the cemetery gate, I was astonished to see Oliver Foster leaning against it, puffing at a cigarette. He looked cold, with the collar of his thin windcheater pulled up round his neck. It was immediately obvious he'd been waiting for me.

'Hello, Jonathan,' he said with a smile.

'Hello. What are you doing here?'

'I wanted to talk to you.' He pulled the gate open to let me through. 'Smoke?' He produced a pack. 'Not Peter Stuyvesant, I'm afraid.'

'Never mind. Thanks.' I took one and he gave me a light. 'Been waiting for me long?'

'Ten minutes or so.'

'How did you know where I live?'

'No other Kellaways with a St Austell phone number.'

'But you didn't want to phone me.'

'Thought face to face would work better.'

'Better for what?'

'Take a walk with me and I'll explain.' He glanced at his wrist-watch. 'Don't worry, I won't make you late for work.'

'I'm not worried.'

'Good.' He led the way at a dawdling pace along one of the paths between the graves. As far as I could see, we had the cemetery to ourselves – unless you counted its permanent occupants.

'What's this about, Oliver?'

'I need you to do me a favour. Naturally, I'll do you one in return.'

'What kind of favour?'

'Well, I reckon you'd like to get to know my sister. I could fix that for you.'

I'd meant what favour he wanted from me, not what favour he could offer me. Already, I'd been outmanoeuvred. 'What makes you think I want to get to know your sister?' I asked cagily.

'All the guys do. Don't pretend you don't. It was obvious, anyway.'

'How?'

'It just was. But you won't get anywhere with her without my help.'

The fact that I believed him was hugely irritating, but I was determined not to show it. 'Maybe I don't need a go-between.'

'You won't get anywhere with her on your own. You're just not in her league. Those who are generally don't get anywhere either. Viv's very . . . choosy.'

'In that case, I doubt she'd let her kid brother do the choosing for her.'

'She wouldn't know I was doing it. She's very protective towards me. You saw how she came to pick me up yesterday. She worries about me, you see. And one of the things she worries about is that I don't have any friends. So, if she thought you were my friend, she'd want to get to know you. You'd have a real chance with her. It's actually the only chance you'll get.'

How satisfying it would be, I thought, to prove him wrong about that. How satisfying, but how improbable. 'Let's just say, for the sake of argument, that I—'

'Do you play chess?'

The question literally stopped me in my tracks. 'Chess?'

'Well, do you?'

I shrugged. 'Sort of.'

'Sort of will have to do. Come to the house Sunday morning around half ten. We'll play a few games. I'll treat you like the big brother I've never had. That'll get Viv's attention. I guarantee it.' He giggled, childishly, reminding me of what was so easy to forget: how young he was. Did I play chess? There was certainly no room to doubt he did.

I knew the sensible thing to do was to turn him down. But it wasn't just the opportunity to meet his sister on her home ground that lured me on. There was also a come-hither hint of mystery about their family that I couldn't resist. Sunday morning at Nanstrassoe House was a far more enticing prospect than anything else a weekend in St Austell was likely to throw my way. Oliver knew that, of course.

'You haven't told me yet what you want me to do in return for this invitation, Oliver,' I said levelly.

'You'll come, then?'

I nodded. 'Yes. I'll come.'

'Good. In that case, this is for you.' He pulled something wrapped in a brown-paper bag out of his pocket and handed it to me.

'What's this?' It was the size and shape of a half-pound pack of butter and weighed about the same too.

'A cake of soap.' He grinned. 'Carefully chosen soap. Just the right consistency. Not too hard. Not too soft. I've cut it in half lengthways. You should get a perfect impression if you compress the key between the two halves.'

'What key?'

I didn't really need to ask. It was only a few days since he'd been locked out of Wren's basement. But even so I could hardly believe he was going to such lengths to gain entry.

'I need access to Wren's records, Jonathan. Greville isn't going to stop me just by locking a door.'

'What are you looking for?'

He smiled. 'It's best if you don't know. Best if no one knows. Until I'm ready.'

I was intrigued. There was no denying it. Intrigued *and* tantalized. A boring holiday job had suddenly blossomed into something much more interesting.

'I need an impression sharp enough for a locksmith to cut a copy from.' Yes. He did. And I wondered what he was offering that locksmith in return. Something else it was best for me not to know, probably. 'Think you can do it?'

'I don't see why not.'

'Good. It has to be done today, though. Bring it to me at the library this afternoon after work. I'll be in the reference section. But remember: no key, no game of chess; no game of chess, no introduction to Vivien. You get me?'

I assured him I did. But as I watched him walk away, leaving me to carry on to Wren & Co., cake of not-too-hard-not-too-soft soap stowed in my duffel bag, I acknowledged to myself that I didn't; I didn't get him at all.

But he got me.

I'd cooked up a cover story for needing to look through the records by the time I reached Wren's: a discrepancy I was trying to iron out for Jim Turner. With any luck, though, I wouldn't need to use it. I'd decided to stage my raid on the basement straight after the mid-morning coffee break, when Joan Winkworth was likely to be in one of her mellower moods. She'd arguably be even mellower after lunch, but it was Friday, so several pints with Pete at the

General Wolfe were virtually mandatory. I needed to be sober for this.

In the event, the whole thing went off with absurd simplicity. I got the loan of the key from Joan without having to proffer an explanation and, during a five-minute sojourn in the basement, produced what looked to me like a good enough impression for any competent locksmith to work with. Glancing round at the shelfloads of dusty box-files before I left, I wondered what Oliver could possibly want with them. But I reckoned he was right. It was best for me not to know. Certainly not if Vivien Foster was to be the reward for stifling my curiosity.

But on one point I didn't have to remain curious for long. Pete had news, eagerly imparted to me over his first lager and lime. His sister worked as a chambermaid at the Carlyon Bay Hotel. Among newly arrived guests were Francis Wren and his glamorous Italian wife, retired opera singer Luisa d'Eugenio.

So, the late George Wren's brother was in town. And he wasn't staying at Nanstrassoe House.

Now I knew what Oliver and Vivien had been doing prior to my encounter with them at Charlestown. They'd been paying a call on their great-uncle. I mentioned this to Pete, without of course going on to mention a second encounter with Oliver that very morning. Pete fed the information into the spicy mixture he was stirring of surmise and speculation. As he saw it, the Wren clan was gathering – none too cordially, given that Francis preferred a hotel to the family home. They were gathering to decide the future of Wren & Co. Nothing else could explain Francis's willingness to return to Cornwall only a matter of months after attending his brother's funeral. 'Let's face it, Carlyon Bay's not a patch on Capri, is it?' Pete reasoned, as if personally qualified to compare the two. 'He's here because he has to be.'

I didn't argue. It was probably true. But, naturally, Pete didn't stop there. 'Olly must have known he was coming. I bet that has something to do with whatever he was looking for in the basement. Francis worked in the company before the war, until about twenty years ago, y'know. Then he suddenly left. No one knows why. Maybe Olly's on the track of an answer.'

I couldn't see any mystery there myself. Francis had swapped Cornwall and the china clay business for Italy and a life of luxury with some Sophia Loren lookalike. Who wouldn't have? Not me. Not Pete either. Except that he maintained there were rumours of past scandals attached to Francis *and* his wife. 'The Wrens are a dark lot,' he assured me, spluttering the words through a mouthful of lager and crisps. 'Always have been.'

There was more evidence to support Pete's contention than he knew. My rendezvous with Oliver at the public library late that afternoon was a prime piece. I found him hunched over a bound set of *Cornish Guardian* back copies. He heaved the massive volume shut as I approached and pulled a chair back for me to sit down beside him.

The atmosphere was warm and torpid, dust-moted shafts of sunlight slanting down from the building's glass-panelled roof. There were only a couple of other readers in the reference section and they were both too far away to catch our whispered exchanges.

'How did it go?'

'Fine. Here it is.' I took the bag of soap out of my pocket and placed it directly in front of him. 'I think your locksmith will be pleased.'

'He better had. Otherwise you won't get past the door on Sunday.'

'There won't be a problem.'

'Good. Here's something to be going on with.' A book I hadn't noticed till now was lying face down on the table to his right. He turned it over and slid it across to me.

The cover illustration was of a chessboard set up for a game. The title above it was *Chess: A Novice's Guide*. 'Very funny,' I said ruefully.

'It's not a joke. You should borrow it. You don't want to look a total idiot on Sunday, do you?'

'Just how good at chess are you, Oliver?'

'Not as good as I'd like to be. But better than anyone I can find to play against. Ever heard of Bobby Fischer?'

'No.'

'He's a genius. Won what they call the game of the century when he was thirteen. You'll find the moves in that book. Just brilliant. He should be world champion.'

'Why isn't he?'

'Because he'll never compromise, never back down from what he thinks is right. I suppose that's what makes him such a great player.' Oliver thought about what he'd said for a moment, as if it had some particular significance for him. Then he pushed back his chair and stood up. 'I'm off.' He pocketed the bag of soap and picked up the newspaper volume. I spotted the dates it covered embossed on the spine: *July–Sept 1959*. And 1959, I recalled, was the year his father had died. 'Coming?'

'No. I'll . . . take a look at this first.' I held up *Chess: A Novice's Guide*.

'Good idea. See you Sunday, then.'

'Yeah. Sunday it is.'

He sloped off and I began leafing through the book. A few minutes later, I saw him through the window, wandering away along Carlyon Road, in the direction of Nanstrassoe House.

That was my signal to cut along to the enquiries desk and ask to see the volume he'd just returned. To win at chess, I reckoned you needed to study your opponent every bit as much as the game.

Luckily for me, Kenneth Foster had died in early July rather than late September. The *Cornish Guardian* of Thursday, 9 July 1959, carried a fuzzy photograph of him which struck me as an eerie preview of what Oliver would probably look like in middle age, beneath the headline **Local businessman found dead in car**. This was surely what Oliver had been reading – what he'd read many times before, if I was any judge.

27

Kenneth Foster, 43, a director of Walter Wren & Co. Ltd, one of St Austell's foremost china clay businesses, was found dead in his car, parked near the end of a rough track on Goss Moor, on Monday. Detective Inspector Hancock of Cornwall Police said the engine of the vehicle was running, with a tube feeding fumes from the exhaust into the car, when two hikers came upon the scene. They pulled Mr Foster from the car and attempted resuscitation, to no avail. An inquest into Mr Foster's death was opened and adjourned on Tuesday.

Detective Inspector Hancock added that Mr Foster's seven-year-old son, Oliver, was discovered in the boot of the car in a distressed condition. How the boy came to be there is presently unclear. His grandfather, George Wren, chairman and managing director of Walter Wren & Co., said the family was deeply shocked and saddened by Mr Foster's death and that nothing in his recent behaviour had prepared them for such an event.

Mr Foster was originally from Kent. He met his wife, Muriel Wren, during wartime service at RAF St Eval. They were married in 1945. He worked at Wren & Co. from then until his death.

I imagined what it must have been like for a seven-year-old boy to be pulled from the boot of his father's car and to see, as Oliver surely must have, his father's lifeless body stretched out at the side of the track – the exhaust fumes catching in his throat, tears filling his eyes, fear and panic gripping him. But who was I kidding? I couldn't really imagine what it must have been like. And I couldn't ask either. It was locked away in Oliver's mind. He wasn't letting go of it. The memory hadn't faded or lost its sting. It was there, raw and real. It was part of him. Just as it was part of whatever he was trying to accomplish now, nine summers later.

I leafed on through the volume and found a report of the inquest. It added little to the original article except a verdict of suicide and some words from the coroner that Oliver might, it struck me, have taken as a challenge, as soon as he was old enough to understand them. *'We cannot hope to discover what led Mr Foster to take such a desperate course. The truth will rest with him.'*

Or not, of course.

There were several large houses dotted along Carlyon Road. Most of them were, or had been, the residences of china clay magnates. There'd never been many other routes to wealth and status in St Austell. I walked as far as the pillared entrance to Nanstrassoe before heading home that evening. The drive to the house curved away past trees and shrubs that screened the building itself from view. All I could glimpse was a stout-chimneyed roof. There was nothing to see and less to learn – until Sunday.

FOUR

I gave some time to *Chess: A Novice's Guide* in the course of Saturday. It made me realize just what a novice I really was. I played through a few sample games, including Fischer's 'game of the century' against Donald Byrne in 1956, when he was thirteen. Poor old Byrne was all I could think. He just never saw that seventeenth move coming. Still, I consoled myself, chess was just a pretext. I was going to Nanstrassoe for other reasons altogether. As Oliver well knew. But Vivien didn't.

Sunday morning was quiet and gently sunny. I'd dressed to look as if I didn't care about appearances, though I'd actually taken a lot of care, of course. Casualness isn't easy to project when you don't feel casual. And I didn't. Not remotely.

I walked through the gates of Nanstrassoe a few minutes before 10.30 and headed along the drive. By now I was expecting nothing but a let-down of some kind. Vivien wouldn't be at home. Maybe Oliver wouldn't be either. The deal I had with him wasn't the sort I could actually enforce. He'd got what he wanted and I didn't know him well enough to tell if he could be trusted.

That self-pitying train of thought carried me nearly as far as the house, which came into view as I rounded the curve of the drive: a stolid rather than elegant three-storeyed Victorian building of ashlar stone with a pillared porch. A car was at that moment moving away from the porch: a maroon Rover, with a middle-aged woman at the wheel and an older woman next to her. Seeing me, the driver slowed. And an overweight Labrador who'd been watching their departure from a recumbent position jumped up and loped towards me, barking and wagging its tail.

The car halted beside me. The driver wound down her window. She was about my mother's age – mid-forties – but more chicly dressed than Mum could ever be, with a certain hauteur embedded in her features and bearing. She was Muriel Lashley. She had to be. The passenger, who peered at me curiously through small, round glasses, was a lot older, seventy or so, with a calm, peaceful face that seemed set for a smile, even though she wasn't actually smiling: Muriel's mother, perhaps? No. I remembered Pete had said Vivien and Oliver's grandparents were both dead. Her aunt, then? Harriet Wren? Yes. That fitted. She too was smartly dressed, albeit in a strange, slightly bohemian style mixing yellow tweed with a beret and vividly patterned scarf, whereas Muriel could have stepped straight out of a magazine fashion shoot for the maturer woman.

The Labrador had reached me by now and was amiably licking my hand as Muriel looked me up and down. 'Can I help you, young man?' she asked sceptically.

'Mrs Lashley?' I ventured.

'Yes.'

'Pleased to meet you. My name's Jonathan Kellaway. I'm a friend of Oliver's. He invited me over for a game of chess.'

'Really?'

'Wonders will never cease,' remarked Harriet, beaming at me.

'Oliver hasn't mentioned you,' said Muriel.

'But then he doesn't mention much at all, does he, dear?' put in Harriet, unhelpfully in her niece's opinion, to judge by the pursing of her lips.

'Is he in?' I asked airily.

'Oh yes,' said Harriet.

'Yes,' confirmed Muriel levelly. 'Yes, yes. Well, go along and see him, then. Enjoy your game.'

'Goodbye, Jonathan,' said Harriet as the car pulled away.

I went on patting the dog while the car thrumbled off along the

31

drive. But already he was losing interest. He didn't follow as I made my way to the porch and rapped the dolphin door-knocker.

The door was answered by a plumply curvaceous girl with black pigtailed hair and olive skin. Her ''Ello' carried some kind of Mediterranean accent. The au pair, I reckoned. Introducing myself as a friend of Oliver's seemed to surprise her as much as it had his mother. But it got me past the door. She directed me towards the drawing-room and called ahead of me. 'You 'ave a visitor, Oliver.'

The house was as Victorian inside as it was out, with lots of heavy curtains, murky oil paintings and flock wallpaper. The drawing-room was vast, but crammed, nonetheless, with fat-cushioned armchairs, bureaux, sideboards and cabinets. Sunlight flooding in through high windows relieved the gloom and made a halo of Oliver's fair hair as he lounged on a couch, flicking through the *Sunday Times* colour supplement. He didn't get up or even look in my direction. But he did consent to bid me a courteous good morning.

'Hello, Oliver. How are you?'

He flung down the magazine and looked at me almost challengingly. 'Bored. That's how I am.'

'Well, it's Sunday. What d'you expect?'

'You just missed Mother and Great-Aunt Harriet.'

'No. I met them as they were leaving, actually. Church?'

'Got it in one.'

'What about your . . . stepfather?'

'Golf.'

'And Vivien?'

'Not up yet. Well, not down yet.'

'When does she normally get up?'

Oliver smiled lopsidedly. 'She'll show herself around eleven. So, until then . . .' He swung his feet to the floor and waved me towards an armchair on the other side of the low table in front of him. There was a chessboard on the table, as yet bare of pieces. They were still in the box beside it. Oliver slid the lid half-open and unceremoniously dumped the white pieces on my side of the board. 'You can have white to start with.'

32

To start with? I didn't like the sound of that. But I didn't argue. 'Fine.'

But it wasn't fine, of course. Within a dozen moves, I was like Byrne against Fischer, heading for defeat. I had a terrible feeling some of Oliver's moves were identical to Fischer's in that famous game. I couldn't remember exactly, though I had no doubt Oliver remembered very well.

'The Gruenfeld Defence is a crackerjack, isn't it?'

'A favourite of Fischer's, presumably,' I sighed.

'Absolutely.'

'Maybe I'll be better off with black.'

'Maybe.'

We set the pieces up again. I pushed the queen's pawn two squares out. Oliver responded in kind. So far so safe.

Then I suddenly became aware that we were being watched. A little boy of five or six, dressed in a cowboy's outfit, complete with Stetson and gunbelt, was staring at me from a few yards away. His chubby cheeks and the fringe of golden hair visible beneath the brim of his Stetson gave him a cherubic appearance, but his set, stubborn frown and a gleam of hostility in his eyes spoilt the effect. He pulled out his plastic revolver and pointed it at me. 'Hands up,' he chirped.

I obeyed theatrically, but Oliver merely grimaced and said, 'Go away, Adam.'

'Hands up or I shoot.'

'Just go away.'

Adam didn't seem disposed to issue a second warning. He took aim at Oliver and pulled the trigger. A cap detonated, making me jump with surprise. But Oliver wasn't surprised at all. '*Maria*,' he bellowed, without looking up from the chessboard.

Adam had fired two more caps and added a cackling laugh before the au pair came hurrying into the room. 'Adam,' she called. 'Stop bozzering your brother.'

'Half-brother,' Oliver murmured.

'The varmint won't surrender,' Adam objected.

'I will,' I said, raising my hands again.

Adam glared at me. 'You don't matter.'

'Well, that puts me in my place.'

'Come wiz me, Adam,' said Maria, beckoning to him. 'You should be out of the 'ouse in the sunshine.'

Adam looked unpersuaded by the argument, but he went anyway, sticking out his tongue at his brother – *half*-brother – as he left.

'He hates me,' said Oliver neutrally as soon as we were alone again.

'He was just playing.'

'If you gave him a real gun, he'd be happy to shoot me.'

'Come off it.'

'It's true. But I shouldn't complain. The feeling's mutual.'

'You don't mean that.'

'Yes, I do. Now, are you going to move?'

I tried to turn my attention to the board, but it wasn't easy. I advanced a knight and bishop. Oliver did the same. I made a few more moves. Oliver's responses were swift and subtle. I sensed he was taking control again. The game was somehow beginning to slip away from me.

Then another interruption came to my rescue. And it was doubly welcome. Vivien wandered in, tousle-haired and yawning. She was wearing a loose silky dark-blue shirt and a pair of tight, faded jeans. Unlike me, she really was dressed casually. And she looked devastatingly lovely as she wandered towards us through a pool of sunlight.

'Oh, hello,' she said, stifling her yawn as she caught sight of me.

'Saved by the bell,' Oliver whispered to me across the board. '*La belle dame sans merci*, that is.'

'Hello, Vivien,' I said, smiling in what I thought was a debonair way. 'Your brother's giving me a chess lesson.'

'Don't worry,' she replied, returning my smile. 'He beats everyone.'

'Jonathan's actually quite good,' said Oliver.

'Wow! That's high praise.'

'Do me a favour, Viv. Make sure he doesn't sneak any pieces out

34

of position while I go up to my room, will you? I've promised to lend him one of my books. It could take me a while to find it.'

I couldn't complain that Oliver had failed to honour our deal. The wink he gave me as he bounced up from the couch underlined the point. He'd gift-wrapped an opportunity for me. What I made of it was up to me.

Vivien watched her brother leave with a slightly bemused expression, then sat down on the couch. 'You two only met on Thursday, right?' she said, mixing a frown in with her smile.

Reckoning my near-collision with Oliver on Tuesday was a subject best avoided, I nodded.

'Well, it's good to know he's found someone he can play chess with.'

'You don't play, then?'

'Not any more. Getting beaten – no, thrashed – by my kid brother time after time rather put me off. I prefer tennis.'

'Between you and me, so do I. How about a game some time?'

'All right. Why not?' It wasn't the most enthusiastic of responses. I wondered if I'd gone just a little too fast. 'So, you're working at Wren's?'

'Yes. Until September.'

'Then off to London?'

'The LSE.'

'I bet you're looking forward to it.'

'I certainly am. I expect you feel the same about Cambridge.'

'I suppose so. At the moment, though, it just seems so far away.'

'Going on holiday before then?'

'I've nothing planned. Normally, Mother and Greville go to Scotland and we go with them. But they're staying here this summer. Greville's too busy to get away.'

If he was, it could only be because of his rumoured negotiations with Cornish China Clays. Vivien would surely only think me stupid if I pretended I hadn't heard about them. 'A lot of the staff think they're going to be taken over by CCC.'

'Do they?'

'Yes. They do.'

35

'Well, I can't say, I'm sure.' She smiled awkwardly. 'Perhaps we could talk about something else.'

We could. And we did, starting with a lament about the assassinations of Robert Kennedy and Martin Luther King. We'd progressed to music – she was into Bob Dylan and I was doing my level best to pretend I was too – when Oliver strolled back into the room, conspicuously empty-handed.

'Sorry, Jonathan,' he announced. 'Looks like I must have left that book at school.'

I shrugged. 'Never mind.'

He zeroed in on the chessboard and snapped out a move, then flashed a disingenuous grin at his sister. 'Was that the great god Dylan's name I heard as I came downstairs, Viv?'

Vivien rolled her eyes. 'Oliver has no interest in music.'

'She's right.' Oliver turned his grin in my direction. 'But thanks to the volume she plays Dylan's records at, I'm word perfect in his lyrics. She tells me they're what makes his stuff worth listening to. But I don't really get it. The times they are a-changin'. A hard rain's a-gonna fall. I mean, we all know that, don't we?'

'I think I'll leave you to it,' sighed Vivien. She got up to go. As she did so, the sickening realization hit me that I'd passed up the chance to ask her out.

Then Oliver said, 'About Tuesday night, Viv.'

She stopped and frowned at him, puzzled, I sensed, that he was raising the subject – whatever the subject was – in my presence. 'What about Tuesday night?'

'I'm not going.'

'Oliver, *please*.'

'I don't want to go.'

'But I told them you'd be there.'

'You should have asked me first.'

'How could I? You'd already flounced out.'

Oliver looked across at me. 'Our Great-Uncle Francis is staying at the Carlyon Bay, Jonathan, with his wife, *la stupenda* Luisa. We'd been over to see them when I met you on Thursday. After I'd left, without the hint of a flounce, I might add, Vivien accepted an invitation to dine with them on Tuesday – an invitation that included me. The evening will be gruesome. I'm not going to put myself through it and that's that.'

'I can't go alone,' Vivien protested.

'Find someone to escort you, then. Someone other than me.'

'How can I do that? It's you they want to see, not some non-existent boyfriend.'

'Well, they're not going to see me. Hey, Jonathan, could you stand in for me?'

'Oliver, please don't be difficult,' said Vivien. 'Jonathan doesn't want to go.'

'Well, you either go with him or you go alone.'

'I don't mind,' I said, trying to sound casual. 'Really.'

'Are you sure?' Vivien asked, looking at me sympathetically, believing her brother had pushed me into volunteering. 'I mean, if Oliver's going to dig his heels in' – she shot him a glare – 'I'd be . . .'

I smiled at her. 'It'll be my pleasure.'

'All right, then. It's a date.'

Oliver and I returned half-heartedly to the chess game after Vivien had gone. My thoughts were already fixed on Tuesday night. I'd have to share her with Great-Uncle Francis and his wife, of course, but it was a start – a very good start, in fact. Thanks entirely to Oliver.

'I want you to do something for me during your dinner *à quatre* on Tuesday, Jonathan,' he said, as he idly manoeuvred me towards defeat.

'What's that?'

'You do know why he's here, don't you?'

'Your great-uncle? No. Should I?'

'Come on. You can put two and two together.'

'All right. Something to do with CCC taking over Wren's.'

'Everything to do with it. There's a full board meeting fixed for Thursday to vote on the deal. It's sure to go through. Barring some last-minute hitch.'

'Is there likely to be one?'

'Not so long as Great-Uncle Francis votes in favour. His and Mother's shares will swing it whatever Great-Aunt Harriet thinks.'

'She's opposed?'

'She wants the family to stay in control of the company.'

'What do you want?'

'It doesn't matter. I don't have a vote. Grandfather left Vivien and me some of his shares, but they're held in trust until we're twenty-one.'

'By which time Wren's will no longer exist.'

'Exactly.'

'You're not looking for something that will . . . wreck the deal, are you, Oliver?'

He looked at me oddly. There was a shadow behind his eyes. 'If only it was as simple as that.'

'What is this really all about?'

'I told you. It's better for you not to know. That way, your question will sound . . . innocent.'

'What question?'

'The one I want you to put to Great-Uncle Francis.' He lowered his voice. 'Mention to him that we've played chess a few times. Say you can't understand why I always win. Tell him I've explained why, but you can't understand my explanation: that you have to be able to see what each piece – what any object – truly represents. As an example, I've said to most people a pig's egg—'

'A *what*?'

'A pig's egg. Clay workers' slang for a large feldspar crystal. But never mind. The point is for you to pretend you don't know what it means. Tell Great-Uncle Francis I said that to most people a pig's egg is just a grey pebble, but to someone who really looks at things it can be the key to everything. Naturally, you asked me what a pig's egg is, just like you did a moment ago. But all I'd say was: ask my great-uncle; he's an expert.'

'An expert in what?'

'Crystallography. He has a small collection of crystal specimens found by Wren's workers over the years. So, he can easily tell you what a pig's egg is. But I want you to study his expression carefully

38

while you relate to him what I said to you. I'll want to know exactly how he reacts.'

'How should he react?'

'Just study him, Jonathan. Form your own opinion. Then report to me. I'll meet you in the cemetery on your way to work Wednesday morning. You can tell me then how it went.' He paused, then sat back on the couch. 'And checkmate, by the way.'

According to Oliver, it was a bad idea for me still to be with him when his mother and great-aunt returned from church. They were likely to ask me a lot of questions and, for the moment, the less they knew about me the better. I had the impression there was nothing unusual in this. His secrecy wasn't just a stratagem. It was his natural state.

I considered saying goodbye to Vivien, but we'd already made an arrangement for Tuesday evening and I was irrationally afraid she might change her mind if I gave her the chance, so I left Oliver to the Sunday papers and slipped out of the house.

The dog was still parked in a sunny patch on the drive. He gave me one rather lazy farewell bark as I passed. Then I heard a first-floor window slide open and Vivien called down to me: 'Jonathan!'

I looked up and met her wide, disarming smile. 'I'm just off, Vivien,' I said. 'I'll—'

'Wait there.' And with that she vanished.

She reappeared, breathless, at the front door, no more than a minute later. I started back to meet her, but she signalled for me to stay where I was.

'I'll walk down the drive with you,' she said, glancing over her shoulder at the house as she caught up with me. There was a per-plexing hint of furtiveness to her behaviour.

'Your brother's a real demon on the chessboard,' I said, smiling at her and noticing how the breeze moved a stray lock of hair across her forehead.

'Not just on the chessboard. Look, about Tuesday—'

My heart sank. She *had* changed her mind. 'When I said it'd be my pleasure, I meant it.'

'It's nice of you to say that.'

'It's true.'

'You might regret it when you meet Uncle Francis and his wife.'

'I'll risk it.'

'OK, but you don't know them. Or me. Or Oliver, really. Which could be awkward. I mean, they'll wonder what on earth you're doing there – *why* I've brought you. So . . .'

'So?'

'Maybe we should meet before then. Just the two of us. To get properly acquainted. What do you think?'

What I thought was I could hardly believe my luck. But all I said, with a mighty effort of self-control was, 'That's a good idea.'

Vivien said she was free that evening and I assured her I was too. In St Austell on a Sunday, even in August, there was little chance I'd be anything else. We agreed to meet at the Rashleigh Inn, by the beach at Polkerris. It was the other side of Par but I declined Vivien's offer to collect me in her car. Mum's curiosity, once aroused, was formidable.

I caught a bus to Par and walked along the coast path from there to Polkerris. I was sitting outside the Rashleigh with a drink, watching the last swimmers and sunbathers drifting away from the beach, when Vivien arrived. She was wearing a sleeveless blue and white sweater-dress and huge diamond-shaped sunglasses that she immediately made a joke of. 'Diamonds are a girl's best friend,' she said, whipping them off and laughing. She looked inexpressibly lovely.

She let me buy her a Cinzano and accepted a cigarette. She talked about how at Cambridge she'd miss the sea and insisted I tell her what I did at Wren's, despite my assurances that the work was even more boring to describe than to do.

Girton College – girls only and two miles out of Cambridge – promised to be boring too, she insisted. I offered to visit her there. 'I might take you up on that,' was her encouraging response. She was funny and light-hearted and captivating through all of this. Her serious, fretful side only emerged when Oliver cropped up

40

in the conversation. I suspected he was going to when I returned with a second round of drinks and saw a change in her expression. She'd thought about her brother – and a cloud had crossed the sun.

'Since you work at Wren's,' she said, 'you've obviously heard about what happened to our father.'

'Yes. It must've been . . . terrible for you.'

'It was. But it was much worse for Oliver than for me.'

'Because he was in the car?'

'He was so mischievous when he was a little boy. Hiding in places you'd never think of was one of his favourite games. He'd been off school with measles for several weeks. Otherwise he wouldn't have been there when Father came home in the middle of the morning. Father left the boot of the car open while he took something into the house. That's when Oliver jumped in and hid under the picnic rug, so Father wouldn't see him when he came back. And he didn't, of course.' A distant look came into her eyes. 'He closed the boot and drove away.'

'Why did . . . your father . . .'

'No one knows.' She gazed past me towards the sea-drawn horizon. 'There was no note. No explanation of any kind. He came home with a book of fabric samples from Broad's that Mother had asked him to collect. She wanted to choose some new curtains for the dining-room. She thought it was peculiar he hadn't waited until he finished work. There was no particular hurry. It only made sense later. He obviously . . . wanted to make sure she had the samples . . . before he . . .'

I suddenly noticed there were tears glistening in her eyes. She stopped and fingered them away. 'I'm sorry. It's been nine years, but I still miss him so much.'

'I'm sorry too.' I patted her forearm gently. 'I didn't mean to upset you.'

'It's OK. I'm all right.' She took a sip of Cinzano and smiled at me. 'Father was sometimes depressed. Not for any obvious reason. It was just . . . the way he was. I suppose it was much worse than usual and he . . . decided he couldn't bear it any more.' She sighed.

'I'm sure he wouldn't have done it if he'd known how it was going to affect Oliver.'

'How has it affected him?'

'Well, he was a pretty normal seven-year-old. But you wouldn't say he was a normal sixteen-year-old, would you?'

'People do change . . . as they grow up.'

'He changed overnight, Jonathan. Since that day nine years ago, he's been . . . obsessed is the only word . . . with what happened to Father. *How* it happened. *Why* it happened. He won't let go of it. I sometimes think it's all he lives for.'

'It can't be as bad as that.' I certainly hoped it wasn't, since I might recently have helped him feed his obsession. A queasy realization struck me. If Vivien ever found out what I'd done for Oliver – and why – she'd want to have nothing more to do with me.

'There are a couple of minor mysteries about what Father did the day he died. Oliver's spent years trying to solve them. He's got nowhere as far as I know. But he won't give up.'

'What are the mysteries?'

'Well, I know Oliver thinks they're basically the same mystery. Father's briefcase wasn't in the car with him and he didn't leave it at home or in the office. So what happened to it? According to Oliver, Father stopped the car somewhere for about ten minutes on the way from St Austell to Goss Moor. He thinks Father got rid of the briefcase then.'

'Why would he do that?'

'Oliver doesn't know. And he doesn't know where Father stopped either, so there's no question of looking for the briefcase. He could have stopped in one of the villages and dumped it in somebody's dust-bin, if he dumped it at all. It might have been overlooked somehow at Wren's. Of course, we don't even know the exact route Father took to Goss Moor. Naturally, Oliver's been over every yard of every possible route. But he's found nothing. I want him to stop. So does Mother. He isn't going to, though. He just can't seem to.'

'Maybe when he leaves school . . .'

'That's what Greville tells Mother. "He'll grow out of it eventually." '

'How did you and Oliver feel about your mother remarrying?'

'I was pleased for her. I think Oliver was too. In his way. Greville's never tried to replace Father. He's . . . quite sensitive, actually. And he's given Mother Adam, of course, who's adorable.'

'I'm not sure Oliver agrees with you there.'

'Oliver tries to ignore him. But you can't ignore a five-year-old.'

'Did Greville know your father?'

'Yes. They served in the RAF together. It was through Father that Greville got a job at Wren's in the first place. According to Aunt Harriet—' She broke off. 'But she tends to exaggerate everything, so . . .'

'What has she exaggerated in this case?'

'Oh, well, according to her, Greville was in a bad way after the war and Father did him a big favour by persuading Grandfather Wren to take him on. Now he's in charge of the business and look what he's planning to do with it.'

'Sell it to CCC, Oliver tells me.'

'Ah.' She looked mildly surprised. And something else: impressed, I think. 'He said that, did he?'

'He also mentioned the special board meeting on Thursday. It's what's brought your great-uncle home, isn't it?'

'Yes. I was going to tell you myself. You see, Uncle Francis doesn't like Greville. Never has. He and Mother have fallen out over it. That's why he and Luisa are staying at the Carlyon Bay rather than Nanstrassoe. I don't want you to be surprised if he says anything nasty about Greville over dinner.'

'I'll try not to be. Families, hey?'

'Exactly . . . Actually, Greville's doing the best he can for the family with this deal. Wren's has no future as an independent business.' Says who? I wondered. Everyone except unworldly exaggeration-prone Great-Aunt Harriet, I assumed. 'Uncle Francis knows it's finished. But he might still want to let off some steam.'

'Thanks for warning me. I think I'll be able to cope.'

'Yes.' She studied me for a disarming moment. 'I think you will, too.'

FIVE

I lay awake for an hour or more that night agonizing over the position I'd put myself in. Oliver was up to something. I knew that much for certain. If I told Vivien what I knew, she'd be grateful. It might even draw us closer together. But Oliver would rightly feel betrayed. I couldn't predict how he'd react. And I didn't want to betray him, anyway.

By the following morning, I'd decided what to do. I'd say nothing to Vivien until I'd given Oliver fair warning. When we met on Wednesday, I'd put it to him that his sister was worried about him and so was I; that I hadn't appreciated how difficult it had been for him to recover from the shock of his father's death; and that unless he told me what he was after in Wren's records I'd have to let Vivien know he was certainly after something.

That still left me committed to putting the question Oliver had prepared for me to his great-uncle on Tuesday night. But taken at face value it was an innocent enquiry. And I *was* interested to see what effect it had. The more I discovered about the Wren family, the better I understood Vivien. And the better I understood her . . .

I expected Monday to be quiet and uneventful. But since the close of the previous working week I'd ceased to be just another anonymous temporary employee and become, as I was shortly to understand, someone Greville Lashley had decided he needed to take the measure of.

It was pushing towards noon in the accounts section, the atmosphere composed of equal parts dust, cigarette smoke and lethargy, when Maurice Rowe took an internal call that brought a scowl to his unlovely face. 'Mr Kellaway,' he barked across the room at me after banging the phone down, 'get yourself up to Mr Lashley's office.' (He would never normally have addressed me as *Mr Kellaway*. It was a sure sign that he viewed the summoning of menials under his charge to the boss's domain as deeply suspicious.)

'Mr Lashley . . . wants to see me?' I asked incredulously.

'Evidently.'

'But . . . why?'

'Ours not to reason, boy. Cut along.'

I cut.

'Go on in,' said Joan Winkworth when I arrived. My hesitant knock at the door of the inner office received no answer, but Joan nodded for me to proceed, so on I went.

The managing director's office doubled as the boardroom, accommodating a long polished conference table overlooked by framed photographs of scenes from Wren's corporate past: workers filling clay sacks at the Charlestown dry; a clay ship with sails rigged nosing out of the dock; a digging gang posing for the camera, shovels in hand, in a new pit; a Wren's lorry loaded with children on a Sunday School outing; and old Walter Wren, whiskered, waistcoated and merely middle-aged, shaking hands with the Prince of Wales some time before the First World War.

I had the opportunity to peruse these because Greville Lashley was in the middle of a telephone conversation when I entered. He waved a hand casually at me, signalling for me to stay, and continued with the call, leaning back almost horizontally in a well-sprung swivel-chair. His desk was set across one end of the conference table, forming a T. Behind him was a large crescent window overlooking the yard. His rockings on the chair carried him in and out of a broad shaft of sunlight that gleamed on his collar-length Brylcreemed hair and the gold band of his wristwatch. He looked his normal suave self – and younger than his fifty years. It took no great effort of the imagination to picture him in sheepskin-lined jacket and flying helmet, climbing into the cockpit of a Spitfire to do battle with the Luftwaffe. He had manliness and style in bucketloads.

'Tell them it comes with my personal guarantee,' were his closing words in the telephone conversation. Then he dropped the receiver into its cradle, causing the bell to tinkle, and treated me to a frowning smile of scrutiny. 'Jonathan Kellaway?'

'Yes, sir. I—'

'Sit down.' He pointed to a chair. 'You're a fast mover, I must say.'

'I'm sorry, sir?'

'Less than a month in our employ and already you're playing chess with my stepson and dating my stepdaughter.'

'Well, I . . .'

'Not that I object to fast movers. Quite the reverse. I find they're essential if you're to get anything done in this world. I'm one myself. Obviously.'

I couldn't see why it should be obvious, but Lashley's wolfish grin almost defied me not to draw the conclusion that he was referring to the ultimate reason he'd succeeded George Wren as chairman and managing director of Walter Wren & Co. – marriage to his late friend's widow, no less: a smart career move, as it had turned out.

'Now look, Jonathan, the thing is this.' His ready use of my Christian name was doubtless calculated to put me at my ease, though somehow it didn't. 'My wife worries about Oliver. Small wonder, considering what he experienced when his father died. I'm sure you know all about that. It's common knowledge. So, I'll say no more about poor old Ken. A sad loss, though, especially for his children. I can certainly never replace him and I've never made the mistake of trying. Oliver spends too much time alone and probably too much time thinking. Never think more than you act. That's my motto. The reverse also applies. Balance, you see. Balance in everything. The point is that if you can . . . bring

46

him out of himself . . . we'd be grateful. All of us. Me included.'

Whether he'd actually winked at me then I wasn't sure. I some-how felt he had. The implication was clear: Greville Lashley's gratitude was a thing worth earning.

'Vivien's an attractive girl, Jonathan. *Very* attractive. I wouldn't blame any red-blooded young fellow setting his cap at her, as I gather you have. Well, happy hunting is all I can say. She's fussy. I can tell you that much. Now, here's my concern. These are . . . delicate times . . . in Wren and Co.'s affairs. Change is in the air. And change is good. Worrying for some. Exciting for others. But good, overall. Without it, business stagnates. And a stagnant business isn't a prosperous business. You understand?'

'Er . . . yes, sir.'

'I gather you're going to study economics at university.'

I was surprised and more than a little disturbed by how much he seemed to have found out about me. 'Er, yes. I am.'

'So I don't need to lecture you about the need to upgrade British industry. The white heat of the technological revolution and all that. In short, the future. It's what I have to plan and prepare for. It's what I *am* planning and preparing for. Delicately, as I say. Sensitively, I like to think. The staff are wondering what's going to become of them if we merge with Cornish China Clays. Actually, they should be wondering what's going to become of them if we *don't* merge with Cornish China Clays. There's a board meeting later this week. Has Oliver mentioned it to you? Or Vivien?'

'As a matter of fact, they both have, sir.'

Lashley nodded thoughtfully. 'I see. And have you mentioned it to your . . . colleagues in Accounts?'

'No, sir.' It was true. I hadn't. But they'd find out about it with-out me well before Thursday. I had no doubt of that. In all likelihood, neither did Lashley.

'Good. That shows . . . restraint on your part. But I'd like to think you might also be capable of something more . . . active.' He smiled at my puzzled expression. 'You're on good terms with Oliver. With Vivien, as well. And I gather you'll soon be meeting my wife's uncle and his *signora*. As a result, it's possible you may learn something over the next few days that has a bearing on the outcome of Thursday's board meeting. Some . . . obstacle to progress. You follow?'

'I . . . suppose I do. But—'

'It may even be something you don't realize has a bearing. Something . . . apparently insignificant but . . . strange, odd, inexplicable.' His smile urged me to see through the opacity of his words. 'If anything remotely of that nature comes to your attention, Jonathan, I want you to alert me to it. A quiet word, nothing more. In complete confidence.'

Something strange, odd, inexplicable. Such as Oliver's determination to gain access to the basement. Yes, that would certainly count as all those things. Except that maybe to Greville Lashley it wouldn't be inexplicable. If I confessed what I'd done now, how would it end? The sack? Or recruitment to some charmed circle of his acolytes?

'You probably think Wren's is a dead-end outfit and china clay's no business for a clever and adventurous young man,' Lashley continued. 'I wouldn't blame you. But you have to see the big picture. The future is written, Jonathan. In words and numbers. We generate more every single day. And that means more paper. Good God, that computer CCC have spews out scrolls of the damn stuff. So, worldwide demand for china clay to fill and coat paper is only going one way: up. And it's not just about paper. A growing population needs more of everything. Coffee cups. Toothpaste. Pill capsules. Condoms. Particularly condoms, if it isn't going to grow too much, hey?' He laughed and I made an effort to join in. 'Well, there's china clay in all of them. That's the point. Them and hundreds of other products. It's going to be a worldwide industry. And I aim to be at the heart of it. Along with a few people who have what it takes to support and, who knows, one day succeed me. The sky's the limit. No . . . wait. There'll be dozens of components containing something manufactured using china clay in whichever Apollo makes it to the Moon. So you see? The possibilities are literally limitless. Think about it, Jonathan. Just think about it.'

*

48

Greville Lashley evidently saw merger with Cornish China Clays as his stairway to success – his and anyone's who clung to his coat-tails. It sounded like pure bombast to me. He was surely too old and too marginal to CCC's concerns to gain anything from the deal beyond a comfortable run-in to retirement. He called it a merger, but it was really a takeover. Wren's would be swallowed whole. And that would be that.

By then, I'd be on the lower rungs of my own stairway to success, in London. The only reason I had to tread carefully at Wren & Co. in the interim was Vivien. I was half in love with her already and we hadn't so much as kissed. I couldn't bear the thought of alienating her by antagonizing her brother or some other member of her family. But the secrets I was keeping were piling up alarmingly. Something had to give. I just had to hope it wasn't something Vivien would blame me for.

Pete Newlove naturally demanded to know what Lashley had wanted with me. I was forced to admit I'd been to Nanstrassoe at the weekend. But chess with Oliver was the limit of my contact with the family in the version of events I treated him to. I claimed not to have seen Vivien at all. Pete seemed to accept this, partly, I think, because it reinforced his impression of her as utterly aloof. He also accepted that Lashley hadn't said a word to me about Thursday's board meeting, of which, as I'd anticipated, word had reached him on the jungle telegraph.

'It all gets settled this Thursday, Jon. Nothing for you to worry about, of course. But for the rest of us toilers it's D-Day. D for decision. D for dole queue. We'll all be sweating on the top line.'

I felt sorry for Pete. He had every right to be worried and obviously hadn't the least suspicion I might be holding out on him. It was just as well his sister was a chambermaid at the Carlyon Bay Hotel rather than a waitress. I was in the clear, I reckoned. For the time being, at least.

I did some juggling of the facts for my parents' benefit as well: Oliver had asked me to accompany him and his sister to their dinner with Great-Uncle Francis and his wife; I'd barely exchanged two words with Vivien on the subject. Mum was so pleased to see me togged up in my one and only suit come Tuesday evening that she accepted the story at face value. Likewise the arrangement I'd supposedly made to walk up to Nanstrassoe and set out with them from there.

In fact, I only went as far as Alexandra Road, where I loitered outside the Capitol cinema until I saw Vivien's bright yellow Mini bearing down on me.

She was beautiful whatever she wore, but the elegant brocaded velvet jacket and fern-patterned silk trousers she'd chosen for our evening at the Carlyon Bay added a new level of maturity to her appearance that I found almost as intimidating as it was alluring.

'Uncle Francis didn't sound pleased when I told him Oliver had turned down his invitation,' she said as we sped away. 'He cheered up a bit when he heard he'd be meeting my new boyfriend, though. Well, that's what he sort of assumes you are and I didn't like to complicate things by disillusioning him. I hope that's not going to be awkward for you.'

'Desperate,' I said with a smile. 'It'll be sheer hell.'

She took one hand off the steering-wheel long enough to slap my shoulder. 'Beast.'

'Actually, I think the role's perfect for me.'

She cast me a sidelong glance. 'Do you now?'

The Virginia creeper-clad Art Deco palace of seaside relaxation that was the Carlyon Bay Hotel was hardly my normal stamping-ground. Entering it that evening with Vivien made me feel as if it easily could be, though. Her company carried with it a charge of life-changing possibilities.

The weather was warm enough for parties to be sitting under parasols out on the terrace. But Francis Wren, we were informed, was waiting for us in the lounge. 'Cold by Capri standards,' Vivien murmured as we went through.

And so it clearly was, to judge by the light sweater Francis was wearing under his blazer. He was a ruddy-faced, white-haired man in his mid-sixties, with too much fat on his stocky frame. But his handshake was firm and there was a hint of steeliness in his blue-eyed gaze. His blazer, cravat and weatherbeaten complexion gave him the look of a veteran yachtsman whose best yachting days were behind him.

'Luisa's still titivating,' he explained, urging us to be seated and to join him in a gin and tonic. 'Women, what, Jonathan?'

I smiled, as if drawing ruefully on extensive experience of the fair sex, which won me a sharp look from Vivien before she diverted Francis into a rambling account of how he and Luisa had been passing their days. Idly was the sum of it. A little reading; a little swimming; a lot of sun-lounging; and a minuscule amount of tennis. If he'd been studying a merger proposal document in advance of Thursday's board meeting, he didn't mention it.

That subject disposed of, he'd just turned his attention to the minor mystery (to him) of my sudden appearance in Vivien's life when Luisa arrived in a cloud of perfume and a shimmer of mid-night blue. Gowned, stoled and multiply pearled, she had the full voice and stage bearing of the opera-singer she'd once been. She also had instantly infectious jollity, pinching Francis's cheek, triple-kissing Vivien and clasping my hand while gazing at me with big, brown, spikily lashed eyes. Her hair was dark and glossy, drawn back to show off the fine bone structure of her face. She was no longer young, but she still had glamour as well as charm.

I wasn't to be spared an account of myself, but I kept it as brief – and factual – as possible. Vivien and I had met through Oliver (true) and hadn't known each other long (also true). Vivien intervened deftly to insist Luisa describe to me the setting of their villa on Capri.

But that proved difficult. 'You have to see it to believe how heavenly it is,' Luisa explained. 'Have you ever been to Capri, Jonathan?' I shook my head. 'Ah, but you will, now you and Vivien are friends. And then . . . you will understand.'

Capri with Vivien: a dream of everything that was delicious and unattainable. But it wasn't unattainable. And I willed myself to believe it could actually happen.

Meanwhile, there were the hazards of fine dining to be braved. I was more of a stranger to four-star hotel restaurants than I wanted Vivien to realize, but dinner passed without my using the wrong cutlery or drinking too quickly. I managed to make some contributions to the conversation that weren't completely stupid. And I even caught Vivien smiling at me on several occasions in a way that seemed, well, affectionate.

Francis said nothing directly about the travails of Wren & Co. and remained tight-lipped when Luisa referred to 'Thursday's meeting'. He was happier bemoaning the state of his homeland under a Labour government and took it in good part when Vivien said he sounded like a reactionary old colonel, pointing out that he really was an old colonel and was entitled to be reactionary. Altogether, he wasn't anything like as crusty as he looked.

When I asked him why he'd settled in Italy, he explained he'd served there during the war with the Eighth Army ('all the way from Sicily to Venice') and had fallen in love with the country even while fighting in it. Returning to work at Wren & Co. after the war was 'just one god-awful anticlimax' and after a few years he 'simply couldn't stick it any longer'. It was easy to believe. As for Luisa, 'meeting her was the best thing that ever happened to me'. And that too was easy to believe. Unless you noticed, as I felt I did, the tightness of Luisa's smile as she listened to him. Everything was superficially right about this adoring couple. Yet something was also subtly wrong.

The story of their first meeting, which it was clear Francis had told many times before, was a case in point. They'd found themselves sharing a carriage on a train from Rome to Naples one warm spring afternoon in 1949. This was a few weeks after Francis's departure from St Austell. He was wandering down through Italy at a leisurely pace, hoping some opportunity with a salary attached would present itself before his money ran out. 'It was just a few days after you were born, my dear,' he said to Vivien. 'I had a telegram from your grandfather in my pocket informing me of the happy event.' His greatest asset, he explained, was his utter ignorance of opera. 'I had no idea who Luisa was.' And that, after many a tedious encounter with fans and fortune-hunters, was a huge relief to her. Before the end of the journey, she'd offered him free bed and board in her villa on Capri in return for his services as handyman-cum-chauffeur. 'I suppose you could say nothing's changed since.'

'Nothing – and everything,' Luisa contributed on cue, before Francis eased into an account of how the adoring effusions of the taxi driver in Naples who took them from the station to the Capri ferry dock first alerted him to Luisa's fame.

I couldn't have said exactly what struck a false note in this paean to happenstance and true love. But something did. It wasn't so much that I doubted the story was true. It was more a case of feeling there was a part of the story – the crucial part – that Francis wasn't telling.

Maybe that's what finally prompted me to ask Oliver's planted question. Luisa gave me the perfect excuse by enquiring after him. I recounted my futile attempts to beat him at chess in a light-hearted, self-deprecating way calculated to lower Francis's guard, then came sweetly to the point.

'"To most people a pig's egg is just a grey pebble," he said, "but to someone who really looks at things it can be the key to everything."' I kept my eyes on Francis as I spoke and there was no missing his flinch of dismay. Oliver's arrow had hit the mark. 'When I asked him what a pig's egg was, he just said, "Ask my great-uncle; he's an expert."'

'"An expert",' said Francis, manufacturing a smile. 'Is that what he called me?'

'Yes.'

'Expert in what?' asked Vivien, frowning in puzzlement.

Luisa was also puzzled. 'What does he mean, *caro*?'

Francis said something to her in Italian that contained the word *cristalli*. It seemed to satisfy her. But not Francis himself. His wine-glass shook faintly as he raised it to his mouth.

'So,' I went on, 'can you tell me what a pig's egg is?'

'I can,' Francis replied, dabbing at his mouth with his napkin.

'It's a large crystal of potash feldspar – a phenocryst, to use the correct mineralogical term – preserved within a softer matrix during kaolinization. The clay workers find them in the pits from time to time. They're geologically interesting and often quite pretty. I have one in a small collection of crystals I put together while I was at Wren's.' I felt he was regaining his confidence now. Whatever the nature of the shock Oliver had given him through me, he had swiftly absorbed it and probably believed no one had noticed anything amiss. 'Now I think about it, I recall I showed Oliver the collection when you and he came out to Capri with Harriet last summer, Vivien. The "expert" description rather flatters me, however. I used to have a coin collection as well. That doesn't make me any more of a numismatist than I am a crystallographer.'

'But how can a pig's egg – a feldspar crystal – be the "key to everything"?' asked Vivien, genuinely bemused.

'Ah,' said Francis, beetling his brow thoughtfully. 'I believe Oliver is referring to the way in which the rocks at our feet, of which a pig's egg is merely one particularly decorative example, reveal, if properly studied, the history of our planet over hundreds of millions of years. Climate changes. Rises and falls in sea level. Movements in the magnetic poles. They're all recorded geologically. And the record is there to see, for someone who really looks.'

'Sounds like you *are* an expert, Uncle Francis,' said Vivien.

'Not at all, my dear. Far from it.' He looked across the table at me. 'I'm afraid none of this is going to help you beat Oliver at chess, though, Jonathan. Perhaps nothing can.'

'Have you ever played him yourself?' I asked.

'Once. Last summer, in fact.'

'Who won?'

Francis smiled. 'I believe it was stalemate.'

'You do realize Oliver set you up with that business about the pig's egg, don't you?' Vivien asked as we drove away from the Carlyon Bay at the end of the evening.

Looking back, I could see Francis watching us from the hotel doorway, puffing at his after-dinner cigar, his free hand half raised in farewell. Did he also realize it was a set-up? I wondered. And, if so, did he think I was a party to it? 'Perhaps Oliver thought your great-uncle would enjoy displaying his mineralogical knowledge,' I suggested.

'Rubbish. It was a code for something.'

'What could a lump of feldspar possibly be code for?'

'I don't know. But then I never know what's going on in Oliver's mind.'

'Do you want me to try and find out?'

'Think you can?'

'Maybe. What's my reward if I succeed?'

She thought about that for a teasing moment, then said, 'Don't get ahead of yourself. I'd be grateful, though. Very grateful. That should be incentive enough.'

We kissed goodnight before I got out of the car at the end of Eastbourne Road. It was only a little more of a kiss than the occasion required. But I walked the short distance home as if I was walking on air, the heady promise of knowing her driving far from my thoughts the problems knowing her brother might yet cause me. She'd agreed enthusiastically to my suggestion of an evening at the cinema on Friday. I didn't actually care what film was showing. If Vivien wanted to see *Thoroughly Modern Millie*, so did I.

SIX

I was all set to deliver an ultimatum to Oliver when we met in the cemetery the following morning. As it turned out, I never got the chance. He was waiting for me by the chapel near the north gate, pacing up and down and smoking a cigarette with nervous intensity.

'You're late,' he announced, as if we'd fixed a definite time. He looked so impatient and distracted I was tempted to point out we were rendezvousing at his request, not mine.

'And good morning to you, Oliver,' I said coolly.

He acknowledged the reproof with a scowling smile. 'Have a good time last night, did you?'

'I did, yes.'

'And you asked Great-Uncle Francis what a pig's egg is, so it was mission accomplished for both of us.'

His certainty momentarily puzzled me. 'How can—'

'Vivien told me when she got home. Accused me of "setting you up". Understandably, I suppose, since she doesn't know about our deal. And I'm sure you'd like to keep it that way.'

'Well, about that, I—'

'Save it. I'm in a hurry. And I don't want to make you late for work, do I? Viv said the old boy looked like he'd seen a ghost when you put the question to him. You'd agree?'

'Yes, I suppose so. Although—'

'Shut up and listen. We have to move fast. I think they're on to me.'

'Who's "they"?'

'Never mind. But if you really want to know, ask him.' Oliver pointed past me with his cigarette.

Turning, I saw nothing at first but the phalanxes of gravestones standing easy in the thin morning light. Then I spotted a brown-clad figure in the middle distance, moving slowly along one of the paths between the graves. It was hard to be sure, but he seemed to be scanning the inscriptions on the stones as he went. Certainly he didn't seem to be paying us any attention.

'His name's Strake. He used to work for Wren's. Now he works for . . . well, that's the sixty-four-thousand-dollar question. But he's been following me for the past couple of days. I can tell you that.'

'Come off it.'

'If you don't believe me, wait and see what happens when we leave.'

'You need to relax, Oliver. This is—'

'Just listen to me,' he broke in, grasping my forearm for emphasis. 'I've got good news for you, Jonathan. I'm letting you off the hook. I want you to tell my stepfather I've confided in you. And this is what I've confided: I'd already got some valuable inform-ation from the records before he gave the order for the basement to be kept locked; I'd have gone back for more if I'd been able to, but it doesn't matter: I've already got enough.'

'Enough about what?'

'Tell him I wouldn't say any more than that. "I've already got enough." You can tell Vivien too. And Great-Uncle Francis, if you run into him. Say you're breaking my confidence because you're worried about me.'

'I *am* worried about you.'

'No need. I know what I'm doing. This puts you in the clear. No furtive key-copying means no secret deal between us. Generous of me, don't you think?'

It was – suspiciously so. 'Why don't you tell me what this is all about, Oliver?'

'Maybe I will. Later. If you'll do one more thing for me. I know you can drive, but have you got a car?'

57

'No. I can't afford one.'

'Could you borrow your father's?'

'Probably.' In fact, it was generally quite easy to persuade Dad to let me use the car, as long as I didn't ask too often. He had little enough use for it himself. 'Why?'

'I want you to drive me somewhere this evening.'

'Where?'

'Pick me up at Nanpean. Park in front of the pub. Be there by seven o'clock. I'll be getting off the bus from Newquay. When you see the bus pull in, start the engine. We'll need to make a quick getaway.'

'Quick getaway? What exactly—'

'Just be there, OK? Or at least warn me if you're going to let me down.'

'Who said anything about letting you down?'

His blue eyes bored into me. I noticed his pupils were un-naturally dilated. I wondered, not for the first time, whether he was entirely sane. 'Can I count on you, Jonathan?'

I felt the force of his will, urging me to assure him he could. 'Of course,' I said. 'I'll be there. But why—'

'No more questions. I'm heading that way.' He pointed towards the gate in the lower corner of the cemetery. 'Wait here and watch what Strake does, will you? That should tell you whether I'm being paranoid or not.'

He spun on his heel then and strode away. I watched him go, stepping back into the lee of the chapel so that I could watch Strake as well without making myself conspicuous.

By the time Oliver was halfway to the gate, Strake had broken off from his perusal of inscriptions and started moving in the same direction. There wasn't much doubt he was following Oliver. He accelerated steadily, cutting between the gravestones to maintain his diagonal route across the cemetery, his short brown mac billowing out behind him.

He had a trilby worn askew on his head and I couldn't see his face for the brim, but I caught a movement of his arm and a drift of smoke that told me he was smoking a cigarette.

Oliver reached the gate and went through. Strake stepped up his pace a little more and was soon hurrying through the gate himself. Then I was alone.

In a sense, Oliver had given me exactly what I wanted: a cover story that would persuade Vivien – and her stepfather – that I wasn't to blame for the consequences of Oliver's actions, whatever they might turn out to be. But in another sense, of course, he was still manipulating me, still using me to serve some devious purpose of his own. And I hadn't the first idea what that purpose was. As I walked the rest of the way to Wren & Co., I pondered the logistics of conveying Oliver's message to Greville Lashley. My colleagues in Accounts would grow suspicious if I became a frequent visitor to the managing director's office with a crunch board meeting pending. I decided to seize my chance, therefore, when I encountered Lashley in the yard, striding purposefully towards his car. It wasn't yet nine o'clock, but already he was leaving rather than arriving. Evidently he'd made an early start – a sure sign of the tumultuous times in Wren's affairs.

'Could I have a quick word, Mr Lashley?' I asked, intercepting him.

'It'll have to be damned quick,' he said without break of stride.

'It's about Oliver.'

He winced, as if a rotten tooth had suddenly pained him. 'Get in the car. You can tell me on the way.'

I was in the plush-leathered passenger seat of the Jag and Lashley was making a roaring exit from the yard before I thought to ask where we were going.

'I have a meeting at Cornish China Clays. You'll have to walk back from there, I'm afraid. I'm operating on a tight schedule today.'

He was also operating without regard to speed limits. We were going to be at CCC in a matter of minutes, traffic permitting. I had no time for subtle preambles. 'I've been thinking about what you said on Monday, sir, concerning . . . unusual events.'

'Have you now? I take it there's been something unusual, then. And that Oliver's involved.'

'Yes.'

'Well, no surprise there. That boy's a specialist in the unusual. So, what is it?'

'It was, well . . . something he said . . . on Sunday.'

'Out with it, then.'

'He said, well . . . he said he'd already got some valuable information from the records before you gave orders for the basement to be kept locked and, although he'd have liked to go back for more if he'd been able to, it didn't matter, because he already had enough.'

Lashley's initial reaction was to drop his speed and nod thoughtfully. I began to wonder if he was going to say anything at all and ended up filling the gap myself.

'I suppose the real reason I'm telling you this isn't that I think it has any bearing on . . . Wren's negotiations with CCC but . . .'

'Because you're worried about Oliver's state of mind.'

There was no denying it. He'd taken the words out of my mouth. 'Er . . . yes.'

'So am I, Jonathan, so am I. I don't suppose he said what he was looking for in the basement, did he?'

'No, sir.'

'Or what he already had enough *of*?'

'I asked, but . . .'

'You got nowhere.'

'Exactly.'

'Well, I'd be grateful if you kept trying.'

'I will.'

'It's to do with his father's death, of course. You realize that much, I'm sure.'

'I guessed it had to be.'

'Muriel thinks he believes his father would never have countenanced a merger with CCC. And Ken would be in charge now, of course, if he hadn't . . . taken his own life. That may be so, for all I know. Ken always had a sentimental streak. But the fact is he isn't in charge. I am. And there's no place for sentiment in this business.'

I'd ceased to be aware of our surroundings as our conversation had proceeded and was suddenly surprised to see the sprawling concrete and glass headquarters of Cornish China Clays looming ahead. A uniformed attendant in a booth touched his cap to Lashley and raised the barrier to admit us to the car park and we cruised to a halt near the main entrance.

'Thanks for being so candid with me, Jonathan,' Lashley said, as we climbed from the car. 'It's much appreciated.' This last remark he addressed to me across the roof of the Jag, with his accompanying smile mirrored in the gleaming paintwork. 'How did dinner with Francis and Luisa go, by the way?'

'Oh, fine, thanks. They were . . . very friendly.'

'Ah. On their best behaviour, then. Let's hope that continues.' He glanced at his watch. 'Well, you'd better step on it, lad. Or Maurice Rowe will have your guts for garters.'

I did step on it, though I made myself later than ever by stopping at a call-box and phoning Dad at the bank to ask him if I could use the car that evening. My explanation that I was doing a member of the Wren family a favour impressed him. Buttering up one's employer was something he very much approved of. Use of the car was agreed.

Maurice Rowe actually made little of my tardy arrival, largely because the following day's board meeting was now preoccupying people to the exclusion of most other topics. Certainly Pete could speak of nothing else when we adjourned to the General Wolfe at lunchtime. Until I distracted him with a question about a former Wren's employee.

'Strake? Gordon Strake? Oh yeah. I remember him. How d'you come to hear of him?'

'I just heard his name mentioned a few times . . . down at Charlestown.'

'That so?' He looked faintly surprised, as well he might. 'Well, Lashley laid him off last year. He was one of our reps. Not bringing in enough business, I suppose.'

61

'What's he doing now?'

'Haven't a clue. He's still in St Austell, though. I've seen him in the betting shop.'

Then, before I could pump him for any more information about Strake, he was back on the topic of the hour: Wren's merger with – or takeover by – Cornish China Clays.

The sun strengthened and the blue of the sky deepened as the day progressed. The evening I drove out into from St Austell was still and clear, with every line of hedgerow and house sharply etched. I reached Nanpean with plenty of time to spare and parked in front of the pub. I bought a half of bitter and sat outside, watching the traffic and waiting for the Newquay–St Austell bus to nose round the corner at the edge of the village.

Seven o'clock came and went. It was nearly ten past, in fact, when the dusty green 58A lumbered into view. I stood up as it passed and caught a glimpse of Oliver's face, close to the window, staring out at me. I drained my glass and made a move for the car.

The bus stopped by the post office a short distance down the road from the pub. Several people got off, Oliver among them. He jogged towards me, frowning in what I took for irritation that I still wasn't ready to go. But by the time he'd piled into the passenger seat of the car, I'd started the engine and lacked only directions.

'Back the way I've just come,' Oliver snapped, slapping the dash-board for emphasis. 'Quick.'

Fortunately, the road was clear. I pulled out straight away and put my foot down, to which the car responded with its normal sluggishness. I glanced back at the pub in the rear-view mirror and saw a familiar figure hurrying up from the stop and squinting after us: Strake.

'See him?' asked Oliver.

'What's he doing here?'

'He's been on my tail all day.'

'He followed you to Newquay?'

'Yes.' Oliver gave a nervous, whinnying laugh. 'A nice waste of his time. I hope he enjoyed the ice-cream he had while I sat on the beach.'

'Where are we going now?'

'St Dennis. I'll direct you from there.' I hadn't noticed until then that he was carrying a small army surplus knapsack on his shoulder. He turned away from me to unbuckle it and rummage inside.

'Why did you go to Newquay?' I asked as we left the village behind and our speed picked up.

'To tire Strake out so I could more easily give him the slip.'

'Well, you've done that all right.'

'Yes. Pretty neat, don't you reckon?'

'Who's he working for?'

'Ask him next time you see him. I'm sure you won't have long to wait.'

'Where *are* we going?'

'You won't have to wait long to find that out either. Just drive.'

Oliver was right. As soon as we reached St Dennis and he told me to take the side-road to Enniscaven, I knew our destination was Goss Moor. It stretched ahead of us, flat and featureless, dun-brown in the lengthening shadow of the clay peaks.

We followed the narrow road north through Enniscaven and crossed a cattle-grid. Another half mile or so and Oliver instructed me to pull in where a rough, rutted track led off between stunted trees and bushes into the heart of the moor. This was it. This was where it had happened, nine years before.

'Your father died here, didn't he, Oliver?' I asked.

I got no reply for a full minute or so as Oliver stared ahead through the windscreen, watching the scenes his memory recalled to him. Then he said, 'Let's get out.'

The air was still and silent. There was a distant murmur of traffic from the A30 and the rumble of a train on the Newquay branch line, but closer to . . . nothing. Oliver opened his knapsack and took out a camera.

'I want you to take my picture, Jonathan,' he said matter-of-factly.

63

'Here?'

'Yes. It has to be here.'

'Why?'

'Just do it.' He handed me the camera. 'It's wound on. All you have to do is point and press.'

'OK.'

'Stay where you are.' He walked a few yards down the track and turned to face me. 'Go ahead now.'

He looked small and vulnerable in the viewfinder, a slight, pale figure in blue jeans and a green sweater, the khaki knapsack hanging at his side, his blond hair gilded by the sun, his expression blank, eyes gazing at the camera, calmly it seemed, resolutely, but also, I sensed, wearily. Behind him the track wound away between gorse and bracken towards a line of electricity pylons and an ill-defined horizon. Nature was neutral here: the ghosts gathered only in Oliver's mind.

I took the picture and lowered the camera.

'I want a couple more,' he said, walking back towards me.

'I can take as many as you like.'

'No, you can't. There are only two left.'

As he moved past me, I glanced down at the exposure counter. It was on 22. I couldn't help wondering what the other pictures on the film contained. But I knew better than to ask.

'I'm ready.' He'd positioned himself in the road, at some precise spot of his choosing. I wound the film on and took the picture. Then he pointed to the grass verge on the other side of the road. 'Take one from there.'

'Sure.'

I moved across to where he'd indicated. He stood by the car and signalled with a nod that he was ready. I took the picture – the last one. 'That's it,' I said.

'Good.' He climbed into the car.

He was holding the knapsack open when I joined him. I handed him the camera and he stowed it away, buckling the knapsack carefully.

'How much do you remember of what happened that day, Oliver?' I asked as gently as I could.

64

'The day my father died?'

'Yes.'

'Everything.'

'But . . . you were only seven years old.'

'It doesn't matter. I made sure, you see. I made sure I never forgot any of it.'

'Do you . . . revisit this place often?'

'As often as I need to.'

'And—'

'Can we go now, please? I've got what I needed.'

At Oliver's direction, I drove back towards Enniscaven, then cut across to Roche and took the St Austell road from there. He showed no inclination to talk, but I allowed him only a couple of miles of silence before I probed a little further.

'Why did you want those photographs taken, Oliver?'

He gave no immediate reply, though he frowned thoughtfully, as if pondering what to say. But in the end all I got from him was a question of his own. 'How did my stepfather react when you told him I'd already got enough?'

I laughed drily. 'Don't you think I deserve an explanation?'

'No.'

I laughed some more at the blitheness of his refusal to play by any of the normal rules. 'You're impossible, Oliver. You know that, don't you?'

'How did my stepfather react?'

I sighed. 'He said he was worried about your state of mind.'

'Really?'

'He thinks you believe your father would never have let CCC take Wren's over.'

'Interesting hypothesis.'

'Do you believe that?'

'Like I say, it's an interesting hypothesis.'

'Why do you suppose your father killed himself?' I asked, thinking I might catch him off guard.

'I don't need to suppose. I know.'

'You do?'

'Yes.'

'Why, then?'

'To keep a secret.'

'What secret?'

'If I told you, it would devalue what he did. It would mean the secret wasn't kept. So I can't tell you. Sorry.'

Determined not to let him see how exasperated I was, I let a few seconds pass before asking, 'How long have you known why he did it?'

'Good question, Jonathan. Perceptive line of inquiry.'

'Are you going to tell me?'

'The answer is: not long.'

'In that case, I'd guess your recent activities – the search of Wren's records, the question about the pig's egg you had me put to your great-uncle, the photographs I took back there – were prompted by whatever it was you discovered.'

'You'd guess that, would you?'

'Yes. Would I be right?'

'Well, let's put it like this. In tournament chess – serious chess – you play against the clock as well as your opponent. Forty moves in two and a half hours is the norm. So, you can't afford to do all your thinking during the game. You have to prepare yourself properly. You have to play the game in your head before you move a single pawn.'

'But you can't plan your opponent's moves as well as your own.'

'You'd be surprised how often you can.'

'And anyway, that—'

'Could you take the Scredda turning up ahead? It's a quieter route into St Austell.'

I guessed there was some other reason for his choice of route than its quietness, but I didn't press the point and the reason soon emerged anyway. Before the narrow lane had wound its way as far as the hamlet of Scredda, he asked me to pull in by a grassy shelf of land, crowned by a mass of tangled hedge and undergrowth.

'I'm going to walk from here,' he announced.

66

It was certainly one way of ensuring he didn't have to fend off any more of my questions. I turned and looked at him. 'Whatever's going on, Oliver, coping with it alone isn't the answer. I'd like to help you, I really would, but—'

'You have helped me, Jonathan. And I'm grateful. You drive on. I'll be fine.' With that he opened the door and jumped out, stepping on to the bank. Then he slammed the door and knocked the roof to signal I could go.

I considered getting out myself and trying to reason with him. But I was irritated by having successive offers of assistance rejected. I couldn't force him to confide in me. And at that moment I didn't even want to try. I put the car in gear and pulled away.

I saw him in the rear-view mirror, watching me, one leg bent against the slope of the bank, his left hand resting on his knee while with his right hand he pulled the strap of the knapsack over his head on to his other shoulder.

Then the lane curved away uphill towards Scredda and he was out of sight.

SEVEN

The sole topic of conversation and all-consuming object of attention at Wren & Co. the following morning was the fateful board meeting. It was due to start at ten o'clock and during the hour beforehand the arrivals of the board members were carefully and none too discreetly monitored from the windows of the accounts section.

Greville Lashley was already present, of course, his green Jag stationed in its normal berth. Soon a maroon Rover was parked beside it, confirming Muriel and Harriet had joined him. Then a taxi delivered Francis Wren from the Carlyon Bay and the gathering was complete. Pete took a few sly bets on how long the meeting would last and the waiting game began.

The meeting had been in progress for about half an hour when Polly, to whose phone the few calls I had were generally put through, reported breathlessly that there was 'a young lady' on the line for me.

It was Vivien. And that was only the first surprise.

'Do you have any idea where Oliver might be?' she asked. There was an edge of anxiety in her voice.

'Er . . . no.'

'He didn't come home last night. Maria thought he was sleeping in this morning, but when she took a cup of tea up to him she discovered his bed hadn't been slept in.'

'Well, I . . .'

'No one's seen him since yesterday afternoon. I don't know what to do, Jonathan. Mother and Aunt Harriet are at the board meeting.'

'I know. Look . . .' What was Oliver playing at now? The question bounced around in my head. 'I saw him last night, Vivien. He asked me to drive him out to Goss Moor. And I did.'

'*Where?*'

'Goss Moor.'

'You mean . . .'

'Yes.' The exact location didn't need spelling out. Vivien knew there was only one place on the moor Oliver would want to be taken.

'Why on earth did you agree to do that?'

I sighed. 'I couldn't see any reason not to.'

'You didn't . . . leave him there?'

'No, no. I drove him back. Well, most of the way back. I dropped him near Scredda. He said he'd walk home from there.'

'*Scredda?*'

'Yes. It's not far. Only a mile or so.'

'When was this?'

'Oh . . . a little after eight, I suppose.'

'You just dropped him at the side of the road?' There was reproachfulness in her voice now, along with the anxiety that was mounting all the time.

'It's what he asked me to do.'

'You can show me where you dropped him, can't you – *exactly* where you dropped him?'

'Of course. But—'

'I'll pick you up in five minutes.'

Fortuitously, Maurice Rowe was out of the room when Vivien's Mini pulled into the yard. She beeped the horn and peered up at me. I signalled I'd be right down and exited before anyone else had a chance to react, pausing only to ask Polly if she'd tell Rowe I had to deal with a family emergency. It was nothing less than the truth, except that it didn't concern *my* family.

69

If I hadn't already begun to regret taking Oliver to Goss Moor, the expression on Vivien's face would have caused me to. It was clearly only her concern for her brother that was holding her anger with me in check. 'I don't understand why you didn't tell me what Oliver was doing,' she said tightly as we started away.

'I honestly didn't think there was anything to worry about,' I said lamely.

'Tell me what happened.'

I stuck to the line I'd fed her stepfather about Oliver's search of Wren's records but supplied otherwise what was a complete and accurate account: Oliver's belief that Strake was following him, our rendezvous at Nanpean, the photo-shoot on Goss Moor, our parting near Scredda.

'Why should Strake be following him?'

'I don't know, Vivien. But he is.'

'And these photographs – what did Oliver want them for?'

'I don't know that either.'

'Where could he be?'

'A friend's home, perhaps.'

'He doesn't have any friends in St Austell.'

'A friend from school, then. He could have caught the sleeper up to London – or somewhere on the way to London.'

This was to my mind the likeliest explanation. And I sensed Vivien very much wanted to believe it. 'Let's hope so,' she said as she accelerated up Menacuddle Hill – the quickest route to Scredda.

We pulled into a field gateway just short of the spot where I'd dropped Oliver and got out of the car. The scene was as I remembered it: a simple curve of the lane beneath a grassy bank, topped with trees and bushes. It held no apparent significance.

'Which way did he go?' Vivien asked, hugging herself as she glanced around.

'I don't know. He was just standing there on the bank as I drove away.'

'Which way was he looking, then?'

Yes. Which way had he been looking? It was a good question. 'Up . . . I think.'

'Up the bank?'

'Yes.' There'd been something in the way he'd lifted the strap of the knapsack over his head, now I thought about it. It was as if . . . 'I think he went up there.'

The bank was steep and slippery. I scrambled up, leading Vivien by the hand. At the top was a trampled-down fence of rusty barbed wire, then a thick belt of low trees and thorny bushes. The land fell away sharply beyond them and I could see the surface of a lake winking and shimmering below us.

'This is Relurgis Pit,' said Vivien, releasing my hand as she squinted down at the water.

'You know it?'

'It was the first clay pit my great-grandfather excavated as an independent operator.'

So, Oliver's choice of dropping-off place hadn't been random. It was futile to go on believing that. He'd come here – to the pit where Wren & Co. had started its commercial life back in 1895 – for a reason: a highly specific reason.

'*Oliver*,' I shouted, without seriously expecting a response. '*Oliver*.' After the echo faded, there was only silence.

'We must get down there,' said Vivien, plunging on ahead.

The water was a milky blue, still discoloured by the clay despite the pit's long disuse. The slopes above the lake were steep and heavily wooded, though away to our left the land shelved more gently and I could see a small jetty at the end of a track that I assumed led in from some point further along the road.

It would have made more sense to drive round and try to reach the lake from there, but Vivien was beyond such reasoning, preferring to force her way down through the barriers of under-growth and brushwood from where we were – the route, it had to be supposed, Oliver had taken himself. I followed as best I could.

71

When I saw Vivien pull up on the crest of a small ridge where the tree cover thinned, my first thought was that she couldn't see a way down from there. Only when I was nearly at her shoulder did I realize she'd stopped because she'd caught sight of something floating in the water below us.

The green of Oliver's sweater must have told her at once what it was: a body, *his* body, drifting face down, arms and legs spread wide. It was just what she'd feared she would see, of course. It was the discovery we'd both dreaded but hadn't spoken of. Oliver was dead. She must have known that at once. And grief must have swallowed her – a grief darker and deeper than the shock I felt.

'Vivien,' I said, clasping her shoulder. 'I'm with you.'

She turned and looked at me. There was horror and incomprehension in her gaze. Her lower lip was trembling. And there were tears in her eyes. She frowned, as if unaware for a moment who I was – or why, as I'd needlessly said, I was with her. 'I must save Oliver,' she murmured.

He was past saving. She must have been well aware of that, even though she couldn't bring herself to admit it. 'Let me,' I said, moving past her and hurrying on down the slope. I took the descent in long, sliding strides, sure it would be much for the best if I reached Oliver first. I heard Vivien scrambling after me, but I didn't look back.

The slope ended in a small arc of shaly shoreline buttressed by the tangled roots of nearby trees. Oliver was no more than ten yards out in the water. There was no doubt now that it was him – the blond hair, the slight figure, the green sweater and blue jeans – nor the least doubt he was dead. I pulled off my shoes and jacket and waded into the water, breaking into a swim when the ground fell away beneath my feet.

Oliver's hands and what I could see of his face were marble-white, the skin corrugated by long immersion. I clasped him under one arm and pulled him behind me as I struck back to shore, where Vivien was waiting.

She helped me turn him over as I dragged him out of the water.

He lay between us, pale and still, his wet hair clinging to his brow. His eyes were closed and he looked, it struck me, entirely at peace. Vivien put a hand to his face and stroked him gently as if he were a sleeping child.

'I'm sorry, Vivien,' I said, longing but not quite daring to put my arm round her. 'I'm so sorry.'

She didn't respond. Her attention was fixed on Oliver. Tears flowed freely down her cheeks as she stared at him, and went on staring, as if by sheer force of will she could bring him back to life.

A minute swelled into a frozen space of time while we crouched beside her dead brother in the silent bowl of the pit. Then she said, quietly but firmly, 'Please go and fetch some help.'

The realization that Oliver's death would leave its mark on the rest of my life seeped into me as I fought my way back up the slope to the road. I didn't know whether he'd drowned accidentally or by his own design, though already I suspected the latter, but the fact of his death – the extinction of all his youthful promise – was unalterable. He was gone. And I was implicated in his going. He'd made sure of that. '*You have to play the game in your head before you move a single pawn.*' His words – his very own, carefully chosen words. He'd foreseen this. I felt sure of it. He'd foreseen everything that was going to happen.

I asked to use the phone at the first house I came to. The elderly woman who answered the door was alarmed by my appearance – my saturated clothes were clinging to me and numerous twigs and leaves were clinging to them – and then shocked when I explained what had happened. Her late husband, it transpired, had worked for Wren's. 'Is the boy who's drowned the son of Mr Foster, God rest his soul?' she gasped. I had to tell her that he was.

The police said they'd be there as soon as possible. I was to wait for them at the end of the track leading from the road to the pit, which was the way they'd go in. They'd bring an inflatable with them to retrieve the body. I thought of Vivien then, sitting by her dead brother, alone with her grief, and decided to let the police find their own way. I had to get back to her as fast as I could.

But first I had to phone Wren's and break the news. I got through to Joan Winkworth and asked to speak to Mr Lashley 'urgently', but she said the board meeting was still in progress and she couldn't interrupt. Only when I told her why I was calling did she change her tune. And then I used the need to meet the police at the pit as an excuse to let her be the one to inform the family that Oliver was dead.

'This is awful,' said Joan. 'Simply awful.' And there was no disputing that.

It was only on my way back to the pit that I remembered the knapsack Oliver had been carrying, containing his camera, but not, it was my impression, just the camera. Where was it? It hadn't looked too heavy to float, so maybe it was on the shore somewhere, some distance, perhaps, from where we'd pulled him out of the water.

But what about the camera? If Oliver had planned to drown himself, the photographs I'd taken of him on Goss Moor began to look like part of a calculated farewell. If they were, what story were the other photographs on the film intended to tell? I had to find the knapsack. It was probably my only chance of making sense of what had happened – and making Vivien understand that I was willing to do everything I could to help her cope with the loss of her brother.

When I finally struggled back down to the lakeside, however, I soon realized making Vivien understand anything was beyond me. I felt weak and light-headed, chilled by my wet clothes and what was probably delayed shock. But Vivien was afflicted by something altogether more profound. She was sitting on her haunches, with Oliver's head cradled in her lap, smiling down at him and combing his hair with her fingers, humming to herself as she did so. She looked almost . . . contented.

'The police are on their way,' I said, crouching beside her. 'They'll be here soon.'

She didn't so much as glance at me.

'Vivien?' I touched her shoulder. 'Can you hear me?'

She very slowly turned her head to look at me. She frowned faintly. Then she returned her gaze to Oliver.

'Oliver had a knapsack with him. The camera was in it. We should see if we can find it.'

No response.

'Vivien?'

Another slow turn of the head. Another frown. But still she said nothing.

'Speak to me. Please.'

The frown deepened. Several long seconds passed. Then at last she spoke. 'I asked you . . . to fetch help.'

'It's coming.'

At that moment, as if summoned by my words, there was the growl of a car engine from the direction of the jetty. I looked across the lake and saw a Landrover pull up at the end of the track leading in from the road. Two policemen, their uniforms black in the harsh light thrown up from the water, climbed out and walked on to the jetty. One of them raised a pair of binoculars to his eyes and scanned the shore.

'Here they are,' I said, standing up and waving to attract their attention.

'Everything's going to be all right now,' Vivien murmured. 'You just wait and see.'

Looking down, I realized that she was talking not to me but to Oliver.

'Everything's going to be just fine.'

But it wasn't, of course. Nothing was going to be just fine ever again.

EIGHT

The passage of events following the arrival of the police at Relurgis Pit that warm August morning are obscure in my memory. I can picture a WPC comforting Vivien and wrapping a blanket round her as she sat in the back of a patrol car; I can reconstruct the face of the officer who jotted my replies to his questions in a notebook between sucks on his pencil; I can still smell the diesel fumes of the inflatable that carried us across the lake, still hear the crackle of the police radios; and I will never forget my last glimpse of Oliver's pale, peaceful face as the zip of the body bag closed over him: the rest is a blur.

At some point, Greville Lashley was present. He spoke to me, though what I said I have no idea. Oliver's body had been removed to the mortuary by then, I think, and Vivien had been driven away. He was presumably anxious to follow. I was taken home by the police myself soon enough. My mother was dismayed by what they told her. It was doubtless more coherent than what I was able to tell her. She insisted I have a hot bath and consigned my clothes to the washing machine.

Lying in the bath at that unfamiliar hour, gazing up at the whorling reflections of sunlight on the ceiling, I tried to force my mind to review what had happened over the previous twenty-four hours and understand why it had led to Oliver's death. But the effort was in vain. There was just so much I didn't know. Only Oliver could have explained it to me. And he was never going to do that now.

Mum gave me soup for lunch, as if I was some kind of invalid – which I suppose I was. She'd taken a call from the police while I was in the bath. They wanted me to go to the station later that afternoon and make a formal statement. She'd said I'd be there at five. She'd phoned Dad, who was going to leave work early to accompany me. I didn't have the strength to argue.

After dutifully downing the soup, I rang Nanstrassoe House to ask how Vivien was, but the line was busy, as it was each time I tried. I went into the garden and smoked a sly cigarette – Mum disapproved of smoking – then sat in a deckchair and listened to the birdsong and sniffed the creosote a neighbour was applying to his fence and wondered how life could be so normal for some when for others it had changed so utterly.

I was about to go in and ring Nanstrassoe again when Greville Lashley suddenly strolled round the side of the house. 'Your mother said you were out here,' he explained, a second before Mum herself appeared at the kitchen door.

'Get the table and a chair out of the shed, Jonathan,' she said. 'I'll make some tea.' It was immediately apparent to me that Lashley's arrival at the door had left her overawed and slightly flustered.

'I was a little worried about you after our conversation out at Relurgis,' said Lashley, as I fetched the wicker table and a chair. 'To be honest, you weren't making much sense.'

'Sorry. I was . . . confused.'

'Shocked is what you were, Jonathan. And I can't say I'm surprised. I'm glad you've recovered, though. You have recovered, haven't you?'

'Pretty much, I think, yes. I've been trying to phone you, actually. How's Vivien?'

'Ah, Vivien.' Lashley sat down and lit a cigarette. He offered me one and implied with a wink and a glance at the house that he quite understood why I didn't accept. His stepson's death hadn't made the least dent in his sangfroid. 'She's in a bad way, I'm afraid. She was bound to take it hard, of course, seeing how close she and Oliver were. The doctor's prescribed some sedatives. We'll . . . see how it goes.'

'And Mrs Lashley?'

'Not too good either. This is an awful thing for the family. Bloody awful.' I couldn't help noticing that he referred to the family as if he wasn't quite part of it.

'You all have my . . . sincere condolences, sir.'

'Thank you.' He nodded solemnly. 'You're a good lad, Jonathan. I'm sure you'd have done anything you could to avert this tragedy.'

'Yes. I would.'

'I never doubted it for a moment.' Something in his narrow-eyed gaze suggested, nevertheless, that the issue *was* in doubt.

This was the moment Mum chose to deliver the tea – and a plateful of biscuits. She stammeringly added her condolences to mine as she manoeuvred the cups and saucers and sugar bowl. Lashley soothed her nerves with his earnest appreciation and then, when she'd left us alone again, slipped a silver flask out of his pocket and poured a slug of whisky into his tea *and* mine.

'We both need this, I reckon,' he said, taking a sip. 'The police gave me a fairly garbled account of what you told them, Jonathan. Drownings aren't that uncommon in these pits, you know. Steep sides. Deep water. Lads larking about. So, their first thought was it was an accident. But they said you seemed to think Oliver killed himself. And that he was being followed by a former Wren employee called Strake. Have I got that right?'

'I don't know how Oliver died,' I said, drinking some of my tea and tasting mostly whisky. 'But, yes, Strake had been following him. I'm fairly certain about that.'

'And you were with Oliver yesterday evening?'

'Yes. I was.'

'I'd be grateful if you could fill me in . . . on exactly what happened.'

'I'll try.'

And so, for the second but not the last time that day, I recounted as much as I knew of the final hours of Oliver Foster. Repetition didn't reveal previously hidden significance. It was as bewildering in retrospect as it had been to live through. Lashley listened intently between sips of fortified tea and draws on his cigarette. His

78

furrowed brow suggested he was seeking what I was helpless to supply: the true meaning of all that had occurred.

'I'm sorrier than I can say,' I concluded, 'that I just . . . drove away and left him there.'

'It's what he asked you do, Jonathan,' said Lashley consolingly. 'And if he was planning to do away with himself, you couldn't have stopped him. He wasn't the kind of boy you could stop doing anything he was set on.'

'Even so . . .'

'This business with Strake is baffling. I persuaded George to let me get rid of him last year. The fellow simply wasn't pulling his weight. I believe Francis took him on originally. They were in the army together. When Francis left, Strake stayed on – far longer than he should have been allowed to. If he really was following Oliver, it'll have been because someone was paying him to. But who'd do such a thing? And why?'

'I asked Oliver that. He wouldn't say. He called it the sixty-four-thousand-dollar question.'

'The photographs are equally baffling. Oliver was unhealthily obsessed with his father's suicide, as we know. But why pose for pictures at the site now, nine years later?'

'I don't know, sir.'

'There was no sign of the knapsack at the pit?'

'Not that I saw.'

'It's a gruesome coincidence, I have to say.'

'Coincidence?'

'Ah, perhaps you don't know that Ken's briefcase went missing at the time of his death.' I did know, of course. Vivien had told me. But till now I'd forgotten. 'It was never found. Odd. Damned odd. Like Oliver's knapsack. And his choice of Relurgis Pit.'

'The first one Wren's ever worked, according to Vivien.'

'Exactly. Ancestral ground, you could call it. If you had a mind to.' He drained his cup and poured himself some neat whisky. 'The police will simply go through the motions, Jonathan, take my word for it. They don't suspect third-party involvement, so they'll leave it to the coroner to decide whether it was an accident or suicide. They won't waste any of their time, as they see it, looking for Oliver's knapsack. That's why I'm wondering . . .' He broke off and cleared his throat, then leant across the table towards me. 'I'd do this myself if I weren't so damnably busy. The board approved the takeover by Cornish China Clays this morning just before your message reached me. There are all manner of legal arrangements to be set in train and discussions I have to have with CCC management. Quite frankly, this couldn't have come at a worse time. The knapsack, Jonathan. Do you think you could go out to Relurgis and see if you can find it? Not today. You're done in. I can see that. But tomorrow. Don't bother about work. I'll tell Maurice Rowe not to expect you back before Monday. Our best hope of learning why Oliver did whatever exactly he did do is laying hands on that bag and its contents. Can you give it a go?'

'It's just what I was thinking of doing anyway, sir. I mean, the knapsack has to be there somewhere.'

'The police are happy to assume it sank.'

'I don't believe Oliver would go to the bother of posing for those photographs if he didn't think they'd ever be developed.'

'Neither do I. So, be as thorough as you can. It's pretty much a jungle round that pit, but there's a good chance that not far from where you found him . . .'

'I'll find the knapsack – with the camera inside.'

'And maybe more besides.' Lashley polished off his whisky and stood up. 'I appreciate this, Jonathan, I really do. Sorry I have to dash off. There are a lot of calls on my time today, as I'm sure you can imagine. Thank your mother for the tea. Let me know how the search goes, won't you? Phone me at the office. Joan will see I get the message.'

I got up out of the deckchair and he shook me by the hand. 'I'll miss Oliver,' I said.

'So will I. He could be as infuriating as all hell, but . . . you had to love him.'

'Perhaps tomorrow I could . . . call round and talk to Vivien.'

Lashley grimaced. 'Best leave it a little longer. These sedatives have really knocked her out. And Muriel . . . Well, I wouldn't want her saying things to you in the heat of the moment, if you know what I mean. In situations like this, people tend to look for someone to blame.'

Yes, I supposed, they did. And in the eyes of the Wren family I was the obvious candidate.

'One step at a time, Jonathan. That's how we should play this.' At least it sounded as if he wasn't about to blame me. 'And the first step is: find that knapsack.'

It's a measure of how shaken I was by the day's events that I didn't insist on going to the police station on my own. There was little my father could contribute to the proceedings, after all, but I knew he wanted to do his best for me and I was grateful for his support, though, naturally, I didn't tell him so.

The completion of my statement was a long-winded and at times tedious process. I mentioned the knapsack and extracted grudging confirmation that it hadn't been found. I also mentioned Gordon Strake and, when I pushed the subject, was told he'd be questioned in due course. There was no sense of urgency and it was generally implied that as a mere witness – and a young lad to boot – I should be supplying information, not seeking it.

Dad took much the same view, predictably enough as a defender of the establishment in all matters. 'Let the police get on with their job, Jonathan,' he advised me on our way home. 'They'll do what needs to be done.'

'Mr Lashley doesn't seem confident they will.'

'Then it's for him to challenge them, not you.'

'I can't just . . . do nothing.'

'Yes, you can. What's happened is a tragedy for the boy's family, of course, but you'll be off to university in a month. New friends. New horizons. You'll soon put all of this behind you.'

Poor old Dad. I think he really believed that.

I headed out early next morning, shortly after Dad had left for the bank. I told Mum I was going to kill some time at the beach and play tennis with a schoolfriend at the Lido, a diet of harmless fresh-air fun she heartily approved of.

In reality, of course, I was going nowhere near the Lido.

I entered the pit the way Vivien and I had the previous day. There was no way of walking round from the entrance track to where we'd found Oliver. The slopes above the lake were simply too sheer to allow it. So, it took another scramble down through the trees and undergrowth from the bank near Scredda to reach the shore.

There was nothing to indicate what had occurred there just twenty-four hours previously. The police had amassed what evidence they wanted, which I suspected was very little, and gone on their way, leaving Relurgis Pit in peace. The lake shimmered opaquely in golden sunshine. A buzzard circled on a thermal high above. And nothing more than a gentle breeze stirred the greenery.

I tried to be meticulous and systematic, descending slowly and by a winding route in case Oliver had discarded the knapsack on the way down. Once at the gravelly patch of shore where Vivien and I had crouched beside his body, I extended the search as far round the perimeter of the lake on either side as I could reach, narrowly avoiding falling in on several occasions.

There was no sign of the knapsack. Oliver could have hidden it, of course. There were plenty of loose rocks available to conceal it. Or he could have loaded some of those rocks into the knapsack, thrown it into the lake and watched it sink. But even by Oliver's standards such behaviour, after going to all the bother of having me take pictures of him at Goss Moor, seemed senseless. So, where was it?

I decided to check the jetty area before giving up, although how Oliver might have found his way over there I couldn't imagine. I heaved my way back up to the lane and walked along to the turn-off.

To my surprise, a taxi was parked at the start of the track. The driver was smoking a cigarette and studying racing form in his newspaper so intently that he jumped when I greeted him.

'Mornin',' he said gruffly, but then smiled genially. 'Headin' for the lake?'

'Yes.'

'Watch your step. Some young feller drowned there yesterday.'

'Really?'

''Fraid so. Could be why I'm here. Got the meter running on an old gent from the Carlyon Bay. You'll find him down by the jetty. Well, I hope you will. Lessen he's in with fishes an' all.'

Francis Wren, hatted and lightly overcoated as if for a fickle early spring rather than high summer, was leaning on the rail by the jetty, puffing at a pungent cigar and gazing out thoughtfully across the lake. He gave no sign of hearing me approach.

'Mr Wren?'

He turned round slowly and looked at me. 'Why, it's young Jonathan.'

'Yes, sir. Good morning.'

'Good morning.' At his instigation, we shook hands. 'Well, well, this is an unexpected meeting. Even though . . . we both have cause to be here.'

'I'm terribly sorry about what happened to Oliver, Mr Wren.'

'Of course. Understood. Damnably upsetting for you as well as the family. I've been knocked sideways by the news, I don't mind admitting. Like father, like son. Dreadful. Just dreadful.'

'It wasn't necessarily suicide.'

'Kind of you to say so, but from what Harriet's told me – I've had to rely entirely on my sister for information, of course – there's not much room for doubt, now is there?'

'No. Not really.'

'You wouldn't be out here looking for Oliver's knapsack, would you?'

'Ah. You know about that.'

'Harriet's a thorough informant. The parallels with his father's missing briefcase are . . . eerie, I must say. Perhaps deliberately so. The workings of that boy's mind are hard to fathom.'

'Yes. They are. And, yes, I have been looking for the knapsack.'

'But I see you're empty-handed. I can't say I'm surprised. I don't think it's here to be found, Jonathan.' Francis cast a glance back across the lake. 'Oliver's sent us a message. But we don't seem to be able to read it.'

'This was the first pit Wren's worked?'

'That it was. It's strange to see it now, so green, so . . . tranquil, when I remember it as a vast white hole in the ground, with men looking no bigger than ants from here, hewing away at the bottom with picks and shovels. It was still operating when I left the company, though it was on its last legs by then.' He was lost for a moment in a reverie of remembrance, then he looked at me sharply. 'Now, what's all this about Gordon Strake?'

'Oliver said Strake was following him. And he was. I saw that for myself.'

'You're sure it was Strake?'

'Well, that's who Oliver said it was. A man was certainly follow-ing him.'

Francis frowned. 'Baffling. Quite baffling.'

'Mr Lashley told me . . . Strake was an old comrade of yours.'

'He served under me in Italy. "Old comrade" is stretching it. He's a Plymouth man. Came down here after the war looking for work. I took him on as a favour to someone who'd seen a lot of hard action. I gather Greville sacked him last year.'

'Apparently so.'

'Well, no doubt the police will find out what he's been up to.'

'As his old CO, you might be able to get more out of him than the police.'

Francis smiled faintly, as if entertained and tempted by the idea of taking a personal hand in the investigation. 'Interesting suggestion, young man. I'll certainly consider it. Now, I think I must be getting back. Luisa will be wondering where I've got to. Would you like a lift into town?'

I declined his offer, explaining that I wanted to continue search-ing for the knapsack, although in truth I no longer seriously expected to find it. I watched him potter away along the track towards his waiting taxi and found myself wondering just what his connection with Strake signified.

Only after he'd vanished from sight did I remember the takeover of Wren's by Cornish China Clays. I should have asked Francis how he felt about the demise of the family firm. It was strange how unimportant that now seemed. Oliver's death had overshadowed everything else. As perhaps he'd meant it to.

A fruitless hour of delving in gorse bushes and picking my way around the treacherous shore of the lake had passed when I abandoned the search and headed back to St Austell. I arrived tired, thirsty and dispirited. It was nearly one o'clock and I wondered if I'd find Pete Newlove in the General Wolfe. His uncomplicated slant on the world of Walter Wren & Co. suddenly seemed like the tonic I needed, along with the several pints he'd be happy to join me in.

First, though, I stopped at a call-box and rang Wren's. I got through to Joan Winkworth, who was lunching at her desk. Lashley was in a meeting at CCC (no surprise there) but had left word I was to come and see him at six o'clock. I asked her to tell him I'd be there.

It was a short step to the General Wolfe, where, disappointingly, Pete was nowhere to be seen. I retired to a corner with my beer, lit a cigarette and pondered the futility of my morning's efforts. The person I most wanted to talk to about what had happened was Vivien, but I'd more or less agreed to leave her be for a while, although part of me was beginning to suspect Lashley had manoeuvred me into that agreement for reasons of his own. There was always the chance, if I rang Nanstrassoe House, that Vivien would be the one who answered. Somehow, though, I didn't reckon it was a very good chance.

'Mind if I join you?'

The question caught me unawares. Looking up, I was astonished to see Gordon Strake standing over me, though not much over, thanks to the shortness of his stature.

He was a small, ferrety sort of fellow, with a narrow,

sallow-skinned face and dark, greasy hair. He looked an unhealthy fifty or so, his cheap brown suit and stained tie doing nothing to improve his appearance. He had a roll-up wedged at the corner of his mouth and was holding a half-finished glass of stout.

'They said I might find you here,' he said, sitting down next to me without waiting for my response. 'You're Jonathan Kellaway, aren't you?'

'And you're Gordon Strake.'

'That I am.' He took a gulp of stout and set the glass on the table. There was a stale smell to him, detectable even through the beer and cigarette fumes. 'I've got a bone to pick with you, sonny.'

'Who's "they"?' I asked, determined not to let him gain the upper hand. He probably thought it would be easy to intimidate me.

'What?'

'The "they" who said you might find me here.'

He gave me a sneering frown. 'Don't get clever with me, sonny. I've had the Old Bill on my back this morning thanks to you.'

'Good.'

His frown deepened. 'What did you say?'

'I'm glad they've been to see you. Did you tell them who paid you to follow Oliver Foster?'

'Who paid me?' The frown became a bemused smile. 'Come off it, sonny. You knew what he was up to. Which is more than I did. I wouldn't have got mixed up in this if I'd had any inkling how it was going to end. That friend of yours was cracked, if you want my opinion. He must have been, to do what he did.'

'Who paid you?' I pressed.

'You trying to tell me you don't know?'

'Of course I don't.'

'Pull the other one.'

'I've got no idea who you're working for.'

'*Was* working for, you mean.'

'OK. *Was*. What difference—' I was silenced by the sudden

realization of what Strake's insistence on the past tense might signify.

'You really don't know, do you?'

'You mean . . .'

'Oliver Foster hired me, sonny, scheming little head case that he was. Paid me twenty quid for that bloody pantomime on Wednesday. Easy money, I thought. Not so sure about that now.'

'But . . .'

'Why? Good question. Reckoned you might be able to tell me. Thought you were in on it. Looks like I was wrong. In which case . . . we've got nothing to say to each other, have we? Bloody Wrens. I wish they'd leave me alone. If you see any of them, don't give them my condolences, will you?'

With that he was out of his chair and away across the pub. He finished his stout in one long swallow and plonked the glass down on the end of the bar without breaking his stride. A moment later, he was gone.

Leaving me to contemplate the ring his glass had left on the tabletop in front of me – a ring like a frozen ripple, radiating from nothing.

NINE

By the close of a miserable afternoon I'd concluded that Strake was right, damn him. Madness of some kind had driven Oliver to end his life in mysterious circumstances of his own orchestration. Francis Wren believed he'd sent us a message we weren't equipped to understand. I was beginning to believe he'd sent us a message he didn't want us to understand. And what that meant for Vivien I preferred not to imagine.

I arrived at Wren's as instructed, promptly at six. I was immediately puzzled by the emptiness of the car park. Lashley's Jag wasn't there, which tended to imply he wasn't there either.

The rest of the staff had all gone. That was no surprise on a sunny Friday afternoon. The only people on the premises turned out to be the cleaners, Ethel and Mavis. Ethel reported that Lashley had left no more than ten minutes previously. She had no idea where he'd been going, of course. 'But he was in a tearing hurry, I can tell you that.'

I considered phoning Nanstrassoe House, then decided it was time I grasped the nettle and called there in person. I hurried off.

There was no sign of the Jag at Nanstrassoe either. But the garage was big enough to accommodate several cars. I glanced up at the first-floor windows of the house as I approached, half expecting to see Vivien watching me from one of them.

She wasn't, of course. But to my surprise someone else was. Adam Lashley, who must have been standing on a chair to reach the windowsill, was peering down at me, frowning as concentratedly as only a small child can.

I raised my hand and waved to him, smiling as I did so. To which he responded by sticking his tongue out and ducking down out of sight.

The door was answered by Maria, who seemed bewildered to see me and undecided whether to invite me in. 'Zere is . . . a lot trouble,' she said.

Then Harriet Wren appeared in the hall behind her. 'It's Jonathan, isn't it?' she said. 'You'd better come in.' As I stepped through the doorway, she went on: 'See what Adam's up to, would you, Maria? I heard a loud thump just now.'

Maria hurried off up the stairs, leaving me to follow Harriet into the drawing-room. She closed the double doors carefully behind us.

'Is something wrong?' I asked. 'I had an appointment at the office with Mr Lashley. He wasn't there.'

'He was called away, Jonathan,' she said, gazing at me studiously through her round silver-framed glasses.

'What's happened?'

'Vivien . . . took an overdose of sleeping pills.'

'*What?*'

'She's at the hospital. Muriel's with her. I expect Greville is as well by now.'

'Are you saying . . .'

'No, no. Muriel found her in good time. She's going to be fine, I'm sure. Physically, that is. As for her mental state . . .'

'Why would she do such a thing?'

'She's spent her entire adolescence trying to protect Oliver. His death has been a dreadful blow for all of us. But for Vivien . . .'

'I must go and see how she is,' I said, turning towards the door.

'Before you do . . .'

I looked back at her. 'What is it?'

'You won't get a very good reception, Jonathan. Muriel thinks you're partly to blame for what's happened.'

'Perhaps I am.'

'I don't think so.'

'Well, I'm going anyway.'

'So I see.' She smiled, approvingly, it seemed to me. 'Good luck.'

I had no doubt Harriet's warning was amply justified, but it was actually a relief to trust my own instincts rather than other people's. I had to see Vivien, now more than ever. Her mother's opinion of me was simply irrelevant.

Vivien's was the only occupied bed in a small side-ward. My first thought was how pale she was. I hadn't been prepared for that. It reminded me of Oliver, when we'd pulled him from the lake.

She was lying propped up on several pillows, with a drip attached to one arm. Muriel Lashley was sitting beside the bed, holding her daughter's hand and talking in an undertone. Greville Lashley was standing next to her, staring into space, with a faintly pained expression on his face.

Vivien was in fact the first to see me. There was something abject in her soulful, wide-eyed gaze. She shook her head, as if to tell me I shouldn't have come – I really shouldn't.

Muriel noticed me an instant later. 'What's he doing here?' I heard her say. And Lashley swung into action.

'Let's step outside for a moment, Jonathan,' he said, striding forward to meet me and extending an ushering arm around my shoulder. 'There are one or two things I need to explain.'

'I'd really like to talk to Vivien,' I protested as he virtually propelled me along the corridor.

'I fully understand, but she's not up to it yet. They've washed out her stomach and she's feeling very weak. We need to take things gently. The doctor's told us she mustn't be put under any stress.'

'I'm not going to put her under stress.'

'Not intentionally, of course. But it's not as simple as that, I'm afraid.'

By now we were passing through the reception area and heading for the exit. 'Mr Lashley,' I protested, 'I just want to—'

'I know, I know. But it's going to have to wait.'

Then we were out in the clear evening air. Lashley released me and instantly produced his cigarette case.

'Smoke?'

'All right,' I said warily. 'Thanks.'

The short ritual of cigarette lighting felt as if it was also a declaration of his confidence in me. This was how men of the world behaved: a restrained conferral over expensive Virginia tobacco, while the womenfolk indulged their frailties indoors.

'How is she?' I ventured.

'Not too hot. I'd no idea she was so distraught she might try to kill herself. It's beginning to look like an hereditary weakness, isn't it? I can't imagine how Muriel would cope if she'd succeeded. It simply doesn't bear thinking about. Anyway, as I'm sure you can imagine, my wife is *very* worried about Vivien, as well as grieving for Oliver.'

'Of course. But—'

'Listen to me, Jonathan. Vivien's welfare has to be our prime concern. They'll discharge her tomorrow – there's nothing physically wrong with her now they've flushed the pills out of her – and we'll take her home. But she's in a very fragile state. That's clear. I'm sure she'll want to see you at some point. Probably not for a few days, though. Until we've got her over the worst of her reaction to Oliver's death and are satisfied there isn't likely to be any repetition of this . . . suicidal impulse . . . I must ask you to be patient.'

It was difficult to frame an objection to his request without sounding selfish. He must have known I was bound to agree to whatever was in Vivien's best interests. 'I don't want to do anything that would upset her.'

'Of course you don't.' He squeezed my shoulder. 'We're all on the same side in this. That's fully understood.'

'So . . .'

'We'll be in touch. Or Vivien will. Just give her a little time. They say it's the best healer.'

'I should tell you that I couldn't find the knapsack. I searched high and low. Nothing.'

'Thanks for trying, anyway. I'm not altogether surprised. Information I received from the police this afternoon suggests Oliver was playing some kind of elaborate game with all of us. It appears *he* paid Strake to follow him.'

'I know. Strake told me.'

'You confronted the fellow, then?'

'Not exactly. I—'

'You're a spirited and determined young man, Jonathan. Resourceful and resilient. I like that. So, don't think I take any pleasure in what I'm about to say. The fact is that I have to terminate your employment at Wren's. With immediate effect.'

I was taken aback. Nothing had prepared me for this. 'But . . . why?'

'Muriel insists. She blames you for helping Oliver carry out his suicide plan. Officially it may be concluded that he drowned accidentally. But we know better, don't we? We also know you couldn't have anticipated what he was intending to do. My wife doesn't see it that way, though. She regards it as intolerable that you should remain a Wren's employee. And in the circumstances I don't feel inclined to argue with her about it.'

That at least I could understand. 'I see.'

'I'm sorry. But there it is. However,' he dropped his voice confidentially, 'I could fix you up with something at Cornish China Clays, if you like. They're always in need of holiday cover. Muriel couldn't object to that. And you have a chemistry A level, don't you, so they're bound to be able to make good use of you.'

It was surprising in its way, even flattering, that Lashley was willing to go to such lengths to help me. Laying off one student worker wasn't a big deal, after all. But apparently he really did like me. 'Well . . . that's kind. I . . .'

'Call Ted Hammett at CCC Monday afternoon. I'll have spoken to him by then. He'll fit you in.'

I shrugged. 'Thanks.'

'I could be doing you a bigger favour than you think. CCC is going places. I intend to make sure of that.'

On my way home, I passed the Capitol, where people were going in for the 7.45 showing of *Thoroughly Modern Millie*, the very showing Vivien and I had arranged to go to. Vivien's world had been knocked off its axis since then – and mine with it. What the future held for us I couldn't have begun to guess.

It promised to be a miserable weekend. And the reality lived up to the promise. I mooched around on Saturday and in the evening went to a party I'd intended to cut, hoping, of course, to have fixed something up with Vivien. I soon wished I'd stayed at home. I left early.

I went for a long and exhausting walk down the coast to Mevagissey on Sunday. Holidaymakers were out in the sun. Well, bully for them. I was well on the way to convincing myself I'd never again be capable of such a simple thing.

When I finally arrived home late that afternoon, I vaguely registered the gleaming condition of the car as evidence that Dad had given it its weekly wash. This further proof that the banal routines of everyday life went on being observed without regard to individual tragedies only deepened my depression.

Dad was oblivious to this and seemed determined to twist the knife by actually describing the cleaning of the car to me.

'The turtle wax gives it a really nice sheen, doesn't it?' he asked, to which I couldn't summon a response. 'I vacuumed the interior out as well, you know.'

I managed a glum nod at that.

'Came across this in the glove compartment. Know anything about it?'

I belatedly realized he was holding something in his hand: a smooth, creamy white, roughly hexagonal stone – or rather, I saw as I looked closer, a pentagon and hexagon superimposed, fused together, as it were. It was several inches across and I knew at once what it was: a feldspar phenocryst – a fine example of a pig's egg. And I also knew how it had found its way into the glove compartment of the car. I knew that with utter certainty.

I told Dad I'd got the pig's egg from someone at work and had intended to show it to Oliver, but had forgotten. A direct connection to Oliver might have prompted him to insist I report it to the police and, for some reason I couldn't properly have explained, I didn't want to do that. It was clear to me the pig's egg was some kind of parting gift: my gift, no one else's.

When I examined it more closely, I noticed that the letter Z had been etched in one corner, too sharply and precisely to be mistaken for any kind of natural marking. There was nothing else unusual about the stone. Typically of Oliver's communications, it was as intriguing as it was impenetrable.

My first impulse was to tell Vivien about its discovery. But the only person I wanted to confide in was the one person I wasn't allowed to confide in, at least for the moment. I'd have to wait for her to contact me. And the waiting would be agony.

I rang Ted Hammett at Cornish China Clays on Monday afternoon, as Lashley had advised me to, and was instantly hired to do a few weeks in their research department as some unspecified form of dogsbody. The whole point of working at Wren's had been that it wasn't Cornish China Clays, of course, so there was more than a little irony attached to this. But it was only for a few weeks. *And* they paid ten shillings more than Wren's.

I started on Wednesday and pushed my luck by immediately requesting Friday afternoon off. There was no objection. It was probably more generally known than I was aware that Oliver Foster had been a friend of mine. And Friday was the day Oliver's funeral was set to take place at Holy Trinity Church at three o'clock.

I was beginning to wonder if I'd hear from Vivien before then. I didn't want our next meeting to be at her brother's funeral, surrounded by friends and relations. But there wasn't much I could do about it. I'd agreed to give her as much time as she needed. And how much that was I had no way of judging.

The answer was waiting for me in the car park when I left CCC that Wednesday, however. Vivien tooted the horn of her Mini and waved me over.

She was wearing her white safari-suit and looked outwardly every bit as carefree and glamorous as the first day I'd set eyes on her. Only the shadow behind her gaze and the nervous tremor I felt as we exchanged a brief, uncertain kiss suggested otherwise.

'Can we go somewhere and talk, Jonathan?' she asked.

'Of course.'

'I know . . . you've been wanting to talk to me ever since . . .' She shook her head. 'I'm sorry . . . so sorry I couldn't . . .'

'It's all right.' I touched her hand. 'I understand.'

'Do you?'

'I think so.'

We headed for Porthpean, the nearest beach to St Austell. On the way Vivien asked me about my first day at CCC. I heard myself faithfully describing the many contrasts with working practices at Wren's, as if she might really be interested – or as if any of it mattered at all.

There was a shared sense that we couldn't really communicate until we'd reached Porthpean and walked out on to the beach and faced the cleansing sea air. The evening was cool and grey. There weren't many people about. We lit cigarettes and wandered out towards the gentle surf.

'I'm on probation, you know,' said Vivien. 'This is my first trip out alone since . . .'

'I'm sorry, Vivien. So sorry I didn't . . .'

'You've nothing to apologize for. It wasn't your fault that Oliver . . . did what he did.' She sighed. 'Or that I fell apart.'

'How are you feeling now?'

'Delicate. Isn't that what they say? Yes. Delicate. That's exactly how I feel.'

Several waves slowly broke while I sought the right words in vain.

Then, as if taking pity on me, Vivien said, 'I think I've feared Oliver might kill himself ever since Father died. I tried so hard to stop it happening, but in the end . . . there was nothing I could do. And confronting my failure was like staring into a pit. A black, bottomless pit. That's why . . . if there is a why . . .' She shuddered and I longed to put my arm round her. But something held me back. 'The truth is a painful thing, Jonathan. And the truth about Oliver is this. He wanted there to be some deep, dark secret that would explain what Father did. He wanted there to be people who'd driven him to it that could be exposed and punished. He wanted that so badly that when he realized there was no secret beyond Father's own depressive temperament he decided to . . . manufacture one. The information he found in Wren's records; the missing knapsack; the man following him: all designed to suggest a mystery . . . where there was actually only a sad, mixed-up boy.'

'Is that what you really believe?'

She nodded glumly. 'Yes. I believe it. Don't you?'

'I suppose . . . I have to.'

I told her then about the pig's egg, news which she received as if it was yet further confirmation of her brother's elaborate campaign of mystification. 'I wonder what he intended the Z to signify? The end, perhaps.'

'You're assuming he inscribed the Z.'

'Oh, I think he did, yes.'

'Would you like . . . to have it? I could . . .'

'No. You keep it, Jonathan. It'll be something for you to remember him by.'

'I'm sure I'll always remember him.'

'Will you?' She smiled weakly. 'That's nice.'

'What are you going to do . . . between now and Cambridge?'

'I'm going away.' It was the answer I'd dreaded. The realization had begun to seep into me that we were here to say goodbye. 'Mother and I are going to Egypt. I've always wanted to see the pyramids. It'll be hot and dusty and completely different from everything I know. It's what I need at the moment. A foreign land.'

'When do you leave?'

'Saturday.'

'So soon?'

'It has to be soon. I can't stay here. After the funeral . . . I have to get away.'

Another silence, timed by the sussurous swash of the sea. It deepened around us as we stood there, two figures on a beach, that early evening of late August, when we were young and thought the future was unwritten.

'I'm sorry, Jonathan,' Vivien said at last.

'Me too,' I murmured.

TEN

Oliver's funeral was attended by large numbers of people he could barely have known. Greville Lashley gave a eulogy that skirted adroitly round the specifics of his stepson's death. From my place towards the rear, all I could see of Vivien was the back of her head. I didn't see much more of her at the gathering afterwards, held in the function room at the White Hart. She knew I was there, of course. But we'd already said all there was to be said. I didn't linger.

And then she was gone. To Egypt, to Cambridge, to places out of my reach. I soldiered on at Cornish China Clays, where I got a crash course in computing and an insight into just how far behind the times Wren's had really been. The takeover soon took effect. To LET signs were up at Wren's East Hill offices within weeks. Pete Newlove confounded his own pessimism by securing a clerical post at CCC and we had a drink at the General Wolfe to celebrate. He asked what I thought the chances were that I'd end up working at CCC after university. I put them at zero and he bet me five pounds I was wrong. I reckoned my money was safe.

Then I was gone too, to London. I had to return briefly to St Austell after a couple of weeks, though, to appear as a witness at the inquest into Oliver's death. Vivien had supplied her evidence in writing. 'Thought it best on medical advice not to have her relive the whole terrible business in court,' Lashley explained to me over lunch at the White Hart. 'She's settling down well at Cambridge. No sense putting that at risk, is there?' I was in no position to disagree. The verdict – death by misadventure – happily avoided the conclusion that Oliver had emulated his father by taking his own life. All in all, the outcome from his family's point of view was, as Lashley described it, 'Satisfactory – really quite satisfactory.'

I wrote to Vivien, reporting how the inquest had gone, wishing her an exciting time at Cambridge and floating the idea of visiting her there, as we'd once discussed I might. I phrased it merely as a possibility. She didn't have to say yes or no. In the event, she said neither. My letter went unanswered. 'I have to get away,' she'd told me that last day at Porthpean. And now I knew for certain I was part of what she had to get away from.

Student life in London brought enough novelties to distract me from the loss of what I'd hoped might blossom between Vivien and me. Resilient, Lashley had called me. And maybe he was right. Or maybe I was just young and eager to expand my world. New friends; new scenes; new experiences: I welcomed them all. The LSE was a hotbed of student activism in those days and finding myself on the fringe of the Grosvenor Square riot was a revelation of just how stultifying my existence in St Austell had been. Other revelations followed. This was 1968, after all. And I was where it was happening.

I went home for Christmas with long hair, a 'Hey, man' drawl I cringe to recall and plenty to talk about – but none of it with my parents. I did a couple of weeks as a relief postman and it was on Christmas Eve, after finishing early and downing several pints in the Queen's Head with my fellow posties, that I encountered Vivien, walking along Fore Street with an irritatingly good-looking young man who was introduced to me as Roger and had public school, not to mention Cambridge, written all over his fine-boned features. Our conversation was brief and on my part muddled. I was too drunk to be taken for sober, but not drunk enough to be unaware how oafish I must have appeared. A light rain was falling, I remember. My breath was misting in the air. A busker was strumming a soggy guitar outside the Midland Bank. The dank grey afternoon was suddenly heavy with unspoken regret. 'Merry Christmas, Jonathan,' said Vivien, kissing me on the cheek. And then they moved on, hand in hand, strolling along the street, bound for Nanstrassoe House, I assumed, and tea beside a roaring fire. I watched them go – and bade Vivien a silent farewell.

2010

ELEVEN

Dr Fay Whitworth was a slim, plainly dressed woman in her forties, with short, dark, grey-flecked hair, a calm, patient face, and brown, soothing eyes. Something in her tone and bearing conveyed practicality as well as intelligence – in ample doses.

We met in a chicly minimalist restaurant in Bristol's tarted-up harbourside district. Intercontinental Kaolins were paying, of course, and I'd been happy to let her choose a more comfortable (and expensive) venue for our discussion than the university canteen. I'd spent many of the long hours of my journey from Augusta struggling to comprehend how and why Greville Lashley had allowed the stand-off with Dr Whitworth to develop and sat down to lunch with her exasperated by the conundrum – and by the need not to appear so.

'I gather from Mr Beaumont's PA that you've worked for Intercontinental Kaolins and Cornish China Clays before it for more than forty years, Mr Kellaway,' Dr Whitworth said, as she perused the menu. 'I'm glad your superior saw the sense of sending someone with experience that goes back so far.'

'For more than forty years we'd have to count some casual spells as a student,' I said, downing a mouthful of white wine. 'But I do have a lot of experience, however you tot it up.'

'It was implied to me that you're the corporation's senior troubleshooter.'

'I'm not sure there is such a designation.'

'But if there were, you'd be it?'

I smiled. 'I'm certainly here to help solve your . . . research problem.'

'And how do you propose to do that?'

'It'd be useful if you told me the exact nature of the problem first. Presley – Mr Beaumont – was a little hazy on the particulars.'

'It's quite simple, really. I—' She broke off as the waitress came to take our order. Dr Whitworth plumped for salad and white fish. I opted for something from the less healthy end of the menu.

'So,' she resumed, 'my problem. Well, *our* problem. I'm bound to say it's rather confirmed my reservations about becoming involved in commercially contracted work. In the academic world, you see, there's a . . . presumption of cooperation . . . that's been generally lacking in my dealing with IK, despite the fact that your own former chairman commissioned my study.'

'The staff you've dealt with have been uncooperative?'

'There's certainly been some obstructiveness, camouflaged, quite convincingly at times, by smiles and sundry blandishments.'

Sundry blandishments, indeed. The mind boggled. 'Could you be more specific, doctor?'

'Please call me Fay. I never persuaded anybody in St Austell to drop the "doctor". I hope for better from you . . . Jonathan.'

'Well, Fay . . .' I smiled. 'Let's hope you get it.'

She returned the smile. 'Now, you asked, quite rightly, for specifics. I'm happy to supply them. I made it clear from the outset in accepting Mr Lashley's offer that I'd only be able to spare a limited amount of time from my university commitments. To make best use of that time I needed to be able to conduct my research in discrete, concentrated packages. I proposed to start in Cornwall and move on to the American side of things later. As matters currently stand, however, my work in Cornwall is incomplete, suspended, if you like, with no prospect of resumption before I'm provisionally scheduled to visit Georgia.'

'Have you met Mr Lashley, Fay?'

'No, no. Discussions were conducted through intermediaries. I gather he's quite infirm. But is it important whether I've met him or not? My clear understanding is that he wants the history of the company to be written and published, preferably while he's still alive to read it.'

'An old man in a hurry.'

She looked surprised, if not shocked, by my disrespectful tone. 'Is that how you see him?'

'It's probably how he sees himself. He's a realist if nothing else.'

'Well, we can agree he wants me to make progress with the project, yes?'

'Absolutely.'

'Good. So, after familiarizing myself with the general history of the china clay industry, I went down to St Austell to amass detailed information on the origins and development of Cornish China Clays. Of course, as you'll know, that effectively means the origins and development of half a dozen separate companies that eventually became Cornish China Clays through a series of mergers and acquisitions. I was somewhat surprised to discover that Mr Lashley didn't start his career at CCC, as I'd supposed, but with one of the smaller outfits they took over in the nineteen sixties: Walter Wren and Co.'

'Why did that surprise you?'

'Because, speaking as something of a specialist in the field of corporate studies – the reason Mr Lashley hired me, after all – it's very unusual for the principal of an acquired entity to become the principal of the acquirer.'

'That didn't happen overnight.'

'No. But that it happened at all is remarkable. And not just once. From Wren and Co. to Cornish China Clays. From Cornish China Clays to Intercontinental Kaolins. Of course, I appreciate his ascent to seniority at Intercontinental Kaolins was smoothed by his marriage to Jacqueline Hudson.' She paused, perhaps hoping I'd make some unguarded comment on Lashley's highly advantageous second marriage. When it became obvious I wasn't going to, she went on. 'No such factor applies to his rise within CCC, however.'

'No one's ever doubted Mr Lashley's expertise. Or his energy.'

'Indeed not. He's fifty years old when CCC takes over Wren's, an obvious candidate for back-numbering. Instead, he works his way to the top – and stays there. It's remarkable. Quite remarkable.'

'A testament to the man.'

'I agree. Which is why I felt I should give Wren's rather more attention than the numerous other small companies CCC bought out over the years. Happily, Wren's records are archived along with CCC's in St Austell, as you know.'

'I'd have assumed they were, Fay, certainly. But there could have been all sorts of clear-outs and disposals I'd know nothing about. I haven't been to the St Austell office in years.'

'Too busy carving a hole the size of the Isle of Wight out of the Amazonian rain forest, I suppose.'

I winced. 'I believe we're both in IK's pay one way or the other.'

'You're right, of course. IK's ecological credentials – or the lack of them – are a subject for another day.' She smiled appeasingly and the arrival of our starters consolidated the pacifying effect. I wondered as the waitress delivered our plates how Fay Whitworth was going to approach the thorny issue of environmentalism in her history of the company. Would the anti-deforestation protesters who'd disrupted the last AGM get a mention? I rather hoped so.

'It's ironic, don't you think,' I ventured, 'that you've found researching a long defunct minnow of a company like Wren's so troublesome, when IK is a worldwide concern employing thousands of people and turning over millions of dollars?'

'Yes. It is ironic. Very. Any idea why it's happened?'

'None. How could I have? You still haven't told me what went wrong.'

'No. I haven't, have I? Very well. I was directed to the Wren's section of the archive and initially made good progress. Documentation from the early years of the company is surprisingly extensive. Walter Wren was an unusually good employer for the period. His pits worked throughout the clay strike of 1913, for instance, thanks to the higher wages he paid. But it was a small company and it stayed that way, so it was bound to be vulnerable when consolidation swept through the industry. I'd like to be able to attach some facts and figures to its vulnerability, but that's where I struck a major snag. All the Wren's material is box-filed by financial year: 1895/96 through to 1968/69. And all the box-files, neatly labelled, are there to be seen on the shelf. But those covering the last twelve years of the company, from 1956/57 to the end, contain mostly blank paper.'

'Blank paper?'

'Yes. Some inconsequential documents at the top, then reams of unused sheets of paper – the flimsy kind once used for carbon copies. It's the same in every file. From CCC records I know Wren's directors voted to accept the CCC takeover offer at a meeting held on the twenty-second of August 1968. But the report of that meeting, along with everything else during the run-up to the takeover, is missing.'

'That . . . can't be right.'

'Those were more or less the same words used by Mr Newlove when I complained to him.'

'Pete Newlove?'

'Yes. You know him?'

It really shouldn't have come as any surprise that Pete was still clinging to a desk in St Austell. He was the same age as I was and probably planned to soldier on until he was sixty-five. He was also, in all probability, the only former Wren's employee still on the payroll. Other than me, of course. 'Pete and I go back a long way,' I admitted cagily.

'In that case, you'll be well placed to say whether his ineffectiveness in addressing my complaint was deliberate or not.'

'I'm sure he'd have tried to be helpful.'

'I found him trying, certainly. Suffice to say I never got much more out of him than a shrug of the shoulders.'

'Then no doubt you went over his head.'

'And fared no better. Which I thought odd, given I was working on a project personally backed by your former chairman.'

It *was* odd. There was no denying it. 'I can go down to St Austell and crack a few heads together, Fay. But if everyone's genuinely baffled . . .' She'd already managed to consume her salad, I noticed, leaving an entirely empty plate, while I was still squeezing lemon on my gravlax. The woman was a fast worker, no question about it. 'There's a limit to what I can do.'

'And to what I can do in terms of a comprehensive history of IK/CCC. Perhaps I haven't made myself clear to you, Jonathan. This isn't a simple case of material lost, discarded and inadvertently disposed of over the years, which isn't at all uncommon in my wide experience of archival research. It's a deliberate filleting of the files, compounded and confirmed by the substitution of blanks for the documents removed. Quite an elaborate exercise, considering we're talking about the records of a company you described in an accurate if decidedly mixed metaphor as a "long defunct minnow".'

'Well, I . . . guess we don't know when it was done, do we? It could have been many years ago.'

'The paper used would suggest that. Alternatively, it may have been used *in order* to suggest that.'

I tried to look and sound more dubious than I actually felt. 'You seem to be formulating some kind of conspiracy theory here, Fay. It all seems highly improbable.'

'Oh, I agree. But, improbable or not, something of the kind has occurred. Intriguing, isn't it?'

'Is it really such a big obstacle to your work, though? Wren's is a very small piece in the IK/CCC jigsaw.'

'You're developing an interesting habit of saying what others have already said to me, Jonathan. "Ignore such a trifling problem and concentrate on the big picture" was the advice given to me – unsought, I should mention – by Mr Lashley's son.'

Adam? How the hell had he got mixed up in this? He was supposed to be in Thailand . . . doing whatever he did in Thailand. 'You've met Adam Lashley?'

'No. We had a telephone conversation a week or so ago. Well, not much of a conversation, to be honest. More of a monologue on his part. The gist of it was that he thought I was making a fuss about nothing and was being paid more than enough not to. I had the impression he may not have been completely sober. Or does he always speak with a slur?'

I was saved having to dodge that question by the waitress's removal of our starter plates. I drank some water and tried to sound curious but unfazed as I asked, 'Where was he phoning from?'

'London, he said.'

London. Damn. Too close for comfort. Too close altogether. 'Adam can be a little abrasive at times. He probably thought he was doing his father a favour by encouraging you to proceed.'

'Well, he was wrong. The more people tell me to disregard the Wren's puzzle, the more determined I become to solve it. And as far as I can see, the best way to do that is to insist it be dealt with . . . by someone like you.'

'And here I am. Ready to deal with it. As best I can.'

'Any preliminary theories?'

'None.'

'There's nothing you know of in the last twelve years of Wren's independent existence that anyone might want to . . . cover up?'

'I can't think of anything at all.'

'Nothing I should be told about that might have a bearing on this?'

'No.'

'I see.' A sip of wine. A narrowing of the gaze. She didn't look as if she believed me. 'I'm surprised you say that, Jonathan. Surprised . . . and a little disappointed.'

'Really?'

'Yes. Really. It suggests you underestimate me, which, professionally speaking, I find hurtful. It should be obvious to you that in the conspicuous absence of most of Wren's records for the period fifty-six to sixty-eight, I'd look to other contemporary records for anything that might shed light on the company's activities at the time.'

She was right, of course. Suddenly and sickeningly, I saw where this was going. I saw the bound sets of the *Cornish Guardian* in St Austell public library. Microfilmed long since, no doubt. But still available for study.

'Kenneth Foster, husband of Walter Wren's granddaughter,

Muriel, and a director of the company, generally considered number two to the chairman and MD, George Wren, committed suicide in July 1959, a suicide witnessed by his seven-year-old son, Oliver. Nine years later, on the twenty-second of August 1968 – the very day Wren's board voted to accept the takeover offer from Cornish China Clays – Oliver Foster was found drowned in a flooded clay pit. Death by misadventure was the verdict, though on a strict reading of the facts suicide would have been equally plausible, if not more so. The body was discovered by Oliver's sister, Vivien, and a friend by the name of . . . Jonathan Kellaway.'

There wasn't much I could say to that. I smiled uneasily. 'I'm sorry, Fay. I should have realized you'd find out about Oliver – and his father before him. Oliver's death isn't an event I have any wish to recall, to be honest. But I really don't think it has any bearing on this problem of missing records.'

'Why did Kenneth Foster kill himself?'

'No one knows. He suffered from depression, but . . .'

'And Oliver? Why did *he* kill himself?'

'He didn't. You said yourself the verdict was death by misadventure.'

'But was that the correct verdict? The report of the inquest said you were the last person to see him alive. I can understand why for his family's sake you'd want to suggest he drowned accidentally. But perhaps you'd like to tell me now, all these years later, what you really believe happened.'

'I don't know. I've never known.' It was comforting in its way to have a simple truth to cling to: I didn't know.

'In that case, you can have no reason for saying the deaths of Kenneth Foster and his son are irrelevant to the issue of the missing records.'

She had me there, of course. 'I guess you're right. It's just . . . my opinion.'

Our main courses arrived. That and the topping up of our wine and water glasses gave me a couple of minutes to consider how to counter Fay's undeniably sound line of reasoning. Nothing sprang to mind, not least because I was already beginning to suspect with queasy conviction that the deaths and missing records were related – very closely related.

'I'm going down to St Austell this afternoon,' I said. 'I'll do all I can to get to the bottom of this.'

Fay eyed me over the rim of her wineglass. 'Thank you.'

'But you must understand I can't guarantee I'll succeed.'

'And you must understand I can't guarantee I'll continue with the project if you don't.'

She couldn't guarantee she'd continue. But she didn't rule it out either. There was wriggle room for both of us if we needed it. 'Very well. I'll let you know what I find out.'

'Please do.'

'Just between you and me, Fay, I'm not privy to the terms you were hired on, of course, but I imagine they're generous. Are you sure—'

'I want to risk missing out on a bigger pay day than I'll ever see in academia?' She smiled wryly at me.

I smiled back. 'Exactly.'

'I won't put my name to a whitewash, however fat the fee is. It's as simple as that.'

'You're a woman of principle.'

'Yes. Something you and Mr Lashley are going to have to get used to.'

A couple of hours later, I was standing on the platform at Temple Meads station, waiting for the Plymouth train and considering just how I was going to 'get to the bottom' of the mystery Fay Whitworth had uncovered. The bottom, as I well knew, was a lot further down than she could possibly imagine. Over the years I'd come to assume I'd never reach it. But my hopes and assumptions had never counted for much. So maybe they were going to be confounded again. Maybe this time – this last time, surely – I'd find the truth that had previously eluded me. Whether I wanted to or not.

1969

TWELVE

I fondly imagined, after nine months in London, that I'd done as much growing up as I needed to, knew the sinful ways of the capital inside out and understood how life should be lived. This delusion enhanced my self-esteem just when it needed enhancing, so I suppose it's not entirely to be regretted, even though many of the things I said and did make for painful recollection.

I'd moved out of the grim university accommodation I'd initially been consigned to at the invitation of a girl who deserves to remain nameless, joining her and her various supposedly worldly-wise friends in a crumbling house in Walworth, where most weekends and quite a few midweeks descended into druggy disorder to a soundtrack of Emerson, Lake and Palmer.

The sobering experience of a police raid and the nameless girl's departure to her new boyfriend's bedsit ushered in a more restrained regime during the second half of the summer term. In a corner of my mind I was also aware that drab reality awaited me in St Austell, where I'd arranged to spend part of the holiday working at Cornish China Clays. Even a student in the sixties couldn't live on air, far less the fumes we normally substituted for it.

Another reminder of St Austell was waiting for me when I returned late one cool, grey Saturday morning in early June from a reluctant expedition to the local shops. I thought at first the bright yellow Mini parked near the house merely resembled Vivien's, though that alone made my heart miss a beat. Then, as I stepped indoors and heard her voice, I realized it really was her car and it really was her, talking to Terry in the kitchen.

She'd changed too, of course. But in her the change had added a translucence to her beauty and a regality – yes, I think you'd call it that – to her bearing, in wondrous contrast to the smart-arse hints of hippydom I'd tacked on to my persona. Her hair was slightly shorter, swaying around the base of her neck as she turned to look at me, her style of dress more individualized – velvet jacket with silver buttons, embroidered blouse drawstrung at the throat, knee-length pleated skirt: all in different shades of blue. She looked, as Terry accurately put it later, as if she was from another planet – one he badly wanted to land on.

I could hardly disguise the fact that it was a surprise to see her, nor how wonderful a surprise it was. Terry was in the process of cack-handedly percolating some coffee for her, but after a few minutes' brittle small talk he got the message and slunk off to the bathroom with his favourite combination of the *Guardian* and the *Daily Mirror*.

'I'm sorry I didn't answer your letter last autumn,' Vivien said, as soon as we were alone. 'It was mean of me.'

'Don't worry about it,' I responded, clearing a crumb-free space for her coffee mug at the kitchen table. 'It can't have been an easy time for you. I understood that.' I gathered a couple of chairs together and we sat down. 'How's Cambridge?'

'Every bit as preposterous as I'd expected. But glorious as well.'

'I'm glad. Smoke?'

'Thanks.'

I gave her a cigarette and we lit up.

'What happened to the Peter Stuyvesants?' she asked with a smile.

'I had to ditch them. No good for my working-class credentials.'

'Your father's a bank manager, Jonathan. You don't have any working-class credentials.'

'Shush! Round here they think I come from a long line of tin miners. None of them knows I was actually born in Norwood.'

116

We laughed. And the sound of our laughter – easy and genuine, yet brief – was somehow shocking. We fell into an equally brief silence, then Vivien said, 'It's good to see you again.'

'Not as good as it is to see *you* again, I'll bet.'

'I'm sorry I . . . cut you out of my life.'

'Easily forgiven. If you're back in it now.' But was she? What had prompted her unannounced visit was still unclear. 'How did you track me down?' (I hadn't been living there when I'd written to her the previous October.)

'I sweet-talked your address out of a clerk in the college office.'

'I'm impressed you went to the trouble.'

'And you're wondering why. Is that it?'

'Well, when we last met, I . . .'

'I wasn't myself. Hadn't been, really, since Oliver's death. The psychiatrist Greville found had me on all sorts of drugs – my only excuse for hanging around with that drongo, Roger. You met him in St Austell.'

'Ah, he *was* a drongo, was he? I thought so.' We laughed again.

'I'm over all that now. I'm me again, seeing clearly, facing facts . . . and very much hoping you'll help me.'

A pause. A weighing of words. But the weighing meant little. She'd never looked lovelier. There wasn't much I wouldn't have been prepared to do at her bidding, as she probably knew. 'You only have to ask,' I said, holding her gaze.

'Then I will. At Easter, I helped Mother clear out Oliver's room at Nanstrassoe. It was something we had to do sooner or later if it wasn't going to turn into some kind of shrine. So, we . . . did it together. There was a trunk he stored all his old toys in from child-hood – teddy bears I'd passed on to him: that kind of thing. At the bottom, we found . . . well, something we never expected to see again.'

'What?'

'Father's briefcase.'

I made no effort to hide my astonishment. 'I thought . . . Oliver had spent years looking for it . . . to no avail.'

'We all thought that. But no. There it was. It was in a bad state, stiffened and misshapen, the lock and clasp rusted through. It had clearly spent a long time in water.'

'Water?'

'Relurgis Pit, Jonathan. I think Oliver finally worked out to his satisfaction that Relurgis was where Father dumped the case the day he died. I think he somehow managed to find it and retrieve it from the lake, though how I can't imagine. But it's surprising what can be achieved through single-minded obsessiveness. And Oliver certainly had plenty of that.'

'Was there anything in the case?'

'Papers, as you'd expect. But the water had turned them to mush. You couldn't make out what had originally been written on any of them, or what sort of documents they were at all, in fact.'

'If you're right, Oliver could only have found the case by . . . diving into the lake over and over again until he succeeded.'

'He was a good swimmer.'

'But why tell no one, not even you, that he'd found it?'

'I don't know.'

'And why . . .'

'Kill himself there? You can say it. I never thought it was an accident. And neither did you.'

I looked straight at her. This was the Vivien I'd known while her brother was alive: vibrant, determined, *honest*. This was the Vivien I knew it was dangerously easy to fall in love with. 'Why would he do such a thing?' I asked, knowing very well there could probably never be a definitive answer.

'He had a reason. I'm sure of that, if of little else. And I sense he wanted me – us – to understand his reason. Mother's decided it's best not to try. She's afraid the most – or rather the worst – we could achieve is a change in the inquest verdict from misadventure to suicide. She wants to avoid that at all costs. Greville agrees with her. So, the consensus in the family is: leave well alone.'

'But you're not going to.'

'The coroner's never going to reopen the case, Jonathan. Mother's worrying over nothing. The verdict doesn't matter, anyway. I just want the truth. Oliver deserves that, don't you think?'

'Of course. But—'

'And that's why I need your help.'

So. We'd come to the crux. We'd come to what had brought her to me. 'What can I do?'

'Do you still have the pig's egg Oliver left in your father's car?'

'Yes. But not here. It's at home in St Austell.'

'Never mind. You're sure it's a Z inscribed on it?'

'No question about it.'

'I think there is, you see. If I'm right, it's not a Z. It's the Greek letter zeta. A capital Z and a capital zeta look the same.'

'Greek?'

'Oliver took it at O level. I'd forgotten until I saw the dictionary in his bookcase.'

'OK. Zeta not Z. Does it make a difference?'

'It's a coded message. I'm certain of it. Zeta is the sixth letter of the Greek alphabet. The sixth letter of the English alphabet is F. So, maybe the Z on the pig's egg actually stands for F.'

'And that means?'

'F for Francis.'

'Your great-uncle?'

'He was a Greek scholar in his day. Greats at Oxford, no less. He collects crystals. He knows what a pig's egg is. And Oliver told you he could explain why a pig's egg is the key to everything.'

Yes. Oliver had told me that. And Vivien and I had both seen how taken aback Francis had been when I'd asked him to explain it to us.

'He played for time before he answered, if you remember. In the end, he suggested Oliver meant it as a metaphor for the nature of geology. But I don't think it has anything to do with geology.'

'What, then?'

'I don't know. But I think Uncle Francis knows. Which is why I've taken him up on a standing invitation to visit him and Luisa in Capri. I'm going out there as soon as term ends. Want to come with me?'

A trip to Capri with Vivien? Had I really heard her ask me along? It promised to transform the summer, perhaps more than

119

the summer. There was no way I'd even try to resist the idea and the watermelon-slice of a smile that was my immediate reaction must have made that abundantly obvious. 'Of course I want to go with you.'

She laughed. 'You're not exactly playing hard to get.'

'Well, there'd be sacrifices, obviously. I'd planned to give myself a few weeks off before starting a holiday job at CCC and thought I might spend part of the time with Terry and some mates, camping in the Peak District. Capri with you is obviously second best to that, but I can't let you go alone, can I?'

'Idiot.' She flicked a dead match in my general direction.

'Seriously, though, won't your mother have something to say about your choice of travelling companion?'

'There's no reason why she has to find out about it. Don't worry. I'll make sure Francis and Luisa don't breathe a word to her.'

Exactly how she was going to do that was unclear to me, but I wasn't about to demand an explanation. Nor was I inclined to point out the flaws in her theory that Francis knew more than he was telling. He might have been genuinely baffled by the question Oliver had had me ask him. And the Z on the pig's egg really might be a Z after all. It didn't matter to me if the trip proved to be a wild-goose chase. Better in some ways if it was. Oliver couldn't be brought back from the dead. Vivien had lost him whatever we discovered on Capri. But I hadn't lost Vivien. She was back in my world. And this time I wasn't going to let her go.

I persuaded Vivien to delay her return to Cambridge until the evening. We took a boat trip from Charing Cross upriver to Kew and wandered round the gardens in warm June sunshine. We talked about our contrasting slices of student life and gently re-established the rapport there'd been between us while Oliver was still alive. Eventually, over tea, we discussed Oliver himself and the dark thoughts that had engulfed her in the wake of his death.

'I never actually decided to kill myself,' Vivien said of her over-dose. 'I just wanted to make the . . . the despair . . . go away.'

'I badly wanted to help you through that, you know.'

120

'I do know. And I'm sorry I shut you out. I suppose I blamed you for what had happened, even though I knew you weren't to blame. It was a terrible time. Not just for me, of course. Mother had to bear her own grief as well as cope with me. Going to Egypt was probably the best thing we could have done.'

'How was it?'

'Ancient. Alien. And indifferent to our . . . piddling anguish.' She smiled. 'Just what we needed.'

'I'm glad it worked for you.'

'The psychiatrist did his bit too. He made me understand I could never have saved Oliver.' She gazed thoughtfully towards the Palm House. 'He'd be horrified by what I'm proposing to do now.'

'Why?'

'Because he said it was important that I accept there was no grand secret behind Oliver's self-destruction; that I let his . . . paranoia . . . rest with him.'

'But you don't think it was paranoia, do you?'

'I'm not sure. I *was* sure. But since we found the briefcase . . .' She whipped off her sunglasses and looked at me intently. 'I need to be certain. Or at least to feel I've done all I can to achieve certainty. Does that make sense to you?'

'Yes, Vivien. It does.'

She leant forward and kissed me. 'Thanks for saying that. You don't know how good it is to have someone believe in me.'

By the time I said goodbye to Vivien that evening, we'd laid our plans. Term ended at Cambridge a week earlier than London, so she'd travel to Capri alone and prepare the ground for my arrival. The only money I had to find was for my train ticket. The generous allowance she enjoyed would cover everything else. From my point of view, the prospect was altogether delicious.

All I had to do in the meantime was back out of the camping holiday and explain to my parents that I was accompanying some anonymous friends to Italy instead, then grit my way through to the end of term. It seemed to take for ever to arrive, but eventually the morning came for me to pack my few essential belongings in a rucksack and head for Victoria station. A postcard had reached me from Capri the day before. '*Arrived safely and looking forward to seeing you. Phone the villa when you know the time of your train into Naples and I will come and meet you. Love, V.*' The contents hadn't gone unnoticed by Terry and my other remaining housemate, Robin. Their nakedly envious opinion was that I was luckier than I had any right to be. And I was inclined to agree.

That morning, they both rose unwontedly early – well before eleven – to see me off. It was as I was literally opening the front door to leave that Terry snapped his fingers and announced he'd just remembered he had something to tell me that had slipped his mind over breakfast.

'Haven't got into debt to fund this Mediterranean jaunt, have you, man?' he asked.

'No, Terry, I haven't. Why do you ask? Thinking of offering me a loan?'

''Course not. I'm borassic. You know that. It's just . . . well, last night, down at the Builders' . . .' (The Builders' Arms was our unlovely local, which Terry was keener on than the rest of us.) 'There was this bloke asking about you.'

'Asking what?'

'Where you were going over the summer. What you were planning to do. I'd never seen him before. Wondered if he might be a . . . y'know, debt collector?'

'What did you tell him?'

'Oh, nothing. I played it cool as ice, man.' (If only I'd found that easy to believe.) 'Well, when I say nothing . . .'

'*What?*'

Terry shrugged. 'I might've mentioned you were going abroad with your girlfriend. But that was it. No details.'

'Couldn't you have told him to mind his own business?'

'I was a bit pissed. Before I twigged what was going on . . .' He shrugged feebly.

I glared at him, little impression though it made. 'You're sure you've never seen this bloke before?'

Even certainty on that point was waning. 'Not that I can recall.'

122

'What did he look like?'

Another shrug. 'Like . . . your average middle-aged square. Not tall, not short. Not fat, not thin. Smoked a pipe. Fussy little 'tache. Never took his hat off, so he might've been bald . . . or he mightn't have been.'

'Sounds like my dad,' said Robin. 'He's bald as a coot under his trilby.'

Whatever association the description had set off in Robin's mind, it meant nothing to me, though whether that was good news or bad I couldn't decide. It was difficult to resist the suspicion that the man's curiosity about my plans for the summer had something to do with Vivien's reappearance in my life. But I was at a loss to understand why.

'D'you know him, then?' asked Terry.

'I don't think so, no.'

'But he knows you,' said Robin.

'Yeah. Well, maybe, maybe not. Look, I've got to go or I'll miss my train. If this bloke turns up again, or anyone else asks about me . . .'

'We'll say you've joined the Foreign Legion.'

I sighed. 'Just say nothing.'

THIRTEEN

I didn't know what to make of Terry's revelation. Nobody had any reason to be interested in my plans for the summer. Yet someone was. The knowledge formed a small dark cloud in the blue sky of my immediate future. It was disturbing, yet also, I'd have to admit, faintly thrilling, as if I'd stepped into an episode of *The Saint*.

I was, in truth, far more excited than I was worried. The train to Dover and the Channel crossing were a drab prelude to a journey of delights. Calais didn't look much, but it was the beginning of abroad. Nothing else mattered. And Paris was Paris, even if all I had time for on my way across the city was a circuit of Notre-Dame and a Brie baguette on the banks of the Seine.

The sleeper to Italy should have been an ordeal, especially since I didn't have a berth, but with every kilometre I covered, extra layers of novelty and exoticism added themselves to the experiences I was eagerly anticipating. In Rome, I missed one train to Naples so I could see the Colosseum bathed in stridently clear morning light. It was a moment of magic: a sunburst of understanding that for me, at nineteen, the world's wonders were open for exploration.

I didn't want to explore them alone, though. Paris and Rome were grand and impressive places. But in Naples Vivien would be waiting. I called the Villa Orchis from Termini station, after a titanic struggle with the eccentricities of a Roman pay-phone. The call was answered by someone sounding young, male and Italian, who switched to fluent if heavily accented

124

English when I bawled my name down the fuzzy, crackling line.

Reassuringly, it was apparent he'd been expecting to hear from me. I assumed he was some kind of servant. He said he'd tell 'Miss Foster' the time of my train and wished me *'Buon viaggio.'*

Three hours later, I was plodding along the platform at Napoli Centrale in a sweaty crowd of disembarking passengers, wishing I'd been able to take a shower at some point since leaving London. And suddenly there was Vivien ahead of me, smiling and waving.

She looked cool and radiant in a white dress, her blonde hair half a shade fairer than I remembered. Men were glancing at her appreciatively as they passed – and enviously at me, I imagined, as we hugged and kissed. I felt the warmth of her skin through the thin fabric of her dress.

'Naples is a madhouse,' she said, threading her arm through mine as we headed for the exit. 'Capri, on the other hand, is paradise. Let's get you over there.'

We took a taxi down through the city to the ferry port. The sunlight fell in glaring slabs between deep gulfs of shadow, revealing a jostling chaos of street life beneath laundry-hung tenements that might once have been fine *palazzi*. Everything was louder and brighter and dirtier than London, but also more vitally human. I opened my eyes and ears to the grubby glory of it all, laughing and shaking my head at our driver's antics as scooters dodged and weaved around us.

'See Naples and die of nervous exhaustion,' said Vivien, laughing along with me.

'I can hardly believe we're on the same planet as St Austell.'

'We're not. We're orbiting a different sun here.'

We reached the port just in time for a Capri ferry and soon, as it chugged out of the harbour, I was able to gaze back at the conical mass of Mount Vesuvius and the wide, languorous sweep of the Bay of Naples. I felt shocked by the abundance of colour and light, as if I was looking at a picture rather than a reality of which I was part. I tried to explain the sensation to Vivien and she said she'd felt something of the same herself on her first visit.

'For some reason, despite all those modern port buildings you can see, it's easy to imagine you've stepped back into Ancient Rome – that Vesuvius hasn't yet buried Pompeii.'

'It's amazing.'

'Luisa told me I'd be a different person here. I didn't know what she meant. I soon realized she was right.'

'Different in what way?'

'Tell me when it happens to you.'

Capri appeared ahead of us, growing slowly from a hazy blob to a looming chunk of cliff and greenery. The ferry closed in on the harbour at Marina Grande and the passengers, most of them tourists clutching cameras and guidebooks, began massing near the stern. We brought up the rear when they were released on to the jetty. I for one was in no hurry. I wanted to savour every step of my arrival.

Where the Villa Orchis was in relation to Marina Grande I had no idea, of course. As we ambled along the jetty, Vivien explained that it was on the other side of the island. 'It's quieter there and more peaceful.' That was easy to believe. Ahead of us was a phalanx of crowded cafés and trinket shops. People were already queuing for the funicular up to the main town.

But for us transport was waiting in the form of Luisa's car, an elegant old Alfa Romeo cabriolet with white-walled tyres, parked on the crowded harbourfront, where it seemed to occupy a bubble of tranquil privilege. Waiting also was Luisa's chauffeur-cum-manservant, Paolo. He was the man I'd spoken to on the telephone – young for his trade, handsome and well-groomed, with a mane of dark hair and a dazzling smile. His deferential greeting carried with it a hint of narcissism. He appeared to have been admiring himself in the rear-view mirror as we approached and I didn't doubt he thought himself superior to me in many important ways that only his employment prevented him from revealing.

The display of fast, expert driving that followed was as

impressive as it was probably intended to be. We sped up the steep, winding road towards the heights above Marina Grande, a view of the harbour and the Sorrento peninsula opening up behind us as we climbed. The wind blew Vivien's hair clear of her neck and, looking at her, I realized once again just how beautiful she was. I gave thanks for the tricks of chance and fate that had landed me there, beside her. With days of her company to look forward to on our very own island in the sun.

The Villa Orchis lay south-west of Capri town, in the foothills of Monte Solaro, the peak that reared above Marina Piccola, Marina Grande's smaller, humbler sister on the southern side of the island. The villas hereabouts, viewed from the road, were bright white pockets in a lush green undulating sward, with little of the houses themselves visible behind high, creeper-draped walls.

But the stone pineapples on the gate pillars of the Villa Orchis symbolized welcome and my first impression was of comfort and homeliness rather than wealth and grandeur. The flagstoned drive carried us through a tunnel of dappled light formed by a fat-columned pergola of luxuriant wisteria to the foot of a short flight of steps that led up to a wicker-roofed terrace and the main body of the house: white-walled like its neighbours, terracotta-roofed, some windows shuttered against the sun, others standing open to the sweet-scented air.

Francis and Luisa were waiting for us on the terrace, where they were taking tea. I was greeted more warmly than I had any right to expect, like someone they knew well and were genuinely delighted to see again. As Paolo vanished with my bag a small, plump, elderly cook-cum-maid addressed as Patrizia brought out more tea and cakes. All was suddenly ease and good cheer. It was only when I was in the middle of recounting a mishap on the Paris Metro, to my audience's gratifying amusement, that I was brought up short by a fleeting seriousness in Vivien's eyes as she looked at her great-uncle. It reminded me of the real purpose of my journey to Capri – the real purpose, that was, from Vivien's point of view.

*

127

I'd been given a room at the side of the house, opening on to a balcony from which the view was shared between an emerald-green flank of Monte Solaro and a sapphire-blue wedge of the Tyrrhenian Sea. I stepped out to admire my surroundings after unpacking and noticed that two other rooms also opened on to the balcony. Through the French windows of one, I glimpsed, folded over a chair, a candy-striped dress that was surely Vivien's. We were close. And perhaps the rooms had been chosen in the knowledge that we might be closer still. A splash of sunlight illuminated the title of a paperback standing on her bedside cabinet: *Catch-22*. But there was no catch I could see.

A close neighbour and old friend of Luisa's was joining us for dinner. But there was still time for Vivien and me to walk down into Marina Piccola for a drink at one of the seafront cafés, looking out over the bay dotted with yachts and small boats. Late-afternoon light sparkled on the wavetops and my moisture-beaded glass of beer and gilded the dark-skinned sunbathers on their loungers below us, drugged by the heat and the rhythmic plash of the surf.

'You may have had a wasted journey,' said Vivien, smiling at me apologetically with pursed lips, as she set down her glass.

'How d'you mean?'

'It's just that I've been here a week and learnt nothing – absolutely nothing – to suggest Uncle Francis is harbouring some dark secret.'

'No?'

'I should be relieved, I suppose. I don't want to think of him as anything more than the kindly old chap he's always seemed.'

'Well, I guess I'm relieved too. And don't worry on my account. It's smashing to be here . . . with you.'

'Flatterer.'

'It's true, Vivien.' I looked at her. 'You must know that.'

She blushed slightly and waved the compliment aside. 'It was nice of you to come, Jonathan. And it's good to see you again. We can . . . try to put last year behind us.'

'Sounds fine to me.'

'But first prepare to be impressed. I was right about the Z on the pig's egg. It is zeta. And it does stand for Francis.'

'Really?' I *was* impressed. And puzzled. Confirmation that the Z stood for Francis implied the existence of some kind of secret after all. 'How did you find out?'

'It's marked on all the minerals in his collection. I asked to see them, which delighted him, and there it was. He stores the samples in a cabinet in his study. He'll happily show you. You only have to ask.'

'The Z – or zeta – is on all of them?'

'Yes. I told him we'd found a pig's egg with a Z on it in Oliver's bedroom. I didn't want to land you in it by saying where it was really found. Anyway, Uncle Francis wasn't fazed or surprised. He said he'd given it to Oliver when we were both here two years ago.'

'Which explains how Oliver came by it. But not why he hid it in my father's car.'

'Perhaps he didn't want it to be lost in the lake. He couldn't simply hand it over to you without giving a reason.'

'And Uncle Francis's reaction when I asked him about pigs' eggs that night at the Carlyon Bay?'

'He actually mentioned that without my needing to raise the subject. Apparently, he'd forgotten giving the sample to Oliver. His old noddle, as he called it, had let him down. Being reminded like that . . . threw him for a moment.'

I wasn't as convinced as Vivien seemed to be. But I didn't need to be. It was all about her. If she was happy to let sleeping dogs lie, so was I. Because in her happiness I saw the promise of my own.

'I think there is a secret at the Villa Orchis, though,' Vivien continued, lowering her voice conspiratorially. 'But it has nothing to do with Oliver.'

'What is it?'

'Paolo, our chauffeur today. He lives in, you know. He has the room over the garage. A very vain fellow, our Paolo.'

'I noticed that.'

'He's an addition to the establishment since I was here with Oliver and Aunt Harriet. When he's not polishing the Alfa Romeo

129

and racing it round the island, he's supposed to be Luisa's secretary, whatever that means.'

'What *does* it mean?'

'I think he attends to all her needs, not just secretarial ones.'

Catching her drift, I instinctively laughed. 'You can't be serious.'

But clearly she was. 'I saw him coming out of her bedroom one afternoon when Uncle Francis was in town. I could tell from his self-satisfied smirk what had been going on.'

'I must look out for it.' I grinned. 'His smirk, I mean.'

She failed to stifle a grin of her own. 'It's not funny.'

'Sorry.'

'Actually, I think Luisa may know I'm on to her. She gave me a little talk later that day. She described how trying retirement was for her. "I put so much passion into my performances and I received so much adoration," she said. "It is hard to live without such things."'

'But you reckon she isn't living without them.'

'Apparently not.'

'Well . . .'

'Live and let live?'

'Or love and let love.'

I let the ambiguities of that float in the air for a moment as I swallowed some beer. Sex in the afternoon, when the villa was quiet and the day at its hottest, took dreamy form in my mind. But it was a dream in which neither Luisa nor Paolo played any part.

I cleared my throat. 'Does Francis know?'

'I'm not sure. Maybe, maybe not. But he's no fool, so . . .'

'He probably does.'

Vivien nodded. 'Yes.'

'They put on a good show, considering.'

'They do, don't they? And as their guests I suppose we should do our best to keep the show on the road. So, now I've told you, try to pretend I haven't.'

'All right. Any other . . . rules of the house?'

'Not really. Pleasure seems to be the guiding principle of life at Villa Orchis.'

'Uhuh. Well, I can see I'm going to have a hellish time of it, then.' I raised my glass. 'Here's to pleasure.'

She giggled, more girlishly than usual. 'I'm glad you're here, Jonathan. I really am.'

'So am I.'

And so I was.

Luisa's friend and neighbour turned out to be a member of the Italian aristocracy, at least so her introduction to me as la contessa Margherita Covelli led me to believe. She certainly looked the part: tall, thin, velvet-gowned and discreetly bejewelled, her aquiline nose and keen eyes giving her a wonderfully predatory appearance, though her manner was actually all softness and gentility. Her grey hair made her look older than Luisa, though according to Vivien that was probably an illusion wrought by the beauty salon Luisa regularly patronized.

Countess Covelli gave the impression of being more contented than Luisa, less effusive but also more thoughtful. She was a widow of long standing, with a family in Milan and a wide circle of acquaintances, who nonetheless valued her solitary existence on Capri. 'There is a rhythm to my life here that I have come to value,' she said at one point, which was as much in the way of introspection as we had from her. She was altogether keener to hear Vivien recount the joys of punting and picnicking in Cambridge and insisted I give a blow-by-blow (and somewhat exaggerated) account of my part in the Grosvenor Square riot. She even wanted to know what I thought of the situation in Northern Ireland. And I somehow wasn't surprised to discover she knew more about it than I did.

'Margherita has a formidable intellect, don't you think?' asked Francis, after persuading me to join him in a brandy and a cigar following the countess's departure and Luisa's and Vivien's retirement to bed. I hadn't needed a lot of persuasion. It felt good to be treated as an equal by him: a fellow man of the world, as it were, even though I wasn't. My spluttering debut as a cigar-smoker soon demonstrated that.

131

I agreed with him about Margherita, naturally, and asked how long she and Luisa had been friends.

'More than thirty years. They met before the war, in Milan. Margherita's late husband was a great admirer of Luisa's singing.'

'Did you know him yourself?'

'Ah, no. Count Covelli's story is rather tragic, I'm afraid. You're familiar with the events that led up to Mussolini's overthrow in 1943?'

I confessed I wasn't.

'Let me fill you in, then,' said Francis, benignly unsurprised by my ignorance. 'The Italians were sick of the war by the end of 1942. It had brought them nothing but disaster. Most of the generals and politicians wanted to renounce the alliance with Germany and make peace with the Allies. But Mussolini would have none of it. So, he had to go. The trigger was the Allied invasion of Sicily in July 1943. Not a cakewalk, let me tell you from personal experience, but ultimately decisive. The King, Victor Emmanuel, started secret talks through intermediaries with leading members of the Fascist Grand Council to have the Duce deposed. Count Covelli was one of those intermediaries. And the talks soon bore fruit. The Council voted to restore the King as commander-in-chief of the armed forces. Effectively, that was a vote to sue for peace. Mussolini was arrested on the King's orders and held as a prisoner. Hitler had no intention of allowing Italy to surrender, of course. The Germans carried on fighting regardless. They rescued Mussolini and installed him as president of a puppet Italian republic. Those who'd betrayed him and were unlucky enough to find themselves in German-occupied territory were for the chop. And Covelli was one of the unlucky ones. He went into hiding, but was soon tracked down. In January 1944, he and five other prime movers in Mussolini's deposition were given a show trial in Verona, then executed by firing squad.'

'Poor man.'

'Quite so. And poor Margherita. She loved him dearly, according to Luisa. At the end of the war, Mussolini tried to escape to Austria, but he was captured by partisans, along with his mistress,

Claretta Petacci, and shot. Their bodies were strung upside down in the Piazzale Loreto in Milan – you probably know this bit – as a demonstration of what the partisans thought of their former Duce. Margherita once told me she went to the square that day to look at the man responsible for her husband's death. She saw a woman beating Mussolini about the head with a stick and ranting about the loss of her son, killed serving in the army in Greece. Margherita said she was almost as horrified by the violence Mussolini inspired in his victims as she had been by the viciousness of his regime. When Luisa bought this villa, Margherita came to visit her and soon decided Capri was where she could find the peace she craved. I believe she's succeeded, much to her credit.'

'It certainly seems a peaceful place.'

'It does, doesn't it? Islands, especially those as small as this, have a special quality about them, I think. They exist a little apart from the world and tend to attract people in need of . . . refuge and healing.'

It seemed to me he might be talking about himself rather than Margherita Covelli. A wistful tone had come into his voice, as if he'd begun reflecting on his own reasons for settling there. He took a thoughtful puff at his cigar and gazed beyond me into some shadowy recess of his past.

Then he rallied and gave me a jaunty grin. 'Capri has more than its fair share of idlers and lotus-eaters in retreat from nothing more than the obligation to earn a living, of course. I should damn well know. I'm one of them.' He laughed his growling laugh. 'A splash more brandy, my boy?'

FOURTEEN

It's hard now, looking back, to recall just how happy I was for most of the few weeks I spent on Capri in the summer of 1969. I recall it as a fact, of course, with the reasons clear and simple in my mind. But memory is always overlain with the knowledge of what follows. And what followed then erased many happinesses, not just mine.

You could say tragedy came out of the blue, for Capri was truly and brilliantly blue in the high, strident Mediterranean light, an intoxicating blend of limitless sky and encompassing sea. And no one anticipated what was going to happen. No one set out – as far as I know – to bring it about. So, yes, you could say it came out of the blue.

It wouldn't quite be true, though. I never saw it coming – never guessed how the dominoes might fall. But I pushed them. There's no denying that. This tragedy was man-made. I should know. I was one of those who made it.

I wanted Vivien so badly I couldn't think about much else, certainly not the mystery her brother had bequeathed to us. Even Vivien had lost her determination to pursue an answer since arriving on Capri and concluding that Great-Uncle Francis held the key to nothing but a contented, if very possibly cuckolded, lifestyle. Capri itself was partly to blame for this. Its heat and stillness, compounded for visitors like us by its seductive otherness, made the cares and preoccupations we'd brought with us seem distant and futile and ultimately unimportant.

Vivien didn't give up without a struggle. She recalled that during their previous stay at the Villa Orchis, while she'd done little but swim and sunbathe, Oliver had gone off on solitary hikes around the coast. He'd been particularly interested in the Roman ruins at either end of the island and so we began our aimless search for his secret by walking out to the remains of the Villa Jovis, on the eastern headland.

From here the Emperor Tiberius had ruled the Roman Empire, but all that remained of his clifftop palace was fallen walls and roofless halls. We wandered the site, surprising basking lizards that scattered before us as we went. The sun blazed down and the pine woods around the villa shimmered in a heat haze. I looked at Vivien as she walked ahead of me, her legs and arms bronzed and her hair bleached from the week and a bit she'd already spent on the island. She was wearing cut-off jeans, a thin-strapped top and a straw hat. Her hair fell beneath the hat to just above her shoulders, bouncing slightly as she walked. A bangle on her wrist winked dazzlingly at me. At intervals, she glanced round and smiled, as if she knew what I was thinking and understood perfectly.

We came to Tiberius's Drop, a sheer cliff, from which, according to the guidebook, those who'd mortally offended the Emperor were required to throw themselves to their deaths. I imagined leaping out, arms spread, into the void and asked, almost rhetorically, 'Did they really jump – or were they pushed?'

'Oh, they jumped,' Vivien said with utter certainty.

'How d'you know?'

'Because I've just remembered Oliver describing this place to me and telling me that if you annoyed the Emperor by forcing the guards to push you, your family would suffer for it. So, they jumped.'

'A cruel choice,' I said, gazing out to sea.

'Not according to Oliver. He reckoned stepping out into thin air would've been easy. As long as you didn't think about what happened when you stopped falling.'

Our eyes met. Oliver was there, between us, an invisible but palpable presence. Whether he was blessing us or cursing us I couldn't have said. Nor, I suspect, could Vivien. Perhaps it made no difference. Perhaps there *was* no difference.

I took her hand and we moved away from the edge. 'I'm so glad you knew him, Jonathan,' she said. 'I'm glad it's you who's here with me.'

And so, it didn't need saying, was I.

We headed back along the narrow paths and alleys of the island towards Capri town, stopping on our way for lunch at a sun-shaded trattoria, where the wine tasted all the fuller to me for the headiness of sharing it with a beautiful young woman who was nearly, oh so nearly, mine.

From Capri we descended to Marina Grande, where we strolled through the crowds to the beach and swam a little and lazed a lot as the afternoon wore on.

I must have fallen into a doze brought on by wine and heat. When I woke, with the shadow of the bluff above us stretching across the towel on which we lay, I found Vivien propped up on one elbow beside me, staring intently into my eyes. She was still in her bikini from our swim. There was a frown of concentration on her brow, as if she was debating something very seriously.

'Jonathan . . .'

I didn't wait for her to say any more. I raised my head and kissed her. I felt her hair tickling my neck, her breasts compressing against me. I put a hand to her shoulder and ran it down her flank, tracing the curve of her waist and hip.

We broke the kiss and gazed at each other. Our course had been set now. We weren't lovers yet. But soon we would be. The realization carried solemnity as well as desire.

'Let's go back to the villa,' she said. 'It'll be cooler there.'

I wished we could have been transported to the Villa Orchis instantly, to the shuttered privacy of her room or mine. But wishes aren't wings. We had to take the funicular back up to Capri and walk from there through the late-afternoon heat. There were many kisses along the way. I hardly knew how we'd manage our arrival.

To my dismay and frustration, it became apparent as we walked up the drive that Francis and Luisa had been entertaining a visitor to tea, who'd been hoping, we were told, to meet us. We had no choice but to sit down on the terrace and socialize.

The visitor was an Italian man of about Francis's age, portly and jet-black-haired, well-tailored and syrupy-voiced. Valerio Salvenini, it transpired, was a garrulous native of the island, who claimed acquaintance with numerous famous Capri residents, both living and dead, and proceeded to reel off a succession of well-worn anecdotes about them.

His wife, he artfully lamented, was away, prompting Luisa to invite him to stay for dinner. All I could do, when he accepted, was swap a rueful little smile with Vivien. We were trapped.

The need to shower before dinner supplied a brief respite from Salvenini's tall tales. I went out afterwards from my room on to the balcony and found Vivien waiting for me, barefoot, wet-haired and wrapped in a bathrobe. We exchanged eloquent smiles and a lingering kiss.

'I think all that sunshine and fresh air we've been out in today means I'm going to need an early night,' she whispered in my ear.

'Me too.' I slipped my hand inside the robe and fondled her breast.

'Some things are better if you have to wait for them.'

'Provided you don't have to wait too long.'

'Go on doing what you're doing,' she gasped, 'and I'll have to take another shower.'

'I could join you.'

She gently lifted my hand away and pressed a finger to my lips. 'Later.'

*

137

I have little memory of what Salvenini told us that evening. Maxim Gorky, Hugh Walpole, Compton Mackenzie, Jean-Paul Sartre, Thornton Wilder, Norman Douglas, Graham Greene, Gracie Fields: they all received a mention, I think. The possibility of an introduction to Greene, Salvenini's close neighbour in Anacapri, was held out to us at some stage: a ripe fruit we failed to pluck. If he was disappointed by our unresponsiveness, he didn't show it. Perhaps he guessed we had only each other on our minds. Perhaps Francis and Luisa guessed as well. Perhaps it was plainly obvious. They'd all been young once. Whereas we'd never been old.

If I could choose one night from my whole life to live over again, it would be that night at the Villa Orchis with Vivien, the French windows of her room standing open to the soft island air, moonlight rippling across her body as I wrapped my arms around her. There was a single moment of rapture and incredulity as I climaxed inside her for the first time that in some part of my mind I realized even then would never be surpassed.

The week that followed passed in a haze of sensuality. By day, Vivien and I swam and walked and explored the island. By night we made long, languorous love and slept late into the morning. I was hers and she was mine. It was a taste of heaven.

Our hosts could hardly have missed the ample evidence of how intimate our relationship had become, but never drew attention to it or interfered in any way. As perhaps befitted partners in an unconventional marriage – assuming as I did that Vivien was right about Paolo's role in it – they appeared genially tolerant of us, if not approving. 'We were put on this planet to enjoy what it has to offer, my boy,' Francis said to me one evening. '*Everything* it has to offer.'

A similar sentiment was expressed by Countess Covelli when she met us in Capri one afternoon and offered us tea at her villa as a reward for carrying home the bags she'd accumulated during a tour of the town's smartest boutiques. 'I adore the company of young people,' she said as we reached her elegant, secluded residence, the Villa Erycina. 'It helps me remember what it was like to be young myself.' She smiled at us deliberately. 'Young *and* in love, of course.'

It was true. We were in love. Well, I certainly was. And Vivien had given me every reason to think she was too. But neither of us had actually declared our love. It had taken a third party to do that. I suppose I was afraid it was simply too good to be true. And Vivien? My *belle dame sans merci*, as her brother had called her? Or someone who merely shared my fear? I didn't know which she was. I still had to find that out.

The Villa Erycina was smaller than the Villa Orchis, but architecturally more distinguished, with fluted columns, high, vaulted ceilings and gleaming marble floors. The countess, it became apparent as she gave us a brief tour of the house before tea on the terrace, had no patience for clutter. All was restraint and order – comfort on the level more of a hotel than a home.

The most personal touches were an array of silver-framed photographs on the drawing-room mantelpiece. Children of two or three different generations – to judge by their clothing and hair-styles – were variously pictured, some formally in a studio, some casually grouped in a domestic setting. The woman at the centre of one such group was clearly Margherita several decades younger. And the stiff-backed, handsomely sleek man pictured separately in evening dress was, I guessed, her late husband.

'*Si, si,*' said Margherita, nodding in confirmation. 'That is Urbano.'

'Francis told me how he came to die,' I said. 'It was . . . a sad story.'

'Yes.' She gazed at the photograph for a moment. 'But not so sad as if I had been married to a Fascist.'

'You must be very proud of him,' said Vivien.

'Of course. But I am still angry with him sometimes also. For leaving me to live the rest of my life without him. For having to explain to his grandchildren why they cannot know him. Perhaps I

139

should have listened to my mother. She advised me not to marry him.'

'What did she have against him?'

Margherita laughed fondly. 'She said he was a man of principle. She said he could not be relied on to put his family first. And she was right. But that was partly why I loved him. For his sense of honour. The last thing he said to me was, "It is better to be betrayed than to be a traitor."' Tears glistened in her eyes. 'Forgive me. That is enough about the past. Let us go and have tea.'

I wanted to ask Margherita how the count had been betrayed, but she obviously preferred not to dwell on the subject, so I left it there, confident as I was that Francis would satisfy my curiosity.

I wasn't disappointed. The count, Francis later told me, had only reluctantly gone into hiding following the Germans' restoration of Mussolini in September 1943. Margherita had, after much cajoling, persuaded him to take refuge with a distant relative near Vicenza, while she laid a false trail by decamping with the children to their holiday home in San Remo. 'But someone tipped the Germans off and Urbano was arrested. Margherita was allowed to visit him in prison before his execution. She told me once how infuriatingly philosophical he'd been. She said it was almost as if he was glad to have been captured, as if he considered hiding from the Germans . . . undignified. A true gentleman, even to the end.'

Vivien and I spoke of Oliver less and less as the days slipped past deliciously. We didn't forget him, of course. But he'd drifted into the dead's natural habitat of unvoiced memories and neither of us, I think, wanted to risk breaking the spell Capri had cast on us by recalling too often the supposed reason for our presence on the island.

That reason seemed more than a little ridiculous now, anyway. Francis obviously had no better idea than we had why and how Oliver had ended his life. I asked one day to see his famous mineral collection and he happily obliged. As I knew from Vivien's description, it was housed in a large four-drawered cabinet in his study. He pulled the top drawer open and drew my attention to the zeta cipher straight away.

'Can't resist showing off my classical education, I'm afraid,' he laughed. 'Has Vivien told you she found the pig's egg I gave Oliver in his bedroom at Nanstrassoe House?'

'She mentioned it, yes,' I replied nonchalantly.

'I still don't understand what he meant by that question he had you ask the first time we met, you know. That evening at the Carlyon Bay. You remember?'

I assured him I did. 'Will you be wanting the pig's egg back?' I asked.

'No, no. I have several. I keep only one sample of each mineral in this cabinet. The choicest examples.'

The specimens were carefully laid out and labelled. Quartz. Biotite. Muscovite. Tourmaline. Haematite. Limonite. Cassiterite. Luxullianite. And humble kaolinite – good old china clay. Fascinating stuff if you were interested in mineralogy or crystallography – which I wasn't. I peered at the painstakingly mounted lumps of rock, but saw only lumps of rock.

'The Duke of Wellington's sarcophagus in St Paul's is made of luxullianite, you know. The Victorians were very keen on it. Ah, there's my pig's egg.' It was slightly larger and more finely formed than the one Oliver had left in my father's car. But it bore the same telltale zeta. 'Hard to know what all the fuss is about, isn't it?'

'Well, it's not the most eye-catching piece in your collection, admittedly. Did Oliver choose a pig's egg specifically? Or did you choose it for him?'

'Er ... I'm not absolutely sure.' Francis's memory seemed curiously fallible on the subject. 'I believe ... he chose it. Of course, I couldn't offer him the pick of the whole collection. Quite a few of the specimens are unique.'

'Are they all from Cornwall?'

'By no means. This part of Italy has much to offer. I have a particularly fine example of vesuvianite, for instance. Here, let me show you.'

He slid the drawer shut and opened the next one down. More

141

rocks met my gaze. I began to wish I hadn't asked to see the collection in the first place. It had told me nothing.

It was a relief, in a way. I didn't really want to turn up any clues to whatever Oliver had been trying to accomplish. I was in love with Vivien. I believed she was in love with me. We were good for each other. We were happy together. And our future looked brighter if her brother was left to rest in peace.

But that wasn't for me to decide. As I was soon to find out.

FIFTEEN

The first straw in the wind was an announcement by Paolo one morning that there'd been an attempt to break into the villa during the night. Splintered paint and wood around the French windows that led from the drawing-room on to the rear terrace suggested someone had tried to force the doors open. There was also some trampled ground in the shrubbery near the part of the wall where the gradient of the alley on the other side made it easiest to climb over.

Francis pooh-poohed the idea, dismissing the evidence as inconclusive and advising us not to worry. Luisa followed his lead, albeit with less conviction. Paolo seemed miffed not to be taken seriously and did a lot of shrugging and muttering. I joked to Vivien that someone might be after Francis's vesuvianite.

A couple of days passed without any further attempt and I for one forgot all about the incident. Then a morning came when Francis and Luisa headed out early, bound for Naples. Francis had a monthly appointment at a private clinic in the city with a cardiologist ('He listens to my ticker and tells me it hasn't stopped yet – money for old rope, of course, but it keeps Luisa happy') and Luisa always used the occasion, she told us, to visit some favourite shops and remind herself there was a world beyond Capri. Paolo was also going to Naples, where apparently he had friends and relatives to catch up with. He drove them down to Marina Grande in the Alfa Romeo: the thrumbling note of its engine and the clanging of the gates as Paolo closed them were what woke me, though Vivien slept on peacefully beside me.

I dozed lightly for twenty minutes or so, then decided to surprise Vivien by bringing her breakfast in bed. Patrizia wasn't in yet, so we were alone in the house. I threw on a dressing-gown and espadrilles and went downstairs.

I was halfway along the hall, ambling towards the kitchen, when I passed the open door of the drawing-room. I caught a blur of movement at the edge of my vision and swung round.

What I saw momentarily rooted me to the spot. There was a man outside on the terrace, crouching by the French windows, holding a crowbar. He was wearing a scruffy brown suit and trilby and had frozen in the act of attempting to prise the doors open. He'd seen me just as I'd seen him. And we recognized each other. Except that I could hardly believe the evidence of my eyes.

'Strake,' I gasped. I simply couldn't credit it. But it was true. Gordon Strake was there, in front of me.

He moved first, jumping up and taking off across the lawn at a lope. I covered several yards after him across the drawing-room before I remembered the French windows were locked, then I turned and ran for the front door.

By the time I'd made it round to the lawn at the back of the house, Strake had vanished. I followed in the direction I'd seen him take. The lawn was bordered by ilex bushes, some as big as trees, with branches extending over the top of the boundary wall. There were enough bent and broken stems to suggest Strake had exited that way. I scrambled up on to one of the stouter branches and peered over the wall. There was a street-lamp bracket within reach that he'd probably used as a handhold. But there was no sign of him. He could have gone up the alley or down and I knew it forked a short distance ahead. Going after him would have been hopeless, even if I'd been wearing more than I was. I retreated to the house.

I woke Vivien with coffee and the full, perplexing story. She was understandably incredulous.

'Strake? Here? That's crazy.'

'I agree. But it was him, Vivien, believe me. Without a shadow of a doubt.'

'What can he possibly want?'

'I don't know. It beats me. Something in this house, though. That's clear.'

'But *what*?'

'I've no idea. Maybe Francis knows. Strake did serve under him in the army.'

Vivien sat up suddenly, spilling some of her coffee into the saucer. 'This is about Oliver, isn't it?'

'Whoa. We don't—'

'No, it *is*. Strake was following him. We only have his word for it that Oliver hired him. Maybe he was working for someone else.'

'But who?'

'Uncle Francis? Maybe that's what Oliver was trying to tell us by planting the pig's egg.'

'Why would your uncle want to have Oliver followed? And why, if Strake was working for him then, would he be trying to break into his house now?'

'*I don't know.*' There was something more than exasperation in the way Vivien looked at me then. There was a hint that she knew I wanted her to let the mystery of her brother's death lie – and why. For a sickening moment I was afraid of losing her. Then she softened. 'I just don't know, Jonathan,' she said, clasping my hand. 'It's inexplicable. But there *is* an explanation. There has to be.'

'I agree. But how do we find it?'

'Well, we tell Uncle Francis what happened this morning and see what he says. What else can we do?'

'Nothing, I suppose. Meanwhile we'd better stay here. Strake might try again if he sees us leaving. He probably saw Paolo drive Francis and Luisa away and reckoned that left the house empty. We don't want him thinking he's got a second chance.'

'You think he's watching the house?'

'It wouldn't be easy without showing himself. But it's possible, I guess. He's a sly customer.'

'Oh God.' She put her cup down and gazed at me sadly. 'I've felt so . . . carefree . . . this past week. And now . . .'

'I'm sorry.'

'It's not your fault,' she sighed. 'I only wish I knew whose fault it really was.'

I kept watch while Vivien took a bath. I'd opened several ground-floor windows by now – the house would have been an oven otherwise – but I didn't expect Strake to return. He wouldn't have fled in the first place if he'd been willing to tackle me. But the fact that he'd attempted to break in had sullied the tranquil atmosphere of the Villa Orchis. It was no longer the haven it had seemed.

Patrizia's arrival restored a measure of normality. I didn't tell her what had happened, partly because her English and my Italian just weren't up to it and partly because her cheerfulness was so comforting. It pushed Strake and whatever sinister forces he represented back into the shadows.

Then the telephone rang. I left Patrizia to answer it. No one ever called me at the villa. But this time, it transpired, someone had.

'*Per te*, Jonathan,' she said, waggling the kitchen extension. '*Per te.*'

I took it in the drawing-room. My first thought was that it was Mum or Dad, checking to see all was well with their little boy. My first thought was wrong.

'You gave me quite a fright, sonny. I didn't know you were here.'

'Strake?'

'I reckon you and me can do each other a favour.'

'I'm not doing you any kind of favour.'

'You might change your mind when you hear what I'm offering.'

'And what's that?'

'You know the Bar Due Mare, by the junction at the western end of town?'

'Yes.'

'Meet me there at noon.'

'Why? What—?'

But I was talking to myself. He'd hung up.

'You have to go,' said Vivien, when I told her what he'd said.

'It could be a trick, to lure me away from the villa.'

'Gordon Strake doesn't frighten me. I'm sure Patrizia would be more than a match for him, anyway. This is our chance to find out what's going on, Jonathan. We have to take it.'

She was right, of course. I knew that. And so, apparently, did Strake.

He'd chosen, perhaps deliberately, just about the noisiest spot on the island. The roads to and from Marina Grande, Marina Piccola, Capri and Anacapri all met in the tight intersection at the very door of the Bar Due Mare, beneath the looming peaks of Monte Solaro and Monte Cappello. Lorries, buses, taxis, private cars and scooters contested the narrow junction, with a bus stop and a filling station adding to the congestion. Exhaust fumes swirled, horns blared, engines roared. It was the closest Capri could boast to Neapolitan mayhem.

Inside the Bar Due Mare wasn't much more peaceful than outside. Vivien and I'd drunk a couple of thirst-quenching Cokes there one afternoon without feeling the least inclination to linger. Strake was waiting for me at a table in the corner, slurping a beer and dragging on a roll-up. He didn't look like a tourist in his cheap suit and faded trilby and he didn't look like a local either. He looked, in fact, exactly what he was: a man up to no good.

I bought a Coke and sat down next to him. 'How do, sonny,' he greeted me.

'What are you doing here, Strake?'

'It's Mr Strake to you.'

He wasn't going to get a *mister* out of me. I ignored the rebuke and reminded myself that this derelict china clay salesman was no tough guy, whatever he pretended. 'Why were you trying to break into the villa?'

'Why d'you think?'

'I can't imagine.'

'No. 'Course you can't. Well, it wasn't to admire the nightingale's taste in curtain tassels, I can tell you that.'

It took me a second or so to realize that by the nightingale he meant Luisa. The implication that he knew her was strangely disturbing. I decided it was time to assert myself – as best I could. 'I'm willing to tell the police about you, Strake. OK? You should understand that.'

'You wouldn't go to the cops without the colonel's say-so. And you wouldn't get it.'

'Rubbish. He's not going to go easy on you just because you were in his regiment.'

'It wasn't his regiment. He only made it to major in the war. The colonelcy – lieutenant-colonelcy, at that – was a demob handout. Reward for services rendered. Special services. Most of which I did for him. With no official thanks. But you're right. He's not going to go easy on me on account of any of that.' Strake took a last drag on his roll-up and started another. 'Our more recent dealings, sonny – they're what'll stop the colonel having my collar felt.'

'What dealings?'

'Ah, well, that brings us to it, doesn't it?' Strake gave me a crooked little smile. 'That brings us to the favour we can do each other.'

'I told you on the—'

'Stuff that. You wouldn't be here if you weren't willing to parley.'

I sat back and looked at him. 'Say what you have to say.'

He leant forward, restoring the narrowness of the gap between us. 'You asked me last summer who paid me to follow Oliver Foster and I told you it was the lad himself. Remember?'

'Of course.'

Strake shrugged. 'Not true.'

I sighed. 'Who, then?'

Another shrug. 'The colonel.'

So, Vivien's surmise was correct – apparently. 'Francis Wren hired you to follow Oliver?'

'That he did.'

'Why?'

'I could tell you. I could tell you the full murky tale. But we have to trade, sonny. That's how this kind of deal works. You scratch my back. I scratch yours.'

'What d'you want?'

He lowered his voice to a smoky rasp. 'A sample of the nightingale's handwriting.'

'What?'

'You heard. A page or so should do. Not just a few lines, mind. Enough to keep an expert happy.'

'Expert?'

'Handwriting bloody expert. Don't play dumb with me, sonny. You know what I mean.'

'You were trying to break into the villa to get a sample of Luisa's *handwriting*?'

'Yeah. And now you can spare me the effort. I'm getting too old for that kind of thing, anyway. So, you do it for me. Come up with what I want and I'll spill the beans on what the colonel was so concerned young Olly shouldn't drag into the light of day. Well? You want to know, don't you? You badly want to know.'

It was true. I did. But I told myself to act cool. I mustn't let Strake believe he had the upper hand. 'What would this . . . sample . . . prove?'

'D'you take me for a sap, sonny? You get nothing more from me till you deliver the goods. And just in case you get some crazy idea of double-crossing me, bear in mind I already know what the nightingale's handwriting looks like, so I'll spot a fake straight off.'

'If you already—'

'I need an example, OK? I need it for comparison. It shouldn't be too difficult. You're under the same bloody roof as her. I'll give you forty-eight hours. Meet me here at noon the day after tomorrow. Then we'll trade.'

'Well, I—'

'This is the only chance you'll get to find out the truth, sonny. Are you going to sit there and tell me you're not interested? Well, are you?'

No. I wasn't.

149

*

Vivien's reaction was in a sense what I'd feared. Her determination to discover what had led to her brother's death was rekindled – and with it her suspicion that their great-uncle was somehow responsible.

'Strake could be stringing us along,' I cautioned. 'Remember, we have no idea why he wants a sample of Luisa's handwriting.'

'But we can find out, can't we? Before we hand it over. We have to do this, Jonathan. Creep though Strake is, he's our best hope of uncovering the truth.'

'You make it sound simple.'

'It is. I'll ask Luisa to write me out the recipe for that apple cake you liked so much. I'll say I want it to send to Mother. That'll please Luisa. She'd like Mother to think better of her than she does.'

Vivien seemed to have fixed on a solution almost before I'd finished outlining the problem. There was a gleam in her eye and an eagerness in her voice I didn't like. We were playing fast and loose with other people's secrets without any idea of what those secrets actually were – or what the consequences of their exposure might be. 'There could be another way,' I said lamely. 'If I told Francis what Strake said, he—'

'No. We can't breathe a word about Strake to Uncle Francis. Or anyone else. This has to stay between us. Don't you see, Jonathan? This is our opportunity to achieve what we came here for.'

What *she'd* come here for, I wanted to say. I'd come for quite a different reason. 'We must be careful, Vivien. We don't know what game Strake's really playing.'

'If he gives us what we want, it doesn't matter.'

But it did. I felt sure of that. It mattered a lot. 'I still—'

'Hush.' She silenced me with a kiss. 'You worry too much. This is going to work. I know it is.'

SIXTEEN

I felt increasingly anxious as the forty-eight hours Strake had allotted slowly unwound. The unknown and the unpredicted jostled disturbingly in my thoughts. Vivien continued to insist there was nothing to be alarmed about. We had Strake where we wanted him, not the other way round.

She exploited my infatuation with her to quench my fears. I realized what she was doing, but hadn't the will or the wish to resist. She let me do things to her I didn't even know I wanted to do until the pleasure of them had exploded in my mind. Then I was her prisoner and she was my plaything. It was a dangerous path to tread. And her readiness to tread it should have been a warning to me.

Obtaining a sample of Luisa's handwriting was, as Vivien had predicted, a simple matter. The apple cake ploy worked perfectly. In the fond hope of ingratiating herself with her stand-offish niece-in-law, Luisa obligingly wrote out the recipe for her *torta di mele* and even went so far as to supply the details of a variant using pears instead of apples. It ran to two and half pages in the end.

So, we had what we needed. Now it was only a question of using it to extract the truth from Strake. Though how we could be sure whatever he told us *was* the truth was another concern of mine Vivien didn't share. We were both going to meet him this time. And she seemed confident she'd be more than a match for him. 'He may talk big, but that's just an act. He's a spineless little shit. We won't have any trouble with Gordon Strake.'

151

That remained to be seen. Meanwhile, there was minor trouble, though nothing we couldn't cope with, from a different source. Paolo spotted signs of Strake's second intrusion: mortar dislodged from the wall, more trampling of the shrubbery. We assured him nothing had happened while they'd been in Naples, an assurance he met with sullen scepticism. But his employers' insouciance left him without a leg to stand on. Francis and Luisa remained resolutely unflustered.

Perhaps suspiciously so. It seemed to me they were determined to close their minds to the very idea that somebody had tried to break into the villa. And I couldn't help wondering if that was because they knew what it might portend.

I stayed up late with Francis over brandy and a cigar the night before Vivien and I were due to meet Strake. I told Vivien later that Francis had been so eager for my company I hadn't liked to disappoint him. But that wasn't true. I wanted to talk to him. Maybe I couldn't tell him about the deal I'd struck with Strake. But that didn't mean I couldn't discuss Strake with him. Whatever Vivien said, I was convinced we needed to know more about the man. And Francis might just be the man to enlighten me.

It wasn't difficult to lure the old soldier on to the subject of his wartime experiences. He'd had a lively time of it with the Eighth Army, though he was happy to admit his involvement in the great battles of El Alamein and Cassino was hardly central. 'The powers that be thought because I could read Latin I could speak modern Italian, so, after the landings in Sicily, I was transferred to intelligence duties: liaising with the locals and so forth. Sometimes that work was great fun, sometimes dull as bloody ditch-water, but it was seldom dangerous. I got off lightly, my boy. Otherwise I'd probably never have lasted the course from Alexandria in May forty-one through to Venice four years later. Too many bullets to dodge, what?'

This was my chance to steer the conversation towards Strake. 'When I met Gordon Strake last summer, he said he'd assisted you on what he called special duties. He made it sound . . . hush-hush.'

152

'The fellow's exaggerating. Where was it you met him? The General Wolfe, didn't you say? Well, put a drink in Strake's hand and an unvarnished account of himself isn't what you'll get. He was my driver for the last six months or so of the campaign. There were a few . . . sensitive situations. But hush-hush is pushing it.'

'Sounds exciting, even so.'

'Not really. The trickiest time was actually after the war ended. Venice was a wonderful place to celebrate the ceasefire, let me tell you. Not too many people can say they've driven a Jeep round St Mark's Square, but Strake can. I was sitting beside him swigging champagne. We were in a procession of Jeeps, as a matter of fact. Within a week, though, most of the Eighth Army had been moved up into Austria to police the border with Yugoslavia. I was part of a Field Army detachment left behind to mop up German fugitives and try to keep a lid on Partisan reprisals against collaborators and Mussolini loyalists. Not easy, not easy at all. Strake made himself quite useful, actually. He had a way of ferreting out information that had eluded everyone else. Not sure what his secret was. A devious mind, probably.'

'Did Strake ever meet Luisa?'

Francis gave me a baffled look. 'Luisa? Of course not. I didn't meet her myself until I'd quit Wren's and come back to Italy in forty-nine.'

'Ah, yes, of course.'

'You seem to have a bee in your bonnet about Strake, young Jonathan. Why are you so interested in him?'

'Oh . . .' I had to backtrack now. I couldn't afford to arouse his suspicions. 'No particular reason. I just . . . didn't get the feeling he was telling me as much as he could have . . . about Oliver.'

'Poor Oliver should never have had anything to do with Strake. The man had his uses, as I say, but I wouldn't trust him further than I could throw him.'

'Yet you took him on at Wren's.'

'Before becoming my driver, he'd been in the front line. He'd risked his life for his country, whatever one cares to say about his character. So, I couldn't just turn him away, though maybe I should

153

have. Maybe I would have, if I'd known what he was going to get up to eventually. But we can only see the future when it's turned into the past. And what use is it then, eh? You don't know it yet, my boy, but life's too short for regrets. Take it from me. Far too short.'

So, Francis told me nothing except what I already knew: Strake wasn't to be trusted. But as Vivien saw it, and as I tried my level best to see it as well, we didn't have to trust him. We just had to use him.

There was no sign of Strake when we walked into the Bar Due Mare shortly before noon. We bought a couple of Cokes, sat down and lit cigarettes. I felt nervous and uncertain. But Vivien remained serenely confident. 'Leave this to me, Jonathan,' she said. 'Strake isn't going to put anything over on us. I simply won't let him.'

Five minutes passed and still Strake didn't show. Vivien told me to stop looking at my watch. 'He probably thinks we'll be easier to deal with if he keeps us waiting. It isn't going to work.'

Another five minutes ticked slowly by. Then the telephone behind the counter rang. The man who'd served us answered it. '*Pronto?*' He looked across at us. '*Si.*' He scowled. '*Si, bene.*' Then he beckoned to me and gestured with the receiver. '*Per lei.*'

I looked at Vivien. She nodded for me to go ahead. I walked to the counter and took the phone. I didn't have any doubt who was on the line. 'Strake?'

'Still not grasped the fact that you need to be more respectful towards me, sonny?'

'Why aren't you here?'

'Because you didn't tell me you'd be bringing your girlfriend. Or that Vivien Foster *is* your girlfriend.'

'It's none of your business.'

'I'll be the judge of that.'

'We have what you want, Strake. Are you going to come and get it?'

'No. Leave little Miss Foster there and get yourself down to Marina Grande. I'll meet you on the jetty.'

I knew Vivien would never agree to be left behind. And I wasn't about to let Strake dictate terms. 'You deal with both of us,' I said, as coolly as I could. 'Or the deal's off.'

'You mean she has the handwriting sample and won't trust you with it, don't you, sonny? Maybe I should meet her and leave you out of it.'

'We'll both be coming, Strake. The question is: will you be there when we arrive?'

He mulled that over for a few seconds, then growled, 'All right. Have it your way. I'll be waiting for you – both of you – on the jetty. But I won't be waiting for long. So, move it.'

With that he cut me off. I put the phone down and hurried back to the table. 'Come on,' I said to Vivien. 'We have to go.'

'Where?'

I answered that question as we bustled out of the bar. The quickest route to Marina Grande was via the series of alleys and steps that cut across the zigzag course of the road leading down to the harbour from Capri town. We turned in to the first of the alleys a few yards along the street.

'He must have been keeping watch on the bar,' I reasoned as we went. 'Though why he wasn't prepared to met us there . . .'

'He's trying to wrong-foot us,' said Vivien. 'We mustn't let him. Stay calm.'

'I am calm.'

'You don't sound it.'

'I'm just not sure we really know what we're getting into.'

'We're not going to give Strake what he wants unless he gives us what *we* want.' She sounded immovable on the point and it crossed my mind that Strake could well have been right when he said she'd never have entrusted the sample of Luisa's handwriting to me. The all-important pieces of paper were currently tucked away in her shoulder-bag. And that was clearly where they were going to stay until she was satisfied Strake had something valuable to offer us. 'Any funny business and we walk away, Jonathan. OK?'

I nodded. 'OK.'

We came to the first crossing of the road, emerging on to it blindly from steep, high-walled steps. A pair of scooter-riders swerved round us. One of them shouted something. Then they were gone, the mosquito-buzz of their engines fading rapidly as we hastened on down the next stretch of alley.

'Let's try not to get run over,' laughed Vivien. 'Strake will raise all sorts of objections to meeting us in hospital.' I laughed with her. The near miss had somehow succeeded in lightening our mood.

We reached the next stretch of road within a few minutes and stepped out more cautiously. Two scooters were again bearing down on us, but they were going more slowly and slowed still further to let us cross.

We'd nearly made it to the other side when the scooter engines suddenly roared. As the riders accelerated towards us, I saw they weren't just similar to the first pair we'd encountered. They *were* the first pair: a couple of standard-issue young Caprese males on Vespas, who shouldn't have taken as long to ride to that point on the road as we had to walk there. The realization struck me too late that they'd waited for us. I turned to shout a warning to Vivien, but one of the scooters cut between us. In a flash of movement, the rider grabbed the strap of Vivien's shoulder-bag and pulled it off her. She was tugged off her feet, falling to the ground as the scooters sped past.

I started to run after them, but they were going downhill, picking up speed all the time. The boy who'd taken the bag looped the strap over his head to secure his hold, swerving as he did so. But he soon recovered his balance and caught up with his partner. Then they were gone, at full throttle, on towards the next bend.

I stopped running after them and raced back to Vivien, who was still lying on the road, winded by her fall. 'Are you all right?' I asked, crouching beside her.

'They took my bag,' she said, pushing herself up on to her elbow. 'It all happened . . . so quickly.'

'I know. They took it and they're gone. Let's get you out of the road.'

She winced as she stood up, clutching the knee she'd fallen on. I helped her hobble back to the steps we'd just descended. She sat down gingerly, massaging her knee.

'How are you feeling?'

'Bruised . . . and a bit shaken. Nothing worse. But . . . where did they come from?'

'They were waiting for us, Vivien. They sized us up on the last straight.'

'That was them?'

'I'm sure of it. They must have spotted your bag and decided we were easy pickings.'

'*Scippatori.*'

'What?'

'The local name for purse-snatchers on motorbikes. Luisa warned me about them. But she said they were a hazard in Naples, not here.'

'Looks like they've arrived on Capri.'

Vivien let out a deep sigh. I thought it was to cope with the pain from her knee, but when she opened her eyes again she immediately stood up, supporting herself against the wall.

'You'd better take it easy.'

'We weren't a natural target, Jonathan,' she said, grasping my arm for emphasis. 'Too young to have enough money for it to be worth their while. All they'll have got from my bag is cosmetics and a measly few thousand lire. Plus Luisa's recipe, of course. Don't you see? *That's* what they were after. The sample of her handwriting.'

'You mean . . .'

'Strake put them up to it.'

'He can't have.'

'Can't he? If he did, he won't be waiting for us on the jetty in Marina Grande, will he? He'll clear off once they've delivered the bag to him. So, let's go and see if he's there or not.'

We hurried on down to the port, going as fast as Vivien's jarred knee would allow. The jetty was busy with the arrivals and departures of ferries. It was impossible to tell from a distance if

Strake was waiting there. But the conviction that he wasn't grew within me as we descended. Vivien was right. The *scippatori* hadn't been opportunistic thieves. They'd been put up to it. They'd stolen to order. Strake had got what he wanted without supplying anything in return.

As I'd feared, he was nowhere to be seen. We made our way along to the far end and stood there, looking back glumly the way we'd come. There was no sign of him. He'd taken us for fools and that's what I for one felt: an utter fool.

'He was never going to trade with us, was he?' Vivien asked, her voice sounding hollow and despairing.

'No.' I shook my head and clutched her hand, as much to draw comfort as to give it. 'He wasn't.'

'Do you think he had anything to trade?'

'I'm not sure.'

'Either way, we've been conned into doing his dirty work for him.'

'I know.'

'What does he want the handwriting sample for?'

'Nothing good. That's for sure.'

'What are we going to do, Jonathan?'

'I don't know. I suppose . . . we should start by reporting the theft to the police.'

'What's the point? They won't catch the thieves. And they certainly won't catch Strake.'

'Check the hotels, then? If we could find out where he's staying . . .'

'Who's to say he's staying on the island at all? He could just be waiting for us to give up and go away before getting on a boat to the mainland.'

'It's still worth a try.'

She turned and looked at me. 'All right. We'll try. But we're not going to find him. You know that, don't you?'

I suppose I did know it. And a trawl of the hotels and *pensione* of Marina Grande, Capri and Anacapri eventually snuffed out the

158

slightest doubt. Gordon Strake wasn't registered anywhere. Searching for him was pointless. He was artful enough to ensure the search would be in vain.

We sat at a shaded table outside one of the cafés in the centre of Anacapri at the end of our afternoon-long hunt, hunched anxiously over a couple of Peronis. A fretful silence grew heavy between us. Then I said, 'I'm worried about what Strake plans to do, Vivien.' It was true. I *was* worried. Our humiliation was one thing. Far worse might be in store for Luisa.

'Whatever he plans to do,' said Vivien bleakly, 'we can't stop him.'

'He's going to use the handwriting sample to prove something. Something . . . discreditable. This has to be about blackmail, doesn't it?'

'Maybe. I don't know. Like I say, we can't stop him.'

'But we can warn Luisa. Or Francis.'

She stared at me, aghast. Warning them clearly hadn't crossed her mind. 'For God's sake, Jonathan. We'd have to explain how we know about Strake. And how he obtained the sample. That'd be as good as saying we're his accomplices.'

'The only way to prove we aren't is to tell them now, before Strake makes his move.'

She went on staring at me, baffled, I sensed, by my naivety. 'We can't do that. They'd be horrified. They'd accuse us of betraying them.'

'And haven't we betrayed them?'

'Not intentionally. Strake tricked us.'

'Yes. That's right. He put one over on us. Which you said he wasn't going to be able to do under any circumstances.' Vivien's stare hardened and I instantly regretted my words. 'I'm sorry. I didn't mean—'

'Yes, you did. You meant it. So you think I'm to blame for this mess, do you?'

'No. Of course not.'

'It wouldn't have been any different if you'd gone to meet him without me. He'd have found some way to outwit you too.'

'I'm sure he would.' But part of me wasn't sure. Part of me *did* blame her.

She stood up abruptly, wincing as her knee twinged. Intimacy, I suddenly realized, was a tender thing, slow and hard to gain, quick and easy to lose. 'I'll get a taxi back to the villa,' she said, anger tightening her voice. 'I'll see you there later.'

I rose and moved round the table towards her. She backed away, forbidding me to touch her. 'Vivien?'

'I need to think about what's happened, Jonathan. I need some space. OK? Just . . . leave it for now, will you?'

She turned and hurried away, down the broad steps from the café to the piazza, where there were taxis to be had. I sat slowly down, feeling utterly miserable, torn between a wish to please Vivien in any way I could and a sick certainty that I'd regret it if I failed to alert Francis to whatever it was we'd set in motion.

A minute later, I'd decided I mustn't let Vivien go without trying to persuade her to see things as I did. We surely only needed to talk it through to find a way forward – together. I left a note to cover the bill and ran down to the piazza.

But Vivien was gone.

SEVENTEEN

When I got back to the Villa Orchis an hour or so later, I found Vivien sitting on the balcony outside our rooms. She looked pensive and drawn, but she jumped up, smiling, as soon as she saw me. The kiss she gave me and the hug that followed suggested all might be well and I soon realized that to her mind it easily could.

'We mustn't fall out over this, Jonathan,' she said, enveloping me in the drowning gaze of her wide blue eyes. 'Strake's made idiots of us, I know, and it's sickening, but I don't want to lose you because of it.'

'Same here.'

'It's to your credit that you want to warn Francis and Luisa that Strake's up to something, but ask yourself what good it would do. He has the handwriting sample and we don't know where he is. There's nothing they could do except worry, assuming they have cause to.'

'So, you think we should leave them in the dark?'

'Well, it's what we intended to do, isn't it? It's what we would have done if Strake had honoured our deal.'

'Only because he promised to tell us what Francis was trying to stop Oliver discovering. But we no longer have any reason to believe Strake was working for Francis. In fact, I'm sure he wasn't. He's been stringing us along, using us to get what he wants.'

'I know. But what's done is done. We have to think of ourselves.'

161

There it was: a ruthless side to her character I didn't want to believe existed. 'Vivien . . .'

'Listen. We'll go out all day tomorrow. We'll take a trip to the mainland. We've talked about visiting Pompeii. Well, let's go. When we get back, I'll tell Luisa the recipe she gave me has vanished from my room. I won't make a big thing of it, but it'll put us in the clear if Strake lets them know he has it. You see? That way, we can't be implicated. You do see, don't you?'

Oh, I saw. I saw very clearly.

'I'll never hear the end of this if Mother or Greville find out what we've done, Jonathan. They'll insist I see that wretched psychiatrist again. They'll probably ask Girton to keep a closer eye on me. What they won't do is understand. Only you can do that, my love.'

And so, inevitably, I assured her I did.

But later, in a sleepless stretch of the night, my understanding changed to guilt. Strake's only consistent trait was to lie. By his own admission, he'd lied to me about Oliver hiring him. It followed that he'd lied to me again about Francis. Either he'd been working for someone else or for himself all along. The probability was that we'd given him the means to profit from some piece of dirt he'd dug up about Luisa. And now, if Vivien had her way, we were going to pretend we hadn't.

But I'd grown fond of our hosts. I'd accepted their hospitality and returned it by aiding and abetting a burglar who was surely about to become a blackmailer – or worse. It was too much to bear. To my surprise and dismay, I realized my conscience simply wouldn't let me do it.

It wasn't until we were standing on the jetty at Marina Grande the following morning that I finally nerved myself to tell Vivien what I'd decided to do. Passengers were already boarding the ferry for the short run to Sorrento, from where we could take the Circumvesuviana train to Pompeii. It would have been easier and maybe, I couldn't help reflecting, wiser, to hold Vivien's hand

162

and follow them on, to enjoy the crossing, to revel in her company. But I wasn't going to take that course.

'I'm not going,' I blurted out.

'What?' Vivien frowned at me, as if she'd thought she'd misheard. She probably hoped she had.

'I have to warn Francis about Strake.' I steeled myself to meet her gaze. 'I'm sorry, but I have to.'

'We talked this through yesterday.' She seemed genuinely bemused. 'I don't understand. You know what's at stake.'

'I'll tell Francis I bamboozled you into getting me a sample of Luisa's handwriting but that you had – still have – no idea what I wanted it for. You'll be in the clear, Vivien. I'll take the blame.'

'He won't believe you.'

'I'll make sure he does. I can be very convincing.'

'You certainly convinced me you agreed it was best to say nothing.' She was angry with me, as I'd known she would be. I dearly wanted her not to be. But I couldn't do what it would take to appease her: I just couldn't. 'It didn't seem as if you had any regrets last night. You remember last night, don't you, Jonathan?'

'Of course I do.'

'I didn't get the feeling then that anything was preying on your mind, except me.'

'I'm sorry, Vivien. I'm going to have to do this. You go to Pompeii. I'll handle Francis. I'll take the flack. It'll be all right.'

'No, it won't. He'll see through your story. He'll know I was party to the deal with Strake. It'll all come out. It's bound to.'

'It doesn't have to. Trust me.' But she wasn't going to trust me. I knew that.

The ferry sounded its hooter. It was about to leave. The last remaining passengers were hurrying up the gangway. 'Are you coming with me?' There was finality as well as urgency in Vivien's question.

'No.'

'Don't, then.' She turned and ran on to the gangway just as the crew were preparing to pull it in. She was the last to board. The engine rumbled. The water churned. The gangway was slid on to the deck and the aft rail closed. The ferry started to head out

163

into the harbour. Vivien glanced back at me, her eyes red, her face crumpled. I felt suddenly desolate, overwhelmed by an awareness of everything I was putting at risk. Then she turned and vanished into the cabin. And I was alone.

There was another ferry to Sorrento in an hour. I must have spent half of that time pacing the jetty at Marina Grande, wondering if I should go after Vivien. I might catch her at the station in Sorrento, or find her somewhere amongst the ruins at Pompeii. Then we could be reconciled. Then we could be happy again.

How would I feel later, though, when we returned to Capri and the Villa Orchis? The knowledge that we'd betrayed Francis and Luisa would gnaw at me as the loss of Vivien gnawed at me now. But if I could persuade Francis that Vivien wasn't to blame and then make her believe I'd persuaded him . . . I had to try. I had to see if I could make it work.

I found Francis in the garden, quietly pruning roses, a common mid-morning pursuit of his. The Alfa Romeo was nowhere to be seen, suggesting Paolo had driven Luisa off somewhere, leaving Francis on his own. He was understandably surprised to see me, especially since Vivien wasn't with me. 'I thought you were gone for the day, my boy.'

'I persuaded Vivien to go without me. I need to talk to you, Francis. Alone.'

He frowned. 'This sounds serious.'

'It is.'

He weighed me up for a moment, then said, 'We'd better go indoors.'

He abandoned his gloves and secateurs and led the way across the lawn to his study, where he waved me towards an armchair. But I stayed where I was. Sitting down for what I had to say just didn't seem right.

'Well?' He smiled benignly. 'You and Vivien are, er, taking appropriate precautions, I assume. If it's advice on where to buy some johnnies, I—'

164

'It's nothing like that.'

'Ah. Sorry. Jumping to conclusions. Bad habit.'

'It's about you and Luisa.'

'Really?' His smile faded. 'Are you sure . . . whatever's on your mind . . . is really any of your business?' Perhaps he thought I was going to tell him what he clearly already knew about Luisa's relationship with Paolo.

'What I have to say involves . . . Gordon Strake.'

'*Strake?*'

'I'm afraid so. Someone really did try to break into the villa recently. It was Strake.'

'What nonsense is this? How can he have?'

'If you'll hear me out, I'll explain.'

Francis beetled his brow at me ominously, then grunted in reluctant agreement. 'Very well. Let's have it.'

There was no way round it now. I'd cut off my own retreat. Francis had to be told. And so I told him. The account I gave wasn't the whole truth, of course. I claimed Strake had promised me the identity and motives of the person who'd hired him to follow Oliver, omitting to mention that Strake had accused Francis of being that person. I also claimed Vivien had had no idea why I wanted the sample of Luisa's handwriting and that a pickpocket at the Bar Due Mare rather than *scippatori* on the road to Marina Grande had stolen it from me. But I left him in no doubt that Strake was planning some sort of move against him through Luisa and that I'd been duped into supplying him with the material he needed.

Francis listened to me in an ever louder silence. He moved to his desk and sat down in his studded leather chair as I spoke. From there he eyed me rather as Mr Brinkworth, my old headmaster at St Austell Grammar, might have done while I tried to justify some gross disciplinary infraction: ire and disappointment mixed in a baleful frown.

'I'm very sorry,' I concluded lamely. 'I should never have tried to do a deal with Strake. It was . . . stupid of me.'

'*Stupid?*' Francis's tone made it obvious he thought this fell a long way short of an adequate description of my behaviour. 'No, no, Jonathan. Let's not write it off as mere stupidity. Callous. Ungrateful. *Unfeeling*. We could say you've been those and still not capture the inexcusable deceitfulness of your conduct.' He struggled to his feet and glared at me, his face colouring deeply. 'What in God's name did you think you were doing?'

'I . . . I thought Strake would tell me the truth . . . about Oliver.'

'The truth? The truth is that the poor boy filled his head with fantastical theories to explain his father's suicide and ended up drowning himself when those theories turned to dust. Strake knows that as well as I do, and evidently much better than you do, which is why he was able to take you for an utter bloody fool. This truth you were after, this secret that doesn't exist, this key to an empty box – that's what you made Vivien your unwitting accomplice in the hope of gaining, was it? And why? To impress her, perhaps? Was that the ultimate object of the exercise?'

'I suppose . . .'

'We welcomed you to our home, Jonathan. We trusted you not to abuse our hospitality.'

'I know. I'm terribly sorry. I shouldn't have done it. Maybe I was trying to impress Vivien. But I . . . really thought Strake was going to give me some valuable information.'

'Instead he's given you nothing. Except a lesson in knowing when you're out of your league.' He sighed and rubbed his forehead. 'A lesson it seems I'll have to pay for.'

'If there's anything I can—'

'You've done enough.' He flapped a hand at me dismissively. 'Get out of my sight. I need to think.'

'I'm awfully sorry, Francis.'

'Yes, yes. So you said.' He slumped back down in his chair, propped one elbow on the blotter in front of him and sunk his chin into his palm.

He was no longer looking at me. I doubted, if I said any more, that he'd even be listening to me. There seemed nothing to do but to leave. I turned and took a step towards the door.

166

'*Wait*,' came his imperious instruction.

I stopped and turned back to face him. There was a marginal softening of his expression. Already his anger was ebbing and with it the redness of his face.

'What you've done, Jonathan,' he growled, 'is unpardonable. However, I give you some credit for coming forward in this fashion. It must have taken a deal of facing up to. And it's decent of you to have absolved Vivien of blame. Nevertheless, I'd be inclined to send you packing if it weren't for the fact that I don't want to alarm Luisa. I've no doubt Strake will contact me soon enough with whatever demands he has it in mind to make. I'll deal with him as I think best. But *I'll* deal with him. I'd be obliged if you conducted yourself as normal in the meantime. I prefer Luisa to know nothing of the matter. You understand?'

'Yes. Of course.'

'Likewise Vivien.'

'I won't breathe a word.'

'Good.' He nodded, grimly satisfied. 'That's all for now. You can go.'

I went for a walk to clear my head and repair my nerves. I wasn't sure, on reflection, that confessing what I'd done had achieved anything beyond clearing my conscience. Francis hadn't given much sign that forewarned was forearmed where Strake was concerned. Nor had he revealed whether he had any idea what kind of threat Strake could bring to bear. But at least the secret was out. At least I'd done the little I could to limit the damage I'd caused.

I ended up in Marina Grande, watching the ferries come in from Naples and Sorrento. Vivien had to be on one of them. When she came ashore, I could tell her Francis had believed me: she was in the clear. That would surely count for something.

But the ferries kept on coming. And she never appeared.

I slunk back to the Villa Orchis with the evening well advanced, baffled and confused. The hours I'd spent at Marina Grande had been in vain. My best guess now was that Vivien had returned to

167

Capri on the ferry she'd left on, without ever disembarking in Sorrento. I expected her to be waiting for me at the villa.

But she wasn't. Instead, Luisa greeted me with news I could never have predicted. 'Vivien telephoned an hour ago, Jonathan. She met some friends from Cambridge at Pompeii today. *Un caso fortuito*. She decided to go with them to Rome. So, she will be away . . . a few days, I think. She said to tell you sorry.'

Friends from Cambridge? A chance meeting at Pompeii? I didn't believe it for a moment. I remembered something she'd said to me that morning. 'We must take our passports with us today, Jonathan. You're supposed to carry one with you at all times in Italy. According to Luisa, the police on the mainland can be quite pernickety about it.' Police pernicketiness, I now realized, had nothing to do with it. Vivien had planned to make herself scarce. She'd obviously reckoned on persuading me to go with her. And why not? A few days in *la città eterna* seemed vastly preferable to me right now than sitting out events at the Villa Orchis. Maybe I'd have gone along with the plan when it came to it. Except that I hadn't left Capri. I'd stayed. And she'd gone.

Francis kept up an impressively unruffled front over dinner, filling the silences created by Vivien's absence and my tongue-tied fretfulness with amusing reflections on island life that I did my pitiful best to suggest I was entertained by. Luisa looked unconvinced. I sensed she thought Vivien and I had had some kind of tiff. As in a sense we had. Though what kind Luisa could hardly have imagined.

Francis didn't need to imagine, of course. He knew. An invitation to join him for his ritualistic brandy and cigar when Luisa retired to bed came, therefore, as a surprise. It was an invitation I'd have preferred to decline. But in the circumstances I didn't feel able to.

I feared a further, more considered dressing-down. It was nothing less than I deserved. But it soon became clear Francis had something else in mind for me.

168

'I seem to have misjudged you, my boy,' he smilingly remarked as he proffered the cigar-box.

His geniality threw me. 'I . . . I'm sorry?'

'This message we've had from Vivien. These friends of hers from Cambridge? Her impulsive decision to accompany them to Rome? Tommy-rot, I'm sure you'll agree. You weren't being quite straight with me earlier, were you?'

'Everything I told you was—'

'No, no. Let's have no more of that.' He peered at me along the barrel of his cigar. 'You gallantly insisted on taking the blame, whereas Vivien favoured cutting and running. That's how it is, isn't it? Her determination to root out the secret she believes lies behind poor Oliver's death made her keener than you on the deal with Strake and less wary of the pitfalls. You could be with her in Rome now, whispering sweet nothings into her ear in some trattoria on the Via Veneto. Instead, you're here, facing the music.'

I was tempted for a moment to admit he was right and bask in the approbation he seemed to be offering. But that would have defeated the purpose I'd set myself. 'Francis,' I said as earnestly as I could, 'I can assure you Vivien knew nothing about my meeting with Strake.'

'Fine. Let's stick to that line, by all means. Vivien knew nothing about it.' He poured me a larger measure of brandy than usual and then did the same for himself. 'My advice to you, my boy, is to go after her. She shouldn't be hard to find. Greville pays her a generous allowance and, as I'm sure you've noticed, she doesn't like to slum it. So it really shouldn't be difficult to track her down in Rome. Try the Hassler. Or the Inghilterra. She'll be in one of the top hotels, I guarantee it. Without a friend from Cambridge in sight. In need of company, in fact. Company . . . and consolation. *Salute.*' He took a sip of brandy. 'Vivien's had more to cope with than any girl of her age should have been asked to, so I'm not going to wax censorious over this unhappy episode. We'll regard it as water under the bridge, shall we?'

'Well, I . . .'

'I should tell you that Strake's been in touch. He's not one to sit on a money-making opportunity. He claims that, armed with the sample of Luisa's handwriting you supplied, he can prove she was the authoress of a series of anonymous love letters sent to a junior member of Mussolini's government. How he came by the letters I don't know and whether the claim's true I don't even care. The newspapers would undoubtedly make a small but embarrassing fuss about it, however. So, to spare Luisa any distress, I'm willing to pay Strake the figure he's demanding. It'll be done through an intermediary, naturally. I don't intend to give him the satisfaction of a face-to-face meeting. I'm confident that will be the end of the matter. In fact, I propose this conversation be the last we have on the subject.' He took another sip from his glass. 'Well, Jonathan? Can I say fairer than that?' He smiled. 'I rather think not.'

Francis's outpouring of goodwill was irresistible. He was convinced his interpretation of events was correct and I knew there was nothing I could say to dissuade him, so, in the end, I didn't even try. 'Least said, soonest mended,' were, I think, his very last words on the subject, before he launched off on assorted brandy-fuelled wartime reminiscences.

By the time I stumbled up to bed, I was convinced all would be well. Strake would be quietly bought off by Francis, while I caught up with Vivien in Rome and assured her she had nothing to fear from returning to Capri. Everything was going to be as it was before. The harsh things we'd said and the foolish things we'd done were going to be forgotten. Life would revert for the remainder of our stay to its happy norm.

Then, as I was undressing, there came a tapping at the French windows leading on to the balcony. In my tipsy state, I had some idea Vivien had secretly returned and was eager to see me. But when I opened the door, I saw Paolo standing outside, the light from the bedside lamp behind me casting shadows on the tight frown-lines of his face.

'What are you doing out there?' I asked, surprised by how slurred my voice sounded.

'I must speak to you,' he answered, in a low, urgent tone.

'What about?'

'I fear something very bad is going to happen. Something . . . *molto terribile*.'

EIGHTEEN

Paolo stepped into the room and padded softly across to the door from the landing, where he listened intently for a moment, then nodded in evident satisfaction. '*Tutto bene*,' he murmured.

'Paolo, what—'

'*Sta' zitto*.' He put a finger to his lips and padded back to where I was standing. 'Keep your voice down, Jonathan. *Il Colonnello* must not hear us.' (He always referred to Francis as the Colonel, though whether respectfully or satirically it was sometimes hard to tell.) 'I am worried about him. How did he seem to you this evening?'

'Fine. Cheery, in fact.'

'More cheery than usual?'

'Yes. I suppose so.'

'*Si*. That is it. An act. He is a good actor.'

'Well, I—'

'There is no one else I can ask to do this, Jonathan. I would do it myself if I could. But it has to be you.'

I stared at him, confused and thoroughly discombobulated. The groomed and preening Paolo normally treated me with a mixture of wariness and contempt, albeit veiled by the deference due to me as a guest of his employers. He had to be very worried indeed, if not desperate, to be asking for my help. 'What . . . is this all about, Paolo?'

'You were gone all day, so you would not know.' (Paolo had of course been absent, driving Luisa somewhere, during my interview with Francis that morning, an interview I naturally had no intention of mentioning.) '*Il Colonnello* was in his study making phone calls most of the afternoon. He did not join *la signora* for lunch or tea. And later . . . he shouted at her. There was . . . an argument. They never argue. It is . . . a thing that does not happen.'

'What were they arguing about?'

'I do not know. I could not . . . make out the words.'

It struck me that, if he really didn't know what the row was about, he had absolutely no business confiding in me. A marital spat, however unprecedented, wasn't a subject he should be discussing with someone he barely knew. Besides, there was an obvious explanation for friction between Francis and Luisa: Paolo himself. 'Why haven't you asked Luisa what it was about?' I ventured.

'I cannot do that.'

I hadn't the nerve to press the point. 'People argue. It's ... no big deal.'

'I think it is a very big deal. There is something wrong with *il Colonnello*. I need your help.'

'What d'you expect me to do?'

'He has told me he wants me to drive him to Marina Grande very early tomorrow morning. He is taking the six-thirty ferry to Napoli. He never goes to Napoli without *la signora* and the first ferry of the day . . . it makes no sense. We must find out where he is going and why he is going there.'

We? Clearly he didn't intend to allow the improbability of our alliance to stand in his way. 'I don't see—'

'You must be on the ferry, Jonathan. Get to the dock early and board before we arrive. I will make sure *il Colonnello* is one of the last passengers. He must not see you. When you reach Napoli, follow him. See where he goes. Then . . . telephone me here.'

'He's probably going to see his solicitor – or his doctor.'

'On the six-thirty ferry? No. It is for something else.'

'Yeah. Something that's none of our concern.'

'It is my concern if there is danger he will get into trouble. *La signora* would want me to stop that happening. I cannot follow him. There is no one else to do it except you.'

'Why d'you think there's a danger he'll get into trouble?'

'I see things. I hear things. I understand things.'

'Such as what?'

'Someone has tried to break into the villa. Now *il Colonnello* is angry and worried . . . and going to Napoli. All this is connected. We need to know how it is connected.' There was that *we* again. Who exactly did he mean? It occurred to me that he might be recruiting me on someone else's behalf. Luisa's, perhaps. 'Will you do it?'

One part of my brain advised me to send him packing. Another urged me to cooperate. It was clear, if nothing else was, that the affable forgive-and-forget routine Francis had treated me to that night was just what Paolo had called it: an act. Something altogether more complicated than buying off Strake was going on. Or else buying off Strake was itself more complicated. Either way, tailing Francis in Naples might lead to the answer. Though whether I'd tell Paolo what I learnt in the process was quite another matter.

'Will you do it, Jonathan?' he pressed.

'You really think it's important?'

'*Si, si.*'

'Why do I get the feeling you're not telling me everything you know?'

'Because you are English. You have a suspicious mind. I am worried about *il Colonnello*. You should be too. Vivien would want you to do everything you can to protect her uncle, I think. And you want to please her, I think also. *Dunque . . .*'

'What are we trying to protect him from, Paolo?'

'I am not sure.' *Not sure*, of course, wasn't quite the same as *don't know*. 'When you see where he goes . . . maybe then I will know. That is why you must telephone me as soon as you find out.'

'What if he spots me?'

'He is old. He does not see so good. He will not . . . spot you. Unless you get too close.'

'Easy for you to say.'

174

'You think I want to rely on you? No. But I have to.'

'Thanks for the vote of confidence.'

'*Basta!* Will you do it or not?'

He was growing impatient. I had to give him an answer and it was never going to be no. Because I'd be following Oliver as well as Francis through the streets of Naples. The truth was a powerful lure. I nodded. 'OK. I'll do it.'

When the alarm woke me at 4.30 the following morning, I was convinced for a moment that I'd dreamt my exchanges with Paolo. But reality repossessed me as I lay staring into the darkness. And when I turned the bedside lamp on, there, beside it, was the small pile of *gettoni* he'd given me for the telephone call he'd be waiting for. He'd also given me several thousand lire to pay for any taxis I needed to take. He wasn't taking a lot of chances with my competence.

The light was on in Paolo's room over the garage when I slipped out of the front door of the villa, showered but unshaven, stomach already growling from lack of breakfast. I hurried down to the gate, opened it carefully to avoid setting off any loud creaks and set off into the thinnest glimmerings of dawn.

I'd never been out and about so early. Capri was dark and quiet, with only a few working folk on the move. The funicular had just started running and I made it down to Marina Grande with more than half an hour to spare before the ferry left. I bought my ticket and a copy of *Corriere della Sera* for camouflage, then dived into a bar for coffee and a pastry.

I was out on the jetty before boarding began, even so, and was one of the first up the gangway. I went to the far end of the cabin, opened the newspaper and kept watch from behind it. A few minutes before the ferry was due to sail, Francis came into view on the jetty, hatted and raincoated against the coolness of early morning. He was carrying a small leather briefcase and looked like a man with business to attend to. Paolo was at his elbow, but was soon waved away. He glanced in my direction as he retreated, though whether he caught sight of me was hard to tell.

175

Shortly afterwards, Francis entered the cabin and took the first free seat he came to, slumping down heavily into it. Dawn starts evidently didn't agree with him. He pulled one of his airmailed copies of the *Times Literary Supplement* out of his briefcase and started perusing it, but was soon doing more dozing than reading, lulled, perhaps, by the sunlight that began to slant in through the windows. My *Corriere della Sera* became an unnecessary prop.

I spent most of the crossing wondering just what Francis was up to. He'd told me there was no question of his meeting Strake, so who was he going to see in Naples? He'd also told me he wished to spare Luisa any distress, which hardly tallied with the row Paolo reported them having. I'd assumed he meant her to know nothing of Strake's threats.

Mulling all that over had got me precisely nowhere by the time we reached Naples and I was soon preoccupied by the practicalities of following Francis. I had to hang well back to let him gather himself together and then hang back again when he disembarked. Fortunately, he was never the swiftest of movers and was even slower this morning. He ambled across the landing area, heading, predictably, though from my point of view, inconveniently, towards the taxi rank.

There was nothing for it then but to let his taxi pull away, before jumping into the one behind and reading out the phrase Paolo had written down for me: 'Follow that cab' in Italian. The driver, a lugubrious, lantern-jawed fellow, grimaced at me. I repeated the phrase more loudly. He shrugged and set off with a lurch.

The morning rush was limbering up on the main road along the harbourside in Naples. It seemed to me that following one vehicle through the jockeying, honking traffic was impossible, but my driver managed it while smoking a cigarette, retuning his radio and casting me the occasional leer that suggested he thought I was too young for whatever game this was.

Before long Francis's taxi took a left into the maze of streets in the old centre. We tagged along behind. I'd have rapidly lost all sense of direction but for the climbing sun periodically dazzling me. As far as I could tell, we were heading north, deeper into the

176

heart of the city. My driver stopped grimacing and leering, as if he was beginning to enjoy himself.

Suddenly, he slammed on the brakes. We skidded to a halt. The other taxi had pulled up about thirty yards ahead of us. Francis clambered out as I watched. I glanced at the meter and shoved enough lire into the driver's hand to cover the fare, then jumped out, keeping my head down, and went after Francis.

He turned into a doorway. As I closed in, I saw the building it served was a hotel: the Albergo Lustrini. It looked cheap but not cheerful. A dusty front window, adorned with an even dustier rubber plant, gave me a partly obstructed view of a drab reception area, across which Francis was steering a straight course for the lift. I slowed, unsure what to do. He reached the lift and pressed a button. The doors slid slowly open. He stepped in.

That was my cue to move. I dodged into the hotel just as the lift doors closed. I kept my eyes trained on the floor indicator as I marched towards it, aware that the stairs were just to the right. The lift stopped at three. Without even a glance in the direction of the desk, I started running up the stairs.

Four flights took me to the right floor. I peered round the corner of the wall next to the lift and there, standing by a door halfway along the corridor, was Francis. He rapped at the door with his knuckles. It opened on a chain. I heard a muffled question from inside. I couldn't have sworn to it, but it sounded like Strake's voice.

'Ways and means,' said Francis. 'Are you going to let me in? We can settle this here and now. On terms I think you'll find attractive.'

There was a pause. Then the door closed and opened again, this time fully. I glimpsed a figure. Strake, almost certainly. Francis stepped into the room. The door closed behind him.

So, that was it. He *was* meeting Strake. Why he'd told me he wouldn't was a mystery. Technically, I'd now accomplished what Paolo had asked of me. But I wasn't keen on phoning him with this information. The less he knew about Strake the better. Maybe I'd just claim I'd bungled the job and lost Francis. I reckoned knowing Strake's room number would be useful whatever I did, though. I trod lightly as I moved along the corridor far enough to see it: 239.

Then, emboldened by how quiet the hotel seemed, I stepped closer. The door looked cheap and thin. It wasn't likely to be very soundproof.

All I could hear was a murmur of subdued voices. I couldn't make out any actual words. Whatever their discussion amounted to, it wasn't a shouting match. Then, quite suddenly, a radio or television came on in the room at high volume. An Italian pop song was playing, bass notes booming through the woodwork. I recoiled instinctively. As I did so, I heard a loud crack that wasn't part of the music and a heavy thump of something hitting the floor. It sounded bad. It sounded very bad.

A few yards further down the corridor was the fire escape. I ran to the door, opened it and stepped through on to a narrow landing on a concrete staircase. Holding the door ajar, I peered through the gap. I couldn't hear the music now. It had either been turned down or off completely. As I watched, the door of room 239 opened. Francis emerged, pulled it to behind him, then hurried towards the lift, tottering slightly as he went. A minute or so later, I heard the lift ping, the doors slide open and close again.

I was tempted to head straight down the fire escape and leave the building as quickly as possible. But I had to know what had happened. I had to find out if Francis had done what I thought he'd done. I stepped back out into the corridor. It was silent and empty. I moved to the door of room 239, hesitated, then pushed the handle down with my elbow and shouldered the door open.

It was true. It was real. It was there in front of me. Strake lay at the foot of the bed. He was half dressed, in trousers and vest. His feet were bare. There was a neat bullet-hole in his forehead. The back of his head rested in a dark pool of blood that was spreading slowly as it soaked into the rug beneath him. I stared at him for a moment, knowing he was dead, yet somehow struggling to believe it. There'd been no deal, no pay-off, no compromise. Francis had executed him. It was as simple and as brutal and as final as that.

I pulled the door shut, nervously grasping my sleeve with my fingers to avoid leaving any prints. The precautions seemed important, though I wasn't quite sure why. I was fighting shock now, but I was thinking hard. What would Francis do? Simply go back to Capri and pretend nothing had happened? I started moving.

The lift was attending to another call when I reached it, so I took the stairs, narrowly avoiding a collision on the next landing with a chambermaid so laden with laundry she never even saw me. I paused at the bottom to compose myself, then walked unhurriedly across the reception area to the door. There was a man behind the desk, fiddling with paperwork. He didn't so much as glance up as I left. I sighed with relief. No one was going to describe me to the police. No one was going to remember me at all.

I turned right outside, for no better reason than it was the direction (as far as I could calculate) of the port. I didn't know how big a lead on me Francis would have. He might be in a taxi by now, though I couldn't see any cruising the street. Maybe he'd headed for the nearest rank. I had no way of knowing where that was, but he might know.

Then I saw him. There was a junction ahead, opening on the far side on to a piazza, with steps leading up from it to a plain-fronted church. At the foot of the steps was an old dry fountain decorated with cherubim. And slumped at the base of the fountain, his back resting against the bowl, was Francis. He was clutching his brief-case tightly in one hand. His other hand was pressed to his chest. His hat lay upside down beside him. His hair was awry, his face unusually pale.

He didn't see me coming as I threaded a path through the traffic to reach him. Then, as I crouched at his elbow, he looked up at me, squinting uncertainly. His breathing was fast and shallow. He didn't look good. I gently jogged his shoulder. 'Francis?'

'Jonathan,' he said weakly. 'What . . . on earth are you . . . doing here?'

'I followed you.'

'You did? How very . . . enterprising of you.' He fashioned a smile. 'Do I take it . . . you know what . . .'

'Yes. I know.'

'I see.' He nodded. 'Oh dear. That rather . . . tears it. I'd be

179

grateful if you'd . . . keep it to yourself, my boy. Unless that . . . offends your conscience, of course.'

'We need to get you away from here.'

'Before the alarm's raised, you mean? Yes. Good idea.' He coughed. 'But I can't . . . move, you see. The whole thing . . . seems to have knocked the stuffing out of me. Not as young . . . as I was. Ticker playing up, I'm afraid. Damn thing.'

A shadow fell over us. A large aproned man still clutching one of the chairs he'd been arranging outside a café at the corner of the piazza peered down solicitously at Francis. '*Va bene, dottore?*'

'*No.*' Francis grimaced. '*Io sto . . . poco bene.*'

'*Dove le fa male?*'

'*Qui.*' Francis patted his chest. '*Qui.*' He was suddenly shorter of breath. '*Il cuore. Un . . .dolore terribile.*'

'*Il cuore?*' The man looked alarmed. '*É un attacco cardiaco, io penso.*'

'*Per favore,*' said Francis, '*chiami . . . un'ambalanza.*'

'*Si, si. Un'ambalanza. Subito.*' The man turned and hurried back to the café, absent-mindedly carrying the chair with him as he went.

By now, two street children had come to see what all the fuss was about. They stood staring solemnly at us as Francis bent his head towards me so that he could whisper in my ear. 'He's going to call . . . an ambulance, Jonathan . . . They'll . . . take me to hospital . . . I'll be . . . all right there . . . Capable hands . . . and all that . . . Now, listen carefully . . . Take my briefcase . . . Go back to the villa . . . Put it in my study . . . Wait, though, until . . . Luisa's gone . . . I'll get them to . . . phone her . . . from the hospital . . . Then the coast will be clear . . . Don't tell her you were here . . . with me . . . or that you know . . . what brought me here . . . Will you do that for me, my boy?'

He was weakening all the time. I felt I had no choice but to do as he asked. 'Yes, Francis. I'll see to it.'

'Thank you. That's . . . decent of you . . . There's . . . one more thing.' He pulled some papers out of his jacket pocket and thrust them into my hand. 'The recipe . . . and something else . . . Luisa

180

wrote . . . a long time ago . . . Not sure . . . how Strake got hold of it . . . I didn't . . . bother to ask . . . If I don't . . . make it through . . . give it . . . to Margherita.'

'Margherita? Countess Covelli?'

'Yes. She . . . deserves to know.'

'OK. I'll give it to her. But—'

'No more questions. Jonathan . . . Take the case and go . . . Please . . . There's a good fellow . . . You've got a . . . sharper brain . . . and a cooler head . . . than I gave you credit for . . . I'll trust you . . . to use them well . . . Now, buzz off, will you? I'll be . . . tickety-boo . . . Just you . . . wait and see.' He reached out and pressed my hand down round the handle of the briefcase. 'You really need to scoot.'

'You're sure about this?'

He nodded. 'Sure . . . and certain.'

I took the case, thrust the papers into my pocket and headed off. The back streets of Naples were an easy place to get lost in. When the man from the café returned, there'd be no sign of me. Francis would spin some convincing story to account for that if he needed to. He'd be covering his own tracks as much as mine, of course. He'd made me his ally in Strake's murder. The chilling reality of that crept slowly into my thoughts as I turned on to Via Duomo, a road I recognized from the taxi ride earlier and was confident would lead me to the harbour. I heard an ambulance siren wailing somewhere to my left, growing rapidly louder. Help was on its way. I tightened my grip on the briefcase and quickened my pace.

NINETEEN

By the time I reached the harbour, a flaw in Francis's plan had occurred to me. If I caught the next ferry to Capri, there was every chance I'd find Luisa, doubtless escorted by Paolo, waiting to board at Marina Grande for the return trip to Naples, after being contacted by the hospital. How would I account for having Francis's briefcase with me? It would be impossible, short of telling them the awful truth.

The only solution I could think of was to stow the case in a left-luggage locker at the ferry office, then hang around in the adjacent café, keeping an eye out for incoming ferries. Settled over a coffee, with a badly needed cigarette on the go, I took a discreet look at the document Francis had given me along with Luisa's recipe for *torta di mele*.

It was a letter, recognizably in her handwriting. It was in Italian, naturally, so made no immediate sense to me. But alarm bells began ringing in my head when I saw the salutation – *Egregio Comandante* – and, above it, an official stamp with German abbreviations round the rim and an eagle and swastika symbol in the centre. The stamp was dated 4.xi.43. As I scanned the letter, I saw a name I knew: Conte Covelli. There was no signature at the bottom, merely the words *da una patriota*.

I pulled out my Italian phrase-book and tried to translate what Luisa had written. I didn't get beyond odd words, but they told their own story: fugitive; traitor; hiding-place; duty; justice. The purpose and meaning of the letter became ever more obvious. It had been sent to the SS commandant for the Veneto region in November 1943 by an anonymous 'patriot', telling him where Count Urbano Covelli was hiding. It was, in effect, the count's death warrant.

It was hard to believe, but it couldn't be denied. Luisa had betrayed Count Covelli to the Germans. Why, I had no idea. But she'd done it. A quarter of a century later, she and the count's widow were still friends. Yet at the heart of their friendship was a terrible secret, a secret I was holding in my hands.

'If I don't make it through, give it to Margherita,' Francis had said. 'She deserves to know.' And so she did. But I didn't want to be the one to tell her. I couldn't make sense of what Francis had done. Killing Strake was understandable: an old soldier's instinctive response to blackmail. But to follow that by telling Countess Covelli Luisa had betrayed her husband? Would he really have summoned the strength of will to do such a thing? I could only hope I got the chance to ask him. If not, it would be for me to decide. And it wasn't a decision I felt equipped to take.

Movement outside the café alerted me to the arrival of a ferry. My earlier reading of the schedule suggested it should be from Ischia. I hurried out to check, only to realize at once that I was wrong. Luisa and Paolo were among the crowd disembarking. Luisa was walking unsteadily, head bowed, eyes obscured by enormous sunglasses. She appeared entirely oblivious to her surroundings. But Paolo, who was at her elbow, one arm hovering protectively around her waist, was glancing ahead as they went. And he spotted me before there was any chance of retreat.

All I could do in the circumstances was shake my head and trust he'd take the hint. He responded with the faintest of nods and walked on with Luisa. She didn't look up. Then a pillar came between us and I moved to keep it there as they headed towards the taxi rank.

I gave them a minute or so's start, then cautiously followed. I reached the corner of the ticket office in time to see their taxi pull away. That was my signal to rush into the office, retrieve the briefcase and buy a ticket for the next ferry to Capri.

Twenty minutes later, as the ferry steamed out into the bay, I opened the briefcase and peered in at the gun, nestling inside Francis's rolled-up copy of the *TLS*. It was a revolver: British Eighth Army officer's issue, I strongly suspected. Strake might not have been the first person Francis had killed with it. But he was probably the last.

I felt anxious throughout the journey, though oddly more on account of the letter I had in my pocket than the murder weapon I was carrying in the briefcase. From Marina Grande I took a taxi to the Villa Orchis, reasoning that the less time I spent on the street with Francis's case in my hand the better, even though no one was likely to realize who it belonged to.

I reached the villa without incident. Patrizia was in the kitchen, preparing a dinner it was unclear anyone would eat. I slipped the briefcase under Francis's desk in his study before facing her and did my best to appear surprised by the news she had for me. '*Il Colonnello*' had been taken ill in Naples and was in the Ospedale di Santa Maria di Loreto. He'd suffered '*un attacco di cuore*'. '*La signora*', escorted by Paolo, had rushed to his bedside. There was nothing to be done but to await word from them. But Patrizia was worried. And so was I. I began to get the feeling Francis's condition had deteriorated after I'd left him. According to Patrizia, he'd been officially described as '*precario*'. That didn't sound good. That didn't sound good at all.

Patrizia rustled me up a pasta lunch, most of which I couldn't eat. I washed it down with a couple of beers, sitting on the terrace and wondering why the brilliant sunshine seemed to have lost much of its warmth. Everything had gone wrong. Strake had outwitted me. Vivien had left. Francis was critically ill. And Luisa . . . I knew too much about some things and too little about others. My confidence that no one had seen me at the Albergo Lustrini was ebbing. My complicity, as the law would see it, in Strake's murder was looming darkly in my thoughts. I felt fearful and insecure.

184

All I knew for certain was that I was way out of my depth.

Then Patrizia emerged from the villa and told me Paolo wanted to speak to me on the phone.

'How's Francis?' I asked as soon as I picked up the receiver.

'He is very ill, Jonathan,' Paolo replied, his voice tight with distress. 'I think . . . we may lose him.'

'Oh God.'

'What happened to him, Jonathan? I need to know. Where is his briefcase? He left with it this morning. But the hospital say he did not have anything with him when he was put in the ambulance.'

'It's here. I brought it back with me. I can explain, but . . . not over the phone. Does Luisa know it's missing?'

'No. I have not told her.'

'Don't. Don't tell anyone. It's vital this stays between us, Paolo.'

There was silence at the other end of the line. I sensed him struggling for self-control. Eventually he said, '*D'accordo*. I understand. We will speak later. I will phone as soon as . . .' He tailed off with another silence. Then: 'I will phone again.'

It was evening before the call came through. I heard the phone ring and Patrizia answer. Then she began sobbing and I knew at once that Francis was dead.

I took the phone from her and spoke to Paolo. 'What happened?' I asked numbly.

'He slipped away. They could not save him.'

'Tell Luisa I'm sorry. This is . . . terrible.'

'*Sì*. It is. I will tell her.'

'Are you coming back here tonight?'

'No. The last ferry has gone already. We will stay tonight at the Excelsior.'

'OK. I'll see you tomorrow. We'll talk then about . . . what happened.'

'*Sì*. We will talk. But there is something we need to talk about now also. Luisa has asked if you can telephone *il Colonnello*'s family in . . . Cornovaglia.'

'Me?'

'She is very upset. She cannot do it. You know them. And they must be told.'

'Yes, but—'

'Will you do it?'

If I'd had any excuse for refusing, however feeble, I'd have used it. The prospect was hideous. But I couldn't see a way out. 'Yes. I'll do it.'

'Tonight?'

'Yes. Tonight.'

It was only after Paolo had rung off that I realized he'd referred to Luisa by her name, not as '*la signora*'. Even he was forgetting himself under the strain of events.

I walked into Francis's study and looked around at the books and the ornaments and furnishings that made it his particular domain. They stood waiting for him, obedient and serviceable as ever. But he would never again fill his fountain pen from the gold-saucered ink bottle, nor prop a cigar in the onyx ashtray, nor slide open the drawers of the mineral cabinet and recall how and where he'd collected each of the samples. My shadow, cast across the Turkish rug by the light from the hall, was not his shadow. His shadow would never be cast again.

I persuaded Patrizia to drink a little of Francis's brandy before she went home. We toasted his memory. She cried copiously and enveloped me in several hugs. It seemed to help her. It didn't do much for me. I drank some more brandy after she'd gone. But I still felt stone cold sober when I picked up the telephone and dialled for the international operator.

To my relief Greville Lashley took the call. I'd dreaded having to speak to Muriel or Harriet, especially Muriel. She didn't know I'd joined Vivien on Capri and certainly wouldn't be happy about it. But her concerns on that score were about to be eclipsed and a doleful pattern was about to be set. For the second time in less than a year, I had to break the news that a member of their family was dead. First Oliver. Now Francis.

186

Lashley reacted with the stoical practicality I'd have expected of him, making nothing of my previously undisclosed presence on the island. 'I'm sorry to hear this, Jonathan. It's not altogether a surprise. I believe he's had a heart condition for some years. But even so . . . the womenfolk will be upset, of course. I'd better go and tell them. How's Vivien? Muriel will want to speak to her.'

I had to explain then why that wouldn't be possible. I recycled the story about friends from Cambridge met by chance at Pompeii and left him to draw his own conclusions as to why I hadn't gone with her. What it amounted to, of course, was that Vivien didn't know Francis was dead. And I had no way of contacting her.

'Are you saying no one knows where she is?' Lashley asked edgily.

'I'm sure she'll call again when . . . her plans are clearer.'

'But meanwhile?'

'We'll . . . just have to wait for her to call.'

Lashley gave a dissatisfied growl. 'We impressed on her the need to keep us informed and to stay in touch. She never mentioned you'd be there. Now this. She can't simply . . .' He sighed. 'Francis and Luisa shouldn't have allowed this to happen. They knew she was ill last year. It's really . . .' Another sigh. 'Well, recriminations at this stage are pointless. And unfeeling. Poor old Francis. I imagine Luisa's taken it hard.'

'I imagine so too, sir, though I haven't actually seen her. She's still in Naples.'

'Of course, of course.' I sensed him rapidly coming to terms with the situation. 'We'll say no more for now, Jonathan. I'm obliged to you for making the call. It can't have been easy. I'll phone you in the morning.'

'OK, sir. Please tell Mrs Lashley and Miss Wren how sorry I am.'

'Will do. Goodnight, Jonathan.'

I slept poorly, waking almost immediately every time I succeeded in dropping off because a noise somewhere in the villa – a creak, a squeak, a scurry of a mouse – made me believe I wasn't alone. I

187

eventually dozed for long enough to dream I'd gone downstairs and seen Strake out on the terrace, trying to open the French windows. To that point it was more of a memory than a dream, but the bullet-hole in his forehead when he looked up and stared at me through the glass was pure nightmare.

By morning, I'd reached a firm decision. It was confirmed for me when Lashley phoned at just gone seven o'clock. That was just gone six o'clock in Britain. He'd presumably had no more restful a night than I had.

'We'll be travelling out there as soon as possible, Jonathan,' he announced. 'Muriel, Harriet and I, that is. We'll probably arrive tomorrow. The day after at the latest. Can you let Luisa know when she returns from Naples?'

'Of course, sir.'

'Tell her we'll stay in a hotel. It'll be less trouble for her.'

'I expect she'll insist you stay here. There's plenty of room, and anyway all the decent hotels on Capri will be full.'

'Mmm. Well, as she sees fit. Now, have you heard from Vivien? Muriel's worried about her. Frankly, so am I.'

'Me too, sir.' That brought us to what I'd decided to do. 'Actually, I'll have left by the time you get here. You won't want me around. I'd only be imposing. So, I'm going home. I hope to catch up with Vivien on the way. In Rome.'

'How will you find her?'

'I have a few ideas.' They were Francis's ideas, actually. I couldn't be sure Vivien was in Rome, but, if she was and if, as I felt certain, she was alone, there was a good chance of tracking her down. If I could make it up with her, something would have been salvaged from the wreckage. 'I'm sure she'll want to join you here once she's heard about Francis.'

'I'd be obliged to you if you could arrange that, Jonathan, I really would.'

'I'll see what I can do.'

'Are you sure you won't come back with her?'

'Probably not. I know Mrs Lashley doesn't approve of me.'

'Nonsense. It's just . . .' He deliberated for a moment, then said, 'Well, maybe you have a point. The atmosphere will be strained enough without . . . You're a sensible young fellow, Jonathan. I appreciate your . . . sensitivity.'

Sensitivity? I was happy for him to credit me with a bucketload. The truth was simpler. I had to get away. I didn't know much. But I did know that.

Patrizia arrived later in the morning. I tried to disguise my eagerness to be gone as we awaited Luisa's return. I'd packed my few belongings and was ready to leave. But I had to speak to Paolo first. Only then could I quit the scene. I sat out on the terrace, listening for the car.

In my bag upstairs I had the letter Luisa had written to the SS in November 1943. I'd studied it several times by then and extracted most of the sense. It was a chillingly callous document. It was proof of an act of betrayal I couldn't believe she'd committed. But she had. And Francis had been unambiguous about what he wanted done with the letter in the event of his death. *'Give it to Margherita. She deserves to know.'* So, there it was: his dying wish; my living obligation. I told myself I had to comply.

But not right away. I'd wait until after the funeral. Then I'd wait another week. And then I'd send it to the countess. I could do it anonymously. She need never know where it had come from.

At that moment the gate opened. And Countess Covelli stepped through it. Seeing me, she raised a gloved hand and advanced along the drive. Something in her expression told me she'd heard about Francis. She looked, as ever, cool and elegant and reserved. She was wearing a dove-grey dress and matching hat. Her low-heeled shoes clipped out a measured rhythm on the flagstones. I stood up.

'*Buon giorno, contessa,*' I said.

'*Buon giorno, Jonathan.*' She took off her sunglasses as she reached the terrace. Her smile was faint and fragile. 'This is a sad day.'

She took my hand and I kissed her on the cheek. 'How did you hear the news?' I asked.

'Luisa phoned me last night. Is she back yet?'

'No. But she should be quite soon. Would you like . . . something to drink?'

'Nothing, thank you. Shall we . . . sit down and wait together for her, Jonathan?'

'Yes. Fine.' I pulled back a chair for her.

She replaced her sunglasses as she sat down. 'It seems worse now I am here,' she said with a sigh. 'To think . . . he will not walk across the lawn again. *Mai più.*' She shook her head. 'I cannot believe it.'

'It's a terrible shock.'

'*Si.*' She frowned thoughtfully. 'Where is Vivien?'

'In Rome.'

'*Roma?*'

'Some friends of hers from Cambridge . . . suggested the trip.'

'But you did not go with her?'

'Ah . . . no. I . . . couldn't.'

The frown remained in place. I sensed her studying me through the darkened lenses. 'Do you know where Francis was when he became ill, Jonathan? Luisa was too upset to . . . make sense about it.'

'I'm . . . not sure.'

'She will need much help. To lose the man you love is . . .' Words seemed to fail her. She looked away, remembering, perhaps, her own loss of a man she loved. How much help, I wondered, would she want to give if she knew Luisa had been responsible for that loss? I was tempted for a second to tell her there and then, to have done with it, to spill the secret.

But I said nothing.

Twenty minutes later that felt more like an hour, Luisa and Paolo arrived. Luisa barely registered my presence amidst the tears and embraces she shared with her old friend. She went into the villa on the countess's arm. I heard Patrizia greet her with a wailing sob. The women in Francis's life on Capri were united in mourning.

Paolo nodded for me to follow as he drove the Alfa Romeo the short distance to the garage. He took the car straight in. I met him

190

as he climbed out. The shadows around us were deep and cool.

'What happened in Napoli?' he asked without preamble.

I told him then how I'd followed Francis to the Albergo Lustrini, where he'd shot dead the occupant of room 239; how I'd caught up with him afterwards in a nearby piazza, where it had become obvious he was seriously ill and an ambulance had been called; and how I'd taken the briefcase at his urging so that the gun wouldn't be found amongst his possessions at the hospital. I claimed to have no idea who Francis had murdered or why. I said nothing about the letter he'd given me. What Paolo knew, if anything, of Francis's dealings with Strake was unclear to me. What was clear was that it was best for me to plead ignorance. Because ignorance isn't a threat. And I didn't want Paolo to think I was any kind of threat, to him or Luisa.

He stared at me intently as I spoke. To my own ears, I sounded shocked by the violent and tragic turn of events, as indeed I was. And nothing in Paolo's reaction to what I said suggested he suspected I was short-changing him.

'Did il Colonnello say why he shot the man?'

'No. He could hardly speak by then, anyway. He just asked me to bring the briefcase back here.'

'Did he ask you why you were following him?'

'There wasn't time for that. There wasn't much time for anything.'

'Si, sì. Capisco.' To my astonishment, Paolo gave me a hug and a kiss on the forehead. 'You did well, Jonathan. I will unload the gun and clean it. There will be no evidence to prove it was fired.' The force of his emotion transmitted itself to me. He'd been devoted to Francis in his own way, however devoted he might be in another way to Luisa.

'Why d'you think he did it, Paolo?' I asked, curious to know what he might say.

'There was a good reason,' he said firmly. 'We can be sure of that. The man must have deserved it. Now we must protect il Colonnello. His . . . reputazione. It was important to him. You must tell no one else what you saw.'

191

'I won't.'

'*Bene*. It will be a secret between us. *Si?*'

'Yes.' We shook hands. I felt I was genuinely giving my word of honour. And that he was too. Even though I knew I might yet confide in Vivien. Just as I suspected he might in Luisa. One unspoken exception cancelled out the other.

'We tell no one,' he emphasized. '*Nessuno*.'

'Agreed.'

He nodded, signalling his satisfaction on the point. 'Have you spoken to the family?'

'Yes. They're on their way.'

'*Si, si*.' He thought for a second. 'There is much to arrange.'

'I'll have to leave you to it, I'm afraid.'

'You are going somewhere?'

'Rome.'

'Ah. Vivien has telephoned?'

'No. But I hope to find her, anyway.'

'You will bring her back here?'

'I'm sure she'll come of her own volition when she hears about Francis. I won't be coming with her, though.'

'No?'

'It's best, I think.'

Paolo nodded. 'Maybe you are right. There will be many questions.'

'Too many.'

'When will you leave?'

I smiled at him. 'Right now. I'm packed and ready to go.'

He returned the smile. 'Then there is no more to say, Jonathan.' He clasped my hand again. '*Buon viaggio*.'

He was pleased to be rid of me, I sensed. And I was pleased to be going. It was a relief for both of us.

192

TWENTY

The train from Naples was more than an hour late when it lumbered into Termini station in Rome. It was a hot, humid evening and I was tired and hungry. I was also paying my own way after a fortnight of generous hospitality on Capri, so had to be content with a shared room in a nearby hostel that the EPT office found for me. One of the other occupants of the room, a Vietnam draft-dodger from Iowa, reminded me over a late-night bottle of paint-stripper wine that in a world of woes and wonders my problems didn't amount to very much.

They remained my problems, however. Next morning, I showered and shaved and spruced myself up as best I could, then headed out, armed with the EPT list of accredited hotels. My plan was to work my way through the five stars, then the fours, then, if necessary, the threes. But I doubted it would be necessary. Vivien wouldn't have stinted herself. It was surely only a matter of time before I tracked her down.

My confidence ebbed, however, as the morning passed. I walked into innumerable marbled lobbies and endured the heavy-lidded disdain of a succession of reception clerks. Their response became wearily familiar. No *Signorina* Vivien Foster was among their guests. And no, they couldn't be mistaken. I began to think I was the one who'd made the mistake: a big one.

It was also an exhausting one, as I extended the search from the historic centre across the Tiber towards the Vatican, then down into Trastevere and across to Termini. By mid-afternoon, I'd more or less concluded that I wasn't going to find her. Either she hadn't come to Rome, or she'd already moved on, to Florence maybe, or some Tuscan beach resort. Rome was a big city and Italy was a big country. She could literally be anywhere.

It was only then that I remembered how much Vivien had said she loved the poetry of Keats. She could recite whole verses of his odes, particularly 'Ode to a Nightingale'. Keats had spent his last few months in a house at the foot of the Spanish Steps, now a museum to his memory. It was a long shot, but I was growing desperate by then. I took the Metro to Spagna.

Vivien wasn't amongst the visitors and my attempt to describe her to the staff was futile. The museum was a magnet for English and American girls of her age. She could have left ten minutes earlier and no one would remember. I retreated to a nearby bar.

Several beers later, and feeling none the better for being slightly drunk, I wandered up the Spanish Steps, with no idea of where to go or what to do. I sat down halfway and stayed there for a miserable hour or so, smoking my last few cigarettes and watching the tourists and locals drifting past me as the afternoon faded slowly towards evening.

For sheer lack of any alternative, I decided to go back to the hostel and book in for another night. In the morning, I'd probably head home. There seemed nothing else for it. I felt utterly miserable by then, baffled and resourceless. I gathered myself together and started up the steps towards the Metro station.

I was nearly there when I saw him, emerging into view round the flank of a tour bus. His long, dark hair, fine-boned features and swaggering gait gave him a Byronic appearance, but the three-piece cream suit was the get-up of an entirely contemporary dandy. He'd been less flamboyantly dressed when I'd last met him. But that had been in St Austell in December. This was Rome in July. And Roger had blossomed exotically in the Italian sun.

He looked in my direction without the least hint of recognition and walked on past the steps leading up to Trinità dei Monti. Instinctively, I veered off course and followed. His presence in Rome was a coincidence I wasn't about to ignore.

I didn't have to follow him for long to find out where he was going. Beyond the church stood the Hotel Hassler, one of my first calls in search of Vivien that morning. Roger went straight in, receiving a forelock-tug of recognition from the doorman. I kept pace ten yards or so behind as he headed across the foyer to the reception desk.

There too he was known. 'Ah, Signor Normington,' said the clerk, reaching for the key-rack.

But the key wasn't there. The probable significance of that chilled my blood. I stopped and listened as Roger said something in Italian I couldn't follow. But it included the words '*la signorina*'. Both men laughed and Roger headed for the lift.

I didn't want to believe the conclusion I'd jumped to, but I was determined to test it at once. While Roger waited for the lift, I followed the TELEFONO sign down a corridor to a wood-panelled booth.

I rang the Hassler switchboard using one of the *gettoni* Paolo had given me. The operator answered promptly.

'*Il signor Normington, per favore.*'

'*Signor Normington?*'

'*Si.* Roger Normington.'

'*Chi parla?*'

I should have expected to be asked for my name, but somehow I hadn't. All I could think of to say was the truth. '*Mi chiamo . . . Jonathan Kellaway.*'

Several moments passed, though not enough for Roger to have reached his room. The question hung in the stuffy air of the booth: who would answer the phone in his place?

And then I heard Vivien's voice in my ear. 'Hello?' She sounded disbelieving and fearful – as well she might. 'J-Jonathan?'

'I'm downstairs,' I said, squeezing all expression out of my voice. 'I'll wait for you outside.' Then I put the phone down. It must have been clear to her that if she kept me waiting long, I'd come to the room. And I reckoned she wouldn't want that to happen at any price.

I stood by the parapet halfway up the steps in front of Trinità dei Monti. Some people had gathered at the top of the steps to admire the vista of Rome that the church commanded. The city was laid out before me in all its luminous beauty. But that beauty only deepened the blackness of my thoughts. I couldn't understand why Vivien had treated me as she had. I couldn't begin to comprehend her behaviour. Did I mean so little to her? Did the time we'd spent together on Capri mean nothing – nothing at all?

I saw her walk out of the hotel and look around. I didn't wave or shout. I waited for her to see me, as she soon did. She walked towards me, pushing back her hair as the gentle breeze wafted a few strands across her face. I remembered running my own fingers through her hair, the memory sharp and painful. She was wearing a yellow dress I hadn't seen before. A gift from Roger, perhaps? It seemed sickeningly probable.

She put on her sunglasses as she reached the steps and started up them. The low sun was bright, true enough. But I knew the glasses weren't to shield her eyes so much as her soul. Already, she was hiding from me.

'This is . . . a surprise,' she said nervously, stopping a couple of steps below me.

'I'm sure it is.'

'How did you find me?' Her voice was tight, her mouth compressed.

'How did you find Roger?'

'It's not . . . what you think, Jonathan. Roger and I—'

'He's sleeping on the couch, is he? Like the perfect gentleman he is. Like the drongo you said he was.' I moved down towards her. She flinched. What did she think I was going to do – hit her? Maybe that would have helped both of us. But it wasn't going to happen. 'Tell me what it is if it isn't what I think, Vivien. Tell me that.'

'I needed to get away. I needed to . . . clear my head. Roger's switching to History of Art next term. I knew he was spending the summer in Italy preparing for it. I had a standing invitation to join him. When I decided I couldn't come back to Capri, I . . .'

'Ran into Roger's welcoming arms?'

'You don't understand.'

'You're right. I don't.'

'If only you'd come with me.' She sounded genuinely regretful. 'If only you'd done as I asked.'

'You mean it could be you and me in a suite at the Hassler instead of you and Roger?'

'You and me somewhere. Together. You turned your back on that.'

'I had to warn Francis, Vivien. I couldn't just let Strake do his worst.'

'So, you did warn him, did you?'

'Yes.'

She sighed and shook her head. 'I wish you hadn't. I asked you not to. I pleaded with you not to. Can't you see what this will mean for me, Jonathan? If you loved me—'

'I do love you, Vivien. That's the worst of it.'

'No, you don't. If you did, you wouldn't have let me in for all the trouble this is going to cause.'

'It's not going to cause you any trouble, actually.'

'Of course it is. Don't make it worse by being obtuse.' Guilt and anger were simmering within her. Somehow, we both felt betrayed. 'My family will never allow me to forget what I've done. It's all right for you. You can walk away from them. *I* can't.'

'Your family know nothing about it.'

'They soon will. Uncle Francis will—'

'Uncle Francis is dead.'

Her mouth opened and closed slowly in silent shock. Then she gasped and steadied herself against the parapet. '*What?*'

'A heart attack. Two days ago.'

'After you . . .'

'After I told him about Strake, yes. And after he killed Strake.'

Silence again. Shock and bewilderment. Then: 'He killed Strake?'

197

'Tracked him to a hotel in Naples and shot him. I followed him. I saw the body. Strake's dead. Francis got clean away with it. But the effort was too much for him.'

'Oh God.' The scale of the tragedy was dawning on her. She took off her sunglasses and stared at me. 'This . . . This is awful.'

'Yes. We set something terrible in motion, didn't we, Vivien? We truly did.'

'What does Luisa think happened?'

'I'm not sure. She and Paolo and I are all keeping secrets from each other. But she won't say anything that might lead the police to connect Francis with Strake's death. Nor will Paolo. You can be sure of that. So, you're in the clear.'

'What did Strake have on Uncle Francis?'

I could have told her then. Maybe I should have told her then. But I couldn't forgive her for running out on me and letting the loathsome Roger back into her life. I couldn't forgive her for not being the person I so wanted her to be. 'I don't know what Strake had,' I said. 'But Francis killed him for it. He wasn't willing to give in to blackmail.'

'Does Mother know yet?'

'Yes. I spoke to Greville. He's travelling to Capri with your mother and your great-aunt. They might already have arrived, for all I know. You should join them as soon as you can.'

'Will you come back with me?'

'What do you think?'

She reached for my hand, but I snatched it away: an instinctive reaction I couldn't deny and she couldn't mistake. She wanted me to be her ally again. Her eyes were soft and imploring. She wanted my help. She needed my help. But finding her with Roger had forced me to confront the flaw in her character I'd happily ignored while we were lovers. She cared too much about her dead brother – and their dead father – ever to give enough of herself to me. I could never be central to her life. Neither could Roger, of course, or any other man alive. But that didn't help. That didn't solve anything.

'I'm going home, Vivien. And you're going to Capri. That's how it is.'

'It doesn't have to be.'

'Yes, it does. We're going in opposite directions.'

'You said you loved me.'

'I do. But you've never said you love me. And if you said it now, I wouldn't be able to believe you.'

'I'm sorry . . . about Roger. I . . .'

'This has nothing to do with Roger. It doesn't have much to do with you and me, either. It's all about your family. Which, as you pointed out, I can walk away from. So, that's what I'm going to do. Goodbye, Vivien.'

I moved past her then, walked hurriedly down the steps and turned smartly right at the bottom, heading for the entrance to Spagna Metro station. I didn't look back to see if Vivien was watching me. Part of me yearned still to be standing beside her. But somehow I knew I had to leave. There'd be too much to pretend if I didn't, too much to forgive and far too much to forget. I had to go. I had to save myself.

Sitting in the cavernous waiting-room that evening at Termini station, with a seat-only ticket for the sleeper to Milan in my pocket, I suspected that if Vivien walked in and asked me to reconsider, I would. I'd go with her to Capri. I'd go with her anywhere. Why not, when she was beautiful and I was penniless and the drunk who'd fallen asleep just along the bench from me smelt of decay and despair? It wouldn't have been a hard choice.

But she didn't walk in. The much harder choice I'd already made was the one I was stuck with. The sleeper arrived. And I climbed aboard.

Self-pity and regret weren't the only feelings I woke to when sallow dawn light seeped through the dirty train window next morning. My neck was stiff and my head was aching. And I knew another decision had to be taken before I left Italy. The letter Luisa had written to the SS in November 1943 was still in my bag. '*Give it to Margherita*,' Francis had said. '*She deserves to know.*' Yes. She did. I could send it to her anonymously and let the consequences take their course. She'd recognize her old friend's handwriting. She'd know who '*una patriota*' was. She'd know the truth at last. The only thing she wouldn't know was who'd sent the letter to her. But if I waited to post it until I was back in England, there was a risk she'd guess it had come from me. I'd have preferred to delay – to wait until Francis's funeral was over and his family had dispersed. But I couldn't afford to. Maybe the notoriously slow Italian postal service would do the delaying for me.

I bought a stamp and an envelope from a *tabaccheria* at Milano Centrale, addressed the envelope carefully in block capitals, put the letter inside and sealed it, then tracked down the post box and stood staring at it for fully five minutes before I lost patience with my own faint-heartedness and thrust the envelope into the slot.

It was done. It was on its way. And so was I.

TWENTY-ONE

The drabness of life in St Austell predictably plunged me into depression. My world was drained of colour and pleasure. I think Mum and Dad were worried I'd been taking mind-altering drugs. It was as useless as it would have been foolhardy to tell them the truth. News of Francis Wren's death had trickled through to his old home town, but neither my parents nor anyone else – not even Pete Newlove, with his taste for conspiracies – thought anything sinister lay behind it.

I latched on to some old schoolfriends I hadn't seen a lot of since we'd left the grammar, drank so much I finished a couple of evenings throwing up and behaved badly enough to get chucked out of a disco at the Lido Club. It wasn't a pretty picture.

I pulled myself together to some degree when I started my summer job at Cornish China Clays. I'd sat up the previous night, sober for once, watching *Apollo XI* land on the Moon. The wonder of the event punctured my self-absorption. It thrilled me, just when I'd convinced myself I could never be thrilled again.

My first day at CCC was also Greville Lashley's first day back from his trip to Capri. He tracked me down and invited me to lunch at the White Hart on Wednesday. 'We have lots to talk about,' he ominously remarked.

According to Pete, Lashley's seat on the board of CCC and his job title of logistics director didn't mean he had a long-term future in the organization. 'They'll ease him out sooner or later. Just you wait and see.' I had no idea whether he was right or wrong and I didn't much care. I couldn't see how the internal politics of CCC concerned me in any way.

I didn't tell Pete or anyone else on the payroll I'd been to Capri with Vivien. It would have raised a lot of questions I'd have found hard to answer. Most of the staff weren't much interested in the problems of the Wren family anyway. Walter Wren & Co. were history now. But not the kind of history anyone wanted to study.

Pete claimed to know exactly how much CCC had paid for the company: £475,000. Why Lashley would want to go on working after grabbing the lion's share of that he couldn't understand. Neither could I. And I didn't expect to find out over lunch at the White Hart. But then I wasn't sure what to expect from the encounter at all. A simple thank you for tracking Vivien down in Rome was my best hope.

Lashley didn't deal much in simplicity, of course, as I was reminded before my first sip of gin and tonic. 'Francis's funeral went off as well as such things can. All the better for your absence, Jonathan, I have to say. You showed admirable common sense in not returning to Capri. You have an old head on young shoulders. It's a valuable asset. One I'm not about to ignore. Discretion and good judgement. They're what I look for in people. They're what I see in you.'

'That's very flattering of you, sir.'

'Not at all. Flattery's a waste of time. I don't need to stroke your ego. You can do that for yourself. Cheers.' He raised his glass and drank. I followed suit. 'A week at the Villa Orchis would have left me with a good deal to ponder, even without the news that greeted me back here in St Austell.' He smiled. 'We'll come to that in a moment.' What news, I wondered, could he possibly be referring to? 'I won't intrude into your relationship with my stepdaughter. It's none of my business. As I understand it, the Normington fellow left the scene, but has now re-entered it, much to your chagrin, no doubt.'

'Well, I—'

'You bear it well. Better than many a man would. Muriel

approves of him. I mention that just so you know. There's a touch of the snob in my wife. No point denying it. Titles impress her.'

'Titles?'

'Well, he's the *Honourable* Roger Normington, isn't he? Son and heir of Viscount Horncastle. One day he'll own half of Lincolnshire. Or a quarter. Or whatever it is. Hell of a lot of acres, though, that's certain. You have met him, I take it?'

'Yes.' I swallowed hard. 'I have.'

'Enough said, then. More than enough. Let's get back to poor old Francis. Luisa's Italian, of course. Tears and wailing are to be expected, though I gather he'd been under the doc on account of his heart for years, so it shouldn't really have come as a surprise. Still, it was my impression there was a little more to it than met the eye. What was Francis doing in Naples that day? I asked, but no one could tell me. In fact, the question seemed to make them nervous. Verdelli, in particular.'

'Who?'

'Paolo Verdelli. The butler, chauffeur, general factotum, or whatever the hell he is.' To my surprise, I realized this was the first time I'd heard Paolo's surname. 'About as forthcoming as a clam. I didn't warm to him, to put it mildly, and the feeling was evidently mutual. What did you make of him?'

'I . . . didn't have a lot to do with him.'

'Very wise. He's a bit too close to Luisa for comfort, if you know what I mean. But that's her affair, possibly literally.' He paused to light a cigarette. He offered me one and I accepted. Then he went on: 'So, can you shed any light on Francis's trip to Naples, Jonathan?'

'Er . . . no. No, I can't.'

'But you knew he'd gone?'

'No. Not exactly. I . . .' I did some swift thinking. 'I went out early that day.'

'Oh yes?'

'Very early. By the time I got back, he was in hospital and Luisa was on her way to see him.'

'You don't think Francis had a mistress tucked away in Naples, do you?'

'I suppose he might have done. I couldn't really say. I doubt it, though.'

'Me too. And he definitely didn't have an appointment with his cardiologist. Or his lawyer. Or even his dentist.' Lashley smiled. 'I checked all three.'

'Really?'

'It pays to check, I find. Check everything. That way you avoid unpleasant surprises. Well, *most* unpleasant surprises, at any rate. But not all. No, not quite all, I'm afraid. Which brings us to someone you and I have discussed before: Gordon Strake.'

'Strake?' It was vital I acted dumb now. I'd hoped Lashley wouldn't have heard about Strake's murder. No one else in St Austell had. (Well, Pete Newlove hadn't, which I took as a good indicator.) 'What about him?'

'You don't know?' There was something almost teasing about the tilt of Lashley's head and the breadth of his smile as he gazed at me through a veil of cigarette smoke. 'Strake's dead, Jonathan.'

'He is?'

'Dead as can be. Murdered, in point of fact. Shot dead in a hotel room in Naples. It happened the same day as Francis's heart attack. Quite a coincidence, eh?'

I frowned, hoping to look baffled as well as shocked. 'That's . . . extraordinary.'

'It is, isn't it? The Naples police don't seem to have made any connection between the two events. I suppose there's no reason why they should. But naturally they informed the British consulate, who contacted Strake's next of kin: a sister in Plymouth. He'd been living with her in recent months, apparently. There was a letter from her waiting for me when I got back. She felt I ought to know he was dead on account of the pension he'd have been due from Wren's if he'd made it to sixty-five. Thoughtful of her. I had the impression she wasn't altogether surprised someone had murdered her brother. I can't say I was, either. He was a dodgy character, however you look at it. But where and when he was murdered *did* surprise me. As it does you, I imagine.'

'Absolutely.'

'Or not.'

'Sorry?'

'It's occurred to me, you see, that you may have been aware Strake was in Naples and that he had some dealings with Francis – his old CO, I believe – in the days leading up to their ... coincidental deaths.'

'Me? No, I—'

'Please don't say any more.' Lashley's smile broadened still further. 'I don't want you to confirm or deny anything, Jonathan. Whatever transpired has been satisfactorily resolved, I'm glad to say. There's been no scandal of any kind. Most importantly, Vivien hasn't been caught up in any police inquiries. And Francis can rest in peace. Now, how exactly all that was managed, I don't know. But I'm impressed it was. Truly I am.'

'I'm not sure I understand, sir.'

'No? Well, it doesn't matter. Incidentally, I haven't told Vivien about Strake. There seems no need to trouble her with that. Have you heard from her since you left Rome?'

I shook my head. 'No.'

'She's gone back there, in case you're wondering. I'm not sure how long she'll stay. But I doubt we'll be seeing much of her down here this summer.'

'That's a pity.'

'Yes. It is, isn't it?' Lashley's contented expression rather suggested the reverse. Perhaps he found life at Nanstrassoe more harmonious without her. His point of view and mine were a long way apart, despite his implications to the contrary. 'We must do our best to keep cheerful in her absence, Jonathan. A bottle of wine with our lunch should help. Where's that waitress?'

I should have been able to enjoy the rest of the meal. The food was good and the wine the finest the White Hart had to offer. But I was weighed down by doubts, regrets and dilemmas, quite a few of which I'd brought on myself. I missed Vivien with a fierce ache. I couldn't gauge how much of the truth Lashley had discovered or deduced or simply guessed. I was beset by the hopeless wish that

Francis was still alive, Vivien and I were still lovers and the Mediterranean sun was still shining on all of us.

But it wasn't. The Cornish sky was more often grey than blue. Francis was dead. Vivien was lost to me. And the only member of the Wren clan who wanted to have anything to do with me was Greville Lashley. He urged me to give serious consideration to a career in the china clay industry and offered to smooth my path. 'CCC is just the start, Jonathan. I have plans. Big plans. You can be part of them. It's a golden opportunity. You should take it. You really should.'

I barely listened at the time. Though, strangely, over the years, the sound of his voice that day has grown in my memory. I had no reason to think so much of my future was bound up in his words. But it was. Oh yes. It surely was.

I knew I wouldn't find it quick or easy to recover from the rift with Vivien. As it turned out, it took me most of the rest of the year. I had to start by accepting there was no way back for us. Thoughts of her with the Hon. Roger Normington didn't help me do that, of course. Nor did my habit of comparing any girl I met with her (unfavourably). My housemates in Walworth soon tired of my lovelorn despondency and tried to snap me out of it with sarcasm. They achieved only fleeting success.

A disastrous trip to Cambridge one Saturday in late November finally broke the spell. I went with some cock-eyed notion of calling on Vivien at Girton and seeing surprise turn to joy on her face when she answered the door to me. A notion was all it remained, however. I decided to work up some Dutch courage in a city-centre pub, overdid it hopelessly and arrived at the college almost too drunk – but not quite – to know how badly any encounter with her was likely to go.

I never made it beyond the porters' lodge. Whether Miss Foster really had gone away for the weekend, as I was told, wasn't entirely clear. Maybe the story was designed to do her *and* me a favour.

On the way back to the station, I passed the Fitzwilliam Museum and saw a girl going in who I was momentarily convinced was Vivien. She wasn't, of course, which was fortunate, given the state I was in. Vivien probably had gone away for the weekend. To Lincolnshire, it occurred to me. To the ancestral pile of Viscount Horncastle.

I took a wrong turning after leaving the Fitzwilliam and found myself blundering along a path beside the Cam, south of the centre. The light was failing and an icy wind was blowing. It began to rain, then to sleet. I couldn't remember feeling colder or more wretched in my life.

I reached the station eventually, after a gigantic detour. Waiting there for the London train over two black coffees and several cigarettes, I came to the conclusion that enough was enough. Chasing something I'd previously turned my back on was as crazy as it was pitiful. It had to stop. And I had to start again.

Starting again didn't involve forgetting, of course. And other issues were left unresolved besides my feelings for Vivien. It was as impossible not to wonder how Countess Covelli had reacted to the letter I'd sent her as it was not to ask myself who had really paid Strake to follow Oliver, or who, come to that, had been on my tail before I'd left for Capri that summer. They were mysteries I eventually reconciled myself to living with. They were questions I had no way of answering. And that, I came to accept, was how they were likely to stay.

2010

TWENTY-TWO

I'd never actually stayed at the White Hart before. Waking the morning after my arrival in St Austell, I looked down from the window of my room at the early risers of the town hurrying along Church Street; then across, through the trees, at the tower of Holy Trinity. The years since Oliver Foster's funeral seemed to roll away as I looked. How could it be more than four decades ago? It wasn't possible, surely. So much time couldn't feel like so little.

But it could. And it did. This was my first visit to St Austell since my mother had moved to Lytham to live with my aunt, a year or so after my father's death. Someone else was growing up now in the house I'd grown up in. Wren & Co.'s old premises in East Hill had been demolished to make way for a supermarket. Nanstrassoe House had gone too, replaced by a cul-de-sac of up-market dwellings called Nanstrassoe Close. Even the General Wolfe, I'd been dismayed to discover the previous evening, had closed down. Nothing seemed to be as I remembered it. Yet what I remembered felt more real to me than the scene I looked out on that morning. The passage of time and the changes it had brought had made me a stranger.

My old school and Cornish China Clays' sixties office block were still standing on the hill above the town, however. All that had changed there was signage. The grammar had been subsumed within Poltair Comprehensive long since and CCC now styled itself Intercontinental Kaolins (Cornwall). But its days were numbered, according to rumours I'd heard during my brief stopover in Augusta. It faced downsizing as Cornish production declined. Smaller premises were being sought for a smaller workforce.

It was certainly obvious that the offices on Tregonissey Road were larger than they any longer needed to be. The car park was a long way short of full when I arrived for my ten o'clock appointment with Pete Newlove and a whole wing appeared to be unoccupied. The weather was suitably nostalgic, though. A soft rain on the heavy side of drizzle was falling from a pewter-grey sky. It had never rained quite like that anywhere else I'd been in all the years of my absence.

The lean, long-haired, droopy-moustached accounts clerk I'd first met at Wren & Co. in the summer of 1968 was now a paunchy, balding man in his early sixties whose post as Resources Manager (St Austell) entitled him to a large office overlooking the town, a six-foot desk and a high-backed leather swivel-chair that squeaked like a trapped mouse at every move.

'Long time no see, Jon,' was his predictable if accurate greeting. It had to be fifteen years or more since we'd last set eyes on each other. 'Still in harness, then?'

'Not for much longer, Pete. I'm on my way out.'

'Yeah? I wouldn't be too sure. You once lost a fiver to me betting you wouldn't work for CCC after university. Strikes me you just can't let go.'

'I'm letting go. You can bank on that.'

He smiled. 'If you say so.'

'Anyway, what's your excuse for still being here?'

'They keep paying me, Jon. Simple as that. Though maybe I should say *you* keep paying me, considering how close you are to the centre of things these days.'

'The only thing I'm close to is retirement. I've handed in my notice. This little damage limitation exercise is my last assignment.'

'Really? Sorry to hear that.'

'Why? It comes to us all.'

'I didn't mean I'm sorry you're retiring. I mean I'm sorry you're going out on a bum note. Damage limitation, did you say? Poisoned chalice, I'd call it.'

'What's that supposed to mean?'

'Don't you know? Oh, before I forget . . .' He ferreted in a drawer, pulled out a car key with an IK-insignia fob attached and slid it across the desk to me. 'Beaumont's PA said we should allocate some transport to you. Freelander near the main entrance is yours for the duration.'

'Thanks.'

'Don't mention it.'

I took the key, wondering how long I'd have to wait for him to expand on his 'poisoned chalice' remark. He wrapped a rubber band round his finger, then unwrapped it, then stared out through the window at the grey sprawl of St Austell. Finally, and to my surprise, he took a pack of cigarettes out of his pocket, flipped up the top and offered it to me.

'Smoke?'

I shook my head. 'I've given up.'

He sighed. 'Naturally.'

'Also, I must have passed at least half a dozen NO SMOKING signs on my way up here.'

'Yeah. I know.' He put the cigarettes away, satisfied, apparently, to have made some kind of point. 'And I actually obey them. It's pitiful, really. That old pension's quite a tyrant.'

'You could start drawing it any time you wanted.'

'True. But to live on it I'd have to cut back on the booze, the fags and the gee-gees. I don't fancy that.'

'You'll have to sooner or later.'

'Yeah. Just like we'll have to get to the point sooner or later, so, why don't we? Doctor Fay Whitworth. You've met her?'

'I had lunch with her in Bristol yesterday.'

'Right. So I don't need to fill you in. I'm sure she did that. Smart woman. And I don't just mean clever. I thought my luck was in when she showed up here, you know. Clever, attractive, single lady, in need of company and, er, evening entertainment . . . Don't look at me like that. A bloke can dream, can't he? Anyway, this dream turned into a nightmare. Missing records. Can you believe it? Missing bloody records from fifty years ago. I mean, who the hell cares?'

'Doctor Whitworth, Pete. And therefore the people you and I both work for.'

'OK.' He held up his hands. 'Point taken. No excuses will do. Somebody's filleted the Wren and Co. files and it's all my fault.'

'I'm not saying that.'

'Not yet you aren't. But when you put your report in to Beaumont, what'll you say then?'

'Depends what I find out while I'm here.'

'Sweet FA. That's what you'll find out. Those files could have been raided any time since the sixties, maybe *in* the sixties. Remember Oliver Foster? Maybe that's what he was up to in the basement over at East Hill.'

'I don't think so. All Wren and Co. documents would have been checked and collated when they were moved here after the takeover in sixty-eight. It has to have happened since then.'

'Which still gives us forty-two years to play with. I bet no one's looked at the stuff in all that time. Why would they?'

'Someone has looked, though, haven't they, Pete? That's the whole point. And you've just asked the right question: *why?*'

'Search me.'

'Oh, I'm sure it won't come to that.'

He laughed. 'Very funny.'

'I should probably start by looking at the files as they presently are.'

'That won't tell you anything.'

'Even so . . .'

'OK.' He levered himself out of the chair. 'Let's step down into the dungeons. Then you can do all the looking you like.'

The basement was a vast, strip-lit concrete cavern, resonant with the hum of the building's boiler. It had been fitted out with lockable wired-off cages, housing different sections of CCC records, along with redundant furniture, office equipment and assorted junk that should have been disposed of many years previously and probably would have been if the size of the basement hadn't made it so easy to stow everything away out of sight. There were typewriters galore, rusty filing cabinets, broken-backed chairs, wobbly-legged tables, bundles of maps, stacks of catalogues and piles and piles of paper.

'There are probably a few fossilized members of staff down here somewhere,' Pete joked as he led the way along the passage between the cages. 'File and forget should be the company's motto. What would that be in Latin?'

He rambled on in a similar vein until we reached our destination: the Wren & Co. cage. The box-files Fay Whitworth had consulted stood on open metal shelving, neatly labelled as she'd described. Some loose files and leather-bound minute books lay on a small table next to the shelving unit, disarranged as if Fay had merely stepped out for a coffee before resuming her researches. But her researches, of course, were not going to be resumed, unless I discovered what had become of the missing records.

Pete opened the padlock on the cage door and we stepped in. I pulled out a box-file dated in the mid-sixties, propped it on the stack of minute books and took a look. It was exactly as Fay had said. Two or three authentic documents, then nothing but blank flimsy paper. I pulled out a couple more, while Pete looked on amusedly, with the same result. Almost everything from the last twelve years of Wren & Co.'s independent existence had vanished. Minute books detailing board meetings from before the First World War were there for anyone to leaf through. But the late 1950s and all of the 1960s was a different story – a different, empty story.

'It's a baffler, isn't it?' said Pete, jingling the padlock key in his hand. 'A real baffler.'

'Has the cage always been kept locked?' I asked with a sigh.

'No. I've only been particular about that since Doctor Whitworth's visit. Shutting the stable door, I know. But there it is.'

'So more or less anyone could have done this, at any time?'

'Pretty much. They wouldn't even have had to be a member of

215

staff. It would've been easy to slip down here from reception if you knew the layout of the building. And what you were looking for, of course.'

'The paper they substituted for the real documents. It's the flimsy stuff we used to use for carbon copies.'

'So it is. But if you're thinking that proves the stunt was pulled before PCs replaced typewriters, think again. There's a pallet-load of that kind of paper in one of the cages further down.'

'Unlocked, of course?'

'You said it.'

'Bloody hell.'

Pete grinned at me. 'It just goes on getting better, doesn't it?'

'Any ideas?'

'Me? Ideas are above my pay grade, Jon. You know that.'

'They were even further above it when you and I worked at Wren's. That didn't stop you having them.'

'True.'

'So?'

'Well . . .'

'What?'

'I've no idea. Honestly. It's beyond me. But . . . no idea doesn't mean no clue.' His grin was becoming mischievous now. 'I, er . . . found something.'

'Found what? Where?'

'I came down here after Doctor Whitworth threw her fit and saw just what you've seen. When I couldn't do anything for her, she stormed off back to Bristol. Then Beaumont peppered me with angry emails. He even phoned me once to give me a bollocking. It didn't get him *or* Doctor Whitworth anywhere, of course.'

'Where's the "but" in this, Pete?'

'Just coming. Last time I was down here, I dropped the key while I was checking the padlock. When I bent down to get it, I noticed something lying underneath the shelving unit. It was a single sheet of paper. A memo, as it turned out, from George Wren to Greville Lashley, dating from late 1959. Now, how did that get there, do you suppose?'

'You have a theory?'

'My guess is it slipped down the back of the unit while our mysterious thief was emptying the files.'

'Which proves?'

'Nothing. Unless the memo is one of the documents the thief was particularly interested in.'

'Any reason to think it was?'

'Maybe.'

'What did the memo say?'

'Thought you'd never ask. See for yourself. It's back where it belongs now.' He pulled down the 1959/60 box-file, put it on the table and opened the lid. 'Here we are.' He turned over the first couple of documents to reveal the memorandum, then leant back to let me see it.

26 November 1959

To: Mr Lashley

Please advise me at your earliest convenience of your conclusions as to how we should best proceed in the matter of the Trudgeon contract in light of the issues arising from your perusal of Mr Foster's correspondence.

G. Wren

At first glance, the memo was notable only for its utter blandness. Kenneth Foster had been dead four months in November 1959. George Wren had presumably asked Lashley to tidy up various pieces of business Foster had been dealing with and wanted to know what he'd done about one of them. Earth-shattering, it wasn't. 'Is this supposed to prove something, Pete?'

Pete shrugged. 'That's for you to say.'

'It's just a memo. George Wren must have sent hundreds of the bloody things in his time, if not thousands.'

'True. But whatever our thief was after would look like this, wouldn't it? It would look insignificant.'

'Maybe. But how do you suggest we distinguish between the *apparently* insignificant and *genuinely* insignificant?'

217

'That's your problem, Jon. I'm just trying to . . . lend a helping hand.' He shrugged. 'It struck me our thief might have separated the stuff he was seriously interested in from the rest as he went through the file. Then one piece of that stuff could have slipped down the back of the shelf. There'd be nothing to stop it finishing up on the floor, would there? Which is exactly where I found it.'

I looked at the shelving unit. It had no back and wasn't fixed to the wall. It could have happened as Pete had suggested. But it was a big *could*. 'Know anything about the Trudgeon contract?' I asked hopefully.

'Not really. Wilf Trudgeon was a haulier based in Charlestown. You must remember his lorries.'

'I don't think so.'

'No? Well, it was before your time, I suppose. He handled most of the transport for Wren's from the dryers to the docks. Wren's bought him out in the end. It was the only way we could get an A licence of our own.'

'A what?'

'An A licence. You needed one to operate as a haulier in those days. They were like gold dust. I was at school with Wilf Trudgeon's son. Dick Trudgeon. Big lad. Built like a brick shithouse. He joined the police. Dick Truncheon, we used to call him. I wonder what happened to him. Retired now, I guess. Like we should be. Like you soon will be.'

'A haulage contract from half a century ago? I don't get it, Pete. It can't possibly matter to anyone, can it?'

'You wouldn't have thought so, would you?'

'Who else have you told about this?'

'No one. It doesn't amount to anything really, does it? Like you said, it's . . . insignificant.'

'I'd better take a photocopy of the memo, even so.'

'I've got one waiting for you upstairs. Seen enough down here?'

'More than enough.'

'Let's go, then.'

We stepped out of the cage and Pete locked it behind us. Then we headed for the stairs.

'There are a couple of things I ought to mention, Jon,' Pete said as we reached them.

'Oh yes?'

'We could talk them over out front before we go back to my office. I don't know about you, but I could do with some fresh air.'

Pete's need of fresh air was heavily qualified. He immediately lit a cigarette once we were outside. We took shelter from the rain in the covered way that linked the main building with the laboratory block and he puffed away tensely for a moment or two before explaining what the 'couple of things' were.

'First off, I guess you ought to know Adam Lashley's in town.'

It was worrying enough that Adam had phoned Fay Whitworth from London. His presence in St Austell was downright disturbing. 'He is?'

''Fraid so. After his father sold Nanstrassoe House he bought a place out at Carlyon Bay. Wavecrest, it's called. About halfway along Sea Road. Absolutely massive, as you'd expect. Empty most of the time, of course, while he's off in Thailand. But he's back now. A woman in the marketing department who walks her dog out on the coast path near there saw him tooling past in his Lotus yesterday morning. Quite a coincidence, hey? You and him showing up in the same week.'

'I doubt it's a coincidence.'

'Me too.'

'Fay Whitworth said he'd contacted her recently. He'd urged her to stop making a fuss about the missing records, apparently.'

'It's a pity she didn't take his advice.'

'What's he up to, I wonder.'

'No one seems to know. I hope it doesn't involve turning up here and throwing his weight around. Of course, he could have come down to . . . er . . .' Pete hesitated and took a fretful drag on his cigarette.

'To what?'

'Well, that's the other thing, Jon. He could be here to see his . . . half-sister.'

'Vivien's in St Austell too?'

'Yeah. Rumour is she's had it pretty rough these last few years. Well, not just these last few, I guess. Losing her son and her husband like she did . . .' He shrugged. 'It's bound to have taken its toll.'

I said nothing. There was nothing I felt capable of saying. The tragic misfortunes of the Normingtons had been amply documented in the tabloid press, where the family had been portrayed as an example of the aristocracy brought low by hard drugs and soft living. The facts were widely known. And the facts were all I knew.

'When did you last see her, Jon?'

'Twenty-six years ago.'

'As long as that?'

'It feels like less.'

'It won't if you see her now.'

I looked at him. 'What's that supposed to mean?'

'She's not . . . looking too good these days.'

'Where's she living?'

'In a caravan . . . out at Lannerwrack Dryers.'

'A caravan?'

'She pitched it there a few months ago.'

'At Lannerwrack?'

'Yeah. I know, I know. It's desperate. But then I get the feeling desperate's what she is. We decommissioned the dryers a couple of years ago. It's basically a derelict site. Ripe for redevelopment as an eco-town, if you believe our press releases. But I'm not holding my breath. Anyhow, Vivien's the only resident at the moment. I consulted HQ and was told to let her be. Whether the old man's been informed I don't know, but no one here's in a hurry to evict her. I'm not sure where we'd stand legally, anyway. I've given her a key to the dryer office, where there's electricity and hot and cold running water. It's not exactly all mod cons, but . . .'

'I don't understand. She could surely afford to live somewhere more comfortable.'

'Cut off by the current Viscount Whatsit. And refuses to take anything from her stepfather. That's the rumour.'

'Bloody hell.'

'Families are, aren't they? Will you go and see her?'

'Yes.' I tried to imagine the state Vivien had been reduced to. But all I could see in my mind's eye was the beautiful young woman I'd fallen in love with so many years before. She was lost to me now. Just as she was lost to herself. It shouldn't have come to this. There should have been a way to make a better future for ourselves. But the future was with us. And it was what it was. 'I'll go and see her,' I murmured. 'Of course I will.'

TWENTY-THREE

Before leaving the CCC building that morning, I instructed Pete Newlove to schedule a series of one-to-one meetings for me with all members of staff in order of length of service. It would take a while to work through them and I wasn't optimistic I'd learn much in the process, but there didn't appear to be any other course of action open to me. I had to start somewhere.

I wasn't optimistic that George Wren's 1959 memorandum to Greville Lashley would lead anywhere either, but I asked Pete to phone round any of his contemporaries from the secondary modern school he was still in touch with in the hope that one of them might know where I could find Dick Trudgeon. Whether Dick would have anything of the slightest value to tell me if I did find him was, of course, open to question.

Also open to question were Adam Lashley's reasons for returning to St Austell. But I felt sure I'd discover what they were soon enough, probably from the man himself. I assumed he knew I'd been sent over from HQ to track down the missing records. Whether he meant to help or hinder was unclear and perhaps unimportant. We didn't like each other. We never had. His presence was bad news.

It wasn't the only bad news, of course. I drove out to Lannerwrack Dryers that afternoon, feeling sick with apprehension. I didn't want to see Vivien looking old and weary and defeated. But that was how Pete had told me she was. Sooner or later, I'd have to meet her, though. And sooner was marginally better than later.

Relief, of a kind, awaited me at the end of my journey. Lannerwrack was a drying and milling plant I remembered as a bustling, noisy place, served from St Austell by road and rail. Disuse had brought an eerie desolation to the site. No lorries rumbled along the approach road. No smoke rose from the chimneys. The elevator towers stood sentinel over an empty drying shed. Nothing stirred beneath its vast roof. And weeds were sprouting through the concrete in the loading yard. I saw the caravan as I drove slowly in. There was no car parked beside it. The old Volkswagen Beetle Pete had said Vivien got around in was missing. And that meant, in all probability, she was missing too. I didn't have to see her yet. There was still a little more time to prepare myself. I was glad of that.

I stopped the Freelander in the lee of the dry and climbed out. Silence and stillness closed in around me. It was no place to be. It was no place to live. Yet Vivien had chosen to come here to hide from the world. I walked across to the caravan. It looked old – twenty or thirty years, I'd have guessed. But the paintwork was in reasonable condition and a couple of hanging flower baskets Vivien had rigged up gave it a homely appearance. There were net curtains at the windows, so I couldn't see in. A wire trailed from the caravan at head height to a half-open vent in the wall of the office lean-to at the end of the dry. Vivien was evidently helping herself to as much electricity as she needed. And why not? Only her stepfather could deny her the right to use it. And I doubted he was about to.

Despite the absence of the car, I knocked on the caravan door. There was no response, of course. Vivien wasn't there. According to Pete, she'd been seen at local markets, selling embroidered handkerchiefs and tablecloths. Maybe that was where she was now. She certainly needed whatever money she could raise if the new Viscount Horncastle had cut her off and she'd refused to take anything from Greville Lashley. Her current existence must have seemed strange to her, if not ironic, after all the privileges and advantages life had bestowed on her. But perhaps that was the point. Her brother, her husband and her son were all dead, in part because of those privileges and advantages. Perhaps what she was engaged in here was a form of penance.

If so, I resolved to tell her, if I got the chance, she should go easy on herself. If there was guilt to be borne, there were other shoulders besides hers to bear it, mine included. I went back to the Freelander, drove it to the other side of the yard and reversed into a position between the milling shed and the slope up to the settling tanks. I couldn't be seen from the approach road there, but I still had a clear view of the caravan. With any luck, Vivien would have no idea when she returned that anyone was waiting for her, least of all me.

I wound down the window and let the cool, moist air waft into the car. Memories drifted in with it: of my childhood in St Austell; of the day at Charlestown when I'd met Oliver and Vivien Foster for the very first time; of Oliver's body floating in the lake at Relurgis Pit; of Vivien as she'd been the following summer on Capri; of Vivien *and* me as we'd been then; and of our fractious parting at the top of the Spanish Steps in Rome.

Pete would have been amused to know how certain I felt then that I'd never end up working in the china clay industry. But certainty has a habit of being confounded by experience. I suppose that's the process we call living.

Most of the living I did at university scored higher in fecklessness and self-indulgence than it did in career-focused academic attainment. The result was that I was still living in Walworth, though in crummier accommodation even than the house I'd shared with Robin and Terry and the others, several months after graduating with a third-class degree. I was working as a porter at St Thomas's Hospital and trying to persuade myself, in the teeth of ample evidence to the contrary, that my on–off relationship with one of the nurses might amount to something serious in the end.

To say I was surprised when Greville Lashley tracked me down at the hospital one day would be a gigantic understatement. He was in London chasing a contract and didn't want to pass up the chance, he explained over a pub lunch, of reminding me there was always an opening for me at CCC. Nor, he emphasized, did such an opening have to be in Cornwall. CCC was expanding all the time. I'd have to prove my worth in St Austell in the first instance, but he reckoned someone with an economics degree and a chemistry A level – someone like me, in other words – would be ideal for the team he was putting together to run new plants in Australia.

Australia. The other side of the world. Land of sunshine and opportunity. I looked up through the clear-glazed top half of the pub window at the grey London sky and knew in that instant I was going to say yes. And Lashley, to judge by the smile playing at the edges of his mouth, knew it too. Pete had won our bet.

Why had Lashley gone to the bother of asking my parents where I was working in London? Why had he made time in his busy day in the capital to seek me out and sign me up? He said it was because I was the kind of reliable, resourceful young fellow he needed about him in the commercial empire he was planning to build. I didn't take him seriously at the time. No one else I knew would have called me either reliable or resourceful. And I didn't think Lashley had it in him to build an empire of any kind.

But he was the better judge of me – and himself. The future was his natural territory. He saw far and he thought long. Within six months, I was in Ballarat, playing my part in CCC's opening up of the high-yielding Victoria china clay deposits. Within a year after that, I was managing a refining plant. Progress, mine and the company's, was, as Lashley had promised, rapid. I was young, as eager to learn as I was to prosper. I enjoyed the rawness of Australia. I thrived on it. I married a local girl, who subsequently divorced me in favour of a local boy. By then seven years had passed and I was thirty.

Lashley himself discussed only business when he visited the Victoria operations. Such news as I had of Vivien reached me indirectly, via my mother, who'd struck up a chatting acquaintance with Harriet Wren. When I heard from her that Vivien had married the Hon. Roger Normington, the future Viscount Horncastle, it was no great surprise. I didn't waste my time dwelling on what might have been. A couple of years later, she gave birth to another future viscount. The course of her existence amidst the landed gentry of Lincolnshire seemed firmly set.

Oliver – and the mystery of how he'd died – faded from my thoughts. I was reminded of him, though, when Bobby Fischer won the World Chess Championship. Oliver had said Fischer deserved to be World Champion and it seemed he was right. But then he was right about most things. He was a great prover of points, even if it wasn't always clear what the point was that he was proving. As it turned out, Fischer never defended his crown. Somehow, I felt Oliver would have approved of that.

I couldn't help wondering from time to time what, if anything, Countess Covelli had done in response to the letter I'd sent her. But there was nothing I could do to find out. And the question was eventually rendered redundant. From the obituaries page of the Melbourne *Age* I learnt of the death in October 1978 of the celebrated Italian opera singer Luisa d'Eugenio. Her most memorable performances were faithfully recorded. Her marriage to Francis Wren merited one sentence. Her dealings with the SS in Mussolini's Fascist republic received no mention.

My mother wrote to me a few weeks later, mentioning that Luisa had died without having changed her will following Francis's death, which meant the Villa Orchis had been inherited jointly by Harriet Wren and Muriel Lashley. They'd decided the family should use it as a holiday home. I instantly imagined Vivien returning there, a wife and mother now, introducing her husband and her son to Countess Covelli, revelling in the status her own title would give her in Capri society, serenely forgetful of the weeks we'd spent there together, content with the cosseted life she'd settled for.

I might have been misjudging her. I might not. There was no way to tell. I'd have had to meet her to form a fair opinion. And I didn't expect that to happen. Nor did I expect that I'd ever return to Capri myself.

But my expectations, not for the first time, were to be confounded.

1984

TWENTY-FOUR

Greville Lashley had told me working in the United States would be geologically simpler but commercially more challenging than the time I'd spent in Australia. As ever, he was right. The china clay deposits of Georgia and South Carolina were ideal for strip-mining. But the presence of a well-established competitor, North American Kaolins, forced us to operate within very tight margins. And Lashley, ever more assertive once he'd manoeuvred his way first to managing director of CCC, then managing director *and* chairman, didn't like the squeeze that put on our profits one little bit.

I'd been number two for a couple of years to Harvey Beaumont at Cornish China Clays (US), based in Sandersville, Ga, when, early in 1984, Lashley came to see us, took Harv and me out to lunch and unveiled the strategy he'd devised to solve the problem.

'Merger, gentlemen. That's the answer. We're going to join forces with NAK. It makes perfect sense. China clay is global business. And CCC plus NAK will dominate it.'

Harv, whom Lashley had poached from NAK, objected that his old boss, Don Hudson, would never consent to a genuine merger. He'd only be interested in a takeover.

'That's what I'll let him think the deal amounts to,' Lashley smilingly responded. 'But it won't. Don's not the man he was. Age has caught up with him. Losing his son in Vietnam has fogged his vision of the future. Don't worry. I can manage Don. And the rest of the NAK board. I can manage this whole thing very sweetly. The important point for you two to bear in mind is that I see you both playing vital roles in the enlarged organization I'll be putting together over the coming years. I trust you. All you have to do is trust me. How does that sound?'

Like a younger man talking, it struck me at the time. Lashley was sixty-five, pushing sixty-six. By rights he should have been contemplating retirement. But not a bit of it. Instead he was contemplating a bold and ambitious corporate coup. No one could say age was catching up with *him*. He didn't look much different from when I'd first met him sixteen years earlier, though it was even harder now to believe the glossy blackness of his hair was genuine. I didn't doubt he could achieve what he was proposing. After all, I'd seen him do it before.

'I'd appreciate it if you kept this under your hats, gentlemen. It's not going to happen overnight. But it *is* going to happen. I'll see to that. I'm mentioning it to you now so you'll understand the thinking behind the changes and . . . the compromises . . . that will be necessary in the months ahead. I want you to keep the boat steady when others are tempted to rock it. You follow?'

We followed. That, I'd learnt, as had Harv, was what you did if you wanted to prosper as a trusted lieutenant of Greville Lashley. He hadn't stopped. He hadn't even slowed down. He was still going places. And we were going with him.

Exactly how Lashley subsequently set about wooing NAK I didn't know. Nor did I need to know. But by early summer there were indications that change was afoot, which unsettled some, though not, obviously, me or Harv. We had to do some minor boat-steadying, as Lashley had anticipated. It didn't prove unduly difficult. We heard nothing directly from Lashley after our powwow over lunch. And we didn't expect to. We knew what was going on.

But what was going on took a sudden swerve in July, just as I was about to head off on holiday. Harv conveyed an urgent message to me from Lashley. I was needed to help him deal with a grave

232

but unspecified emergency. I was to join him as soon as possible – on Capri.

I'd never been back there. Capri spelt loss and regret for me: loss of the happiness I'd briefly known with Vivien and regret for the part we'd played in the events that had led to Francis Wren's death. It was a place I'd have preferred to avoid. But a summons from Lashley couldn't be ignored. My preferences were irrelevant. He paid me well to keep them that way. I was on the next flight.

It was Wednesday afternoon when I landed in Naples. The weather was breezy, but the breeze was blowing from an oven. The runway shimmered liquidly in the heat haze. No one was waiting to collect me and Capodichino was like dozens of other airports I'd jetted into over the years. It stirred no memories.

The taxi ride to the ferry terminal was different, as I'd known it would be. I couldn't stop myself remembering my journey there from the railway station with Vivien. The city looked and sounded and smelt just as it had then: bright and loud and pungent. But Vivien wasn't sitting beside me, glancing at me and laughing as we jolted along. And I wasn't the person she'd glanced at and laughed with anyway. Time had changed me, as I didn't doubt it had her.

I assumed Vivien wasn't staying at the Villa Orchis. I doubted Lashley would have called for me if she had been. Who might be there besides Lashley himself I didn't know. The message had given no details. Muriel, I supposed. Harriet, quite possibly. And Adam too. He was twenty-one, reading English (not a choice of subject I could imagine his father approving of) at Oxford. Since encountering him as a child, I'd met him just once, three years previously, when Lashley had brought him into the office in Sandersville. I recalled a tall, floppy-fair-haired youth who greeted everything he saw of CCC's US operation, including me, with undisguised boredom. Whether Lashley hoped he'd follow him into the business he'd never disclosed. But the signs hadn't exactly been promising.

*

The ferry carried me out into the brilliant blue of the bay. I sat on the top deck, watching Capri slowly assume its familiar shape as we approached. It felt both more and less than fifteen years since my last visit. I'd done a lot of living in those years. But nothing I'd done had eclipsed my memories of the few weeks I'd spent on the island. Nothing ever would. I knew that without the need to tell myself. It was a given. It was a fact of my life.

Facts, of course, were what Greville Lashley dealt in. They were the currency of his commercial existence. He'd summoned me to Capri. So to Capri I'd come.

I didn't know what to expect when I arrived. But seeing Lashley waiting for me on the jetty at Marina Grande still came as a major surprise. In his panama and linen suit, he looked like some ex-pat leading a life of leisure in his retirement. The truth, as I knew, was that he had little use for leisure and even less for retirement. The emergency mentioned in his message had to be just that to bring him down to the port to meet me. Something must be seriously wrong.

There was no way to tell that from his casual bearing, however, or his smile as I stepped off the gangway. He shook my hand and clapped me on the back. 'I reckoned you'd make this ferry, Jonathan,' he said. 'And here you are.'

'Good of you to come down here, sir. I could have . . . made my own way.'

'No need. I brought the car. But actually . . .' His hand was on my shoulder as we followed the other disembarking passengers along the jetty. The gesture was trusting and confidential, almost intimate. 'I'd like us to have a word before we go up to the villa. I need to explain the lie of the land to you. We can talk at the café along here.'

I knew the café he was referring to. Its tables, sheltered from the ferry crowds by the harbourmaster's office, were set out on a terrace overlooking the beach. Vivien and I had stopped there for coffee several times. Customers were few at that stage of the afternoon and by a troubling coincidence Lashley chose the very table where Vivien had always wanted to sit. I tried to tell myself I couldn't be sure it was the same table. But, of course, it was.

The waitress approached as we sat down and we ordered coffees. Lashley lit a cigarette and offered me one. I accepted, rare though it had become for me to smoke. I welcomed this one more as a prop than anything else.

'I'm sorry to have disrupted your holiday plans, Jonathan,' Lashley said as he took a first draw on his cigarette. 'Be assured I didn't do so lightly. A situation's arisen – a dire situation – in which I need your assistance.'

'I'll do whatever I can.' The man had been generous enough over the years for me to give up a week's hiking in the Appalachians without complaint. 'What's the problem?'

'We'll come to that presently. I must emphasize at the outset, however, that this lies well beyond your range of duties at CCC. You won't in any way prejudice your position there by refusing.'

'But I won't refuse.'

'I hope not, certainly. I need someone I can rely on to act for me. Someone reliable . . . and loyal. As I've always found you to be.'

'I'm glad you think so, sir.'

'You may not be glad for long. I—' He broke off as the waitress returned with our coffees. '*Grazie*,' he murmured. He busied himself with his cigarette as she set down the cups and walked away. Then he leant towards me and lowered his voice. 'What I'm about to say must go no further, Jonathan. You understand?'

'Certainly.'

He sighed. 'I didn't think I'd ever find myself saying something was a matter of life and death and meaning it literally. But that is how I find myself.'

'Life and death?'

'Yes. It concerns Muriel.'

'Is she ill?'

'No. That is . . . I'm sorry. I mustn't beat about the bush. The plain fact is that my wife has been kidnapped.'

'*What?*'

'I'd be obliged if you kept your voice down, Jonathan, shocking as I appreciate the news is. I haven't informed the authorities, you see. I wouldn't trust the local police to negotiate a hairpin bend, let alone my wife's release from the hands of the Camorra.'

'Who?'

'The Neapolitan Mafia. They're sure to be behind this, just as they're behind every other crime in the region above the level of pickpocketing and handbag-snatching. Italy's very pretty, as I'm sure you've noticed. But it's all make-up. Underneath there's a very ugly face.'

'But here? On Capri?'

'You'd expect them to leave well alone, wouldn't you, considering what they skim off from the tourist trade? Well, there's a reason we've been targeted and I think I know what it is, but that doesn't help free Muriel. The only thing that'll do that is money.'

'They've demanded ransom?'

'Oh yes. And we're close to agreeing a figure.' Something in my expression must have signalled my surprise that he'd evidently haggled over the price. 'If you cave in straight away, they only demand more. And they have an exaggerated notion of what I'm worth. It's important to show them I'm not a pushover. I have to extract a measure of respect from them to make this work.'

'How long have they been holding her?'

'A week. She went to her hairdresser as usual last Wednesday afternoon, but never came back. Somewhere between the salon and the villa, they grabbed her. She was on foot, which must have made it easy for them. It's only a short walk. And a pleasant one, normally. But it turned out to be neither. They probably had her in a boat heading for the mainland before I even noticed she was late. I had the first phone call that night. There have been several since. They're not easy people to do business with. But to them that's what this is: business. So, I have to play by their rules. It's the only way, believe me. I've taken discreet advice. What I'm doing gives us – gives Muriel – the best possible chance of a safe outcome.'

The calmness with which he'd explained the situation would have surprised me if I'd been listening to anyone else. But Greville

Lashley's self-control was legendary. I'd have expected nothing less. 'This is terrible. I can hardly believe such a thing could have happened.'

'It is terrible, as you say. But wailing and gnashing of teeth won't help Muriel. They sent me a photograph of her holding a copy of last Friday's *Il Mattino* to prove they have her. She looked well, in the circumstances. But frightened. That was obvious. And understandable. The Camorra have a bloodthirsty reputation. Their guiding principle, however, is greed. That's what I have to appeal to.'

'How can I help?'

'First, by saying nothing about this to anyone other than those who already know. There must be absolute secrecy until we've secured Muriel's release. I need your word on that.'

'You have it.'

'Thank you.' He nodded at me solemnly. 'I knew I could count on you. That's why I called you in.'

'Who does already know?'

'Very few, fortunately. Adam's been staying here since term ended at Oxford. He's worried sick about his mother, but he appreciates that what I'm doing is the best way to get her back where she belongs. The only other person in the know is Jacqueline Hudson.'

'Hudson? Is she . . .'

'Don Hudson's daughter. I invited Don here so we could discuss my merger idea in a relaxed and comfortable environment. Jacqueline came with him. The discussions went well, which seemed important at the time but now, of course, utterly trivial. Don flew back to Atlanta the day before Muriel was kidnapped. It was actually Muriel who invited Jacqueline to stay on for a while. They'd hit it off and Jacqueline was enjoying herself, so . . . why not? Well, she's not enjoying herself any more. But she wants to stay until Muriel's released. She's a good-hearted young woman, I must say. She's promised she won't breathe a word to anyone, even her father, until this is over. I believe her. She has a trustworthy nature.'

'Good. What about Vivien? Does she—'

'I haven't told her and I don't intend to, unless, of course . . .' He raised one hand in reference to a contingency he had no wish to put into words. 'You're well aware, Jonathan, that Vivien has had a good many traumas to cope with in her life. But marriage and motherhood seem to have agreed with her. She's found . . . peace of mind. I intend to keep it that way if I possibly can.'

'I understand.' So I did. But that didn't quell a surge of resentment. Marriage and motherhood. Privilege and prosperity. And the title of a viscountess to revel in when her father-in-law dropped off the aristocratic perch. Oh yes. Vivien had peace of mind all right. I should know. I'd helped her get it.

'I haven't told Harriet either. Not least because, as far as Patrizia and Elena are concerned, Harriet's ill, meaning Muriel's had to rush home to Cornwall. You remember Patrizia?'

'Yes. Of course. But Elena?'

'Her daughter. They share the cooking and cleaning. Salt of the earth, both of them. But they'd be incapable of keeping quiet about something like this. Patrizia would be in permanent hysterics. She's very attached to Muriel. So, watch what you say when they're around.'

'I will.'

'We won't have to maintain the pretence for much longer. I'm confident of reaching a final agreement with Muriel's captors within a few days.'

'I'm glad to hear it. But I'm still not clear what—'

'I want you to do? Well, let's deal with that. The thing is, Jonathan, when agreement's been reached, there'll have to be a delivery of the ransom money, simultaneous with Muriel's release. I anticipate they'll insist on separate locations. So, while I go wherever they nominate to collect Muriel, someone else will have to go somewhere else to hand over the cash. It's asking a lot, I know, but I'm hoping you'll agree to be that someone.'

'I see. Well, I—'

'It should be straightforward. Like I say, to them it's just a business transaction. But they're capable of anything. I'd be lying to you if I pretended there wasn't an element of danger in this.'

I'd already guessed he had some such role in mind for me. Why else summon me across the Atlantic? He needed the services of a trustworthy employee – by implication, his *most* trustworthy employee. Quite how I'd ended up with that status I wasn't sure. It was about a lot more than my record at CCC. It was about Francis and Oliver. And Vivien, of course. And maybe even her long-dead father. I'd kept secrets for Greville Lashley without knowing what they really were. They bound us together. They underpinned the trust he was putting in me. And they ensured I wouldn't turn him down. 'I can do that,' I said. And as I said it, in some small, unworthy compartment of my brain, I was already relishing the moment, lodged in an ill-defined future, when Vivien discovered who she was beholden to for her mother's life. 'You can rely on me.'

TWENTY-FIVE

He was grateful. That was clear. And in his gratitude there was also satisfaction that I'd vindicated his judgement of me. But there was more he had to tell. We ordered another two coffees. He lit another cigarette. The heat of the afternoon faltered marginally. A bar of cloud traced a line across the horizon. Evening wasn't far off now.

'There's a complication, Jonathan. One I'd like you to deal with while I finalize the terms of Muriel's release. An Englishman – Thompson's his name – has been looking for Muriel. He's staying at the Gabbiano, up in the town. I gather he's been asking questions about her *and* me in the shops and cafés. He arrived at the end of last week. He called at the villa on Sunday. I'd never clapped eyes on the fellow before. He's in his sixties. Podgy and more than a little truculent. A Londoner, judging by his accent. Anyway, he claimed to have had an appointment with Muriel on Saturday. She didn't show up, naturally. But she'd never mentioned any such appointment to me. He declined to say what they were meeting to discuss. He declined to say very much at all, in fact. I told him Muriel had left the island at short notice and saw him off. But he's still here. And he hasn't stopped asking questions. I had a phone call from Harriet the night before last. He'd been on to her, asking if Muriel was in St Austell. Harriet was puzzled, obviously. I told her Muriel was out playing bridge and would call her later in the week. If all goes well, she'll be able to do that, though what she'll say about friend Thompson I can't imagine.'

'Do you think she really had agreed to meet him?'

'I've no idea. It seems improbable, but since the fellow won't reveal what line of business he's in, if any . . .' Lashley shrugged. 'I'd like you to get him off my back. Find out what his game is and persuade him – pay him, if necessary – to leave Capri. I'd happily ignore him, but given the delicacy of the situation . . .'

'OK. Leave it to me.' Yes. What an invaluable resource I was to Lashley. I'd become a troubleshooter in his personal, as well as his professional, life. 'I'll contact him tomorrow.'

'Excellent. We don't need him making a nuisance of himself in the days ahead, we really don't.' Lashley rubbed his eyes. He looked tired and just a little strung-out. It was hardly surprising. A lesser man and many a younger one would have been in pieces after the week he'd endured. 'I can't tell you how reassuring it is to have you here, Jonathan,' he said, summoning a smile from somewhere. 'I'm indebted to you.'

'You said earlier you thought you knew why you'd been targeted.'

'Ah yes.' He took a lengthy draw on his cigarette. 'Well, maybe you know too.'

I frowned in puzzlement. 'No.'

'It's Verdelli, Jonathan. It has to be.'

'*Paolo* Verdelli?'

'The very same. He expected to inherit the Villa Orchis when Luisa died. Along with the fortune he imagined she'd salted away. She promised him as much, to hear him tell it. But there was no fortune. And the villa went to Muriel and Harriet. All those years he'd catered for her . . . needs . . . were in vain. There was no pay-off for him. Just a thumbed nose from beyond the grave. He didn't like it. Who would, in his position? He consulted a lawyer at one point. But even in Italy there's no law protecting the interests of middle-aged gigolos. He had to swallow his disappointment and go looking for some other wealthy widow. Except that I'm not sure he did swallow it. The last time he spoke to me was just after the lawyer had told him he didn't have a leg to stand on. "You will regret robbing me," he said. And he looked as if he meant it.'

241

'An idle threat, surely.'

'That's what I assumed. But he comes from an old Neapolitan family. A lot of them have connections with the Camorra. He might easily have Camorrista relatives. A word in the right ear. A favour called in. He's probably on a cut of the ransom money. Yes, I suspect he's behind it. The inflated figure the kidnappers initially demanded points to him. I expect he still believes Luisa was a millionairess.'

'Does he still live on Capri?'

'No. He left the island soon after we took over the villa. But according to Patrizia he hasn't gone further than Naples. As a matter of fact, I saw him there myself, at the ferry terminal, when Muriel and Adam and I arrived two weeks ago. He pretended not to recognize us and I was happy to pretend I didn't recognize him. But now I look back on it, there was something ... furtive ... about his behaviour. I think he was already planning to take revenge on us for what Luisa did to him.'

'If you're right ...'

'There's nothing to be done about it. At least not until we have Muriel back home, safe and sound. Then ... Well, we'll see.' A gleam in his eye suggested he didn't intend to let Paolo get away with extorting money out of him. How much money he was planning to settle for he hadn't said, and I hadn't asked. It would have seemed tasteless.

As for Paolo, I knew he had even better reason to be bitter than Lashley supposed. Between us, he and I had covered up the evidence that Francis had murdered Strake. Whether Luisa had been aware of what we'd done, I didn't know. If she did, her failure to leave Paolo anything in her will was spectacularly, perhaps unforgivably, cruel. But Luisa, as I also knew, had been capable of great acts of treachery. Perhaps this had merely been her last.

It was the recollection, never far from my mind, of the part I'd played in events leading up to Francis's death and in its aftermath that prompted me to ask Lashley, as we left the café and headed for his car, whether he was acquainted with Countess Covelli.

242

'The *contessa*? Yes, she's a neighbour. Well, you'd know that, of course. We don't socialize with her, if that's what you mean. Amiable but distant is how I'd describe her. And elegant. *Very* elegant. A great beauty in her youth, I imagine.'

'She was a close friend of Luisa's.'

'That was my impression when we first met her, after Francis died. But she didn't attend Luisa's funeral. They must have drifted apart. Or fallen out. Who knows?'

'I liked her. I might call on her, if you don't mind.'

'Why should I mind? Tell her I've got you over here working on the terms of a big new contract. That can be your cover story. Remember: Muriel's gone home to Cornwall because Harriet's poorly. But not too poorly. Otherwise she'll wonder why Adam and I have stayed put.'

'Don't worry. I won't let anything slip. Maybe I won't have time to see her, anyway.'

But I'd find the time. Oh yes. It was like an itch I couldn't help scratching. What had the countess done after reading the letter I'd sent her? How had she paid her old friend back for betraying her husband to the Nazis? I couldn't come to Capri and make no effort at all to find out.

Lashley's car was a Fiat runabout. It was a far cry from the Jaguars he normally favoured, but convenient for the narrow, winding roads of Capri. As we climbed the hill out of Marina Grande, slowed by a labouring lorry ahead of us, he asked after my parents. Then, when I'd assured him they were both well and that my father was enjoying retirement, he said, almost as if he envied them, 'They must be proud of you, Jonathan.'

'Well, I don't know about that.'

'Oh, I think so. Parenthood is something of a lottery. You never quite know what you're going to get. Since you'll be seeing quite a bit of him, I should prepare you for the fact that Adam isn't easy to deal with.'

'I'm sure I wasn't at his age either.'

'I knew you at his age. There was a big difference. As you'll see for yourself. Just remember: it's all one big pose. He likes to seem flippant and superior. Actually, he's as insecure as anyone else. And he's as worried as I am about his mother. He just has a strange way of showing it.'

'I'll make allowances.'

'Good. Because you'll need to, believe me.'

As it turned out, I had to wait a while for my first encounter with Adam. He'd gone out – destination a beach or a bar or both – shortly after Lashley had set off to collect me. We were informed of this as soon as we reached the Villa Orchis by Patrizia, stouter than she'd been fifteen years earlier but otherwise unaltered. Blithely unaware of what had happened to Muriel, she enveloped me in hugs and kisses and fussed around cheerily.

Lashley introduced me to Jacqueline Hudson, a tall, softly spoken brunette in her late thirties or early forties, whose taut expression hinted at the strain she was under. She might have been cool and aloof on other occasions, but the gravity of the situation had fostered a camaraderie between her and Lashley to which I was immediately admitted.

'Greville's spoken so highly of you, Jonathan,' she said, as soon as Patrizia had left us alone. 'It's a mercy he has someone like you to call on. Lord knows, he needs help at a time like this.'

'I'm here to do whatever I can.'

'I urged him to contact the police as soon as we realized Muriel had been taken. He convinced me that would have been a mistake. You agree?'

For all her courtly southern accent and manners, it was clear she believed in coming to the point. I could hardly disagree, with Lashley standing beside me, but maybe she thought she'd be able to gauge the sincerity of my response even so. 'I've always had the highest respect for Mr Lashley's judgement. I'm sure what he's doing is for the best.'

'Me too.' She smiled stiffly. 'But it's a trial for all of us. And for Muriel . . . well, I don't like to think about what she's going through.'

'It won't be for much longer,' said Lashley. 'I'm very close to an agreement with these people.'

'People? I'm not sure they qualify for the description.'

'Neither am I. But I can't afford to let them know that. Now, if you'll excuse me, I have some things to attend to.'

There was a trace of exasperation in Lashley's words. He headed for Francis's old study, now his, like a man facing up to a painful duty. He'd shouldered the responsibility for freeing Muriel. It was probably the heaviest responsibility he'd ever shouldered. And he couldn't shirk it.

'His self-control is remarkable,' said Jacqueline after he'd gone. 'I couldn't have handled the pressure the way he has.'

'You must have handled a good deal just by being here and knowing what's going on.'

'I've tried to give Greville as much support as I can. It's little enough, though. He carries all the worry and the stress inside him. He's gone to the study now because this is often the time they call. A deal is close, he tells me. The end's in sight. I surely hope so.'

'How's Adam coping?'

'You're acquainted with the young man?'

'Barely.'

'Well, he's another worry for his father. Out a lot, especially late at night. Drinking too much. Probably on drugs as well. He won't . . .' She sighed. 'It's not for me to say. It's hard for him, I know, but . . .'

'He's very young.'

'My brother was risking his life in Vietnam at Adam's age. Risking it . . . and losing it.'

'I'm sorry.' Lame as the sentiment was, it was all I could offer.

'John's death shortened my mother's life and my father's never properly recovered from it either. Such a thing does lasting damage. You can't just . . . shrug it off. I know that from personal experience. So, I'm praying this turns out well, Jonathan. Literally praying. Every night. Because if it doesn't . . .'

She said no more. She didn't need to. Her silence said it all.

TWENTY-SIX

The Villa Orchis was a sombre, anxious place in Muriel Lashley's absence. The changes she'd made to the furnishings and decorations of Luisa's days only emphasized, as her husband freely admitted, that it was much more her home from home than his. She'd always spent more time there than he had, carefully imprinting on it her very English sensibility. Luisa would have objected that there were too many cushions and far too many ornaments. And I'd have agreed with her. That, however, was as Muriel wanted it. I scarcely knew her, though the little I knew I didn't like, which I suspected was just how she felt about me. But her plight was an awful one. I didn't need to work hard at wanting to rescue her from it.

After dinner, and Patrizia's departure, Lashley asked me to step into his study for a word – a conferral, in effect, from which Jacqueline was uncomplainingly omitted. Lashley was old school. This was a man's job. And we were the men to do it.

The room had been altered less than most of the others. It was much as Francis had left it, preserved by Luisa in his memory, I assumed. Lashley, for whom the environments he lived and worked in always seemed matters of little importance, had simply colonized it for his purposes.

The mineral cabinet had gone, though, donated to a museum, maybe. In its place stood a safe, in which, Lashley told me, the money to buy Muriel's freedom was stored in readiness. 'In Swiss francs, Jonathan,' he said. 'The Camorra's currency of choice. They phoned earlier,' he revealed. 'They're beginning to sound almost reasonable. We'll have a deal soon. Twenty-four hours. Forty-eight at most.'

'I'm glad to hear it.'

'Then you'll have to do your bit, I'm afraid.'

'I'm ready for that.'

'Muriel's always been down on you, as you know. She blames you to some degree for Oliver's death. Unreasonably, of course, but there it is. Rest assured I shall point out to her that you're more use to me in an emergency – and to her – than the Honourable Roger could ever be.'

'Horses for courses.'

Lashley chuckled grimly. 'You're a realist, like me. We do what has to be done. We get results. And a result is what we need.' He opened a drawer of the desk and took out an envelope, stamped and franked, with his name and address written on it in large capitals. He handed it to me. 'Take a look,' he said softly.

Inside was a photograph: *the* photograph. Muriel Lashley, smartly dressed, hair coiffured from her visit to the salon, stared grimly at the camera, her face drawn, eyes hollow, fear – and, yes, anger – etched in her gaze; in front of her, clutched prominently in both hands, was the Neapolitan daily, *Il Mattino*.

The print wasn't sharp enough for me to read the date, but from the same drawer Lashley took a copy of the previous Friday's edition. Its front page matched the one in the photograph. 'I was instructed to buy it,' he explained. 'So there could be no doubt.'

'I'm really sorry this has happened, sir.'

'Thank you. I know you are. But don't worry.' He squeezed my shoulder. 'You and I are going to make it *un*happen.'

The bedroom I'd been allocated was the same room I'd been given fifteen years before. Lashley had no way of knowing that and Patrizia had probably forgotten. It was just another coincidence, a minor one at that. But I could have done without it. Beyond the

247

calamity I was there to help Lashley deal with were ghosts of memories I had no wish to meet.

Sleep proved elusive, though whether because of those ghosts or straightforward jet lag I couldn't have said. I abandoned the struggle after a couple of hours and went downstairs to make myself a hot drink.

So it was that I alone of the household was still up when Adam reeled home from wherever he'd spent the evening and a large chunk of the night. It was immediately obvious he was drunk and not hard to guess he was half stoned as well. My presence in the kitchen was no great surprise to him. He'd been told I was coming – and why. He was ready for me. And I was ready for him.

'Waiting up for me, Kellaway?' he slurred, taking a puff on what smelt like a reefer. 'Didn't know tucking the son and heir up in bed was part of your contract. But I guess your contract covers . . . whatever Daddy says it covers.'

He seemed to be even taller than I remembered. Fatter too. His round, puffy face was flushed, his Che Guevara T-shirt stained with red wine. He swayed as he squinted at me, forcing his eyes to focus. I reminded myself that hostility and excess were probably his way of coping with his fears about what might happen to his mother. 'Do you want a cup of tea?' I asked. 'I've just made some.'

'Nah. Not my idea of a nightcap.' He pulled open a cupboard and took out a bottle of brandy that Patrizia probably kept for cooking. 'This is more like it.' He found a glass and poured himself an unhealthily large slug.

'Don't you think you've had enough?'

The question was a red rag to a bull. 'I've had enough of being cooped up here. And pretty soon I'll have had enough of you. You've come for the pay-off, right? You're the bag man?'

'Sort of.'

'So how much is in the bag? I reckon I've a right to be told. It's coming out of my inheritance, after all.'

'Your inheritance?'

'Money Daddy's put away over the years. Intended for me. *Not* intended for a bunch of Neapolitan low-lifes.'

248

Drunk as he was, there seemed no doubt he genuinely resented the family's savings being raided to buy Muriel's freedom. His selfishness was breathtaking. 'We're talking about your mother's life, Adam,' I reminded him.

'What's happened to her isn't my fault.'

'I never said it was.'

'But I'm the one who has to pay for it.'

'Your father's the one who's paying.'

'You still haven't told me how much.' He gulped down most of the brandy in one swallow. His eyes bulged. He shook his head like a dog and grinned inanely at me. 'Ah . . . Perhaps you don't know. Daddy keeping you in the dark, is he? Like a fucking mushroom. When does the next bucketload of shit land on your head, hey?'

'I'll leave you to it.' It was clearly pointless talking to him in his present condition, tempted though I was to say what I thought of him. I picked up my tea and headed for the door. He grabbed my elbow to stop me.

'You should be nice to me, Kellaway. Nicey nice. I'll be in charge of the business one day. Some bootlicking now might stand you in good stead later.'

I prised myself free of his grip. 'Goodnight, Adam,' I said levelly.

He said nothing. But I felt the force of his glare, trained some-where between my shoulder blades, all the way out of the room.

I was up early next morning, thanks only to my alarm clock. There was a moment of shock such as I'd experienced before, a moment when I remembered I was back on Capri. And the Wren family were back in my life, the Lashley branch of it, anyway. Greville Lashley had treated me well over the years and I wasn't going to let him down. Set against that, the fact that his son was an egotistical jerk didn't count for much. I couldn't allow it to.

My intention was to catch the mysterious Mr Thompson at his hotel before he headed out somewhere for the day. The Gabbiano was a small, whitewashed establishment at the eastern end of Capri town. The receptionist I encountered understood enough English to direct me to the small courtyard garden at the rear, where Signor Thompson was enjoying his *prima colazione*.

The breakfasters comprised a German-speaking couple and one bald, paunchy, jowly old Brit stationed at a pink-parasoled table with tea, cornflakes and the only English-language newspaper available to him, the *International Herald Tribune*. He was smoking a pipe and this, together with his severely clipped moustache and his baggy-shirt-and-trouser concept of hot-weather gear, gave him the look of someone stuck firmly in the 1950s.

'Mr Thompson?'

He looked up at me suspiciously. 'I'm Fred Thompson, yes. Do I know you?' As Lashley had said, there was an undertow of cockney in his voice.

'No. Let me introduce myself. I work for Greville Lashley. My name's Jonathan Kellaway.'

Something I can only call a tremor flitted across Thompson's face: a brief narrowing of the gaze, a twitch of surprise, a frown of disbelief. The effect was disquieting, as if he did know me, or knew of me, but hadn't expected to meet me in such a setting. 'What can I do for you, Mr Kellaway?'

'Mind if I sit down?'

'Be my guest.'

I sat down opposite him. 'Sorry to interrupt your breakfast. I didn't want to miss you.'

He took a puff at his pipe. 'What sort of thing does Mr Lashley employ you to do?'

'This and that. I gather you've been asking after *Mrs* Lashley.'

'I've had my ear to the ground, yes. I expected her to be here, see. We had an appointment.'

'Concerning what?'

'No offence intended, but that concerns something between me and her that's none of your business.'

'And what's *your* business, Mr Thompson?'

'Oh, I'm retired. Drawing my hard-earned pension.'

'So, you're here on holiday, are you?'

'Not exactly. I still keep my hand in. And Mrs Lashley . . .' He broke off and grinned at me. 'It's lucky you dropped in, actually. Saves me trudging over to the villa. I was planning to, see. This very morning, as it happens.'

'Why?'

'I wanted to give Lashley a last chance to square with me . . . before I go to the police.'

'The police?'

'What else can I do? Mrs Lashley goes missing when she's asked me to come all this way to discuss an urgent matter. Mr Lashley won't tell me where she is. The word among the tradesfolk is she's gone to look after her sick aunt in Cornwall. But the aunt isn't sick and thinks her niece hasn't left Capri. Which is where Mrs Lashley's daughter also thinks she is. But she isn't. Apparently. *Misterioso*, as the locals would say.'

'Mr Lashley's not obliged to explain his wife's comings and goings to you.'

'That he isn't.' Another grin. 'The police might be a different matter, though.'

'They'll tell you to go away and stop wasting their time.'

'We'll see.'

'You'll certainly have to disclose the nature of your business with Mrs Lashley to them.'

'And I will.'

'So why not disclose it to me first . . . and avoid making yourself look an idiot?'

'That's what you think I'll look, is it?'

'Mr Lashley knows nothing of your "appointment" with his wife.'

'Not unusual in my line.'

It seemed to me that could mean only one thing. 'Are you a private detective?'

'Confidential inquiries agent is what I used to call myself, Mr Kellaway. Retired, like I told you. But still on call . . . for a few trusted clients.'

A private detective, by any other name. Thompson had admitted it. And the significance of his admission was like the disappearance

251

of the ground beneath my feet. Suddenly, I remembered Terry's description of the man who'd been asking questions about me at the Builders' Arms in Walworth back in the summer of 1969. '*Your average middle-aged square. Not tall, not short. Not fat, not thin. Smoked a pipe. Fussy little 'tache. Never took his hat off, so he might've been bald . . . or he mightn't have been.*' It was him, fifteen years older, fatter and balder. It was Fred Thompson, confidential inquiries agent. There wasn't a doubt of it in my mind.

'Are you all right, Mr Kellaway? You look as if you've seen a ghost.'

'I'm fine.'

'Well, if you're sure.'

'Are you saying . . . you've done some work for Mrs Lashley in the past?'

'I have, yes.'

'What sort of work?'

'The confidential sort.'

'Following people? Checking up on them?'

'Confidential means confidential.'

'When did you first work for her?'

'She's my client, Mr Kellaway. You aren't.'

'Fifteen years ago? Or more?'

'Privileged information, I'm afraid.' His smile was more of a smirk now. He was enjoying himself. At my expense. 'Where's Mrs Lashley? That's all I want to know: where she is and how she is. I'm worried about her, see.'

Lashley had instructed me to buy Thompson off if I had to. Perhaps it was what the fellow was angling for. Perhaps he'd tell me everything I wanted to know if the money was right. Distasteful as it was, it had to be attempted. 'You'll have incurred some expenses coming all this way, Mr Thompson. And no doubt you have a standard daily fee. Mr Lashley would be—'

'Don't say it, Mr Kellaway. You'll embarrass me. And yourself. This is what I'll do for you. For your boss, that is. I'll give him twenty-four hours. Meet me in the Piazzetta at ten o'clock tomorrow morning. I'll be at one of the café tables. You can tell me

252

then where Mrs Lashley is and why she isn't here. I'll decide what to do about it. I may still go to the police. We'll have to see. It depends. What doesn't depend is this. Stand me up or feed me a load of bull and I'll go straight to the station and make a full report. Fair enough?'

I hurried back to the Villa Orchis, angered as well as humiliated. I'd been comprehensively outmanoeuvred. To make matters worse, I felt horribly certain Thompson knew more about me than he was telling. The same applied to Lashley, of course. I had nothing but bad news for him.

Jacqueline was breakfasting on the terrace. She invited me to join her. But I had to see Lashley without delay.

'He's in his study, working,' she told me. 'He has business papers faxed to him daily.'

'Of course.' He would have. He was a man who liked to stay in touch. 'I'll have to interrupt, though.'

'Adam hasn't surfaced yet.'

'No?'

'Did you speak to him last night? I'm a light sleeper and he woke me coming in. I thought I heard him talking to someone downstairs.'

'That was me.' I grimaced. 'Maybe he's friendlier when he's sober.'

'Not so you'd notice. Just quieter.' She smiled at me sympathetically. 'But we must make allowances.'

I smiled ruefully back. 'That we must.'

Lashley too would have to make allowances. This he rapidly appreciated when I told him how my encounter with Thompson had gone: just about as badly as it could have.

'Damn the fellow,' he said when I'd finished, stubbing out one cigarette in Francis's old onyx ashtray and lighting another. 'What could Muriel have been thinking of?'

'As to that, sir, I wondered if you had any idea.' I'd omitted to mention my suspicion that Thompson had been on my tail in

London fifteen years before. If he really had been working for Muriel then, Lashley surely had to know.

'I might have, Jonathan. When Vivien went up to Cambridge, Muriel was worried about how she'd cope. Understandably so, in the circumstances. I needn't remind you of the overdose she took after Oliver's death. Anyway, Muriel convinced herself Vivien was likely to "fall in with the wrong set", as she put it. The papers were full of scare stories about drugs and God knows what. Muriel insisted we should . . . well, check up on her. Make sure everything was as . . . stable . . . as she assured us it was. Vivien was seeing a psychotherapist, but she was quite capable of pulling the wool over his eyes. Muriel had just lost her son. She was determined to do whatever she could to protect her daughter. I let her have her way, rather against my better judgement, to be honest. But CCC's takeover of Wren's was making a lot of demands on my attention at the time. She consulted a detective agency in Plymouth. They had some kind of reciprocal arrangement with an agency in London. An operative was detailed to carry out . . . discreet monitoring of Vivien's activities . . . and associations.'

'Thompson?'

'I think we must assume so. If the name was ever mentioned to me, I don't remember it. But Muriel certainly went to Plymouth to be given some reports in person on a couple of occasions. I couldn't spare the time to accompany her. Thompson may have travelled down from London to meet her.'

'Would I have figured in his . . . monitoring?'

'I'm afraid you may well have. I'm sorry, Jonathan. Muriel didn't say and I didn't ask. The exercise seemed to put her mind at rest and I was happy to leave it at that.'

'Why would she contact him again after all these years?'

'That's just what I've been asking myself. I believe there can only be one answer. Paolo Verdelli. I didn't hide from her the rumours I picked up about his Camorra connections. She may have heard things herself. She spends more time here than I do. Perhaps she was worried for her safety. For Adam's, too. Vivien's as well, come to that. And little Dylan's. I can only suppose she decided to call in

Thompson to take Verdelli's measure and assess what threat, if any, he posed. Alas, it seems the threat was greater and more imminent than either of us imagined.' He leant back in his chair and turned to gaze into the sun-dappled garden. 'Muriel's captors have made it very clear to me that if they get wind of police involvement there'll be no deal. They haven't spelt out what that would mean for Muriel, but I think we have to assume the worst. Thompson may be genuinely concerned about her, but any intervention by him could easily be disastrous. He mustn't be allowed to talk to the police.'

'How can we stop him?'

'I don't know, Jonathan. Let me think about it. We have a little time to play with. Let's just hope it's enough.'

TWENTY-SEVEN

I'd never had any liking for Muriel Lashley. She was a cold, proud, narrow-minded woman. It should have been less surprising than it was to learn she'd hired a private investigator to keep track of Vivien's activities. No doubt she really had been worried about her daughter. But she'd also wanted to be assured Vivien was mixing with the right people. And I was one of the wrong people. It was as simple as that. What she'd have done to split us up if we hadn't done such a thorough job of it ourselves, I don't know. But she'd have tried her damnedest. I was sure of that.

The irony was inescapable. The man Lashley had asked for help in freeing Muriel was a man Muriel wanted to have nothing to do with her family. My dislike of her was overridden by the severity of the situation. I'd do my best for her out of common humanity. But after we'd secured her release, would she be capable of thanking me? And how would I respond if she did? There would have to be a reckoning of some kind between us.

The day passed slowly and anxiously as Lashley pondered how best to deal with Thompson. Despite the crushing heat, I took a long walk out round the south-eastern shore of the island. The exercise was a palliative of sorts. But it only smothered my immediate concerns by bringing unwelcome memories to the fore. Every step I took on Capri was shadowed by recollections of the weeks I'd spent there with Vivien.

My route back to the Villa Orchis took me past the gates of the Villa Erycina. I peered through them along the colonnaded drive towards the house. White roses trained round the columns offset the deep red of the surrounding bougainvillea. There was a scent of jasmine in the still air and a murmur of bees. It was the siesta hour and Countess Covelli would be resting. This was no time to call. I beat a retreat.

Siestas hardly figured in the night-owl routine of Adam Lashley. He was in the kitchen, fixing himself a late, late breakfast when I entered the villa. The gutturally dubbed episode of *Bonanza* he was watching on a portable TV while ploughing his way through an enormous bowl of cereal deafened him to my arrival. I went upstairs and took a shower, then fell asleep, lying naked on my bed as the ceiling fan rotated at a slow purr above me. The afternoon vanished.

It was nearly dinner time when I woke. I dressed hurriedly and went downstairs. I found Lashley with Jacqueline in the drawing-room. There was a perceptible lightness to their mood. Something good had happened. 'We'll talk later,' was all Lashley said in answer to my enquiring look. And I knew better than to press him.

Adam deigned to eat with us that evening. Jacqueline dutifully asked him some questions about literature. That his answers stopped short of sullen dismissiveness seemed largely due to his father's presence. I kept telling myself he was masking his fears for his mother with this show of indifference. But I didn't really believe it.

Lashley told Elena she could leave early: we'd clear up after ourselves. Once she was gone, he immediately announced he'd had another phone call from Muriel's captors. Terms for her release had been agreed.

I sensed Adam wanted to ask what figure his father had settled for, but all he actually said was, 'You think this will work, Dad?' He sounded young then, almost like a child – young and vulnerable.

'I'm confident it will,' said Lashley. 'They'll call again tomorrow night with arrangements for the exchange. Remember: it's in their financial interests to ensure this goes smoothly.'

'You'll be seeing your mother again soon, Adam,' said Jacqueline.

If the remark was intended to reassure Adam, the scowl it was rewarded with showed it had failed. Lashley appeared not to notice this. Or else he pretended not to. 'All we have to do,' he pressed on, 'is hold our nerves for a little longer.'

'Not quite all, surely,' I said cautiously, uncertain whether he'd told Adam about Thompson.

But he had. 'He means the private dick, Dad,' Adam said, flashing a scornful glance at me.

'I've given the Thompson problem a good deal of thought,' said Lashley, flattening one hand decisively on the table. 'It's imperative we dissuade him from going to the police. The surest way of doing that, I believe, is to tell him the truth. Once he appreciates the gravity of the situation, he'll fall into line. There's an element of risk in confiding in him, of course, but less than the risks we run by concocting a cover story or simply daring him to do his worst. Do you agree, Jonathan?'

I was surprised. I'd thought Lashley might jib at such a move, but I should have known better. He was ever the realist. 'Yes,' I replied. 'As far as I could judge, Thompson's genuinely concerned for Muriel's safety.' But would he believe me? That was the crucial question. 'Perhaps I could show him . . . the photograph you received.'

Lashley nodded. 'By all means. He needs to be convinced. Which is why I think a suggestion Jacqueline made to me earlier is eminently sensible.'

'I'll go with you when you meet him, Jonathan,' she said. This was a still greater surprise, as my expression must have made obvious. 'I'm a disinterested party. And a woman. My presence will . . .'

'Bolster your credibility,' said Lashley. 'We need Thompson on our side, Jonathan. It's absolutely vital.' He made a fist of his hand, tightening it until his knuckles turned white. It was the first sign I'd

258

noticed of the strain I knew he must be under. 'Do you think you can manage it? I'd speak to him myself, but I fear that might be counter-productive.'

'I'll manage it, sir,' I declared, looking across at Jacqueline. '*We'll* manage it.'

Adam slouched off to his room to watch television. A little later, Lashley announced he needed an early night. He looked exhausted, which was understandable, but nonetheless disturbing, as I admitted to Jacqueline after he'd headed off to bed.

'He's always been so indomitable. And he prides himself on his stamina. I've never known him admit to fatigue before.'

'He's not a young man, Jonathan, though Lord knows he seems a lot more than four years younger than my father. He worries about Muriel constantly. It's hard for him not to imagine the conditions she's being kept in. It's a stressful situation for all of us, but for Greville it must be simply awful.'

She admired him. That was clear. And his strength of mind *was* admirable. If I'd been in the hands of the Camorra, I'd have wanted Greville Lashley to be negotiating my release. Negotiation was in his blood. 'Thanks for offering to meet Thompson with me, Jacqueline. I think he'll believe you a lot more readily than me.'

'I just want to help.'

A thoughtful minute or so passed. Then she said, 'The man Greville believes may have set this up: Paolo Verdelli. You know him better than any of us, don't you?'

'I suppose so.'

'You think he's capable of such . . . monstrousness?'

'Envy and resentment can drive people to do all sorts of things. As for Paolo, I . . .' He'd protected Luisa. He'd been loyal to her. Maybe he'd even loved her. And what she'd promised him in return had been snatched away. Envious and resentful? I'd have bet he was. And then some. 'I think he's capable of it, yes.'

'Then we'd better hope his share of the ransom money will be enough for him.'

'Yes. We better had.' It was a good point, but also, though

259

Jacqueline couldn't know it, an irrelevant one. Lashley didn't intend to give Paolo the chance to come back for more. As soon as Muriel was safe, he'd go after him. I didn't want to think about what that would involve. But that it would happen was a certainty.

The first ferryload of day-trippers hadn't yet arrived when we walked into the Piazzetta the following morning at ten o'clock. The square was quiet and peaceful, with customers at the café tables well spaced. The sun was warm with the promise of later heat, sparkling on the rims of the clock-tower bells as they rang the hour.

Thompson raised a cautious hand in greeting as we moved towards him. He was on the shady western side of the square, cradling a teacup as he perused the *International Herald Tribune*. He frowned suspiciously at Jacqueline, then at me. 'I thought you'd be coming alone, Mr Kellaway,' he said. 'I wasn't expecting you to bring . . . Miss Hudson, is it?' He allowed himself a little half-smile of pleasure at deducing my companion's identity.

'You're well-informed, Mr Thompson,' Jacqueline said, unfazed. She offered him her hand, obliging him to struggle to his feet, which somehow tarnished his small victory.

'Information's my bread and butter.' He grinned at her. 'I expect Mr Kellaway's told you that.'

'Yes. He has.'

'Well, well. Sit down, both of you. Please.'

I borrowed a third chair from another table and we settled. Thompson made a meal of folding up his newspaper. Then he pointed the stem of his unlit pipe at me and cocked his head.

'You a jogger, Mr Kellaway? You look as if you might be.'

The question seemed inane as well as irrelevant. I shrugged. 'I like to keep fit.'

'Big mistake. *Multo errore*. It's in the paper. The bloke who invented jogging's dropped dead of a heart attack while . . . jogging.' Thompson grinned. 'You couldn't make it up, could you?'

'Might we come to the point?' Jacqueline sounded dignified and serious. She looked it too, in her plain sunglasses and lilac dress, her hair tied back, her gaze direct. Thompson's expression suggested he was genuinely impressed. As was I.

'Let's do that. By all means.'

Before we could, though, the waiter appeared. Jacqueline and I ordered coffee. After he'd gone, I sat forward and held Thompson's gaze. 'Mrs Lashley's been kidnapped,' I said quietly. 'It happened last week. Mr Lashley's been negotiating terms for her release since then. He hasn't informed the police.'

'Kidnapped?' Thompson kept his voice down too. His grin had vanished. 'That's very bad news.'

'You've heard of the Camorra?'

He nodded. 'The Neapolitan Mafia. Yes, I've heard of them. They're responsible?'

'I'm afraid so.'

'Good Lord. Well, well, well.' He fingered his moustache. 'Mr Lashley's kept the police out of it, you say?'

'Yes.'

'Which is why, Mr Thompson,' said Jacqueline, 'we implore you to say nothing to them either.'

'A ransom payment was finally agreed yesterday,' I went on. 'Mrs Lashley should be free within days.'

'A happy – if expensive – ending is in sight, then?'

'Mr Lashley's only concern is to secure his wife's safe return,' said Jacqueline.

'Of course. I understand. Otherwise, no doubt, as a law-abiding Englishman, he'd have called in the police straight away.'

'It's easy to recommend such a course of action,' I said. 'But it's a different story when the life of someone you love is at stake.'

'Yes. That's what kidnappers trade on, Mr Kellaway. None of them would ever be caught if all their victims made it so easy for them.'

'The past week's been anything but easy, Mr Thompson,' said Jacqueline.

'I'm sure it's been no tea party for Mrs Lashley, that's for sure.' Thompson's initial shock was giving way, I realized, to something

261

more sceptical. 'Have the kidnappers supplied any proof that she's alive and well?'

Jacqueline took the envelope Lashley had given us out of her handbag and showed Thompson the photograph. 'We've authenticated the paper as last Friday's edition,' I said as he peered at it.

'I hope Mr Lashley knows what he's doing. The Camorra don't mess around.'

'He's aware of that,' said Jacqueline.

She retrieved the photograph just as the waiter reappeared. He delivered our coffees and retreated. There was a brief silence at the table.

Then Thompson said, 'I'm puzzled, though. Why would they have picked on her? The Lashleys aren't an obvious target. China clay doesn't put them up there with oil barons and shipping magnates, does it?'

'We believe there may have been a personal element,' I responded. 'A man who used to work for Luisa d'Eugenio, former owner of the Villa Orchis, apparently believes he should have inherited the property instead of Mrs Lashley. He's made no secret of bearing a grudge. And he's rumoured to have Camorra connections. It's likely Mrs Lashley was planning to hire you to establish whether he posed a genuine threat.'

Thompson thought about all that for a moment, then asked, 'What's the name of this man?'

'I'm not sure we—'

'Verdelli?' My fleeting dismay didn't escape him. 'It is, isn't it?'

'Yes,' I admitted.

He nodded, satisfied on the point. 'The word is Paolo Verdelli was Luisa d'Eugenio's paramour as well as her servant. He supposedly ended up nursing her after she had a stroke a few years before she died. You can see how he might have expected a reward for all that . . . devotion.'

'It's not the Lashleys' fault he didn't get it.'

'No. But it's become their problem. I might have advised a precautionary pay-off if I'd been consulted earlier.'

'Might you, now?' said Jacqueline. It was clearer to me than I hoped it was to Thompson that she disliked him more with every word he spoke.

'Standing on the letter of the law can sometimes be a false economy, Miss Hudson.'

'Can it really?'

'You'll be able to discuss that with Mrs Lashley in the near future,' I said, exerting myself to remain emollient.

'I'll look forward to it.'

'Meanwhile . . .'

'You'd like my assurance that I'll keep all this to myself. Particularly where the police are concerned.'

'Exactly. We've confided in you, because, frankly, you left us no choice. But if Mrs Lashley's best interests really are your prime concern . . .'

'All right.' His pipe had become a pointer again. 'Mr Lashley's in the very devil of a fix. I can see that. Provided I don't learn you've dreamt up this story to keep me off his back, then—'

'Do you seriously doubt the truth of what we've told you?' Jacqueline interrupted. 'My God, we've shown you the photograph. What more proof do you want?'

I wouldn't have been so outspoken for fear of antagonizing the man. But the effect was surprisingly salutary. 'You'll have to excuse me,' he said appeasingly. 'I'm sometimes too suspicious for my own good. Blame forty years of following unfaithful spouses. I don't doubt the truth of what you've told me, Miss Hudson. And I won't do anything to endanger Mrs Lashley. Does that satisfy you?'

'Yes.' Jacqueline treated him to a little nod of gratitude. 'Mr Lashley will be relieved to hear it.'

'And I can expect . . . good news . . . within a few days?'

'You can,' I answered.

'Then we all know where we stand, don't we? I hope . . .' He waggled his pipe vaguely in the air. 'I hope it all goes well.'

A few wordless seconds passed. Then Jacqueline murmured, 'Amen to that.'

TWENTY-EIGHT

The funicular had begun to disgorge the first knots of day-trippers in the Piazzetta when we left Thompson to his pipe and paper and started back towards the Villa Orchis. We didn't want to keep Lashley waiting any longer than was necessary for a report on how our meeting had gone. The undertaking we'd obtained was, after all, crucial to the success of his plans.

We didn't make it to the villa quite as quickly as we'd hoped, however. A chance encounter with Countess Covelli was bound to happen sooner or later. Capri was a small island in a small world. But somehow I wasn't expecting it, even so.

She stepped out of a *farmacia* in Via Roma, directly into our path. She looked almost exactly as I remembered: tall, thin, Roman-nosed, alert and graceful. Fifteen years had made scarcely a mark on her. She was wearing a pale linen dress, a long loose coat and a wide-brimmed straw hat. She smiled when she saw me, a smile that seemed to me to mix warmth with irony.

'Jonathan? *Santo cielo*! It really is you.'

'Hello, Contessa,' I replied, covering my discomposure as best I could by introducing her to Jacqueline.

'Greville's mentioned you, Contessa,' said Jacqueline. 'But only as a neighbour.' She looked curiously at me. 'Clearly you and Jonathan are much better acquainted.'

'We became so when Jonathan was last here,' the countess

explained, glancing towards me. 'I have often wondered whether he would ever return.'

'Mr Lashley has me here on a business matter,' I said, smiling uneasily.

'I see. Well, I am told he is . . . an energetic man of business. And you work for him?'

'I do.'

'Not so hard that you cannot find time to have tea with me, I hope.'

'Of course not. I'd be . . . delighted.'

'Will you come too, Miss Hudson?'

'It's real kind of you to ask me, Contessa. I'd love to join you.'

'Tomorrow afternoon?'

Jacqueline and I glanced at each other. We could hardly tell the countess why making innocent social engagements was so difficult for us. 'Mr Lashley and I actually have a very busy weekend ahead of us, Contessa,' I said hesitantly. 'It may be . . .'

'We will leave it open.' Her smile conveyed something more than her usual charm. There was a purposefulness as well, a determination. Or maybe that was just in my imagination. 'Come if you can. Five o'clock. No one should still be attending to business at that hour. I will hope to see you both then.'

Jacqueline would doubtless have been more curious about Countess Covelli if she'd been less preoccupied. As it was, she asked me nothing about her until later that day. We hurried on to the Villa Orchis and told Lashley the good news: Thompson had agreed to cooperate.

This clearly came as a relief to him. It was one less thing to worry about. But there were still plenty of others. We had to wait for the Camorra to announce how they meant to exchange Muriel for the ransom Lashley had agreed with them. And waiting wasn't easy.

'I've told them I won't release the money until they release Muriel,' he revealed. 'They have to understand we can't be pushed around. But they have the upper hand. They know that.' He sighed. 'It's one hell of a delicate balance.'

265

Delicate it was. And delicate it remained. The day passed with agonizing slowness. Jacqueline sat in a shady corner of the garden, trying to read. Lashley stayed close to the phone in his study. Adam headed out for a swim and returned a few hours later in a condition that suggested he'd done a lot more drinking than swimming. Elena came and went. At some point, Jacqueline persuaded me to relate Countess Covelli's sad history. Naturally, I omitted the saddest part of all. I wasn't supposed to know, and nor was anyone else, that her husband had been betrayed to the Nazis by the former owner of the Villa Orchis.

The call came, as all the previous ones had, in the early evening. Jacqueline and I heard the phone ring through the open French windows of the study as we sat on the terrace. Adam was up in his room. The bass rumbles of the music he was listening to suggested he was unlikely to have heard it himself. I was glad of that and suspected his father would be too.

We sat where we were, waiting in anxious silence as five minutes trickled by, then ten. Finally, we heard the tinkle of the bell as Lashley replaced the receiver. And still we didn't move.

Then he came to the French windows and beckoned for me to join him.

'I'd appreciate your confirmation that you're willing to play your part in the deal I've struck, Jonathan,' he said, ushering me into the room.

'That goes without saying.'

'Nevertheless, you should hear what I've agreed before you commit yourself unequivocally. Sit down.'

He returned to his chair behind the desk. I sat down opposite him. He took a cigarette he'd been smoking from the ashtray and looked at it absent-mindedly, then decided it was too far gone and stubbed it out.

'Are you . . . satisfied with the arrangements?' I prompted.

He pondered the question for a moment, then nodded. 'As far as I can be, yes. I'm to travel to Naples tomorrow and stay overnight at the Excelsior. A room's been reserved in my name. The exchange is set for Sunday morning. That's where you come in. You're to take the money down to Marina Grande. I'll pack it in a briefcase. Arrive no later than eight twenty. You're to meet a man at the boarding point for the eight-thirty ferry to Naples. He'll ask you for a light and give you his name. Bartolomeo. You'll open the case and show him the contents. He'll have an accomplice somewhere on the wharf watching all this, so be careful. When the ferry's ready to leave, give Bartolomeo the case and see him aboard. Stay until the ferry's left. Then come back here. Bartolomeo's accomplice will phone me and tell me where I have to go to collect Muriel, which won't be far from the hotel.'

'As simple as that?'

'We must hope so. The guarantee of their good faith is that if they don't phone, I could contact the police and have Bartolomeo arrested as he leaves the ferry in Naples. With the money, of course. But it won't come to that, I'm sure. The money is what they want. The money is what this has all been *for*.'

'I'll gladly deliver it.'

'Thank you. I'm going to take Adam with me tomorrow, assuming the Excelsior can find a room for him.' Lashley smiled weakly. 'It'll get him out of your hair. I don't want him to cause you any problems. I don't want there to be any problems at all.'

'I'll make sure there aren't.'

'Excellent. Thank you again, Jonathan. This is above and beyond, you know. I won't forget it.' He held my gaze, determined to ensure I understood the depth of his gratitude. 'You can be assured of that.'

Events were unfolding as promisingly as could reasonably be expected. But there would have to be another thirty-six hours of anxious inactivity before Muriel's release. The torpid summer heat and the idle frivolity that ruled Capri made the crime being inflicted on the owners of Villa Orchis seem surreal, if not *un*real. There was no outward sign of it. Its actuality was locked away in the minds of the few who knew of it. And there it took its silent toll.

To my surprise, though perhaps it was a testament to the strain he was under, Adam was up early on Saturday morning. To my even greater surprise, he challenged me to a tennis match. 'We can fit a game in before it gets too hot,' he said, his mood, if not overtly friendly, certainly less hostile than usual. I agreed and we headed off to the courts in town.

Adam served like a cannon, but was about as mobile as one too. I could have won a lot more easily than I did, something that didn't escape his attention. 'Glad to see you've . . . taken my advice,' he panted as we towelled down afterwards.

'About what?'

'Keeping in with me. It's a . . . good idea.'

'Are you really thinking of going into the business?' I asked, unable quite to credit the idea.

'I'm not thinking about anything much . . . beyond tomorrow.'

I stood rebuked. 'No. Of course not.'

'Nor should you be.'

'Everything will be all right, Adam, I'm sure of it.'

There was a flash of anger in the look he gave me then through his sweat-beaded fringe. He didn't want reassurance from me. What he wanted, as he was quick to spell out, was obedience. 'Just do what you've been told to do without screwing up, OK?'

There would come a time, I felt certain, when I'd have to make Adam understand that being Greville Lashley's son didn't give him any natural authority over me. But that time wasn't now. I nodded. 'OK.'

I drove Adam and his father down to Marina Grande that afternoon. Jacqueline came too. We saw them off on the 3.30 ferry. Lashley wanted to leave before the day-trippers began returning to Naples en masse. He shook my hand before boarding, but didn't add any last reminders of what was required of me. I didn't need reminding. He knew that.

Their departure left Jacqueline and me with time on our hands, a good reason in itself to take up Countess Covelli's invitation to tea. 'It'll do us good to talk to someone who's uninvolved in this thing,' Jacqueline asserted. I couldn't disagree, conscious though I was that the countess wasn't, in truth, *completely* uninvolved. There was a trail connecting Luisa d'Eugenio's act of treachery in 1943 with Muriel Lashley's abduction more than forty years later. And we were treading it.

Our earlier encounter with the countess had left me with the disquieting sense that she was in some way stringing me along. It was possible she'd deduced that I'd sent her Luisa's letter. But I had to behave as if she hadn't, especially in Jacqueline's presence. I'd have preferred to meet her alone, with Muriel safely back home at the Villa Orchis. Then we might have been able to speak freely. As it was . . .

Countess Covelli was nothing if not a practised and courteous hostess. We sat on the terrace of the Villa Erycina as the late-afternoon sun stretched its golden swathes across the garden, talking idly, or so it seemed, of Capri and Cornwall and Georgia. She'd given Jacqueline a brief tour of the house beforehand. The sad fate of her husband, whose silver-framed photograph still stood on the mantelpiece in the drawing-room, had been lightly touched on. Jacqueline had responded with an account of her own family's tragedy. The human cost of warfare had been lamented. And the countess hadn't mentioned Luisa once.

It was Jacqueline, in the end, who introduced her name into the conversation as we drank our tea. She knew from me that the countess had been a friend and contemporary of Luisa's and asked, quite naturally, if she missed her.

The countess took so long to reply I thought she meant to ignore the question. But she was merely choosing her words carefully. 'I miss the friend I once believed she was,' she said at last.

'Pardon me?' Jacqueline was clearly bemused.

'I did not speak to Luisa for the last nine years of her life. I had no . . . communication . . . with her at all.'

'Why?'

'Because I discovered that she had done something terrible – something unforgivable – during the war.'

'What?'

269

The countess gave a pained smile. 'I did not accuse her when she was alive. I will not accuse her now she is dead. I never told her why I ended our friendship. But I am sure she knew. That was enough for me.'

The fleeting glance she cast me as she spoke removed all doubt in the matter. She was addressing me, not Jacqueline. And she was answering the question I wanted to ask but couldn't. She hadn't allowed the truth to consume her. She'd dealt with it in her own dignified way.

'It's a sad thing . . . to lose a friend,' said Jacqueline hesitantly.

'*Si*. It is. But I think it would be sadder to be deceived by someone for your whole life.'

'I guess so.'

'Do you think Paolo knew that Luisa had done this unforgivable thing, Contessa?' I asked. I needed to say something if my silence wasn't going to become conspicuous and it had occurred to me that I might be able to glean some valuable information in the process of changing the subject.

'I do not think Luisa told anyone, Jonathan,' the countess replied in measured tones.

'I gather Paolo's left Capri.'

'I believe he has.'

'Do you know where he's living now? I'd like to contact him, while I'm here.'

'You would? You surprise me.'

I shrugged. 'He did me . . . a few favours. If he's fallen on hard times, I'd . . . like to help.'

' A kind thought. But . . . *purtroppo* . . . I do not know where he has gone.'

'He has relatives in Naples, I'm told.'

'Ah. Perhaps Naples, then.'

'It's a big city.'

'*Si*. Bigger, it seems to me, every time I visit it.'

'Sounds like you don't give me much chance of finding him.'

'None at all, on your own.' She smiled. 'But if you like, I could ask . . . Valerio Salvenini. You remember him?'

270

Salvenini. Luisa's gossipy acquaintance in Anacapri. Yes, I remembered him. 'I certainly do.'

'He knows many people in Naples. He is a man with . . . many connections.'

'Really?'

'It is very simple. If he does not know, he will probably know someone who knows.'

'In that case, Contessa . . .' I exerted myself not to sound too eager. 'Please do ask him. I'd be very grateful.'

She smiled at me. 'I will ask, Jonathan. And we will see what he can tell us.'

Fortunately, it didn't appear to have crossed Jacqueline's mind that I might know what the 'something unforgivable' was that Luisa had done during the war. I was glad not to have to deny it. Instead, when we left the Villa Erycina, all I had to do was echo her sentiments where Countess Covelli was concerned. 'She's a great lady, don't you think, Jonathan?' I assured her I thought exactly that.

Another assumption of Jacqueline's I didn't bother to correct was that Lashley had put me up to asking the countess about Paolo. 'Greville's not going to let him get away with this, is he?'

'No. He isn't.'

'What will he do? He can hardly go to the police after telling them nothing about Muriel's abduction.'

'I don't know what he'll do. But he'll think of something. You can be sure of—'

I broke off as we reached the gates of the Villa Orchis. They were standing open and, to my horror, I could see a police car parked on the drive.

'Oh my God,' said Jacqueline. 'What's that doing here?'

271

TWENTY-NINE

My first thought was that Thompson had broken his word and gone to the police. A second thought, which I didn't express, was that something altogether more terrible had happened.

In one sense at least, though, it made no difference. Jacqueline and I had to play it cool. We had to be sure we gave nothing away. 'Don't volunteer any information,' I whispered to her as we hurried along the drive. 'Stick to our cover story until or unless it becomes impossible.'

'Do you think Thompson's told them everything?'

'I don't know. But we'll soon find out.'

Patrizia's voice was the first we heard as we entered the villa. She was in the kitchen, talking at a pitch that suggested she was on the verge of hysterics. There were three men with her, two in police uniform, one in plain clothes. Patrizia saw us first, setting her off on a manic gabble we'd have had little chance of following even if it hadn't been in Italian. Her rudimentary English tended to desert her at moments of crisis and this was clearly such a moment.

As far as I could gather, our return was anticipated. The officers nodded their understanding in response to Patrizia's arm-waving explanations. The older of the two in uniform flashed a warrant card and wearily introduced himself as Tenente Bianconi. His younger junior went unnamed. Bianconi laboriously confirmed we were who I'd already heard Patrizia say we were several times, then gave way to the third man.

He was about the same age as Bianconi, grey-haired and handsome in the Italian style, dressed in a well-cut pale-blue suit. He had an authoritative bearing and a pair of disconcertingly piercing eyes. He too produced some kind of warrant card. '*Commissario Gandolfi, Polizia Guidiziaria, Napoli.*' He sounded as if he was used to taking charge of any situation he found himself in. And he proceeded to do just that.

'Where is Signor Lashley?' he asked me directly.

'He's, er, gone to Rome for the weekend. With his son.' This, I knew, was what Patrizia would have told them, because this was what we had told her.

'And his wife – Signora Lashley?'

This was a trickier question. Patrizia believed Muriel to be in Cornwall. But Thompson – and probably therefore Gandolfi – knew better. 'What exactly is this all about?'

'We have received information that Signora Lashley may have come to harm.' Patrizia began a babbling interjection which he cut off imperiously before returning his attention to me. 'Your housekeeper has told us that Signora Lashley is visiting her aunt in Santa Ostel. We have telephoned her aunt. Signora Lashley is not there.'

'I see.' What Harriet would have made of such a call was hard to imagine. But we could worry about that later. 'Look, do you think . . . we could talk about this in the drawing-room? It's a little . . . difficult.' Jacqueline caught my eye. She knew just how big an understatement this was.

Gandolfi's glance at Patrizia suggested he could see the merits of my proposal. He spoke to Bianconi in Italian, then nodded to me. 'OK. We will go to the drawing-room.'

Jacqueline and I led the way. Only Gandolfi and Bianconi followed. The young policeman was left in the kitchen, to mind Patrizia. I heard him say, '*Caffè, signora?*' in a hopeful tone as we headed along the hall. I was thinking hard as we went, balancing what I had to withhold and could afford to admit. Gandolfi was quite cunning enough to let me tangle myself in contradictions if I wasn't extremely careful.

The way he merely smiled enquiringly at me when we'd gathered in the drawing-room reinforced the point. If I wanted to hang myself, he'd feed me the rope.

'The fact is, officer . . .'

'*Si?*'

'Well, the fact is that Mr Lashley told Patrizia his wife had gone home to Cornwall because . . . he thought that's where she'd gone.'

'But she had not?'

'No. They'd had some kind of row, I gather.'

'A . . . row?'

'An argument.'

'Ah. An argument.'

'A serious falling-out. Mrs Lashley left. They were both . . . upset . . . so . . . exactly where she was going was unclear.'

'And where did she go?'

'I'm not sure. But nothing like as far as Cornwall. She spoke to Mr Lashley on the telephone yesterday, apparently. He set off with his son to see her earlier today.'

'In Roma?'

'Possibly. Possibly somewhere closer. Mr Lashley had to tell Patrizia something. Rome may have just . . . popped into his head. He was . . . embarrassed by the whole episode. He didn't want to discuss the details with me or Miss Hudson. He said he'd be in touch as soon as the situation was . . . clearer.'

'But he has not been . . . in touch?'

'Not yet, no.'

'Is this your understanding also, signorina?' Gandolfi asked, turning towards Jacqueline.

'Yes,' she said, with the faintest tremor in her voice. 'It is.'

'I see. So, there is no possibility that Signora Lashley has come to harm?'

'Not as far as we know,' I said.

'You think we have been . . . misinformed?'

'You must have been.'

'Has someone made any . . . specific allegations, officer?' Jacqueline asked.

'The Questura here in Capri received a telephone call earlier today. The caller said Signora Lashley may have been . . . murdered.'

'*Murdered?*'

'*Si.* It is a serious matter, signorina.'

'Who was this caller?' I asked.

'He did not give his name.'

'Was he Italian? Or English?'

'English. There was some difficulty understanding what he was saying. His Italian was . . . not good.'

'Perhaps he was . . . misinterpreted.'

Gandolfi frowned, as if pained by the suggestion. 'I do not think so. He made a second allegation: that if Signora Lashley *had* been murdered, it was because she knew too much about a previous unsolved murder. Gordon Reginald Strake. Do you recognize the name, Signor Kellaway?'

What was I to say now? If the caller was Thompson, he shouldn't have known about Strake. How could he have found out? *What* had he found out? 'I don't think so,' I said.

'He was shot dead in his room at the Albergo Lustrini in Naples fifteen years ago. I investigated the case.' And that, of course, was why, fifteen years later, Gandolfi had travelled from Naples to follow up an anonymous tip-off received by the Capri police. He looked like a man who disliked loose ends.

'I can't see what that would have to do with the Lashleys,' I said, reasonably enough, it seemed to me. 'They weren't living here then.'

'No. But Signora Lashley's uncle, Francis Wren, was. The house-keeper told us that.' *Thank you, Patrizia*, I thought. *Thank you for nothing*. 'We mentioned the date of the Strake murder to her: the ninth of July 1969. This confused her, because she thought that was the date Francis Wren died. But maybe they died the same day. Perhaps you can tell us, Signor Kellaway. The housekeeper said you were here when he died. That is correct, isn't it?'

Out of the corner of my eye I could see Jacqueline frowning

worriedly. This was more complicated than she'd supposed – and than I'd expected. All I could do now was brazen it out. 'I was here when Francis Wren died, yes. I spent a couple of weeks here in the summer of 1969. The exact date? I'm not sure. Early July sounds right, though.'

'Do you recall hearing of the Strake murder at that time?'

'No, I don't.'

'And have you been a regular visitor since then?'

'No. I, er . . . This is my first return visit.'

'Your first . . . in fifteen years?'

'Yes. As it happens.'

'I think we've told you as much as we can, officer,' said Jacqueline. There was a steely glint in her eyes. Whatever doubts she might have, she'd evidently decided we had to assert ourselves. 'As soon as Mr Lashley or Mrs Lashley is in touch with us, we'll ask them to contact you. They'll be able to clear everything up. We're merely their guests. There's a limit to what we can say. But there's really no reason, is there, beyond this anonymous phone call you've had, to suppose anything's happened that might require your attention?'

Gandolfi looked at Jacqueline curiously, as if only now taking her seriously. 'The phone call is all we have,' he conceded.

'Well, then?'

Gandolfi turned back to me. 'Do you agree, Signor Kellaway? Signor and Signora Lashley will be able to clear everything up?'

'Of course.'

'And there's nothing else . . . you want to tell me?'

'There's nothing else I *can* tell you.'

'*Allora*, we must hope you hear from them soon.'

'I'm sure we will.'

'If you do not, you will hear from us.'

'It's good of you to be so concerned for their welfare,' said Jacqueline. 'But unnecessary, I feel sure.' She smiled at him – and kept smiling. 'Will that be all?'

'*Si*. That will be all. For now.' He signalled to Bianconi with the faintest of nods that they were done. 'I wish you a pleasant evening.'

The imperturbability Jacqueline had displayed in Gandolfi and Bianconi's presence deserted her as soon as they'd gone. 'My God, Jonathan, do you think it could be true? Muriel's dead – murdered?'

'I don't think there's a shred of truth in it,' I said firmly. I couldn't be certain of anything, of course, but it seemed obvious to me who'd set the police on us. 'Thompson's behind this. He can't have believed us when we told him about the kidnapping, but he didn't have the courage to accuse us openly – hence the anonymous phone call.'

'He didn't believe us? What about the photograph?'

'I don't know how he'd account for that. But in his suspicious mind just about anything's possible.'

'And who in hell's Gordon Strake?'

I was clearly going to have to tell her something about Strake. Otherwise she might think there really had been a plot against Muriel. 'It's a long story, Jacqueline. He used to work for Wren's before it was taken over by Cornish China Clays.'

'He did? And he was murdered – here in Naples?'

'Yes. But, look, can we leave this until I've spoken to Greville? I really need to talk to him. And we also need to pacify Patrizia. Could you handle that? I'll explain as much as I can afterwards – I promise.'

It was a promise I knew she'd keep me to. I knew who'd killed Strake and why. Soon she'd know too. But first I had to speak to Lashley.

He'd said I was only to call him in an emergency, which this certainly qualified as. He sounded anxious when he answered the phone in his room at the Excelsior. And what I had to tell him wasn't going to make him any less anxious.

'Damn it all,' was his first reaction. 'I thought you'd squared Thompson.'

'So did I. I'm sorry, sir. He obviously didn't believe us.'

'But he's not sure, is he? Otherwise he'd have given the police his name *and* our explanation for Muriel's absence. As it is, he wants to play it both ways, damn him. And what he's playing with is Muriel's life.' Lashley was angry. And I didn't blame him. 'We just have to hope the Camorra haven't got someone watching the house. If they think we've called in the police . . .'

'Do you think they're likely to have us under surveillance?'

'I don't know. Maybe. Maybe not.'

'What do you want me to do?'

I heard Lashley give a heartfelt sigh. 'Proceed as planned. There's no alternative.' He thought for a second, then added: 'You handled the situation as well as it could be handled. Thank Jacqueline for me. I'll phone Harriet and put her mind at rest as best I can.'

'What about Thompson?'

'Don't go anywhere near him. We'll deal with Thompson when this is all over.'

'How does he know about Strake, though?'

'Good question. Maybe he came across him when he was monitoring Vivien's movements. Since I've never understood what Strake was up to, it's impossible to say how their paths might have crossed. Thompson must have mentioned Strake to the police because he calculated an unsolved local murder would get their attention. It seems he was right.'

'I'm going to have to tell Jacqueline where Strake comes into this. She's wondering what it all means.'

'Naturally. Tell her the truth . . . or as much of it as you've told me. Francis killed Strake, didn't he, Jonathan?'

He'd never explicitly asked me that question before, though I'd long felt the answer was clear to him. 'I think Strake was blackmailing Francis,' I said.

'Good riddance, then. If that has to come out in the wash, so be it. The living are more important than the dead. It's Muriel we have to think of now.'

'Of course.'

'We must hold our nerve. And see this through to the end.'

But what would the end be? I'd thought I'd known. Just as I'd thought I had the measure of Fred Thompson. We had to believe everything would still go according to plan. And we had to behave as if we believed it. As Lashley had said, there was no alternative. Believing and behaving couldn't mould the future, though. Other people's wills and actions were at work. And the outcome couldn't be predicted, only experienced. As it would be. Very soon.

After Patrizia had gone home, calmer but still confused, I sat down with Jacqueline and told her as much of the truth about Gordon Strake and Francis Wren as I could. I didn't reveal I'd been in the Albergo Lustrini at the time of the murder, nor what it was Strake had used to blackmail Francis – and certainly not the blame I'd shared with Vivien for enabling him to do so. Gandolfi's questioning had reminded me how hard I would find it to justify everything I'd done fifteen years before. I'd made a lot of mistakes and mis-judgements then. All I could do now was try my damnedest not to add any more to the list.

'I guess I understand better then ever why Greville called you in, Jonathan,' Jacqueline said when I'd finished. 'You know more about this than he does.'

'I wish I didn't.'

'I bet you do. But he's lucky to have you on his team. As I'm sure he realizes.'

'You stood up to Gandolfi pretty well yourself.'

'All I did was play for time. Which I think we got. And it should be enough, right?'

'It should be, yes.'

'How did Thompson find out about Strake's murder, do you think?'

'I don't know. He'd probably say he's a detective and that's what he does: detects.'

'Well, let's hope he doesn't detect anything else in the near future.'

'Yes. Let's hope.'

Later, I sat on the balcony outside my room, staring up at the night sky. It was pincushioned with stars, save for a large chunk of total darkness ahead of me that I knew to be the soaring bulk of Monte Solaro. There was a truth like that, I felt certain, waiting for me in the day yet to dawn: vast, black and invisible, detectable only by the lesser truths it obscured. '*Ah*,' I'd say if I saw it. '*So that's it. Of course. That was it all along.*'

THIRTY

Before leaving for Naples, Lashley had packed the ransom money in a black leather briefcase. The money itself was in rubber-banded bundles of hundred-franc notes. I deliberately made no attempt to count them, or even estimate their total value. It seemed important, though I'm not quite sure why, for me to be able to say later I genuinely didn't know the size of the payment.

Early on a Sunday morning, even in high summer, Capri was a place of silence and tranquillity. I drove the Fiat down to Marina Grande along an empty road beneath a cloudless sky still free of jet-trails. There were no cars following me. The concern had crept over me that Gandolfi might have detailed someone to keep us under surveillance. I thought this unlikely, if only because he'd had so little time to arrange it and would surely have struggled to justify such deployment of manpower, but the total absence of traffic was a welcome reassurance.

The port was the busiest place on the island, though still a long way short of its midday frenzy. I parked close to the funicular station, got out and headed for the jetty, briefcase in hand. A few people were breakfasting at the harbourfront cafés. A few others, some with luggage, were ambling in the same direction as I was, bound for the Naples ferry, which stood ready at its berth. One or two small boats were moving slowly around the harbour. No one was hurrying or shouting. The atmosphere was calm, the mood relaxed.

But I felt neither calm nor relaxed. I scanned the jetty ahead of

281

me as I walked along it towards the ferry, wondering if Bartolomeo would really show up. For some reason, it was horribly easy to believe he wouldn't. Passengers would board the ferry, but none of them would approach me. Then the ferry would sail and I'd be left, standing on the jetty with the money. And Muriel . . .

Then I noticed, some way beyond the ferry, where the jetty curved right, a man in a dark suit and straw hat sitting on one of the quayside bollards, holding a newspaper open in front of him, but looking at me. As I passed the ferry and moved on towards him, he stood up, carefully folded his newspaper and slipped it into his jacket pocket. He was grey-haired and stockily built with a muscular look to him.

He nodded to me as I approached and said, quite neutrally, '*Buon giorno.*'

'*Buon giorno,*' I responded cautiously.

'Signor Kellaway?'

'*Si.*'

'Bartolomeo.' He offered me his hand and I shook it. His grip was strong and uncompromising. He held my gaze for a moment, then looked past me. '*Tutto bene?*'

'*Si. Tutto bene.*'

I glanced round. There was no one behind me – no one at all, in fact, within earshot. We had this corner of the jetty to ourselves.

He stepped back and pointed to the bollard he'd been sitting on, then the briefcase at my side. '*La cartella. Qui.*'

I stood the case on the bollard and opened it. He leant forward and peered inside, then reached in and fanned through a couple of the bundles of Swiss francs. He gave a grunt of apparent satisfaction and gestured for me to close the case.

'OK?' I asked.

'OK,' he said.

'Let's go, then. *Andiamo?*'

He nodded. '*Andiamo.*'

I grasped the case and we walked back along the jetty to the ferry. When we reached the gangway, I handed it over. He treated me to half a smile, as if appreciative of my caution. '*Grazie*,' he said. Then he went aboard.

I watched him disappear into the cabin and looked at my watch. It was 8.26. The ferry wouldn't sail for another five minutes or so. I moved back towards the wall above the jetty as some more passengers bustled past me and boarded.

Then I was suddenly aware that one of them had stopped. I looked round and met the stern, quizzical gaze of Commissioner Gandolfi.

'*Buon giorno*, Signor Kellaway,' he said.

'*Buon . . . giorno*.' I could hardly force the words out. I knew my shock and dismay must have been obvious. The casual smile I tried to manufacture can't have fooled him for an instant. 'What . . . are you doing here?'

'I'm going home.' He returned my smile, but his was altogether more convincing. 'My investigation delayed me yesterday evening. I missed the last ferry. *Allora*, here I am. You are travelling to Naples?'

'No. I . . .' What was I doing on the jetty if I wasn't travelling to Naples? I felt unable even to begin to imagine a plausible answer. 'No, I'm not.'

'Signora Hudson, then? Is she aboard?'

'No,' I replied. A sullen negative was all I was capable of.

'You enjoy watching the boats, perhaps. Is that it? I understand. There is always something to watch in a port, isn't there? The arrivals. The departures. The meetings. Like ours, this morning.'

It was hard not to read an extra layer of meaning into his words. Had he seen me give the briefcase to Bartolomeo? Had he guessed what the case contained? 'I don't want to hold you up,' I said numbly.

'You are right. I must not miss another ferry. I will hear from Signor Lashley very soon, I hope.'

'I'm sure you will.'

'*Bene. Arrivederci*, Signor Kellaway.' He nodded to me, then headed for the gangway.

*

283

A few minutes later, the ferry sailed. I watched it chug slowly away from the jetty, then turn towards the mouth of the harbour. Neither Gandolfi nor Bartolomeo was sitting on deck. They were both in the cabin. Bartolomeo was presumably unaware that a police officer was on board. But the same mightn't be true of the Camorrista Lashley had been told would observe the delivery of the case from a safe distance. Was Gandolfi known to them? I could only hope not.

As soon as the ferry had left the harbour, I started back along the jetty. There might be an innocent explanation for Gandolfi's arrival on the scene, but I couldn't persuade myself to believe it. Lashley had to be told. As soon as possible.

The phone was busy in the first bar I tried. I bought some *gettoni* and hurried on to another, but the phone there was out of order. Valuable minutes were spilling through my fingers as I ran back the way I'd come.

This time the phone was free. I rang the Excelsior and asked for Greville Lashley. There was a brief delay, then I was put through.

But it was Adam Lashley, not Greville, who answered. 'Kellaway? You're not supposed to be calling. What's gone wrong?'

'Where's your father?'

'They phoned him like they said they would. He's just left. He's going down to the Borgo Marinaro.'

The Excelsior stood on the seafront in Naples, as I knew, facing a small fishing harbour – the Borgo Marinaro – sheltered by the ancient walls and turrets of the Castel dell'Ovo. The harbour would be quiet on a Sunday morning and might have been chosen by Muriel's kidnappers as a convenient place to drop her off by boat. It was certainly easy for Lashley to walk there from the hotel.

'Have you screwed up, Kellaway?' Adam's voice had already risen in pitch. 'I knew we shouldn't have relied on you.'

'There's been no screw-up. I've handed the case over. The man who took it's on the ferry.'

'Why are you calling, then?'

'Listen to me, Adam. I—'

'We've listened to you too fucking much.'

'*Listen to me.*' I had the attention of the nearest espresso-sipping bar-propper even if I didn't have Adam's. I was thinking fast, though not necessarily as carefully as I needed to. Everything might still be all right. *Might.* But I couldn't ignore Gandolfi's presence on the ferry. I had to do something. Or, rather, since Adam was in Naples and I wasn't, *he* had to do something. I lowered my voice. 'Get yourself over to the ferry terminal. You need to be there when the ferry docks. That'll be in about forty minutes, so you've got plenty of time. The man with the case is wearing a dark suit and a straw hat. We need to be sure he isn't being followed.'

'How am I supposed to know?'

'Watch out for a middle-aged bloke in a pale-blue suit, grey-haired, good-looking. He got on the ferry after our man. I don't think he's tailing him, but if he is . . .'

'Yeah? If he is?'

'Then we might have a problem.'

'What d'you expect me to do about it if we have?'

'Nothing.' It was beginning to sound like a bad idea even as I outlined it. I couldn't be sure Adam wouldn't draw attention to himself somehow, which might only make matters worse. 'Don't intervene, Adam. Just watch what happens.'

'Watch some bastard walk away with my money, you mean?'

'I'm sure your father's explained that—'

'Yeah, Dad's explained. *You've* explained. Everyone's fucking explained. OK, Kellaway. Leave this to me.'

'It's not—' But he'd hung up. And I knew calling again was pointless. I put the phone back on the hook and hurried out of the bar.

All was picture-postcard peaceful on the Marina Grande harbourfront. The ferry was still visible, ploughing a white furrow through the deep-blue sea as it headed for Naples. The sun was warm in my face. The air was fresh. It seemed inconceivable that Muriel Lashley's life hung in the balance this summer morning. But it did. And there was nothing – *absolutely nothing* – I could do about it.

I went back to the villa and told Jacqueline what had happened. She wasn't sure it had been wise to send Adam to the ferry terminal and neither was I. But the die was cast. There were still good reasons to think everything would proceed smoothly. The money had been paid. Now, surely, Muriel would be released. I imagined her being helped out of a small motorboat on to a pontoon at the Borgo Marinaro and left to find her way to where Lashley was waiting for her. It wasn't so hard to believe.

Time passed, slowly but inexorably. Then, at last, the telephone rang.

It was Lashley. And the tone of his voice told me at once that all my believing had been for nothing.

THIRTY-ONE

The bad news in Lashley's first phone call was followed by worse in his second and worse still, in its own way, in his third. Jacqueline and I sat in the Villa Orchis struggling to come to terms with all that occurred as the morning elapsed, waiting helplessly for the consequences to reveal themselves. All we knew for certain was that those consequences would be bleak and bitter.

The sequence of events, once it was clear, told its own terrible story. It began with Lashley standing for half an hour outside Piovra, one of the bars in the Borgo Marinaro. He'd been told Muriel would be brought to him there and he assumed she'd be delivered by boat. But nothing happened. Time dragged by. Piovra opened for business. Still nothing happened.

Then the Piovra barman came out, saying there was someone on the phone wanting to talk to him. Lashley went into the bar and picked up the phone. He recognized the caller's voice at once. It was the negotiator he'd been dealing with. But he was no longer negotiating.

'You broke your word, Signor Lashley. The police are on us. You should not have gone to them. The deal is off.'

'I didn't—'

'You will not see your wife today.'

The call ended there, leaving Lashley bewildered and distraught. He wondered if he should phone the police at once, but instead he hurried back to the hotel.

More or less simultaneously, about a kilometre north of the Borgo Marinaro, the ferry from Capri was docking at the Molo Beverello. Adam was watching from the corner of the ticket office as the passengers disembarked. He spotted Bartolomeo at once. And the man in the pale-blue suit – Gandolfi – was close behind. He stayed that way as Bartolomeo headed away from the ferry in the direction of the car park.

A flash of sunlight from a windscreen drew Adam's attention to a car moving slowly round the curve of the exit road, waiting, perhaps, for Bartolomeo. Gandolfi may have had the same thought. He quickened his pace, overtook Bartolomeo and stepped into his path.

There was an exchange of words, inaudible to Adam. Gandolfi flourished some identification and pointed to the briefcase. More words came, tenser and faster. And more pointing. Bartolomeo shrugged and set the briefcase down. Gandolfi looked at it and said something. Perhaps he was expecting the case to be opened. But that didn't happen. Instead, Bartolomeo pulled out a gun and shot Gandolfi in the chest.

A woman screamed. Bystanders scattered. Adam took cover behind the ticket office. Gandolfi fell to the ground. Bartolomeo grabbed the briefcase and ran to the car, which took off with a squeal of tyres, pulled straight on to the main road and sped away.

The shocked bystanders recovered themselves slowly. Gandolfi lay where he'd fallen, bleeding heavily and groaning. Someone ran to call an ambulance. Adam walked away fast, heading for the Excelsior.

By the time he arrived, Lashley had already spoken to me, so he realized at once, when Adam told him what had happened, that the man Bartolomeo had shot was Commissioner Gandolfi. The game was up. He phoned the police.

Adam protested that this wrecked Muriel's chances of being freed. He couldn't seem to understand that the shooting of a senior officer meant the police would soon be coming to us even if we didn't go to them. It was better to tell them everything. Well, maybe he didn't want to understand. And Lashley didn't have the heart to point out that with the money in their hands and a full-scale police investigation sure to follow, the Camorra had no reason now to let Muriel go. He tried to squeeze something hopeful from the negotiator's parting remark – 'You will not see your wife today' – but that was largely for Adam's benefit. He entertained little hope himself, as he admitted to me later.

'Whether Gandolfi followed you from the villa or just showed up to catch that ferry by chance we may never know, but the result couldn't have been worse. The police will want to make someone suffer for the murder of one of their own. They'll do everything they can to catch the people behind it. That makes Muriel a potential witness against them as well as their hostage. To imagine they'll release her in such circumstances is' – he sighed – 'simply unrealistic.'

By then, Lashley knew, because the police had told him, that Gandolfi was dead. Once they'd realized a previously unreported kidnapping had cost their colleague his life, their initial sympathy had given way to hostility, exacerbated by Adam's finger-jabbing demands that they 'fucking do something'. What they'd done, after his finger-jabbing had escalated to shoulder-shoving, was arrest him.

'I should have stopped Adam before he went so far,' Lashley admitted. 'But I was so appalled by how badly wrong things had gone so damn quickly that I couldn't seem to concentrate. The police will probably just detain him overnight. Theoretically, they could charge us all with obstruction of justice. So this fellow the Consulate's sent to see me says, anyway. But he doubts it'll come to that and so do I. Don't reproach yourself for anything you did or didn't do. We all acted in good faith and for the best as we saw it. The fact that the outcome's been disastrous doesn't alter that.'

It was a brave assertion by Lashley, but I wasn't sure he really believed it. He'd booked himself in for a second night at the Excelsior, so as to be on hand when Adam was released. It had been made clear that Jacqueline and I would be required to report with Lashley to Police Headquarters in Naples later on Monday to

289

make full statements. The man from the British Consulate had supplied the name of a lawyer we'd do well to consult. The mechanism of an official reaction to the murder of Commissioner Gandolfi and the kidnapping of Muriel Lashley was cranking into motion.

The blowing of the lid on the kidnap plot meant those close to Muriel who'd hitherto been told nothing about it now had to be informed. There was no way round it. Secrecy had got us nowhere. The awful truth had to be confessed. I knew Lashley would tell Harriet and Vivien without further delay. And I knew that would bring Vivien to Capri, probably by Tuesday at the latest. I could remember a time when I'd have been elated that I was going to see her again. Now the prospect was simply one more layer of dread. As Lashley had put it, things had gone wrong *so damn quickly*.

I had no doubt who was primarily to blame for that. I left Jacqueline to explain to Patrizia and Elena what was going on, a task I didn't envy her, and headed for the Gabbiano. The police didn't yet know who'd made the anonymous call that had prompted Gandolfi to visit Capri. I fully intended to tell them. But not before I demanded an explanation from him myself.

It was mid-afternoon when I reached the Gabbiano. The atmosphere was quiet and somnolent. A man emerged sleepily from a cubbyhole and gave me Thompson's room number. There were no phones in the rooms, which was fine by me. The less warning Thompson had of my arrival the better.

His guttural, belated response to my thumps on his door suggested he'd been asleep himself. He was still asking who I was and what I wanted when I tried the handle and found the door wasn't locked.

'Kellaway?' He was sitting on the edge of the bed when I entered the small, shutter-darkened room. He was dressed only in socks, trousers and a vest. He glared at me blearily. 'What the hell are you doing here?'

'You promised you'd say nothing.'

I moved to the window and pushed the shutters open. The

sunlight that flooded in dazzled him and fell on a dog-eared pink wallet-file lying on the bedside table. The flap was open. Thompson flicked it over, concealing the contents, while shielding his eyes with the other hand.

'Why did you call the police?' I demanded, standing directly in front of him.

'I . . . didn't.'

'No one else knew, Thompson. It has to have been you.'

'I made no call.'

'Didn't you hear what I just said? *No one else knew*.'

'This call was . . . anonymous?'

'Naturally.'

'Then someone else did know. Because I didn't call.' He pulled his shirt off the bedpost and struggled into it. 'When's this supposed to have happened?'

'Yesterday. And there's no "supposed" about it. The police have been on to us. You sabotaged the delivery of the ransom. An officer's been killed and—'

'*Killed?*' That seemed to worry him more than anything else. 'What are you talking about?'

'The kidnappers shot him and made off with the ransom money. They didn't release Muriel Lashley. Chances are they aren't going to now. Thanks to you.'

'A policeman *shot*?'

'*Yes*. Commissario Gandolfi.'

'Bloody hell.' He abandoned fiddling with his shirt buttons. 'That'll have put the cat among the pigeons.'

'More than you bargained on, is it? The police won't thank you for leading Gandolfi on with your crazy allegations about Strake's murder, you know.'

'Strake? What's he got to . . .' He stopped in mid-question, silenced by the realization that he'd just admitted he knew the name.

'How did you find out about him?'

Thompson tried to look puzzled. 'Who?'

'Gordon Strake.' I stepped closer. 'All in here, is it?'

I grabbed the wallet-file a split-second before he did and carried it towards the window. He lurched off the bed and came after me with a growled, 'Give that here'. But all I gave him was an elbow in the stomach.

It doubled him up. His face turned a deep red and, with a groan, he sank back down on to the bed, clinging to the post for support. 'You bugger, you,' he gasped. 'I'm getting over . . . a hernia operation.'

'It's a pity you didn't stay home to recuperate, then, isn't it?'

I opened the file. Inside were pages of scrawled notes, photocopied newspaper articles and a sheaf of black-and-white photographs. The topmost picture was of Vivien . . . and me. We were standing next to her Mini in Walworth the day in 1969 she'd travelled down from Cambridge to ask for my help in exposing the truth that lay behind Oliver's death. We were smiling at each other, blithely unaware that somewhere, not far off, Thompson was training his camera on us.

The other pictures were all of Vivien. They looked to have been taken in Cambridge. The Honourable Roger featured in a couple of them. I held them up for Thompson to see. 'You took these?'

'To show Mrs Lashley.' He winced. 'What's wrong with that?'

'And these newspaper articles?' I glanced through them. They were from the *Cornish Guardian* and the *Western Morning News*: inquest verdicts on Oliver and his father, reports of Wren's merger with Cornish China Clays, an interview with Greville Lashley. Thompson had been a busy boy.

'Background information,' he said defensively. 'I was just doing my job.'

'Did you follow us here fifteen years ago?'

'No. Mrs Lashley called me off when I told her Vivien had contacted you again.'

'Why?'

'Who knows? Maybe she didn't need proof positive that you were porking her daughter.'

I took a stride towards the bed with the fleeting intention of punching Thompson in his foul mouth. Then I stopped. I half

292

suspected he wanted me to hit him, so he'd have a bruise to show off later to the police.

'Beating up an old man is all you're good for, isn't it, Kellaway?' he sneered.

'How did you find out about Strake?'

'All I know is what Mrs Lashley told me fifteen years ago. An ex-employee of her family firm, name of Strake, had supposedly been harassing her son before his suicide. She asked me to keep an eye out for him while I was checking on Vivien in case he was doing the same to her. But I never saw hide nor hair of him. Why would he be of any interest to the Italian police?'

It was a good act. He sounded almost innocently curious. But I was sure he'd made the anonymous call alleging a connection between Muriel's disappearance and Strake's murder. He couldn't fool me. 'You know why he'd be of interest, Thompson. You told them why.'

'You've got the wrong man. I didn't make that call.'

'Of course you did. No one else could have. As you can be certain I'll tell them.'

'Don't do that.'

'Why shouldn't I?'

'Listen . . .' He licked his lips nervously. 'Policemen cut up rough when one of their own gets it. I've seen it happen. I wouldn't trust I-tie rozzers to be too . . . particular. I'm not as young as I was. I need you to keep my name out of this. And I can do you a favour in return.'

'What are you trying to say?'

'Whatever happens – I mean, *whatever* – I'll keep my mouth shut. The police'll hear nothing from me. You've got my word on it.'

'And your word's worth precisely what?'

'As much as yours or Lashley's, the way things are.'

He had me there, as he must have realized. I had no way of gauging how much he knew about Strake's murder and he was too clever to tell me, but I was technically party to a perversion of the course of justice, something I wasn't eager to discuss with

Gandolfi's grieving colleagues in the Naples police. Arguably, the same applied to Lashley. Just how much trouble Thompson could land us in was unclear. But in that lack of clarity lay his bargaining power.

'Does that ugly look on your face mean you'll get down off your high horse and put my offer to your boss?' he asked with a smirk. 'If you think you'd choke on a "yes", I'll settle for a nod.'

Lashley agreed with me that, galling though it was, we'd be wise to say nothing to the police about Thompson. As far as they were to know, we had no idea who'd phoned them, nor why the caller should have alleged Muriel's kidnapping was somehow connected with Strake's murder.

Jacqueline, as supportive as ever, assured us she'd be equally circumspect in what she said. 'It won't be difficult,' she predicted. 'They won't think I know anything useful.'

But she knew a great deal now, of course. Enough to prompt her to ask me, as we faced a blank and anxious evening together at the villa, 'Do you wish you'd gone to the police back in 'sixty-nine and told them everything, Jonathan?'

I didn't have to ponder the question for long. 'Absolutely.' But . . . 'At the time, though, there seemed to be so many good reasons not to. I never imagined Strake would come back to haunt us.'

'Nor that anything like this would ever happen, I guess.'

'You can say that again.'

'Greville sounded awful low when we spoke. Do you think there's any hope for Muriel?'

'I don't know. I just don't know.'

It might have been more accurate to say I didn't want to know. But that was a luxury I wasn't to be allowed to enjoy for long. We were about to set off for Marina Grande the following morning, in time for the ten o'clock ferry to Naples, when the telephone rang.

It was Lashley. 'The police have just called, Jonathan,' he announced, with sombre lack of preamble. 'A body's been washed ashore near Ercolano. They think it may be Muriel. I'm leaving straight away. You and Jacqueline . . . should prepare yourselves for the worst.'

THIRTY-TWO

The body washed ashore near Ercolano that morning was Muriel Lashley, of course. She'd drowned, presumably after being thrown overboard the previous night from a boat somewhere in the Bay of Naples. Technically, according to Cremonesi, the suave and softly spoken lawyer put our way by the British Consulate, there was some question as to whether this could be regarded as murder, especially since there was no hard evidence she'd been kidnapped in the first place beyond the photograph Lashley had been sent. There were no recordings of the phone calls her kidnappers had made and no eyewitnesses to her abduction.

It was not, Cremonesi explained, that the investigating magistrate doubted what had occurred, simply that he had so very little to investigate. Commissioner Gandolfi had certainly been murdered, of course, but rumour had it he habitually played his cards so close to his chest that his colleagues seldom knew what lines of inquiry he was following.

We might have been able to assist the magistrate by naming Thompson as the source of the anonymous phone call to the police or suggesting that Paolo Verdelli had been party to the kidnap plot, but both courses of action threatened to cause us more trouble than they would Thompson or Verdelli. Strake's scrawny shadow stretched a long way.

'If we're to take this further, Jonathan,' Lashley said to me in a reflective moment, 'it must be on our own initiative, without recourse to the authorities.' He had his suspicions, I knew, that the Camorra wielded enough influence in the upper echelons of the Naples police to ensure Gandolfi's murder and Muriel's death (however it was defined) would remain officially unexplained.

Adam, released without charge after twenty-four hours in custody, was a seething bundle of grief, rage, resentment and reproachfulness. I said barely a word while he launched a series of red-faced accusations of stupidity and worse at me in Lashley's suite at the Excelsior. I remember looking past him through the window at the broad expanse of the bay and imagining Muriel's last choking moments of life somewhere out there, near the far blue horizon. It had all gone wrong, for a host of reasons, most of which no longer mattered. It had ended as it wasn't meant to.

Now, suddenly, I was redundant, an unwelcome reminder of the failure to save Muriel. Vivien was on her way, though her departure had been delayed following news of her mother's death. She was waiting in London for the Honourable Roger to join her and for Harriet to travel up from Cornwall so they could fly out together. The problems my presence would cause didn't need spelling out. I believe Lashley would have sent me back to Sandersville straight away if he could have, but the investigating magistrate required us to stay within his jurisdiction until he'd decided whether we should be charged with anything, a possibility Cremonesi assured us was extremely remote.

I booked into the next hotel along the seafront from the Excelsior, the Vesuvio, and tried to reconcile myself to sitting it out there, while Lashley awaited the family's arrival, before he returned to Capri, where Muriel was to be buried. Jacqueline would go with them and doubtless attend the funeral. Only I was *persona non grata*. Lashley apologized to me for this, though I well understood the reasons. I'd been called in to help deal with an emergency. And the emergency was over. It was time for me to go. Unfortunately, I couldn't.

'I'd ask you to keep yourself busy trying to track down Verdelli if I wasn't so sure he'll be lying low till all this blows over,' Lashley

297

said to me before we parted. 'It'll never blow over as far as I'm concerned, of course. I'll use local expertise to trace him once the magistrate's signed off the case.'

'What then, sir?'

'Then, Jonathan, I'll decide what to do. But he's not going to get away with widowing *and* robbing me. I can assure you of that.'

I didn't doubt Lashley meant what he said. But I wasn't sure he'd have to wait as long as he thought to set in motion whatever retribution he had in mind for Paolo. I phoned Countess Covelli to find out if Salvenini had told her anything useful. She'd been horrified to hear how Muriel had died and had sent a letter of condolence to her family. She'd also tried to contact me at the villa, without success.

'I asked Valerio Salvenini about Paolo for you, Jonathan, and he said he would let me know. But I have not heard from him. Would you like me to . . . remind him?'

'Well, thanks, yes, if you could.'

'It is important?' Her tone implied she suspected it was and wouldn't be fooled by any denials.

'It might be.'

'And you are staying at the Vesuvio . . . for now?'

'Yes. I don't want to get in the family's way at the villa.'

'That is very considerate of you.' And not just considerate, she clearly realized. 'Will I see you again before you leave?'

'I . . . hope so.'

'I will be in Naples on Friday to see my *notaio*. Perhaps we could meet then.'

'Yes. By all means.'

So, Countess Covelli at least hadn't ostracized me.

I phoned the Gabbiano as well and was given the unsurprising news that Frederick Thompson had checked out. He'd gone while the going was good, as I probably would have done myself if I'd had the option.

I wondered if I'd hear from Vivien. She was at the Villa Orchis

298

by now, with her husband, her stepfather, her great-aunt and her half-brother: Muriel Lashley's closest surviving relatives, gathered in mourning. Perhaps that would be enough for her to cope with. Perhaps, in the shock of losing her mother, there'd be no space to think of me.

I thought of her, though – a lot. Solitude and idleness made sure of that. On Wednesday, having nothing better to do, I took the train along the coast to Pompeii and followed the hordes of camera-toting tourists round the ruin-lined streets. Vivien and I had planned to go there in 1969, but never had. It was where she'd invented a chance meeting with some friends from Cambridge that was supposed to explain her trip to Rome. She hadn't actually gone to Pompeii at all, I assumed, though she probably had since.

I was in no state to appreciate what I saw. I wandered the stony thoroughfares in a daze and spent a full hour sitting in the amphitheatre, staring into space.

That was where, by a supreme irony, my old Walworth house-mate Terry almost literally stumbled upon me. I hardly recognized him at first. The concavely thin, bushy-bearded student had become a thick-waisted, short-haired auditor, husband and father of two. What kind of impression I made on his wife in my dis-tracted state I dread to think. Terry took it for a signal that I was still enjoying the free and easy lifestyle he'd somehow allowed to slip through his fingers, though he dutifully assured me his sons (at that moment shooting hostile glares in my direction) were an undiluted joy to him.

They were staying on a camp site near the beach at Pozzuoli before heading on down the coast. Terry eagerly suggested I go out there that evening. We could reminisce and compare post-university career paths over a beer or six. I agreed, rather less eagerly. I was in no condition for a boozy reunion, but I didn't exactly have any other plans. It was settled that he'd meet me off the Metro at Pozzuoli station at eight o'clock.

Poor old Terry. I'm sure he was looking forward to our boys' night out. But I never made it to Pozzuoli.

Vivien was waiting for me at the Vesuvio. I didn't see her as I entered. She was in the bar area that adjoined reception. The man on the desk told me I had a visitor and, turning round, I saw her rise from a sofa into a golden shaft of filtered sunlight.

She was looking sombre and drawn. Her hair was slightly shorter than I remembered and maybe a fraction of a shade darker. She was wearing a simple flared blue skirt and belted white T-shirt. There was scarcely a trace of make-up. But that made no difference. Her beauty, if not unaltered, was certainly undiminished.

I walked slowly towards her, struggling to decide how to greet her. A kiss? A handshake? A simple hello. Nothing seemed right. And nothing, in the end, was what I settled for.

'I'm sorry . . . about your mother, Vivien,' I said, surprised by how hoarse my voice sounded. 'I suppose . . . Greville's told you everything?'

'I'm not sure, Jonathan.' She looked at me coolly. 'That's why I'm here.' It was, her tone suggested, the only reason she'd come. 'Can we talk?'

'Of course. Shall we sit down?'

'Not here. Outside. In the air.'

'All right.'

We headed for the revolving door that led out on to the street. Before we reached it, the man on the desk called out to me.

'Ah, Signor Kellaway. If you are leaving . . .' I looked round at him. 'There is a message for you. The caller said it might be urgent.'

'I'll wait for you on the other side of the road,' Vivien said, pressing on towards the door.

I went back to the desk and was handed a small V-monogrammed envelope. Inside was a note addressed to me. '*La Contessa Covelli telephoned. The address you require is Salita Penitenza 33.*'

'Can you show me where this is?' I asked, proffering my street map of the city.

The man peered at the note and then the map before marking it with a cross. 'You will go there, Signor Kellaway?'

'Probably. Why?'

300

'It is . . . not a good area. You should be careful. It is not a place for' – he smiled – '*la bella signora.*'

'Don't worry.' I smiled back at him. 'I won't take *la bella signora.*'

He nodded. '*Bene.*'

Vivien was leaning against the wall by the bridge that led across from Via Partenope to the Castel dell'Ovo and the Borgo Marinaro, apparently oblivious to the surging traffic and the ambling sightseers. I crossed the road to join her.

'Was the message from Greville?' she asked me at once, her eyes concealed from me now behind sunglasses.

'No. It wasn't.'

'Really?'

'No,' I said, more emphatically. 'Why should you think it was?'

'Because he knew I was coming to see you. Maybe he wanted to make sure you'd toe the party line.'

'The party line?'

'You know what I mean.'

'I don't, actually. Look, Vivien, what happened to your mother was—'

'Why did it go wrong, Jonathan? Why did she end up dead?' She turned away from me, suddenly close to tears. 'I'm sorry. I was determined not to do this.' She took a couple of deep breaths, then faced me again. 'An anonymous phone call to the police which Greville believes this man Thompson made ruined everything, he tells me. Is that really how it was?'

'Yes. But for that, I think Muriel would have been released unharmed.'

'Down there?' She nodded to the harbour below us. Its café-lined quays were crowded with people. Pleasure craft bobbed gently at their moorings. Sunlight shimmered on the water. 'Where Greville was waiting for her?'

'It's what was agreed. It's almost certainly how it would have turned out if Gandolfi hadn't intervened.'

'And whose fault was it that Gandolfi intervened?'

'Whoever made the anonymous phone call.'

'Really? It doesn't go any deeper than that?'

'What d'you mean?'

'You don't want to admit it, do you?'

'Admit *what*?'

'For God's sake.' She sounded exasperated. But the tremor in her hand as she looked away and rubbed her forehead hinted at something beyond exasperation. Her grief was tinged with anger, directed, apparently, at me. 'Can we walk, please? Moving . . . seems to help.'

'Sure.'

We headed east, towards the Excelsior and the triple-arched canopy of the Immacolatella Fountain, with Mount Vesuvius looming ahead of us across the bay. Vivien wasn't dawdling. I had to stride out to keep pace with her. 'It's our fault,' she said decisively, as if the point was unarguable. 'If we hadn't helped Strake blackmail Luisa, Uncle Francis wouldn't have murdered him and there'd have been nothing to interest Gandolfi all these years later. And Paolo, much as he might have resented being cut out of what he saw as his rightful inheritance, wouldn't have felt so badly treated by the family whose good name he'd protected. Yes, it's our fault all right, yours and mine. We started this. And we never once warned my mother how embittered Paolo had cause to be.'

'No one could have foreseen what it would lead to, Vivien. We weren't to know he had connections with the Camorra.'

'Greville knew. Or at least he suspected it. I blame him too.'

'And there's no actual proof Paolo was involved.'

'Yes, there is. The phone call. I've heard all about Gandolfi's visit to the villa from Jacqueline. A lot else too. You seem to have been more open with her than you ever were with me.'

'Just a—'

'Forget it, OK? You trust her. Everyone trusts her. Apparently, I have to trust her as well.' There was a strand of guilt in the harshness of her tone – guilt for being far away when her mother needed her. 'Thompson couldn't have made that call without help, Jonathan. He

302

had no reason to suppose Strake had ever come to Naples, let alone been murdered here. There's no plausible way he could simply have stumbled across the information. Somebody must have told him. And from what Jacqueline tells me, it's doubtful he could string together a sentence in good *or* bad Italian. He'd have needed to be instructed what to say. By the same somebody.'

'Paolo?'

'Exactly.'

'Why would he do that?'

'Because his share of the ransom money wasn't enough for him. It probably wasn't much, anyway. No. He wanted blood. And when he heard Thompson was looking for him, he saw a way to get it. He'd have known Gandolfi was still on the force and would spring into action once the call was made. And he'd have known how the people holding Mother would react if they had cause to suspect the police had been called in.'

'You're suggesting he deliberately sabotaged the deal?'

'Yes. And it worked, didn't it? He got what he wanted.'

'Vivien, this is—'

'The truth. That's what this is.'

We'd reached the fountain. She turned aside and stopped, staring out to sea, wondering, I sensed, just how it must have felt for her mother as she thrashed and floundered and drowned out there in the darkness.

'She couldn't swim,' she murmured, hugging herself to suppress a shudder. 'Not a stroke. How can the magistrate say that's not murder?'

'It's a technicality.'

'I want Paolo found. And brought to book.'

'I'm sure Greville will do everything he can to achieve that.'

'Do you know where he is, Jonathan?' She looked round.

'Me?' My instinct was not to tell her about Countess Covelli's message. Not yet, at least. I needed to think very carefully before taking any action. 'How would I?'

'Jacqueline mentioned that you'd asked Countess Covelli for help in tracing him.'

'I did, yes. But—'

'I spoke to the countess a few hours ago.'

'Really?'

'She said she hadn't been able to find anything out.'

What was Vivien thinking? What was the look in her eyes that I couldn't see behind the dark glasses? 'The message at the hotel was from her,' I said, weighing my every word, as I felt Vivien was also doing. 'She wants me to phone her. So she can tell me she's drawn a blank, I suppose.'

'Or to tell you where he is.'

'But you said she—'

'I'm not sure I believed her.'

'Why would she lie to you?'

'I don't know. But there's something between you, isn't there? Some . . . bond.'

'Is there?'

'This terrible thing Luisa's supposed to have done. The reason the countess ended their friendship. You know what it is, don't you?' She raised a hand to forestall my reply. 'Don't deny it. She's probably sworn you to secrecy. And I don't want to know, anyway. Nothing like as much as I want to know where Paolo is. Promise me you'll tell me if you find out.'

'What would—'

'*Just promise me.* Your word, Jonathan.' She took off her glasses and looked directly at me, squinting in the bright sunlight, tears glistening at the corners of her eyes. 'Give me your word, if not for Mother's sake, then for the sake of what you and I once were to each other.'

I couldn't do it. The deceit was more than I could stomach. I shook my head. 'No.'

'No what?'

'I'm not going to promise you anything.'

'Because you already know.' Understanding flashed in her gaze. 'That's it, isn't it? That's what the message was. The countess has told you where he is.'

'If I knew, I'd inform Greville.'

'And I'd have to hope he thought I could be trusted with the information. No, Jonathan. Tell *me*. Tell me now.'

To pretend any longer that I didn't know was futile. 'Why?'

'Because I want to look Paolo in the eye when he denies being responsible for my mother's death. And I want him to know he's not going to get away with it.'

'I suspect Greville would say confronting him now was unwise.'

'And Greville's your boss. So, whatever he says goes. Is that how it is?'

'Of course not. But it would be unwise. You must realize that.'

'I don't care whether it is or not. I want Paolo to understand how much I hate him for what he's done. I'll find out where he lives one way or the other. According to Jacqueline, the countess said she was going to ask Valerio Salvenini. So, he must have supplied her with the address. Well, I can charm it out of him if I have to. Or you can take me to it now. It's your choice, Jonathan. You have to decide . . . which is the least unwise course of action.'

THIRTY-THREE

The taxi driver dropped us in a small piazza off Via Toledo, explaining to Vivien – whose Italian was far better than mine – that it was the closest he could get to our destination.

The city sloped sharply uphill from there, towards the heights of Vomero. The buildings were tightly packed along narrow, steepling streets, many divided by lengthy flights of steps. Washing hung from balconies, while, below, merchandise piled outside shops contested pavement space with double-parked scooters. Grubby, bright-eyed children scurried everywhere. It was late afternoon, clammily hot on sallow-shadowed Salita Penitenza. There was a pervading smell of blocked drains and a garbled jangle of music and jabbering voices from the open windows around us. It was, as the desk clerk at the Vesuvio had warned me, no place for '*la bella signora*'.

It didn't look like Paolo's natural habitat either. And '*la bella signora*' was there at her own insistence. A few adult idlers cast us leery glances as we climbed the winding steps, examining chipped and faded number-plaques on walls in search of 33.

We found it eventually, partially obscured by fencing round part of the steps that appeared to be under repair, though no repair work was taking place. There were five bell-pushes clinging to crumbling stucco beside a decrepit doorway. Four had names of varying legibility recorded next to them. None of the names was Verdelli. Vivien prodded the nameless fifth. There was no immediate response and no way of telling if a bell was ringing any-where. She gave it several more prods.

We were still standing there a few minutes later, wondering what to do, when a barrel-shaped old lady dressed in black, her girth expanded by a bulging shopping-bag, bustled past us and slipped her key into the lock. Vivien at once engaged her in conversation and she seemed neither to notice nor object as we slipped into the gloomy entrance hall behind her. A lot of eye-rolling and head-tossing accompanied her replies to questions about Paolo Verdelli. I couldn't follow much of what she said, but the phrase '*ultimo piano*' was clear enough. Paolo lived on the top floor.

'I don't think she likes him,' Vivien said, as we started up the stairs. 'She said something about him having noisy visitors and there were other things I couldn't understand. Do you know what *mosconi* means?'

'Haven't a clue. You can ask Paolo.'

The house, shabby enough at street level, deteriorated still further as we climbed. The plasterwork was crumbling, with fragments of it lying on the landings and stair-treads. The light was dim, the atmosphere musty. Salita Penitenza 33 was a far and dismal cry from the Villa Orchis, as Paolo must have been painfully aware.

'Are you sure you want to go through with this?' I asked, feeling I should give Vivien a chance to back out.

'I'm sure.'

'He may not be at home.'

'Let's find out.'

We reached the top floor, where it was marginally less gloomy thanks to a skylight somewhere above us. I made sure I was first to Paolo's door. If there was to be an encounter with him, it would best be managed by me.

I realized something was wrong almost at once. The frame was splintered around the lock and, as I approached, the door swung ajar in response to the flexing of a loose board beneath my foot. There was a low buzzing noise from within that I couldn't account for. I knocked on the door and pushed it open. 'Paolo?' I called.

The buzzing was much louder now. I noticed darting movements ahead of me. There were flies everywhere, swarms of them.

'*Mosconi*,' said Vivien from behind me. 'I remember now what it means. The old lady was complaining . . . about bluebottles.'

'Stay here,' I said, advancing into the flat.

I didn't have to go far to discover what was attracting the flies. The noise of them in the kitchen was like the drone of an engine. A naked man lay on his side on the floor, limbs splayed, head bent back. There were flies all over him. And a throat-catching stench of decay filled the air.

Paolo Verdelli was dead. That much was obvious to me as I covered my nose and gestured for Vivien to remain where she was. I took a few hesitant steps closer.

He was as slim as he'd always been, but there was a lot of grey now in his mane of hair. His handsome features were distorted in a grimace. A length of clothesline had been looped several times round his neck. It was resting loosely on the floor, but had clearly been used to strangle him. He wasn't just dead. He'd been murdered.

Vivien hadn't waited at the door. I was suddenly aware of her at my shoulder. 'Oh God,' she murmured. 'Oh dear God.'

Truly, there was nothing else to say.

I telephoned the police from a nearby shop, then stood waiting for them outside number 33. Vivien had rejected my suggestion that she leave before they arrive, just as she'd shrugged off my attempts to shield her from the horror of Paolo's death. She seemed determined to face it and all the questioning we were in for. I knew she was shocked, of course. So was I. She was breathing shallowly and her hands were trembling. But there was nothing I could do to comfort her. The way she held herself and the distance she kept from me made it clear she didn't want me even to try.

'How long do you think he's been dead?' she asked numbly, as we waited.

'I don't know. A couple of days, maybe. Or less, in this climate.'

'They killed him because he sabotaged the exchange. You realize that, don't you?'

'It . . . could be.'

'It must be. He'd made himself unreliable. He might have named names. He had to be silenced.'

'Well, he was silenced all right.'

'Yes.' She bowed her head for a moment, then said quietly, 'All those flies. And the smell. It was awful.'

'I know. Try not to think about it.'

She looked at me strangely, as if the suggestion was absurd, as in its way it was, of course. 'What I'm thinking about is how much to tell the police. We can't name Thompson as Paolo's accomplice without taking the chance they'll discover you helped cover Uncle Francis's tracks after he murdered Strake.'

'Tell them what you like, Vivien. I'm not sure I care any more.'

'Easy for you to say, when you know *I* care too much about my family to drag all that into the open.'

'You'd prefer to keep it simple?'

'What choice do I have?'

'I don't know. It's your secret as much as it's mine.'

She sighed. 'We'll say nothing about Thompson, then.'

'Fine by me.'

The remark seemed to anger her. She glared at me for a moment, then moved suddenly past me, heading towards the shop from where I'd phoned the police. 'I must let Roger know what's happened,' she said. 'He'll be worried about me. I won't be long.'

As it turned out, the police arrived before she returned. Those exchanges were our last chance to make some kind of peace. And we hadn't taken it.

The taking of statements, the answering of questions and the explaining of circumstances occupied most of the evening, even though, as Vivien and I had agreed beforehand, our account supplied no connection with Thompson and Strake. As far as the police knew from what we told them, we suspected Paolo's motive to have been his exclusion from Luisa's will, nothing more, nothing less. They were left to assume he – or an unidentified accomplice – had mentioned Strake's murder in the anonymous phone call

309

because it was unsolved and therefore likely to pique Gandolfi's curiosity.

Lashley caught up with us at Police Headquarters. Roger was with him, exuding disdain and disgruntlement. He contrived to avoid addressing a single word to me. His concern for Vivien seemed synthetic. But maybe I was just prejudiced.

Soon, Cremonesi was on the scene as well, abandoning some social event at Lashley's request. (He was still dressed in his dinner suit.) His intervention smoothed all the wheels and speeded our departure. 'Informally, I gather they believe Verdelli was killed by the kidnappers for the reason you suggested, Signora Normington,' he said to Vivien. 'I am personally sorry you had to see such a terrible thing.' His regrets were a nice touch. But then he was a man who dealt in nice touches.

Lashley booked back into the Excelsior for the night, along with Vivien and Roger. 'I'm worried Vivien may suffer a delayed reaction to what's happened,' he confided to me after seeing them off in a taxi. I preferred to walk to the Vesuvio and he said he'd walk with me. 'She thinks she's tougher than she really is.'

'I couldn't stop her going to see Paolo,' I said, accepting his offer of a cigarette as we headed away from the Questura. 'Of course, I never anticipated what we'd find.'

'How could you? Although, reflecting on the situation, I dare say we shouldn't be unduly surprised. With Verdelli dead, there are no leads for the police to follow. It's even crossed my mind that this might be intended as a sop to me: some twisted form of apology from the Camorra. I feel cheated, even so. I intended to go after him, you know.'

'I do know, yes. So, maybe it's for the best.'

'Maybe. But it'll be a long time before I see it in that light. How did you find out where he was?'

'Countess Covelli.'

'Ah yes. The countess. Not a trusting soul. But she trusts you. Don't worry, I'm not going to ask why. All of us should have a few secrets.'

We walked on in silence for a few minutes, his remark hanging in the air. Then I asked, 'How are things . . . at the villa?'

'Oh, as well as can be expected.'

'And you? After everything that's—'

'I'll survive.' He clapped me gamely on the shoulder. 'You can rely on that.'

And I felt sure I could.

After a restless night, I rose at dawn and went for a run along the promenade to Mergellina. The sea was a mirror of the sky. Naples basked as the sun climbed. I had no place there. Remaining served no purpose. But I couldn't leave. I was a prisoner of procedure, a witness to crimes no one investigating them had any serious expectation of solving. Three people were dead. Yet life went on.

I was grateful when Harv Beaumont contacted me that morning. He wanted my opinion on some problems that had arisen at one of CCC's processing plants. Applying my mind to them was a welcome distraction. But the distraction was short-lived. Vivien and I were due at the Procura later in the day to supply formal statements of evidence for the investigating magistrate. Our appointments were at different times, however. She'd gone, whisked back to Capri by Roger, before I arrived. I was shocked to realize I might well not see her again during my enforced sojourn in Naples. If so, the last thing she'd said to me would prove to be 'I won't be long'.

Next morning, I met Countess Covelli at the Caffè Gambrinus. She had an hour to spare before a meeting with her lawyer. 'I have much money, Jonathan,' she told me, with a self-deprecating smile. 'And it causes me much trouble.'

Most of the customers were sitting outside. The countess preferred one of the cooler, quieter rooms towards the rear, away from the traffic fumes of the Piazza Trieste e Trento. She was curious to know what I could tell her about the death of Paolo Verdelli.

311

That was more than she could ever have anticipated. I related the entire story of Strake's murder and Francis's death – and his dying wish that she should have the letter Strake had been blackmailing him with. Lashley was right. The countess trusted me. And I trusted her. It was a relief to know I could confide in her with no fear as to the outcome.

'I knew that if I waited long enough, everything would make sense,' she said when I'd finished.

'You'd already guessed it was me who sent you the letter?'

'*Si*. I had. But I had not guessed all the . . . circumstances. What a surprisingly high-principled man Francis was.'

'Yes. It surprised me too.'

'And you believe Paolo persuaded the Camorra to kidnap Signora Lashley because she inherited what he thought should have been his . . . reward . . . for all the things he had done for Luisa?'

'That's what it comes down to.'

'*Dio Mio*.' She shook her head. '*La vendetta*. It is an Italian vice.'

'Not one you suffer from though, Contessa. Luisa did you far more harm than she ever did Paolo. Yet all you did was . . . ignore her.'

'But I am a woman. And I have seen too many . . . acts of revenge.'

'Including the desecration of Mussolini's corpse, according to Francis.'

'*Si*. The Piazzale Loreto, in Milano, on the twenty-ninth of April 1945. I regretted going as soon as I arrived, though now I am glad I went – glad for the lesson it taught me. People were kicking the Duce's body. I saw a woman beating him with a stick. And another trying to force a dead rat into his mouth. Many people think the partisans hung the Duce and his mistress from the roof of a filling station to show their contempt for them. But I was there. I know why they did it. It was to protect the bodies from any more punishment. They had seen enough. So had I. I remembered then something my dear Urbano had said to me when I visited him in

312

prison before his execution and I understood at last what he meant. "*La vendetta è il suicidio*." Revenge is suicide.'

'Your husband was a wise man, Contessa.'

'*Si*. He was.'

'Why did Luisa betray him to the Nazis?'

'Because she believed in Mussolini, as did many Italians. More than you will hear admit it now. To her, Urbano was a traitor.'

'Then why did she want to remain your friend – the friend of a traitor's widow?'

'Because after the war she turned her back on her beliefs. She pretended she had never had them. You see? She betrayed herself. I think that was the most contemptible thing she ever did. She suffered for it in the end. I heard from Patrizia that she died a bad death.'

'Something tells me you won't, Contessa.'

'I hope not.' She took a sip of coffee and looked at me earnestly. 'Promise me you'll remember what Urbano said, Jonathan. Revenge is always . . . self-destructive.'

'There's nothing I have cause to avenge.'

'But there may be. Before your life is over. When I am dead and you have forgotten me.'

'I'll never do that.'

'Then . . .'

'I promise.' I looked her in the eye. 'I solemnly promise.'

THIRTY-FOUR

The week ended. I remained in Naples, a prisoner of the Italian investigative process. On Saturday, Jacqueline came to see me. We had lunch at a seafront pizzeria near the Vesuvio. It was from her that I learnt the true scale of Lashley's problems, which he'd played down in our telephone conversations. Adam's reaction to his mother's death was, as Jacqueline described it, an exhausting roller-coaster of weeping and drunken ranting. Harriet's contempt for what she called Adam's 'emotional incontinence' was no help. And Vivien was too absorbed in her own grief to share much of her stepfather's burden. As for the aloof and indolent Roger, 'All he's absorbed in is himself.' That left Lashley 'exhausted, poor man'.

Jacqueline admitted to some envy of my exile from Capri. 'You're well out of it, Jonathan, let me tell you.' I formed the impression that she'd be relieved to leave as soon after Muriel's funeral – set for the following Wednesday – as the powers that be said she could.

That turned out to be sooner than we'd feared it might be. I received the news from Cremonesi late on Monday afternoon. The investigating magistrate had indicated there'd be no charges against any of us, partly, Cremonesi implied, to spare the police embarrassment in the light of Muriel's death. There was consequently no purpose in detaining me or Jacqueline within the magistrate's jurisdiction. We were free to go.

On Wednesday morning, while Muriel Lashley was being laid to rest in the Protestant section of Capri's cemetery, I boarded a plane for Rome, with a connecting flight booked through to Atlanta. I was on my way.

There were things I thought I knew and things I thought I understood about what had happened during the two weeks I'd spent in Italy that summer – two weeks that had encompassed the deaths of Muriel Lashley, Paolo Verdelli and the luckless Commissioner Gandolfi. But, as time passed, I came to realize that what I knew and what I understood were far from clear. There was a sub-text to events I'd failed to see, let alone read. There was a meaning within the meaning I believed I'd grasped. There was an answer to a question I hadn't had the wit to ask.

The merger between Cornish China Clays and North American Kaolins went ahead in October. Many in CCC doubted the wisdom of the move. But I didn't. Not for a moment. Greville Lashley had told Harv Beaumont and me what it would lead to and I for one was confident it would. Bereavement was never likely to put a brake on Lashley's ambition or impair his judgement. Intercontinental Kaolins, as the merged entity was to be called, would be the vehicle for his dominance of the industry worldwide. It would be his fiefdom – and no one else's.

I spent Christmas with my parents in St Austell, wondering whether I shouldn't have devised some excuse to be elsewhere. I was getting a little old for the role of wanderer returning. But it was the role I had to play, nonetheless.

The circumstances of Muriel Lashley's death had excited quite a bit of attention in her home town, but details were elusive and Mum's hopes that I'd be able or willing to supply some were to be dashed. 'Your discretion's a great disappointment to your mother,' Dad jokingly remarked.

Mum had fared little better, it transpired, during her last chance meeting in Fore Street with Harriet Wren. The old lady had mentioned that her family would be gathering for Christmas in Lincolnshire and had made a few waspish remarks about the Honourable Roger, but her only reference to her deceased niece had been indirect, albeit tantalizing.

'She said she didn't think Mr Lashley would remain a widower for long,' Mum revealed.

'She did?' I was surprised, though I did my best not to show it.

'Yes. Then she tapped the side of her nose and pottered off.'

'Any idea who she had in mind as the new Mrs Lashley?'

'That's what I was going to ask you.'

'Well, I don't know.'

'No?'

'No.'

'Really?'

I nodded for emphasis. 'Really.'

And I really didn't. It struck me as wildly improbable that Lashley would remarry in the foreseeable future.

But the improbable, of course, as I should have borne in mind, isn't impossible.

2010

THIRTY-FIVE

When the sound of a car engine broke my reverie, I assumed it was Vivien returning to her home from home at Lannerwrack Dryers, where she'd find me waiting for her. But almost immediately I realized the note of the engine was all wrong for the Volkswagen Beetle that Pete Newlove had told me she drove. It was too low, too throaty, altogether too powerful. It sounded more like a sports car.

And that's what it was: a sleek blood-red speed machine that I guessed belonged to Adam Lashley before I actually recognized him as the driver. He braked to a sharp, pebble-spraying halt beside Vivien's caravan, pushed the door open with his foot and heaved himself out.

Adam hadn't improved with age. I suppose he was never likely to have. The vain, spoilt, tempersome child was still there to be seen in the fat, ruddy-faced, scowling forty-seven-year-old. He was wearing an expensive suit, but bought off the peg. The sleeves of the jacket were too long and I'd have bet against him being able to fasten it. The trousers were too long as well, the bottoms gathered in folds at his ankles. The shirt he'd paired it with seemed designed for a beach holiday. Altogether, the man was a mess.

I suspected the mess was as much psychological as physical. Adam had never played more than a notional role in the running of Intercontinental Kaolins. He lived (and lived well) on the allowance his father paid him, spending most of his time in Thailand. Office rumour left no vice unimagined where his

319

activities there were concerned, though it had always struck me that for a pleasure-seeker Adam never looked as if he was enjoying himself.

True to form, his expression as he glanced round him was thunderous. But, also as usual, he didn't see what was in front of him: me. He took the cigar he was smoking out of his mouth, hawked up some phlegm and spat it out, then slammed the car door and strode towards the caravan.

He must have known, from the absence of the Beetle, that Vivien wasn't there. Perhaps that was why he didn't bother to knock. He just gave the door handle a few futile wrenches, then peered in through one of the net-curtained windows. That got him nowhere, of course, though where he was actually trying to get was unclear.

It didn't stay unclear, however. He stalked back to the car, opened the boot and pulled out a crowbar. Not liking the look of that, I eased the door of the Freelander open and stepped lightly out.

He had his back to me as I hurried across the yard and he didn't hear me coming. He took a last puff on his cigar, threw it to the ground, then stepped up to the caravan and tried to find a levering point for the crowbar between the door and frame. It was a clumsy effort that ended with the crowbar jolting free.

Adam was shaking a jarred thumb and swearing to himself when I called out his name. He whirled round and his face darkened instantly. 'Kellaway?'

'Hello, Adam.'

'What the fuck are you doing here?'

'No harm. Unlike you.'

He looked past me and registered the presence of the Freelander. Then his scowl was back on me. 'Why don't you mind your own fucking business?'

'Business is why I'm here. Boss's orders, you could say.'

'What orders?'

'Those missing records that have held up Doctor Whitworth's researches? I've been sent to find them.'

'The fuck you have.'

320

'Didn't your father tell you?'

The question touched a raw nerve – one of many. He brandished the crowbar as if tempted to attack me with it. I took half a step back. 'Why don't you just retire and give us all a break, Kellaway?'

'I will. After this last job.'

'I don't know where the fucking records are.'

'I never said you did.'

'Maybe Vivien stole them. Has that crossed your pathetic little mind?'

'It has, yes. And it looks like it might have crossed yours, too. Planning to search the caravan, were you?'

'This is IK property. I *am* IK. So, if I want to give an illegally pitched caravan the once-over, I can. And I will.'

'It's here with your father's consent. I can't let you break into it.'

'How are you going to stop me?'

'Don't do it, Adam. It'd be a big mistake. Haven't you made enough of them in your life?'

'What would you know about it? Luckily for me, you've mostly been out of my life since you cost my mother hers.' It hadn't taken him long to remind me of my role in the events that had led to Muriel Lashley's death. But the blame game wasn't one I had any intention of playing.

'Doctor Whitworth told me you'd been in touch with her.'

'So what if I have?'

'I'm puzzled, that's all. Why should you care whether a history of the company gets written? It's not a subject you've ever shown any interest in before.'

'I don't have to explain myself to the likes of you.'

'That's true.' It always had been. One of the first things he'd ever said to me, as a five-year-old boy, was, 'You don't matter.' I remembered then what Oliver had said about him on that occasion: 'If you gave him a real gun, he'd be happy to shoot me.' Nothing had changed. Nothing, I'd lived long enough to understand, ever really changed at all.

'Why don't you just piss off, Kellaway?'

'Why don't you, Adam?'

I don't know if I'd intended to provoke him. The retort was out of my mouth before I'd weighed the words. But the effect wasn't long in coming. Something dark and primitive I'd seen a few times before blazed in Adam's eyes. He strode towards me and took a vicious swing at my head with the crowbar.

He was probably drunk, or drugged. Or maybe he'd ingested so much over the years that he was never free of the effects. Either way, my reactions were quicker than his despite my age. I dodged to one side and he decapitated a chunk of thin air. The force of his swing carried him off balance and he was suddenly sprawling on the ground.

He'd let go of the crowbar in the process. I grabbed it and backed away. He stared woozily around, as if confused about how he'd ended up where he was. Then he noticed me and confusion was evidently dispelled. 'Clever fucker, aren't you?' he panted.

'Go home, Adam,' I said, genuinely hoping he'd take my advice.

He pushed himself up and scrambled to his feet with a lot of help from the wing of his Lotus. The glare he shot at me then was impersonal, I felt. It bore the hostility with which he always confronted the world.

'I'll hang on to this for the time being,' I said, keeping a firm grip on the crowbar.

'You've got it coming, Kellaway. You know that? Some time soon. Oh yeah.' He nodded for emphasis. 'You can count on it.'

'Any message you want me to give Vivien?'

'The same goes for her. You can tell her that.'

'She's got it coming as well?'

'You all have. The fucking lot of you.'

His hatred was indiscriminate. I doubted he could have supplied a coherent explanation of who 'the lot of us' were. Nor could he have said what form his wrath would take. He probably wouldn't remember the threat a few hours after uttering it. But he was angry. That at least was clear. He was very angry. He had been all his life.

'Think I'm joking?' He wagged a finger at me. 'Wait and see.' He staggered round to the driver's side of the car, clambered in and started up. The high-performance engine supplied some of the machismo he'd come up short on. He swept round the yard in an arc, then put his foot down and sped away.

I watched the dust settle in his wake and listened to the fading growl of the Lotus. Then I walked slowly back to the Freelander.

Fate hadn't been kind to Adam's family. That justified some of his bitterness, I couldn't deny. The rest was a product of his own personality. He believed he was entitled to every good thing in life. And his resentment that some of them had eluded him knew no bounds.

His mother's death was a trauma and a tragedy. But at twenty-one he'd been old enough to recover. The fact that he never really had made me wonder if part of him hadn't welcomed the excuse it supplied to gorge on self-pity. His father's prompt remarriage (indecently prompt, many said) couldn't have helped, though I suspect it was nothing compared with Adam's horror when, at nearly seventy, Lashley had sired another child. At least it had been a daughter rather than a son for the old man to dote on.

Michelle Lashley was now, at twenty-three, a top-flight equestrian, with Olympic aspirations much burnished by her mother. The Lashleys' residence near Augusta was large enough to accommodate enough stables, paddocks and training facilities to supply a cavalry troop, let alone one pampered and privileged young woman with a perfect seat. I hadn't seen Jacqueline in years and had never summoned the nerve when I had to ask how and why she'd come to marry a man three decades older than she was. Maybe her (apparently) perfect daughter was the answer. Connubial bliss hardly seemed to be, based on the amount of time they were reported to spend apart. When Lashley was at home, Jacqueline and Michelle would be three-day eventing in Europe. When they returned, he'd take himself off to Capri. He stayed there more and more. The dry heat of the island was certainly better for a man of his age than the humidity of Georgia. But the arrangement may have had more to commend it than that. It appeared to suit all parties.

When Vivien had last been to Capri, or Georgia, I wouldn't have liked to guess. If Adam was feeling sorry for himself, he could always have reflected on how much more fortunate he was than his half-sister. The admission she'd gained to the aristocracy by marrying the Honourable Roger had led to nothing but scandal and catastrophe. Roger's drug habit probably explained his accidental shooting (mercifully not fatal) of a rambler on a foot-path that crossed his father's estate. But six months in prison only made the habit worse. Then their son, Dylan, embodiment of so many of Vivien's hopes for the future, wrote himself off in the Lamborghini he'd been given for his twenty-first birthday. Within two years, Roger was dead of an overdose. How Vivien had coped (or not) I didn't know. Lashley confined his discussions with me to business and I never saw any other member of the family. Harriet Wren was dead by then. My mother could tell me nothing and had preoccupations of her own as my father's health began to fail. All the IK rumour mill reported was what I could easily have guessed. Vivien was a stricken soul.

The rumour mill had it that Roger's father, Viscount Horncastle, did everything he could to support Vivien. But he too was dead now and according to Pete Newlove the new viscount, Roger's younger brother, had sent her packing from the ancestral home. Her estrangement from Lashley, which Pete had also mentioned, was perhaps no great surprise. They weren't blood relatives, after all. And his second wife was the same age as Vivien. It wasn't a recipe for good or close relations. Whether through choice or circumstance, then, she was alone. No longer young, no longer wealthy, no longer a mother, she dwelt now in the ruins of her life.

The afternoon advanced. The greyness of the day deepened. And then she came.

I watched the car come to a sputtering halt next to the caravan. A woman stepped wearily out. She was wearing jeans, trainers and a baggy dark-red jumper, with an unzipped blue fleece on top. Her grey hair was tied back plainly behind her head. Her face was Vivien's, I persuaded myself with an effort, but it was the face of an altered Vivien, puffy and pallid, with loose flesh around the jaw.

She'd put on some weight. There was a bulkiness to her figure the shapelessness of her clothes couldn't conceal. And there was a stiffness to her movements. Someone who didn't know her would see a luckless old woman leading a threadbare existence. I saw the memory of the beautiful girl I'd fallen in love with. And I saw the cruelty of what she'd become.

She peered at the door of the caravan for a moment, then unlocked it and swung it open. She fetched a couple of bulging black plastic sacks from the boot of the car and went in. The door closed behind her. I waited for a minute or so, then climbed out of the Freelander and started across the yard.

When I was a few yards from the door, I heard the key turn in the lock.

I knocked and called her name. 'Vivien.'

'Go away, Jonathan,' she called back. Her voice hadn't changed at all. It was soft and slightly husky, just as I remembered.

'I only want to talk to you.'

'There's nothing for us to talk about.'

'Most of Wren and Co.'s records have gone missing. Have you heard?'

'I didn't take them.'

'I'm not accusing you of anything.'

'Have you been sent to find them?'

'Yes.'

'By Greville?'

'Who else?'

'I don't talk to people who take Greville's orders.'

'We're talking now.'

'Go away. Please.'

It was the *please* that touched my heart. I felt suddenly and deeply moved. And I couldn't think of a damn thing to say.

Vivien didn't say anything either. But she unlocked the door. And pushed it open.

We looked at each other in a frozen interval of silence, all our memories, the good and the bad, compressed between us as something solid but invisible.

325

Eventually, Vivien broke the silence. 'You remember when the circus used to come to town, Jonathan? In our childhood?'

'I remember.'

'There was always a gypsy fortune-teller. One year I pleaded with my father to let me have my fortune told. He forbade it, which was unusual. He never normally forbade me anything. "It's best not to know the future, kitten," he told me. He used to call me that sometimes – kitten. I was disappointed. I couldn't understand why anyone wouldn't want to know the future. Well, I understand now.'

'I'm sorry, Vivien,' I said, genuinely but unavailingly.

'What for?'

'Everything.'

'Most of it's none of your fault.'

'I'm still sorry.'

'It doesn't help. But thank you, anyway.'

'Can I come in?'

'To see if I'm hiding the missing files?'

'If you tell me you didn't take them, I believe you.'

'You shouldn't. I'm the obvious suspect.'

'Because of Oliver?'

'I'm glad you haven't forgotten him.'

'I'll never do that.' I took the pig's egg out of my pocket then and offered it to her. 'I thought you might like this.'

'Oliver gave it to you. You should keep it.'

'Do you have many reminders of him?'

'I have his photograph album. That's about it.'

'Are there any pictures of him in it?'

'A few.'

'I'd really like to see them. If you'll let me.'

She stared at me pensively, then nodded. 'All right. Come in, then.'

She moved back and I stepped inside. The caravan wasn't quite as cramped as I'd expected, largely because there was so little in it. Wherever most of Vivien's possessions were, they weren't there. The kitchenette at one end, the bed at the other and the living area in between were equipped with the barest of essentials. There was a tall cupboard where I assumed the contents of the black sacks had already been stowed, another cupboard under the sink and another, with sliding doors, beneath the bed. Storage space was otherwise non-existent. A pile of stolen CCC files was nowhere to be seen.

'I left just about everything I own in Lincolnshire,' she said, as if some kind of explanation was required. 'I left most of me there as well.'

'Has it got any easier . . . to bear your loss?'

'I suppose it must have. Otherwise I wouldn't still be living and breathing and . . . existing.' She took a deep breath. 'I'd rather not talk about it, Jonathan. Honestly. We can talk about Oliver. Long enough has passed since you and I saw him floating in the lake at Relurgis for us to do that. Time really is some kind of healer.'

'I haven't come here to upset you.'

'No. You've come here to find out if I know who might have removed those files. Who, when and why. Isn't that it?'

'The only person I can think of who ever showed any interest in Wren's records was—'

'Oliver.' She looked at me.

'Yes. Oliver.'

'So, I might have taken them . . . to search for what he was so interested in.'

'You might have.'

'But I didn't.'

'Who, then?'

'I don't know. Someone . . . covering their tracks.'

'Tracks of what?'

'It's your job to find out, apparently. Maybe it always was.'

'What d'you mean?'

'Oliver chose you, Jonathan. I'm not sure why. But he did.'

'Chose me to do what?'

'Finish what he started.' She stepped across to the tall cupboard, opened the door and took something down from a high shelf. It was the photograph album she'd mentioned. It had stiff black covers and a gold tassel at the spine. She laid it on the table that

327

stood in front of the window and flicked through the pages until she found what she was looking for. 'There he is,' she said softly.

It was a snapshot of Oliver as I remembered him: slim-faced and high-browed, his hair straw-blond in the slightly faded tones of the print. He was squinting in strong sunlight, his eyes in shadow. There was the faintest of smiles for the benefit of the camera. Behind him was an overgrown headland and a broad expanse of blue ocean.

'I took that near the Villa Jovis when we went to Capri in the summer of 'sixty-seven,' said Vivien. 'The pictures of Oliver in the album are amateur efforts compared with the others, because he could take those himself, obviously.'

'Was he a keen photographer?'

'In the same way he was a keen chess player. Whatever he did, he wanted to be the best at. Look at these.'

She turned several pages over in slow succession. As many of the photographs were black and white as colour. They were mostly impersonal studies of the clay country: spoil heaps, drying sheds, railway lines, mica lagoons, refining tanks, often pictured from unusual angles and either early or late in the day, to judge by the thin, slightly eerie light. There was an expertise to them that amounted in some cases to true artistry. 'I'm surprised you've never shown me these before,' I said.

'Mother kept the album at Nanstrassoe House. It didn't come into my possession until Aunt Harriet died. It's the only thing of Oliver's I have with me here. And it's the only thing I need. I can summon up his memory – I can see him again – whenever I choose to open it.'

'I'd give a lot to know what was on the last film he ever loaded into his camera.'

'So would I.' She closed the album and put it back in the cupboard.

'Do you really have no idea who might have stolen those files, Vivien?' I asked, hoping she might be just a little more forthcoming now.

She sat down at the table and looked up at me. 'No. Have you?'

I shrugged. 'None at all.'

'I suppose you could ask yourself who you know with any personal interest in them.'

'It's a short list. Most of the people who produced the documents in those files are dead and gone.'

'My stepfather isn't.'

'Your stepfather commissioned the work that led to the discovery that the files were missing, Vivien. Why would he do that if he'd stolen them?'

'I can't think of a reason. But . . .' She broke off and looked away, out through the window.

I sat down opposite her. 'But what?'

'Nothing.' She shook her head. 'There's nothing I can tell you.'

'Are you sure? You can say anything you like to me.'

'As long as I don't mind it getting back to Greville. He's your boss. You said so. You work for him.'

'You can trust me, Vivien.'

'No. I can't.' Her gaze was far more sorrowful than it was recriminatory. 'I can't even trust myself.'

'You're not going to help me, are you?'

'If you need my help, you've already failed.'

'OK.' I nodded. 'I get the message.' I stood up. 'I'll leave you to . . . whatever you fill your time with here.'

'Embroidery. And a whole lot of nothing. That's what my life amounts to now.'

'I should warn you about Adam. He was here earlier. I had to stop him forcing the door open. He was in an ugly mood.'

'So that's why there's some paint missing. Don't worry about Adam. He's always in an ugly mood. I can handle him.'

'He might have thought he'd find the missing records here.'

'He might have. But he was looking in the wrong place. He has a history of doing that. If you're right, you should ask yourself why he'd be bothered about the records in the first place.'

'Why do you think he'd be bothered?'

'I can't imagine.'

'He was worked up about something, Vivien. He was angry.

Potentially dangerous, I'd say. I don't like to think of you, alone here, in the middle of nowhere, miles from help of any kind.'

'Don't think of me, then.'

I wrote my mobile number on one of my cards and put it on the table in front of her. 'You can call me any time.'

'I won't call . . . I don't have a phone.'

'Pete Newlove said the line in the dryer office is still connected.'

'I wouldn't know. I haven't tried to use it.'

'Why not just humour me and say you'll call in an emergency?'

'All right.' She gave a weary half-smile and picked up the card. 'I'll call in an emergency.'

'Thank you.'

She folded her hands together and gazed at me neutrally. Silence accreted itself heavily between us. Then she said, 'Goodbye, Jonathan.'

THIRTY-SIX

I arrived at IK (St Austell) the following morning oppressed by gloomy thoughts about the ravages of time and the seeming impossibility of the task Greville Lashley had set me. I'd considered phoning him to ask exactly how he expected me to pull it off, but I'd known the chances of speaking to him were slim and any message I'd left would have sounded defeatist or, worse, truculent.

Truculent was in fact pretty much how I felt. Pete Newlove would doubtless have said he felt much the same if I'd made the mistake of asking him. But he and I had practical matters to discuss. I found him in his office, grimacing over a cup of coffee, the aroma of which couldn't dispel the strong smell of a recent cigarette. He greeted me grouchily and handed me a printed timetable of the one-to-one meetings with staff he'd scheduled for me.

'Thank God it's Friday, hey, Jon?' he said as I scanned it. 'You'll get two days off to recover from the first load before you tackle the second.'

'You think I'm wasting my time, Pete?'

'Your time. My time. It's all IK time. So, waste away, old chum. No skin off my nose.'

'I see you've only allocated half an hour for lunch.'

'Whip through 'em and you can have longer. You may as well be quick, since you'll have nothing to show for it. I didn't just sit on my backside after Doctor Whitworth raised the alarm, y'know. I

331

did my job. No one here knows what happened to the records.'

'You're sure of that, are you?'

'I'm sure if any of the staff succeeded in pulling the wool over my eyes they'll succeed in pulling it over yours, too.' He grinned. 'No offence, Jon.'

I sighed, unable, try as I might, to be riled by his cynicism.

'How'd it go at Lannerwrack?'

I sighed again. 'I saw Vivien. She's . . . like you said.'

'Learn anything useful?'

'Not about the records. But . . .' I glanced down at the schedule. 'The last few on here may have to stay late. I have to go out around midday. I'll be . . . an hour or so at most. But obviously it'll . . . put things back.'

'Going to the doctor, are you?'

'What?'

'I just wondered. You look as if you've got a pain. In the arse, is it?'

'You don't look so chipper yourself, Pete.'

'No? You amaze me . . . not. Anyway, you can't overrun this afternoon. Anyone you haven't got round to by five will just have to wait till Monday.'

'Why can't I overrun?'

'Because I got busy on the phone last night and fixed you and me an early-evening engagement . . . with my old schoolmate Dick Trudgeon.'

'You did?'

'Spending your whole life in the same miserable town may not broaden your mind, but it does mean you know lots of people. And those people know other people. So, I was able to track Dick down. He hasn't gone far either. Retired, like I said he'd be. And willing to chew over old times. We're meeting him at the Fountain in Mevagissey at half six. He lives down that way.'

'Was meeting in a pub your idea or his?'

'Well, we don't want his missus cramping his style, do we? And you can claim the ale on expenses. My ale, anyway. You'll be driving, so I expect you'll be on orange juice.'

'Of course.'

'A word of thanks wouldn't go amiss, Jon. "Well played, Pete, nice one." Something along those lines. You want to speak to him, don't you?'

'Yes, I do.' I cracked a conciliatory smile. 'Sorry. I'm feeling a bit fed up this morning. I'll soon snap out of it. You've done well, Pete. Thanks a lot.'

'Don't mention it. Except to Beaumont, obviously. I want you to make sure he knows I've been a model of cooperation.'

'I'll do that.' I looked at the clock on the wall behind him. 'Now, how do I get a coffee before I start the interrogations?'

The staff interviews proved as fruitless as Pete had predicted. He and I were the only former Wren's employees still on the strength. Most of those I spoke to hadn't even been born when Walter Wren & Co. ceased to exist. They were eager to please the Head Office troubleshooter they saw me as, but they couldn't help. They genuinely couldn't.

My departure at noon should have been a big relief to me, but I was only swapping a tiresome duty in favour of a potentially hazardous venture. I'd decided I should try for Vivien's sake to make Adam understand she had nothing to do with the theft of the records. It wouldn't be easy, but catching him sober and not long up gave me the best chance of success. From what I knew of his lifestyle, that meant calling by around midday.

Wavecrest was even bigger and more ostentatious than Pete had led me to expect. Set on a hillock that put it one up on its scarcely modest neighbours, and supplied a panoramic view of St Austell Bay into the bargain, it was what its architect would probably have called cutting edge: flat-roofed and white-walled, with walk-around balconies and lots and lots of blue-tinted glass. The garden didn't supply much in the way of camouflage. None of the pines and bushes had yet grown high enough to soften the rectilinearity of the house and would probably never be allowed to. Wavecrest was a statement, not a murmur.

333

The gate at the foot of the drive was electronically operated. There was an intercom for communication with the house set in the driver's-side pillar. But there was also a side gate for pedestrians and, since I was sure any talking to Adam was best done face to face, I parked the car on the grass verge at the side of the road and entered on foot.

There was no sign of Adam's Lotus, but the underground garage that came into view as I climbed the drive looked large enough to hold a whole fleet of cars. Still, I'd have bet on him wanting to exhibit his speedster for the delectation of the locals, so I began to wonder if I'd left my arrival too late.

Closer to, the blue-tinted windows revealed a mirror-like reflectiveness that rendered the interior of the house more or less invisible. Adam could have been staring out at me stark naked as I approached the door and I wouldn't have known. I pressed the bell and waited. The silence was depressingly absolute. It felt increasingly as if I was wasting my time.

Then, quite suddenly, the door sprang open. It was electronically operated, like the gate, and there was no one waiting to greet me. I stepped into a high, circular space, from which an open-treaded staircase curved up to the first floor. Double doors led off into various rooms. Filtered daylight flowed in around me.

'Hello?' I called.

'Hello,' came an echoing response, though not in Adam's voice. A young woman wearing only a short silk bathrobe and a pair of fluffy mules ambled out into the hall from what a distant glimpse of fridge-freezer suggested was the kitchen. She held a coffee mug in one hand and a phone in the other and was texting as she walked. She spared me a fleeting glance – flashing eyes beneath a tousled fringe of dark hair – and a somewhat less fleeting smile. 'You're not the aerial man, are you?'

'No.'

'Pity. Adam's not getting all his satellite channels. Puts him in a bad mood.' She stopped texting and gave me a little more attention. She was small and pretty in a girlish way. I'd have said she was still in her teens. How many like her had Adam worked his way through

334

over the years, I wondered, though I didn't really want to know the answer. 'He just went out. If it's him you wanted.' She grinned. 'He still just went out, though, come to think, even if you didn't want him.'

'It *was* Adam I was looking for. I'm from Intercontinental Kaolins. My name's Kellaway. Jonathan Kellaway.'

'Don't think so.'

'Sorry?'

'I've heard of you. But Jonathan's not your first name.'

I smiled bemusedly. 'I assure you it is.'

'No. It's Fucking. Fucking Kellaway. That's what Adam calls you.'

I had to laugh at that. 'Well, you've got me there.'

'I'm Mad.' She rolled her eyes. 'Short for Madeleine.'

'Pleased to meet you, Mad.'

'You're a friend of the family as well as one of their wage slaves, right?'

'Right.'

'So you must know Adam's sister – Vivien.'

'I do, yes.'

'He says she's *really* mad. Off her head. That so?'

'No. Not so.'

'But she's a countess. And she lives in a caravan.'

'A viscountess, Adam means. And technically she's not even one of those. But she does live in a caravan.'

'Countess; viscountess: same difference.' Mad grimaced at the contents of her coffee mug and plonked it down on a glass-topped table, then looked thoughtfully at me. 'Been here before?'

'Never.'

'What d'you think of it?'

'What do *you* think of it?'

She shrugged. 'It's all right. Come on. I'll show you what I like most about the place.'

She led the way through a large, palely decorated, modishly furnished drawing-room, followed by another room that was barely distinguishable, but might have been planned as some kind of library, to judge by the number of empty bookshelves lining two of the walls.

'How long have you and Adam known each other?' I asked as we went.

'A few months. We met in Phuket.'

Ah yes. Thailand. Of course. 'Were you on holiday there?'

She laughed. 'You could say that.'

We entered a high-ceilinged corridor and headed along it. A faint smell of chlorine told me what our destination was before we reached it.

The swimming pool was as oversized as everything else in the house: a vast rectangle of deep-blue water surrounded by white marble. Tracts of lawn were visible through high windows to either side. Everything was as it might have looked in an estate agent's brochure: lavish and empty. 'Ace, isn't it?' Mad asked, glancing back at me.

'Very nice.'

She tossed her phone into the lap of a nearby chair and kicked off her mules. 'I like to wake up with a swim,' she announced. Then she untied the belt of the bathrobe, shrugged it off and, letting it fall to the floor behind her, advanced to the edge of the pool.

I'd seen no outline of a swimsuit beneath the robe as I'd followed her through the house, so it shouldn't have come as any surprise that she wasn't wearing one. Nevertheless, as she'd doubtless intended, it did. She stood where she was for several seconds, giving me the opportunity to admire her peachy little bum, then dived in.

She swam, fast and smooth, to the far end, turned and swam back, then trod water and waved me forward.

'Why don't you come in, Jonathan? It's lovely.'

'Very tempting, but . . . no, thanks.'

'Adam wouldn't have to know.' She licked her lips. 'If that's what you're worried about.'

'When do you think he'll be back?'

'Oh, not for hours. He's playing golf. Yawn, yawn.'

'Could you tell him I called by?'

'If you want me to.'

'I do, yes. Ask him to phone me. He's got my number.'

'I know. He said so. "Fucking Kellaway. I've got his number."'
She grinned up at me mischievously.

'You're a funny girl, Mad.'

'I certainly like to have fun. Sure you won't join me?'

'I'm sure.'

'Your loss.'

'Probably.'

'Definitely. 'Bye, then.' With that she turned and swam away at
a leisurely pace, the water flowing sinuously around her.

I walked to the side of the pool, watching her for as long as it
took me to reach a set of double doors that led out on to a terrace
– and for a little longer than it took. Then I left.

During an afternoon spent fruitlessly questioning IK staff about
the theft of Wren's records, there were several times I found myself
wishing I'd taken up Mad's invitation. I resented being forced to
pursue such a half-baked investigation and my patience was wearing thin.

Meeting Dick Trudgeon was undeniably worthwhile, though.
And Pete was twitchily eager to set off for Mevagissey as the working day drew to a close. His mood was such a strange mixture of
nervousness and joviality that I began to miss his normal heavy
irony. I eventually demanded to know if something was bothering
him.

'Well, yes, I suppose so,' he admitted cagily. 'Could we talk about
it on the way? I don't want us to be late.'

Punctuality had never been one of his strengths. This alone
should have forewarned me. As it was, he talked about everything
but whatever was bothering him during the drive to Mevagissey,
preferring to distract me with gossip about the proposed eco-town
and the viability of the new shopping centre.

We arrived twenty minutes or so early and Pete proposed a
preliminary drink at the Ship, the first pub we came to after parking the car, before we moved on to meet Trudgeon at the Fountain.
The whisky chaser he ordered with his pint suggested he needed

some Dutch courage to broach a delicate subject. And so it proved.

'While you were out to lunch, Jon, I had a visit . . . from Adam Lashley.'

So, it seemed Adam hadn't been playing golf after all. 'You did?'

'Yeah. He showed up shortly after you left.'

'How shortly?'

'Well, five minutes, maybe. Does it matter?'

'It might.' It occurred to me that Adam could actually have been waiting for me to leave. It was a disturbing thought. 'What did he want?'

'A chat. He didn't come into the office. He phoned up from reception and asked me to join him downstairs. So, down I went. He ushered me outside and we took a turn round the car park while he . . . said his piece.'

'Which amounted to what?'

Pete took a deep swallow of beer. 'I'm doing you a big favour letting you in on this, Jon. A little more . . . appreciation . . . would be nice.'

'Oh, I'm appreciative, Pete, believe me.' I smiled cheesily at him. 'Now, are you going to tell me what he wanted?'

'On one condition, yeah.'

I sighed. Pete playing hard to get was the last thing I needed. 'Name it.'

'You guarantee you'll keep me in the loop on this whole business of the missing records.'

'Are you sure you want to be in the loop?'

'Better in than out, I reckon.'

'Then you have my word, Pete. You're in.'

He paused to think about that, then said, 'OK. So, here's the thing. Adam made me an offer. Ten thousand quid, to be precise, cash in hand, if I'd tell anyone who wants to know that it was me who stole the records – and destroyed them.'

'*You?*'

'Acting, Adam suggested I say, on the instructions of a senior member of staff now pushing up the daisies. There are several to choose from. I'd say I was just following orders, without knowing why the orders had been given. This would've been years back, not long after the takeover, when I was only a dogsbody. It'd mean you could stop looking for the records and Doctor Whitworth would definitely have to make do without them. End of story.'

'You think so?'

'Well, it might work. It makes some kind of sense. It would explain what's happened . . . without really explaining anything.'

'And Adam thinks achieving that's worth ten thousand pounds?'

'Apparently.'

'Why? I mean, why the hell should he care – to the extent of trying to bribe you?'

'He said he was anxious Doctor Whitworth should complete her company history while his father was still alive and well enough to read it and that this would force her to get on with it.'

'You believe that?'

'Of course not. Adam the dutiful son? Do me a favour. He's obviously lying. I let him think I believed him, though. I'd have been stupid not to.'

'And what did you say to his offer?'

'That I needed time to think about it. I pointed out I could get myself into hot water by doing what he wanted. Maybe even end up getting fired.'

'And how did he respond to that?'

'He said he'd make sure I wasn't fired. And he gave me until Monday to mull it over. I got the feeling . . . he might go higher than ten thou if I pushed him.'

'He must be desperate.'

'That's what I reckon. In fact, it's the main reason I'm telling you any of this.'

'How d'you mean?'

'Ten thou – or more – in the back pocket's not to be sniffed at, Jon. Don't you think I'm tempted to take him up on his offer?'

Yes. I did. Between Adam and his girlfriend, there'd been a lot of tempting going on. 'What stopped you?'

'The question you asked a few minutes ago. *Why?* Why should Adam be two bits bothered about missing records, half of them dating from before he was born? It shouldn't matter to him. But it does. Too much for me to overlook – whatever he's willing to pay me. And besides . . . I don't like him. I never have.'

I smiled. 'What are you going to say to him on Monday, then?'

'I'm hoping I won't have to say anything to him. I'm hoping you and me will have figured out by then what he's up to – what it is he's trying to hide.'

'*You and me.*' It was an interesting choice of phrase. Pete evidently regarded us as a team. 'Do you think Adam took the records?' I asked.

'Maybe.'

'Why?'

Pete shrugged. 'He might have been following orders. Like he wants me to say I was.'

'Whose orders?'

'I haven't a clue. Have you?'

'Not yet. Let's hope Dick Trudgeon can supply one.'

'Yeah. Let's hope.' Pete glanced at the clock behind the bar and drained his whisky. 'And let's hope that clock's fast. Otherwise we're keeping him waiting.'

THIRTY-SEVEN

Dick Trudgeon was an archetype of the policemen of our generation: tall, broad-shouldered and slowly spoken. He had white, crinkly hair and a large, crumpled nose that looked as if it had been broken by a Friday-night brawler many years in the past. His expression was a mixture of wariness and contentment. He had a seat by the front window of the Fountain and could, I realized, have seen us enter the Ship if he'd been there early enough, which the inroads he'd made into his pint of HSD suggested he might well have been.

I bought him another pint, and ten minutes of chitchat about our schooldays and subsequent careers carried us to a point where he evidently felt we should show our hand. 'I'm sure Pete here didn't go to all the bother of tracking me down just for the pleasure of a chinwag about old times,' he said, eying me beadily.

'You're right, of course, Dick,' I responded. 'We're actually hoping you'll be able to help us clear up a minor mystery.'

'Oh yes? And what might that be?'

What I told him was accurate as far as it went. Someone had removed from the IK archive all records relating to Wren & Co.'s dealing with his father's haulage company and we wanted to know why.

His reaction was understandably sceptical. 'Haven't you boys got more urgent business to attend to?'

'You'd think so, wouldn't you?' Pete chimed in. 'But our boss doesn't like loose ends. And he pays the likes of us to tie them up for him.'

'Your boss would be . . . Greville Lashley?'

'The very same.'

'Is he still in harness? He must be about the same age as my old dad. That'd put him in his nineties.'

'He officially retired some years ago,' I said. 'But he continues to . . . take an interest.'

'Good for him.'

'What about your dad, Dick?' Pete asked.

'No longer with us. Nor is my brother, Mike. He was Dad's number two in the business till it was sold to Wren's. I was never on the payroll. Saw no future in it.'

'Well, you judged that right,' I said.

'So I did, I suppose. But the Wren's buy-out was a godsend. It funded Dad's early retirement to Spain. And it set Mike up in a business of his own. It was a good deal for them. A very good deal.'

'An A licence was a valuable commodity in those days,' said Pete.

'So I'm told.' Trudgeon frowned thoughtfully. 'Except that Wren's were bought out themselves within a couple of years by CCC. So, it was money down the drain really, wasn't it?'

'I expect Mr Lashley hoped it would boost Wren's profitability in the long run,' I reasoned smilingly. 'Unfortunately, there was no long run.'

'That must have been how it was, yes.' But Trudgeon's tone suggested he was far from convinced. 'Dad did well out of it, though. He always did well out of Wren's. He used to say they were his best customers. Even before the buy-out.'

'Really?'

Trudgeon nodded. '"Good payers; prompt payers". That's what he used to say about Wren's. It was a catch-phrase of his. I was still living at home then. I remember Mike and him making a joke of it.'

'A joke?'

'They'd laugh about it. Mum and I couldn't understand why it was so funny.'

'I'm with you and your mum on that,' said Pete.

342

'How much did Wren's pay for the business?' I asked, looking across at Pete.

He shrugged. 'I don't know. Info like that wasn't doled out to the lower ranks. Dick?'

Trudgeon gave a shrug of his own. 'I wasn't told the exact figure. But you boys could find out if you wanted to, couldn't you? Surely there's a—' He broke off.

'A record of it somewhere?' Pete grinned at me, even though there was nothing to grin about.

'Have you any idea why someone would want to strip Wren's files of paperwork relating to Trudgeon Haulage, Dick?' I asked. It was time to pose the question directly.

He pondered his answer for a long time, then said, 'Dad and Mike are both dead. I suppose it can't do any harm to tell you.' There was another lengthy pause. He drank some beer. He looked at each of us in turn. And then: 'It's strange you two digging this up after so long. I haven't thought about it in donkey's years. I wasn't sure what to make of it at the time. To be honest, I wasn't too keen to get to the bottom of it. I'd only just started with the force. The last thing I needed was . . . dodgy dealing by members of my own family. So, I . . . turned a deaf ear.

'A deaf ear to what, you're wondering.' He sighed. 'Well, this would have been January or February of 'sixty-nine. I can't remember more exactly than that. But it was certainly early in the year. A cold, wet weekday night. The kind of night when you did more standing in doorways than pounding the beat. St Austell was quiet as the grave. Until I heard the sound of glass being smashed down East Hill as I was walking along South Street. I stepped on it then and found this fellow, drunk as a lord, standing outside Wren's old offices. They were still unoccupied after the takeover by CCC. He'd thrown an empty whisky bottle at one of the windows and broken it. There was quite a lot of glass about. He was swaying like a corn-stalk in the breeze and swearing like a trooper. Angry about something, but too far gone to make sense. I arrested him as drunk and disorderly and marched him off to the station.

'It was as the sergeant was booking him that he caught my name.

That really seemed to set him off. "I've done enough for your father and your brother over the years for you to overlook a bit of broken glass." That kind of thing. I didn't know what he was on about, though the sarge raised an eyebrow at me. He was still hollering when we put him in a cell for the night. By next morning, he'd quietened down. But he hadn't forgotten me and mine. He said my brother would go bail for him. And damn me if he didn't. Mike delivered the money straight after the magistrate had remanded him. I remember Mike told me to steer clear of the subject with Dad. "Least said, soonest mended," was how he put it.'

'You're talking about Gordon Strake, aren't you?' Pete cut in. 'I remember reading he'd been fined in the paper.'

'That was his name, yes. Strake. A former sales rep for Wren's. Given the boot for drunkenness, I shouldn't wonder.'

'Did you ever ask your brother what Strake had done for him and your father, Dick?' I pressed.

He shook his head. 'No. It sounded to me as if some form of corruption was involved. I really didn't want to know. Mike told me he'd make sure Strake left town and I was . . . well, not happy, of course, but . . . relieved, I suppose . . . to leave it at that.'

'And this . . . corruption . . . could be the reason the records were stolen?'

'Well, it could be, couldn't it? If I had to name a suspect, I'd go for Strake.'

'Long dead, I'm afraid.'

'Easy to blame, then. That should be good news for you boys. A neat explanation to serve up to your boss.' Trudgeon squinted at me. 'You don't look very pleased about it, though.'

Trudgeon headed home not long after, claiming his supper would be spoiling. He thanked us for the beer and we thanked him for his frankness. Quite where his frankness had taken us was hard to say, however. Pete was gagging for a cigarette by then, so we stepped round to the harbour, where seagulls were feasting from discarded chip wrappers and the setting sun was casting a queasy light on the house fronts of the town.

'It comes back to Strake,' I mused as Pete greedily inhaled his first lungful of smoke. 'It always seems to.'

'You really think he stole the records?' Pete asked through a spluttering cough.

'I'd like to. It'd be . . . convenient. But I'm not sure. He didn't know his way around the building, did he? And there were quite a few people who'd have recognized him and queried why he was there.'

'I've meant to ask you before how you reckon he ended up getting himself murdered – in Naples, of all places. I was surprised when I heard that on the grapevine, I can tell you. You were there at the time, weren't you?'

'I was staying at the Villa Orchis on Capri. I wasn't in Naples.'

'Same neck of the woods, though. What d'you think took Strake there?'

'If I had to guess, I'd say he was planning to touch Francis Wren for a loan, but he got into trouble – fatal trouble – before he had the chance.'

'Well, that would be like him, I suppose. There's no chance his murder's connected to our little mystery, then?'

There was every chance, of course. I knew that. And so, I suspected, did Pete. 'No way to tell,' I said neutrally.

'And forty years too late to ask Strake to explain himself.'

'Yes. It is.' As I spoke, a thought struck me. Maybe, by an indirect route, it wasn't too late. 'Hold on, though. There was a sister in Plymouth. She wrote to Lashley, notifying him of her brother's death. Strake had been living with her prior to his trip to Italy. He must have gone there after Mike Trudgeon gave him his marching orders from St Austell.'

'Got a name for this sister, have you? Or an address?'

'No. But Lashley probably filed the letter in CCC's personnel records.'

'Meaning it wouldn't be in the stuff that's gone missing.'

'Exactly.'

'She could be dead herself, Jon. Or gaga in a home. Or Lashley might have thrown the letter away.'

'Or she mightn't be dead. Or gaga. And the letter might be in the file.'

'Yeah.' Pete drew on his cigarette. 'We'd better check, hadn't we?'

'First thing in the morning?'

He nodded. 'Bright and early.'

And early it certainly was when I drove into the virtually empty car park at IK (St Austell) the following morning. None of the few members of staff planning to spend part of their Saturday in the office had yet arrived, with one exception.

Pete was waiting for me by the main entrance, puffing on a cigarette. His red-rimmed eyes and grimacing expression suggested the whisky chasers had caught up with the pints of beer overnight and formed a head-splitting combination. He didn't look to have shaved either. All in all, he wasn't a pretty sight.

'I hope this'll be worth the effort,' he growled as we went in.

'So do I, Pete.'

'We'll have to go up to my office to get the keys for the CCC cages. Fortunately, that's where the kettle is. I need a strong black coffee.'

'Looking at you, I'd have to agree.'

'Yeah, well, I haven't had the benefit of a full English and a cafetière of the finest Colombian, have I?'

'Chez Newlove doesn't run to that?'

'Take a guess.'

'On the whole, I'd rather not.'

All I got by way of a response as he made a stumbling start on the stairs was a defiant V-sign.

Fifteen minutes later, we were in the basement, heading for the cage containing CCC records from the sixties and seventies, with Pete slurping coffee from a mug as we went.

The box-files looked the same as those used for Wren's records, but we were confident we weren't going to be confronted by sheet after sheet of blank paper, if only because Fay Whitworth had already examined them. And our confidence was rewarded. The records were intact.

Or so they appeared to be. But the personnel files contained no letter written to Lashley by Gordon Strake's sister in the summer of 1969. We checked meticulously. It just wasn't there. Pete unhelpfully repeated his suggestion that Lashley had thrown it away.

But he hadn't. He just hadn't passed it on to the personnel department. When we sifted through the files of the department he'd been responsible for at CCC, Logistics, there it was, with a note in his handwriting: *No action required.* An understandable statement – at the time.

I held the letter under the light to read, with Pete craning over my shoulder.

12 Gascoyne Terrace
Plymouth
Devon

18th July 1969

Dear Mr Lashley,
I am writing to tell you that my brother, Gordon Strake,
died on the ninth of this month. As you were his employer
at Walter Wren & Co., I thought you ought to know,
because I remember he said he would be due a pension from
the company. He lived here after leaving St Austell earlier
this year and remained a bachelor, so there will be no
widow's pension due either. If you need any more
information, my telephone number is Plymouth 68115.

Yours sincerely,
Dora Strake

'Do you think he rang her?' Pete asked.
'Probably not. But I'm going to ring her. Now.'

'She wrote that more than forty years ago, Jon. What are the chances of her picking up the phone and saying, "Oh yes. *That* letter. Thanks for getting back to me"?'

'Only one way to find out.'

'As long as you're prepared to be disappointed.'

'I'm *always* prepared to be disappointed.'

According to Pete, Plymouth 68115 was sure to have acquired an extra digit since 1969, supposing it was still connected. He was right. And it was. The woman who answered sounded much younger than Dora Strake was bound to be. But my luck was in. She knew Dora.

'We bought this house from her three years ago, when she moved into sheltered accommodation.'

'Do you happen to know her address?'

'Oh yes. We send her a card every Christmas.'

'And a phone number?'

'Yes. Do you want it?'

A few minutes later, I was talking to Dora herself. It had been almost too simple. But simplicity wasn't going to carry me much further. Courteous though she was, Dora was also understandably puzzled.

'You're phoning about Gordon? My brother Gordon? And you used to work for Wren's, you say?'

'I know it's all a long time ago, Miss Strake. But—'

'A *very* long time.'

'I knew your brother. Not well, but . . . our paths crossed. I've never quite understood the circumstances of his death. It happened in Naples, I believe.'

'He was murdered, Mr Kellaway. The Italian police never discovered who'd killed him. Or why. It was dreadful. Just dreadful. He's buried there, you know, in Naples. I sometimes wish . . .' There was a silence. Then: 'Never mind.'

'Something's happened, Miss Strake. Something that might – just might – help to explain what occurred in Naples.'

348

'Really?'

'I was wondering if perhaps we could meet.'

As I'd calculated, there was no chance Dora Strake would refuse to talk to me once the bait had been dangled before her of a possible explanation of her brother's murder. I set off for Plymouth a few hours later – alone, despite Pete's pleas to accompany me. I claimed Dora might be alarmed if we arrived mob-handed, although she'd sounded unflappable enough. The truth was that there were aspects of my involvement with Strake I didn't want to have to disclose to Pete. Having him along threatened to cramp my style. I consoled him with the promise of a full account of the trip when I got back.

THIRTY-EIGHT

Hillingdon Court was a purpose-built block of sheltered apartments off Mannamead Road, set in its own leafy, well-maintained grounds. Whatever Dora Strake had done with her life, it had evidently been more remunerative than anything her brother had accomplished, although, of course, she'd wasted much less money than he had on booze, cigarettes and three-legged racehorses.

She was a small, bright-eyed, white-haired old lady, gingerly arthritic in her movements but quite obviously in full possession of her wits. The intense concentration with which she received my account of how I'd tracked her down was a warning in itself. She wasn't to be trifled with.

I suppressed my personal knowledge of what Strake had been up to during the trip to Naples he'd never returned from, but I volunteered everything else – the missing records, the evidence Strake had been following Oliver, the claims he'd made at the time of his arrest by PC Trudgeon. What Dora would make of it all I had no idea. But I felt sure she was intelligent enough to know her brother had been no saint, and candour tends to reward candour in my experience.

'Dear, dear, dear,' was her first response. Her further thoughts were delayed by the fetching of hot water to top up the teapot. Then: 'It would be pointless to deny Gordon had a shady side to him, Mr Kellaway. I could blame it on the war. He spent so long away in the army, seeing things and doing things that may have made him . . . mistrustful of humanity. But it won't quite wash, will it? Thousands of other young men did their bit without losing what my father would have called their moral compass. Gordon was a great disappointment to him. "Your trouble, boy," he used to say, "is that you think the world owes you a living. Well, it doesn't." Now my father had his faults – more than a few – but I fear he was quite right where Gordon was concerned.

'He was my brother. I loved him. But I wasn't blind to his weaknesses. I hoped the job with Wren's would put him on the right road and for a long time I thought it had. He never told me he'd been sacked until he came to stay with me in the early months of 1969. And he never said why he'd left St Austell. I assumed he'd turned to me because he was short of money, though he always seemed to have plenty to spend in the pubs and betting shops. Then he announced that some work had come his way and off he went. To Italy, as it turned out.'

'Did he say what kind of work?'

'No. He was cagey about it, very cagey. Not that that was unusual. He was always one to play his cards close to his chest. To be honest, I was glad to see the back of him. We didn't part on the best of terms, something I've long regretted. When the police told me he'd been murdered, in Naples . . . well, I was dumbstruck. I had no idea he'd been planning to leave the country.'

She looked at me apologetically. 'It's kind of you to have come all this way to speak to me, Mr Kellaway. I dare say Gordon's murder may well have had something to do with these other things you've told me about him. But what it all amounts to – what exactly he was doing and at whose say-so – I'm afraid I simply can't imagine. Do you think he may have stolen the records that have gone missing . . . to cover his tracks in some way?'

'It's possible, though actually I doubt he could have stolen them.'

'Well, you'd know better than me.'

'I was hoping he might have let something slip during his stay with you that could point us towards an explanation.'

'Alas, no. Gordon was terribly secretive. And infuriatingly tight-lipped.' She smiled at some fond memory. 'He was very protective towards me when we were growing up. I suppose that's what made me so tolerant of his . . . prickliness in later life. All I can tell you is this: I felt he was . . . waiting for something while he was here. A message. An order. Then he got it. I don't know how. He never used my telephone. And no one ever phoned him. He never had any post either. But he was careful about things like that. He'd use call-boxes. Or he'd talk some pub land-lord into holding letters for him. That was the sort of man he was. "Always look after number one, Dor," he used to say. "First rule of life." Sadly, he didn't prove to be very good at it, did he? Father often predicted he'd come to a bad end. And so he did.'

'He never mentioned Wilf or Mike Trudgeon?'

'Not that I can remember.'

'Or Oliver Foster?'

'No. Though I may have mentioned Oliver Foster to Gordon. His death was reported in the *Western Morning News*. And the connection with Wren's stuck in my mind. I don't recall anything Gordon said about it, though. Probably because he *didn't* say anything.'

'No. I don't suppose he did.' I sighed. 'It seems to be a recurring theme.'

'I'm sorry to disappoint you, Mr Kellaway. It looks as if Gordon took his secrets with him to the grave. I'd like to know what they were every bit as much as you would. But I don't think we're going to find out, do you?'

I'd arrived in Plymouth optimistic that at last, at long last, I was going to break through to the truth. I left not merely frustrated by a wasted journey but despondent about my chances of ever learning anything new. The secrets I was chasing were too old, the keepers of them too long dead. I'd embarked on a ghost hunt, but the ghosts steadfastly refused to walk.

*

I phoned Pete as promised and he was waiting for me in the bar when I reached the White Hart. He didn't seem surprised I'd drawn a blank.

'I tried to warn you, Jon. Without your own personal Tardis, you're never going to find out what happened, and why, forty-plus years ago.'

'What d'you suggest I do, then?'

'Give up. And drink up. What d'you say to a Saturday night pub crawl?'

When I woke next morning, thick-headed and raw-throated, I wished I'd turned Pete down. All I could recall of the evening was boozy reminiscence and swaying transits of St Austell town centre, hedged about with the troubling conviction that I'd made a fool of myself, though exactly how was, like much else, unclear.

Maybe, I reflected as I stood under the shower, some such outcome was only to have been expected, considering a fool's errand was what I'd been sent on. If so, it was time to accept the futility of what I'd been asked to do. I'd finish my questioning of IK staff, compose some kind of report about the missing records, email it to Presley Beaumont and then . . . go home.

Wherever home was. My peripatetic career and recent domestic solitude hadn't equipped me to pronounce on the subject with any confidence. Retirement would make it a subject I couldn't ignore. Maybe it was one more deserving of my attention than puzzling gaps in the archives of a small and long defunct china clay company. Maybe I should let the past take care of itself.

I cut through the worst of the hangover with a pot of strong black coffee, skipped the rest of breakfast and headed out in the Freelander. It was still early for a Sunday and I had the roads largely to myself. The weather was cool and clear. There was a cleansing freshness in the air. I drove up to Goss Moor, parked where Oliver had insisted I park that last day of his life, forty-two years before, and stood where he'd posed for his photograph.

'Why have me take pictures you knew no one would ever see,

Oliver?' I murmured. 'Why play such an elaborate game when you knew you were never going to finish it?'

'*You can't afford to do all your thinking during the game,*' I remembered him telling me about tournament chess, although chess, of course, wasn't really what he was talking about. '*You have to prepare yourself properly. You have to play the game in your head before you move a single pawn.*'

'Did that mean you knew it was going to turn out like this? Did that mean you knew I'd never understand?'

'*You helped me, Jonathan. And I'm grateful. You drive on. I'll be fine.*'

His final words to me. An acknowledgement. A farewell. A benediction. And maybe the only kind of ending there was ever going to be.

I drove back the same way I had that summer evening in 1968, by way of Roche and Scredda. The route, like everything else, had been chosen by Oliver, chosen for his particular purposes. I didn't stop where I'd dropped him at the roadside, near Relurgis Pit, but I found myself glancing in the rear-view mirror as I drove past, half expecting to see him shouldering his knapsack and starting up the bank. He wasn't there, of course. He was gone, long gone. But still I sensed he was watching me. If so, I felt sure, there was nothing for him to watch.

The road into St Austell from Scredda took me past the IK offices and my old school and then the library, where I'd met Oliver to deliver the bar of soap containing the pattern of Wren's basement key. The younger me kept pace effortlessly with my older, scarcely wiser self.

As I crossed the bridge over the railway line in Carlyon Road, I noticed someone I half recognized hurrying towards the station. A second glance confirmed it was Mad, Adam's girlfriend. She was wearing a short pink mac, jeans and Ugg boots and was struggling along with a large, bulging shoulder-bag, large enough, I suspected, to hold most of her few possessions.

It was too late by then to turn down towards the station myself. I had to head on to the roundabout at the top of East Hill before doubling back. By the time I drove into the station forecourt, Mad was nowhere to be seen. I pulled into a short-stay parking space and hurried into the ticket office.

She was turning away from the counter, ticket in hand, when she saw me. She flinched with surprise. 'Oh, hi,' she said, her voice drained of all the confidence and ebullience I remembered from our previous encounter.

The reason was hard to miss: an angrily swollen black eye. 'What happened to you?' I asked at once.

'I don't want to talk about it,' she said, looking past me towards the platforms.

'Are you leaving?'

'Er, yeah. I'm going . . . to London. To, er . . . stay with a mate.'

'When's the train?'

She glanced at the clock. 'About . . . twenty minutes.'

'Maybe I could buy you a coffee.' I gestured towards the café.

'Nah. That's . . . all right.'

'Come on. You look as if you need one. And I certainly do.'

She weakened. 'I suppose . . . All right, then. Ta.'

I took her bag, sat her down at one of the tables and went to fetch our coffees. I watched her as I waited to pay. She was staring out through the café's picture window at the taxi rank and, beyond it, the grey roofscape of St Austell. She seemed both younger and older than when I'd met her at Wavecrest: weaker and more vulnerable, yet harder and grimmer.

'There you go,' I said, delivering her coffee and sitting down.

'Are you catching the train?' she asked, frowning at me sideways as she tilted her face to deny me a clear view of her black eye.

'No. I was driving past. I stopped when I saw you.'

'Why?'

'You looked like you were . . . leaving town.'

'I am. What's it to you?'

'I was . . . surprised. That's all.'

355

'Life's full of surprises.'

'Such as finding out Adam has a violent temper?'

'I already—' She stopped and chewed her lip. 'I don't want to talk about Adam.'

'No. I don't suppose you do.'

'Could I . . . ask you a favour?'

'Sure.'

'Don't tell him . . . you saw me here.'

'OK. I won't.'

'Thanks . . . Jonathan.'

'How old are you, Mad?'

'Why d'you want to know?'

'It's just a question.'

'All right. Sorry, I'm . . . nineteen.'

'Nineteen. Good.'

'Why's it good?'

'Because you have plenty of time to start again. And again and again, if it comes to it. Forget Adam. Forget all about him. That's my advice.'

'I might take it.'

'You should.'

She raised a feeble little smile. 'I bet you wish you could forget about him.'

I laughed. 'You're right there.'

'He's . . . not always a bastard.'

'I'm sure he isn't.'

'It's just there are . . . lines. When you cross them . . . you wish you hadn't.'

'What sort of lines?'

'Well, like . . . him and that fucking garage.'

'The garage?'

'At Wavecrest. Adam always gets the car out and has me meet him on the drive. Even in the rain. I wasn't allowed to go down there. Made a big thing of it. Such a big thing I . . . well, I decided I would . . . just to spite him. I mean, I waited till he was out, obviously. I'm not stupid. And I didn't touch anything. But . . .

356

somehow . . . he knew.' She shook her head. 'He's so fucking suspicious.'

'Is that why he hit you?'

She raised a hand to her brow, masking her black eye. 'Yeah. He went completely ape. I've never seen him so . . .' Her gaze fell. 'It wasn't just the eye.'

'When was this?'

'Yesterday afternoon. He was all, like, kissy-kissy-make-it-better later. But . . . I'd decided by then I had to clear out. It's golf again this morning, so . . .'

'You grabbed your chance.'

'Yeah.' She took her hand away and looked at me directly. 'It's a joke, really. There's nothing to see in the garage. You'd think he was, like, hiding a body down there, but all that's there are tools and polishes for the Lotus and a pile of boxes.'

'Boxes?'

'Yeah. Half a dozen cardboard boxes, stacked against the wall.'

'What's in them?'

'Dunno. I didn't look. They're sealed with . . . brown tape, y'know? I knew he'd notice if I opened one, so I . . . left well alone.'

'Anything written on the boxes?'

'The name of some removal company. Printed, like. Nothing written. They're all the same. I guess they're stuff . . . he never got round to unpacking.'

'Could be.'

'What is it?'

'Sorry?'

'The way you're frowning. It's like . . . you know what's in the boxes. And it isn't just . . . stuff.'

I shrugged. 'How could I know?'

She took a gulp of coffee and stared at me. 'He's frightened of you.'

'Adam? Never.'

'Yes, he is. And this is why, isn't it?'

'Mad, I can assure you I—'

'I don't want to know,' she cut in. 'So there's no need to deny it.

I'm getting out. I'm finished with Adam. I should never have started. He's too old for me. And too . . .' She flapped a hand dismissively in lieu of analysing Adam's assorted neuroses. 'Can we go outside? I'm dying for a ciggy.'

After she'd smoked her yearned-for cigarette, we went back into the station and I stood with her on the platform, waiting for the London train. She babbled on about the friend she was going to stay with. I listened politely. We said no more about Adam. When the train was announced, I persuaded her to let me give her some money for the journey, though I reckoned what I handed over would last her longer than that. She gave me a preposterously passionate kiss by way of thanks. 'You should have taken that swim with me, Jonathan,' she said, grinning mischievously. I couldn't help grinning back. Then the train came rumbling in.

After it had left, with Mad safely aboard, I walked back to the car and phoned Pete.

He sounded as if I'd woken him up. 'What can I . . . do for you, Jon . . . this beautiful Sunday morning?'

'You can make some coffee. I'm coming straight round.'

'*What?*'

'Coffee, Pete. We have to talk. I'm on my way.'

Pete's flat was conveniently close to both IK and the town centre. He'd admitted to me the night before that he should have invested in somewhere bigger and smarter, but the inertia of the un-ambitious bachelor had got the better of him. I found him wandering around in his dressing-gown, coffee mug in one hand, cigarette in the other, amidst unwashed dishes and flung-aside newspapers. He looked like a man who found the chaos of his surroundings entirely congenial and he sounded as if he'd have much preferred to be left to wallow in them.

'Let me get this straight,' he said when I'd finished. 'You reckon the boxes this girl Mad saw in the garage at Wavecrest contain the missing records?'

'Isn't it obvious? That's why Adam wants you to say you got rid of them. To cover his tracks. And it's why he went berserk when he discovered Mad had disobeyed him and gone down to the garage. Because that's where he's hidden them.'

'Or his pornography collection. You don't *know* the records are there. You can't.'

'No. But I *can* find out, with your help.'

Pete swallowed some coffee and grimaced at me. 'Oh, no . . .'

'Look, all you have to do is phone Adam and say you want to call round this evening to discuss his proposal. He'll think you want to haggle over the price he's offered. Fine. Haggle away. As long as you ask to use the loo first. Leave the window open so I can climb in and cut down to the garage while you keep Adam busy.'

'What if he refuses to see me?'

'He won't. He's desperate for you to agree you'll confess to stealing the records.'

'OK. But what if . . . he sends me to an upstairs loo?'

'For God's sake, Pete, why would he? There'll be one for visitors on the ground floor. Just get in there and open the window. You can leave the rest to me.'

'What is the rest?'

'I take a look inside those boxes.'

'And then?'

'And then we'll know.'

'And Adam will know we know.'

'If I'm right, he has a lot of explaining to do. He may as well start by explaining to us.'

'Great. He'll be delighted to do that, I'm sure.'

'I can't do this without you, Pete. I need your help.'

'Remind me. What do I get out of this?'

'My gratitude. Greville Lashley's gratitude too, if we can put Doctor Whitworth back to work.'

'By exposing his son as a thief.'

'Adam has it coming.'

'I wouldn't disagree with that.'

'So . . .' I clapped him on the shoulder. 'We're on then, are we?'

The only answer I got was a scowl. But there was something about it I took to be affirmative.

THIRTY-NINE

Adam agreed to see Pete at ten o'clock. The late hours he kept worked in our favour, since it meant I could operate under cover of darkness. We travelled out to Carlyon Bay in Pete's Vauxhall, after he'd heroically limited himself to one nerve-settling whisky at the White Hart before setting off.

The gates of Wavecrest stood open and we drove straight in, although I only knew they were open because Pete told me. By then I was curled up behind the passenger seat, with a blanket over my head. 'Here we bloody go, then,' he added, by way of encouragement.

He stopped at the top of the drive, murmured, 'No sign of him yet,' then got out and slammed the door behind him. A few seconds passed. I heard the faint chime of a doorbell. A few more seconds passed. There was a distant burble of conversation. Then silence.

I waited a full, uncomfortable couple of minutes, then untangled myself and got out of the car, crouching low to avoid being noticed from the house, even though there was no reason to think Adam would be in a position to notice me. I closed the car door as quietly as I could, then headed for the side of the house, where a path led round to the back.

I was wearing dark clothes and carrying a torch. It belonged to Pete. I'd bought fresh batteries for it, along with a Stanley knife, in B & Q that afternoon. I'd checked about three times that my phone was off. I was as ready as I was ever going to be.

There were lights on in virtually every room of the house. Adam was profligate in all things, almost as a matter of policy. The swimming pool was fully lit and there were a few lamps dotted around the garden as well, to show off the topiary. I suspected Adam had taken Pete into the drawing-room, on the far side of the house from me. But I took no chances, clinging to the deepest of the shadows.

Several minutes crept by slowly enough for me to realize how cold a night it was, with a keen breeze blowing in off the sea. Then a light came on in a narrow, frosted window just beyond the kitchen. And then the window was opened wide. I saw Pete peering anxiously out, but I didn't move. The plan was simple. It didn't require contact at this stage. He flushed the loo, then left, switching the light off and closing the door behind him.

That was my cue. Steering a curving course across the terrace to avoid the glare of the kitchen lights, I reached the open window and peered in. I could see little beyond the top of the loo cistern. It was clearly going to be a scramble, but it was manageable. Noise was what I had to avoid at all costs. I propped the torch on the cistern, heaved myself up by the window frame, then slowly and gingerly slithered to the floor.

I picked up the torch and eased the door open. An open door to my right led to the kitchen. A passage continued past it towards the entrance hall. I could hear voices somewhere, and a chink of glass. Adam was dispensing drinks. He was probably acting the part of the generous, smiling host, waiting to hear just what Pete had to say for himself. '*Well, make him wait a little longer,*' I silently urged my reluctant accomplice.

I braced myself and entered the kitchen. The lighting was stark and powerful. There was no hiding-place here. I hurried through to the utility room.

The door straight ahead of me led out to the back of the house. Turning, I saw another door that was clearly the one I wanted. I moved across to it, lowered the handle carefully and opened it. There were stairs leading down. There were lights too, of course, but I decided to rely on the torch. I stepped through, switching the torch on as I closed the door behind me.

The stairs were concrete. There was no danger of creaks. I descended in silence and emerged through another door into the garage. The Lotus stood ready for Adam's next outing, slewed extravagantly across a space that could have accommodated three cars with ease. I ran the torchbeam along the rear wall and saw the boxes almost at once, stacked beneath a shelf holding various tins and brushes.

They were as Mad had described them: half a dozen cardboard boxes, all the same size and in good condition, with *Pickford's – the Careful Movers* printed on the sides facing me. There were no labels to reveal their contents. But I felt sure I knew what was in them.

I lifted one down, set it on the floor and, wielding the Stanley knife, slashed through the brown tape sealing the lid. Then I prised it open and shone the torch in.

Walter Wren & Co., East Hill, St Austell, Cornwall. I saw the letterhead and a date beneath: *14 April 1966*. There was no doubt, then. These were the missing documents.

I sifted through them. They comprised a bundle of letters and memos from the spring of 1966. Lashley's signature appeared on several, along with notes in his handwriting. Then came a folder stuffed with receipts and invoices from the same period and another bundle of letters and memos. A mention of the name Trudgeon caught my eye on one of the letters. I pulled it out.

It was a memo from Lashley to George Wren, dated 24 May 1966, headed *Trudgeon Acquisition*:

The urgency which I referred to in my memorandum of the 20th resided in the rarity of such opportunities. The board agreed some time since that we should endeavour by all means to obtain an A licence in order to carry out our own haulage operations. The price I negotiated with Trudgeon was in the circumstances a reasonable one. I believe you will look back upon it in future years as a bargain.

Someone had underlined the word *bargain* in green ink and had added a note in the margin, written in ballpoint with such force

363

that the strokes of the pen had dented the flimsy copy paper. *A bargain for GL, not Wren's!!!*

It was Oliver's writing. I felt absolutely certain of that, even though, as far as I could recall, it was the first example I'd ever seen. But the choice of green ink, the triple exclamation marks and the accusatory tone clinched it. No filing clerk would have done this. It was Oliver. It had to be. I pulled the memo out and stuffed it in my pocket, planning already to ask Vivien to confirm it was in her brother's hand.

But what did it mean? *A bargain for GL, not Wren's!!!* Whoever had stolen the records and hidden them here must know. And that meant Adam knew too.

I cast around with the torch, found a light switch and pressed it down. A few clicks and a hum, then fluorescent light flooded the garage. I considered carrying the box upstairs, dumping it in Adam's lap and demanding an explanation. Then I decided to bring him to me instead. I rounded the vast bonnet of the Lotus and yanked at the driver's door, intending to get his attention with a few blares on the horn.

The door was locked. But that didn't matter, as it turned out, because my attempt to open the door set the car's alarm off: a deafening electronic yowl. I covered my ears and stepped back.

I didn't have to wait more than a couple of minutes. The door from the stairway was flung open and Adam charged into the garage. He stopped when he saw me, his face flushed, his mouth half open, his eyes piggish and angry.

'Turn it off,' I shouted, though the noise meant he'd have needed to lip-read to know what I was saying. '*Turn the damn thing off.*'

He got the message, one way or another. He pulled out the key-remote and silenced the alarm. With the silence came also a strange, expectant stillness. Pete was standing in the doorway behind Adam. He looked worried. Adam, on the other hand, looked on the brink of vein-bursting fury.

'What the fuck's going on?' he demanded.

'You know what's going on, Adam,' I replied coolly. 'I found the missing records in those boxes.' I pointed towards them. 'Where you've been hiding them.'

'You had no right to come down here.' He glared over his shoulder at Pete. 'You helped him, didn't you? I'll destroy you for this, Newlove.'

'You'll destroy no one, Adam,' I said forcing him to look back at me. 'Unless it's yourself. Pete's only done what I told him to do. And I've only done what your father told *me* to do. So, are you going to explain?'

'To you? Why should I?'

'Because I'm here with your father's full authority. And he'll expect an explanation.'

'You don't know what you're talking about. You don't under- stand a single fucking thing.'

'Make me understand, then.'

He stared at me, mouth quivering. But no words came. Then he said, 'All right.' He summoned a defiant smile. 'Have it your way.' He thumbed a button on the remote. The Lotus flashed its indicators in welcome. Then he pressed a switch on the wall behind him and the garage door began to roll slowly upwards. 'There's something I need to show you.'

He reached the passenger door of the car in a couple of strides, opened it and leant inside. I couldn't see what he was doing from where I was standing, but I guessed he was looking for something. When he closed the door and stood upright again, he was holding a gun. And he was pointing it straight at me.

'Tell Newlove to stay where he is,' he said icily.

'What's happening, Jon?' Pete called to me, seeing the change in my expression.

'He has a gun, Pete.'

'Oh, Christ.' Pete looked instantly sick with fear.

'Stay where you are,' I said.

'Sure, sure.'

'Let's all keep calm. Hey, Adam?'

'Yeah,' said Adam. 'Calm as you please.'

'Why don't we—'

'Why don't *you* listen to me? You and Vivien worked this out, didn't you? The two of you, scheming and conspiring against me, plotting to steel my inheritance.'

'Vivien knows nothing about this.'

'Bullshit. She knows everything. You *tell* her everything.'

'No. It's not like that.'

'Shut up. Just do as I say. Move over to the boxes. Both of you.'

There was nothing for it but to obey. I walked across to the stack of boxes, where Pete joined me. Adam moved to the rear of the Lotus, tracking our progress.

What have you got me into? Pete's reproachful gaze demanded. I had no ready answer.

Adam was pointing the gun in our direction as he aimed the remote at the car. The boot sprang open. Then he stepped away, making room for us. 'Load the boxes in the car,' he snapped. 'Start with the boot.'

'What are you going to do with them?' I asked.

'Just load them in,' he replied, the pitch of his voice rising.

'Let's get on with it,' said Pete, fearful, I think, that I meant to goad Adam into firing. He picked up a box and carried it towards the Lotus.

'You too, Kellaway,' said Adam.

'OK, OK.' I picked up the one I'd already opened and followed Pete.

The door of the garage was fully open by now. Adam stood beneath it, gun in hand, face fixed in a twitching frown. He watched as we loaded a box each into the narrow boot, more or less filling it. 'Put the others inside the car,' he said. And we did, two on the rear seat, one on the passenger seat and one in the foot well. 'OK. Go back over there.' He gestured towards the bare stretch of wall where the boxes had stood.

'Don't do anything stupid, Adam,' I said as we retreated. 'Whatever's in those files isn't worth all of this.'

'Worth killing you for, you mean?'

'We'll say nothing about the boxes, Adam,' said Pete, his voice cracking as he spoke. 'We don't really care about the missing records, do we, Jon?'

'Absolutely not.'

'They can stay missing as far as we're concerned.'

'Good,' said Adam. 'Because they're going to.' He strode round to the driver's door, yanked it open and climbed in. The gun was still in his hand, clasped to the steering-wheel as he started the engine. The roar of the throttle filled the space around us. Then he slammed the door and reversed fast out of the garage, the tyres squealing as he slewed the car round at the top of the ramp. Another roar, and he was gone from our sight, down the drive towards the road.

We said nothing for a moment, both of us staring into the dark gulf beyond the glare of the overhead lights. The growl of the Lotus faded into the night. Then Pete puffed out his cheeks in a sigh. 'Bloody Nora,' he murmured. 'I thought he was actually going to shoot us, y'know.'

'I'm sorry, Pete. I had no idea he had a gun.'

'He's mad. Stark staring bonkers. You do realize that, don't you? Mad *and* drunk. He was guzzling Scotch like it was lemonade while we were upstairs.'

'Well, he's gone now.'

'Oh, he's gone, all right. No question about that. Gone where you don't come back from. You can tell the old man from me: his son needs locking up. I mean, what's he going to do now? Who's he going to wave that gun at next?'

'I don't—'

'What?'

'He wouldn't. Surely he wouldn't.'

'Wouldn't *what*?'

'Vivien.' I turned and looked at Pete. 'He blames her more than me. And she's alone out there at Lannerwrack.'

'Call her. Warn her. Tell her to get the hell out.'

'She doesn't have a phone.'

'No phone?'

'Come on. We have to get over there. Fast.'

FORTY

By the time we were on the bypass, heading west, I'd gone a long way to convincing myself I was worrying unnecessarily. Whatever secret Oliver had teased out of Wren's files, it was still safe from us. Keeping it that way had to be Adam's priority, given the lengths he'd already gone to to suppress it. So the likelihood was that he'd put the records conclusively out of our reach before even thinking of going after Vivien. Maybe he'd destroy them this time, though why he hadn't before I couldn't imagine.

That wasn't the only thing I couldn't imagine. The secret itself remained unguessable, despite Oliver's note on the memo in my pocket. *A bargain for GL, not Wren's!!!* GL was Greville Lashley, of course, but he'd sent me in search of the missing records in the first place, so it could hardly be him Adam was protecting. Who, then? Who and – after all these years – why?

Pete's thoughts had evidently been running along the same lines as mine. 'I'm not sure about this, Jon. Adam may be pretty crazy, but he's got the records and we haven't. Won't he—'

'Concentrate on finding somewhere else to hide them?'

'Exactly.'

'I was just coming to that conclusion myself. I don't think he's gone to Lannerwrack.'

'Panic over, then?'

'Sort of.'

'Do you still want to go there anyway?'

368

'Yes. I'll try to persuade Vivien to leave with us. It's not safe for her to stay there any more. If it ever was.'

'Right. I'll enjoy seeing how you manage that.'

But I'd already decided to talk to Vivien alone. It was going to be a difficult enough conversation without Pete as an audience. I told him to stop the car at the entrance to the site and wait for me there. He protested, but his heart wasn't in it. I suspected he was glad to be spared the outside chance of another encounter with Adam, armed and dangerous. That was a small part of my reasoning as well. Whatever was going on in Adam's troubled mind, it wasn't Pete's responsibility to sort it out. Somehow, though, it had become mine.

'There's nothing to worry about,' I said as I prepared to get out of the car. 'Adam won't have come here.'

'I hope we're right about that, Jon.'

'Me too. If anything does happen . . .'

'Like what?'

'Just anything.' I looked towards him in the darkness and sensed him looking at me. 'Call the police and stay put. Don't follow me. OK?'

'You're the boss. Don't be long, hey? I've only got a few fags left.'

'I'll be as quick as I can.'

I walked away from the car, along the curving approach road to the dryers. Their towers loomed ahead, black and bulky against the milky moonlit sky. I heard the crunch of grit beneath my shoes and the rustle of the wind in the hedges bordering the fields to either side. I had the torch with me, but there was no need to use it. I knew the route well enough to find my way.

I saw light gleaming in the caravan windows as I entered the wide, black expanse of the yard. All was quiet and normal. I felt more certain than ever that Adam hadn't come here. I made my way past the Beetle to the caravan. The curtains were closed, but they were thin enough to show a shadow of movement within. Vivien was evidently still up and about. I could hear the faint burble of a radio.

369

I knocked on the door. Instantly, the radio was switched off. But there was no other response. I knocked again and called out: 'Vivien, it's me – Jonathan.'

'Jonathan?'

'Yes. Can I come in?'

There was a long wait, but eventually she opened the door.

I'd seen her only three days before, but somehow I'd still managed to forget how different she was from the Vivien lodged in my mind. She frowned at me. 'What are you doing here at this hour?' she asked.

'I found something I wanted to show you. And . . . something's happened I need to . . . tell you about.'

'What?'

I took the memo out of my pocket and passed it to her. 'The note in green: is that Oliver's handwriting?'

She put on a pair of glasses that were hanging round her neck and moved back into the light to read the note. She gasped in surprise. 'Yes. Oliver wrote this.'

'Can I come in now?'

'Oh, yes. You better had.'

She took another pace back as I stepped up into the doorway. At that moment, there was a sharp crack from somewhere behind me and a ping of impact on the roof of the caravan. It was a gunshot. The certainty of that rammed into my thoughts along with the sickening realization that I'd misread Adam totally. He was here. He'd been here all the time, waiting for my arrival to confirm his belief that Vivien and I were allied against him.

A second shot followed the first almost instantly. This one drilled a hole in the window to my right. I leapt forward into the caravan, pulling the door shut behind me. 'Get down,' I shouted to Vivien. She ignored me, darting back to throw a switch that plunged us into darkness, then forward to lock the door.

'*Down!*'

Now, at last, she dropped to her knees beside me. 'What's happening?' she panted, her face close to mine. 'Who's out there?'

'Adam. I learnt this evening that he stole the records.'

'*Adam?*'

'In his mind, we're his enemies, you and I. God knows what it's all about. I didn't think he'd come here. I only wanted to—'

A third shot shattered the rest of the window and ploughed into the farther wall of the caravan. 'Has he gone mad? For God's sake, Jonathan, why is he doing this?'

'I think he has gone mad, yes. Something's pushed him over the edge.' Pete must have heard the shots. He'd already be on the phone to the police. But how long would it take them to arrive? 'I'm sorry, Vivien. I don't know what to do. There's no reasoning with him.'

'Are there more notes in the files like this?'

'Probably. I never got the chance to check. Adam took them with him.'

'Oliver really was on to something, then.' I had the bizarre sense that she was smiling. 'He wasn't deluded after all.'

'Maybe not. But that doesn't help us now.'

'Yes, it does. It means—'

'*Come out,*' Adam bellowed from no more than a few yards beyond the door. '*Come out and face me.*'

To my astonishment, Vivien started to get up. I pulled her back down. 'What are you doing?' I whispered.

'I'm not afraid of him.'

'Well, you should be.'

'Maybe so. But I've lost too much over the years to hang on to fear, Jonathan. I don't have any left.'

'*Are you coming out or not?*'

'Pete Newlove's waiting for me at the site entrance, Vivien. He'll have heard the shots and called the police. They'll be here soon.'

'Not soon enough, I suspect.'

'You can't go out there.'

'Adam's always hated me. I've never really understood why. Perhaps this is my chance to find out.'

'*I'm not going to wait for ever.*'

Vivien tried to pull away from me again, but I held her fast. 'I won't let you go.'

'There was a time I longed to hear you say that. But that time is past.'

'He means to kill us.'

'I'll take my chances. What do I have to live for, anyway?'

'For God's—' I broke off, my attention seized by unexpected sounds outside the caravan: a metallic clunk, followed by the splashing of something liquid against the door and along the wall. 'What's that?' A whiff of petrol through the smashed window supplied an answer even as I asked the question. 'My God, he's going to try and burn us out.'

'I won't wait for him to do that.'

'Neither will I.' It occurred to me that a fire was Adam's crazed notion of how he could make our deaths look like the work of an unknown arsonist. The fact that there were ample clues to lead the police to him probably hadn't crossed his mind. No matter. He'd just given us our best chance of escape. He couldn't hold a gun, let alone aim it, while he was sloshing petrol out of a jerry can. 'Stay behind me.'

I scrambled to my feet, certain that I had to act fast if I was to get the better of him. I pushed Vivien back, unlocked the door, flung it open and jumped out, turning as I did so in the direction the splashes had been coming from.

I landed awkwardly and, steadying myself, saw Adam as a dark shape ahead of me. He looked to be holding the jerry can with both hands. Petrol vapour caught in my nostrils. There was a tang of tobacco smoke as well. He'd lit a cigar, no doubt intending to use it to ignite the petrol. The tip of it glowed as he looked towards me.

I charged him without further thought – and no idea of where the gun might be. He tried to dodge me, but, drunk and impeded by the jerry can as he was, he was too slow. I took him in the chest and down we went. He grunted as we hit the ground and the cigar fell from his mouth. Exactly where the jerry can ended up I couldn't tell, but I could hear the rest of the petrol gurgling out of it.

I pinned Adam down with my forearm across his throat and cast around with my free hand in search of the gun. 'Fuck you,' he gasped. Then there was a whoosh as the cigar set the spreading pool of petrol alight. Flames billowed up to my left and, an instant later, they were on us. Adam's trousers must have been soaked in petrol. His legs were on fire and so were mine. I rolled off him and, looking back, saw Vivien standing in the doorway of the caravan as a tentacle of flame began to run along its base.

'Get out of there,' I shouted.

But all she did was retreat inside. I sat up and began thrashing at my legs in a vain attempt to put out the flames. Adam was moving too, heaving himself slowly up, apparently oblivious to the flames curling around him. I could smell flesh burning, though whether his or mine I wasn't sure. There was smoke coming from the caravan as well now – an acrid, choking ribbon of it.

Suddenly, Vivien reappeared. She jumped out of the caravan, cradling a bundle in her arms, and rushed towards me. It was a blanket. She dropped it over my legs and beat down on it. The flames went out. But she didn't stop beating.

Then I heard a weird, half-despairing, half-exultant shriek. Vivien's face registered her shock at what she saw behind me. I turned and saw it too.

Adam was on his feet, his clothes ablaze. But he didn't seem to care about that. He'd wrestled the gun out of his pocket and was trying to point it at us. But the flames on his sleeve were dazzling him and obstructing his aim. He cocked his head one way, then the other, in an effort to focus on his target.

At that moment, light flooded over him, swamping the shadows cast by the flames. It was coming from the headlamps of a car speeding along the approach road towards us. I knew the police couldn't have arrived so quickly. It had to be Pete. He must have seen the fire and decided he couldn't just sit where he was and wait for them to turn up.

Adam stared towards the light, as if fascinated by it. His mouth sagged open. And his face registered pain for the first time: a wide, wincing grimace of agony. I'm not sure he could see us any more. He said something, but I couldn't make out the words. He fired the gun. Two shots whistled off into the night a long way wide of us.

'Drop the gun, Adam,' Vivien cried. 'We can help you.'

But he was past helping – way past. He gaped in apparent surprise at the bubbling flesh on his wrist and arm and must have recognized, deep within himself, the finality of the moment. He thrust the barrel of the gun into his mouth and pulled the trigger.

FORTY-ONE

I spent the night in hospital after being treated for the burns to my legs and hands, while the police and the Fire Brigade busied themselves at Lannerwrack and began their painstaking inquiries into what had happened. I answered their questions as best I could, but the truth was that none of us could properly explain why Adam had acted as he had.

The memory kept recurring to me of Adam as a five-year-old, firing his cap-gun at Oliver one Sunday morning at Nanstrassoe House. There'd been hatred in him even then, though I'd done my best to ignore it. Advantages had been showered on him through his life, but they could never erase the central flaw in his character: in his mind, the world had always been set against him.

That wasn't enough to explain the behaviour that had led to his death, of course. The cause of his self-destructive frenzy was to be found, if it was to be found anywhere, in the decades old files of Walter Wren & Co. he'd gone to such lengths to keep from us. The police discovered them in his Lotus, parked in the lane that ran along the far western boundary of the Lannerwrack site. He'd cut a hole in the fence and gone in from there.

The files were impounded as evidence, though soon enough the police did the obvious thing and asked Fay Whitworth to come down and examine them. Nobody from Intercontinental Kaolins was to be allowed a look before she delivered her verdict. Rumours about what she might discover spread freely from St Austell to

375

Augusta. All I could tell Presley Beaumont was that we wouldn't have to wait long to learn the worst.

Meanwhile, there was Adam's funeral to be arranged. But none of his relatives seemed in any hurry to take charge. When I called his father to break the news of his death, I was obliged to do it by answerphone message. According to Beaumont, the old man never took calls directly any more. Evidently, he didn't respond to messages directly either. Jacqueline phoned me from Georgia to report that Greville simply wasn't fit to travel. It was 'difficult' for her to come to Cornwall herself and impossible for Michelle, who was committed to competing in an equestrian tournament in Uruguay. She suggested Vivien could do whatever had to be done.

But Vivien wasn't in any state to deal with the administrative complexities of sudden death. She'd lost most of her possessions in the fire, including Oliver's photograph album, her most cherished memento of him. Homeless and to a large degree helpless, she didn't put up any resistance when Pete persuaded his sister, a kindly soul, to take her in. That left me to deal with the coroner and the undertaker and the family solicitor. My various attempts to talk to Vivien about what had happened – and to thank her for coming to my rescue that night – all ended with her gazing past me and shaking her head and saying simply, 'It doesn't matter.'

She was in shock, of course. To some extent, so was I. The dressings on my legs and hands slowed me down and the drugs the doctor had put me on made me drowsy. I shambled around pitifully, feeling my age, and was grateful when Pete volunteered to run a few errands for me. University commitments delayed Fay's arrival until the end of the week, which consigned us all to limbo. No date was fixed for the funeral. The possibility remained that Lashley would rouse himself and fly in to confront the consequences of his son's suicide. I half expected it to happen. But, as the days passed without word from him, it seemed less and less likely.

I'd booked Fay Whitworth into the White Hart, at IK's expense. She arrived on Friday afternoon and met me for dinner after checking in with the police. Solicitous though she was about my injuries and what Vivien and I had been through, she made no effort to deny her eagerness to see what the records held.

'It's clear, I think, that they must contain something pretty sensational. Otherwise why would Adam Lashley have stolen them in the first place?'

'We don't actually know Adam stole them, Fay. Only that he was storing them.'

'Hiding them, you mean.'

'OK. Hiding.' I shrugged. I had no energy to waste on debating turns of phrase.

'I'm surprised you want to minimize his behaviour. He did try to kill you, after all.'

'I know. It's just . . .'

'What?'

'The whole thing seems so . . . inexplicable.'

'Well, I'm here to explicate the apparently inexplicable.'

'And will you let me know what you find out? Or will that be deemed *sub judice*?'

'I don't see why. Adam's dead. There isn't going to be a trial.'

'Not of Adam, no.'

She frowned at me. 'That's an interesting remark, Jonathan. What are you afraid might come out?'

'I'm not afraid. I'm . . . wary.'

'Well, we'll soon know whether you have good cause to be.'

'How soon?'

'I've agreed to present my findings to the police on Monday. But I reckon a solid day's work tomorrow will get the job done.'

'Tomorrow?'

'Yes. So if I were you, I wouldn't stray far.'

I had no intention of straying. Pete drove me over to his sister's house on Saturday morning and I told Vivien what Fay's timetable was likely to be. She seemed philosophical about the outcome, but she was still so numbed by what had happened that it was difficult to tell what she was really thinking. I suspected it was similar to what I was thinking myself. It was almost impossible to believe we might be about to learn, after so many years, why and for what Oliver had died. The past was shifting ground beneath our feet. But the truth was no longer necessarily out of reach.

Pete took me down to Charlestown for lunch at the Harbourside Inn and set out his stall. 'If any shit is going to fly fanwards because of what the doc digs up, Jon, I want early warning. I think having a gun waggled in my face by the late lamented barking mad Adam Lashley puts me ahead of the likes of Presley Beaumont in the queue for info.'

I didn't argue. In fact, I agreed with him. One hundred per cent.

Late that afternoon, I was resting in my room at the White Hart when there was a knock at the door. I can't have been a glorious sight when I opened it, but Fay Whitworth didn't seem to notice as she strode in.

'I could use some coffee,' she said, flapping her notebook meaningfully. 'It's been a hard day.'

'But rewarding?'

'You could say that.'

Seeing me fumbling with the kettle, she took charge and told me to sit down, pointing to the armchair rather than the upright by the desk. I had the impression she wanted that for herself.

While she made the coffee, she complained about the vending machine at the police station and the grim lighting in the room they'd allocated to her. I waited patiently, gazing through the window at the wind-stirred trees in the churchyard on the other side of the road. I felt no eagerness for the truth. If it was coming, it would come. And I would hear it.

'It wasn't what I was expecting, Jonathan,' Fay said, settling herself at the desk and taking a first sip of coffee. 'Not that I knew what to expect, of course. But this . . .' She shook her head. 'It was a surprise.'

'Are you going to tell me what it amounts to?'

'That's as much for you to say as me. I can give you the facts. What they amount to is to a large degree conjectural. I suppose it depends on how far you want to take it. Maybe it's more than what it appears to be.'

'And what does it appear to be?'

'Fraud, of a subtle kind. I haven't had time to study every single document, but the conclusion to be drawn from those I have examined is clear. Oliver Foster has been my guide. There are lots of notes in his hand and his distinctive green ink – like on the memo you abstracted – and lots more underlining and asterisking by him that identify the key figures and passages in invoices and letters that would be easy to miss otherwise. He was a clever boy. Very clever. Very . . . analytical. A chess player, you said?'

'Yes. A good one.'

'That doesn't surprise me. Though he'd probably have admitted he was up against a better one.'

'Who?'

'Greville Lashley.'

I'd known she was going to name him. It had seemed inevitable, even if it was still – for a little longer – incomprehensible. 'You're accusing our mutual employer of fraud?'

'I shan't be accusing anyone of anything. And I doubt the police will be interested in pursuing a nonagenarian expatriate based on the kind of evidence the records contain. They might've wanted to ask him a few questions, though. If he was in the country.'

'He's too ill to travel.'

'So they tell me.'

'What exactly are you saying he did?'

'Nothing that the untrained observer – or even the incurious accountant – would notice. But Oliver Foster knew what he was looking for. And he found it.'

'Which was?'

'Over the twelve years covered by the files – 1956 to 1968 – Greville Lashley slowly but surely ruined Wren's.'

'Ruined them?'

'They were viable as an independent outfit and could have gone

379

on being viable. That's one of the surprises. They didn't have to sell out. Lashley forced it on them.'

'How?'

'By manoeuvring the company into buying new equipment when the old was still serviceable, paying more than they needed to for supplies and services, bidding excessively low to secure contracts, purchasing land they had no immediate use for and generally throwing good money after bad. The Trudgeon deal was a case in point. Wren's had always paid Trudgeon's more than the going rate, on the grounds that CCC would gobble Trudgeon's up if they didn't have Wren's business and there was no one else with sufficient experience of loading operations at Charlestown. It was a weak argument, but George Wren was a weak man. And a poor reasoner. Lashley regularly bamboozled him. When they finally bought Trudgeon's to acquire an A licence for transport of their own, they paid far too much. And that's not the worst. It looks like they'd regularly paid Trudgeon's two or three times over for the same work. Lashley was a master of tricksy paperwork. But Oliver tracked him through the maze he'd constructed. And I've followed Oliver. There's really no doubt that what I'm saying is true.'

'Trudgeon's must have connived at this.'

'I imagine they must.'

'Gordon Strake was the go-between, wasn't he?'

'Oliver certainly thought so, based on the note he wrote on the copy of the letter Lashley sent to Strake at the time of his dismissal. Even pliable George Wren had finally had enough of the man and insisted he be got rid of. But what does Lashley say in the letter? "Your loyalty and discretion remain greatly appreciated." "I'll bet", Oliver scrawled next to that. With multiple exclamation marks.'

'Why would Lashley want to run Wren's into the ground, Fay? What was the object of the fraud?'

'I assumed at first he was taking cuts of the overpayments and undercharging – backhanders from Wren's suppliers and customers. But no. It was cleverer than that – and worse. There's no actual proof, but the warm tone of letters Lashley received from

Percy Faull, managing director of CCC and chairman of the china clay trade association, gives the game away. Wren's had a good workforce and some of the most productive pits. Properly managed and developed, they could have been profitable enough to rival CCC and Faull knew it. So, he engaged Lashley to sabotage Wren's. His reward was to be a prominent position in the merged operations, with a promise of further elevation in due course. Faull adopted Lashley as his successor at CCC and pushed the appointment through the board when he retired. That's no secret. But why he favoured an outsider has puzzled me from the start of my researches. Now I have the answer. In a handwritten postscript to one letter, he says to Lashley, "Keep up the good work." Oliver gives that double underlining and an asterisk. He knew what it meant. Thanks to him, so do I.'

'You're sure about this?'

'Having seen what I've seen today, yes. Greville Lashley was employed by Wren's. But he was working for Cornish China Clays. And he seems to have recruited Gordon Strake to assist him. The extent of Strake's role is hard to discern, of course. That's where we enter the realm of speculation.'

'Go on, then. Speculate.'

'There are memos from Kenneth Foster in the early months of 1959 that suggest he'd smelt a rat. Then, conveniently for Lashley, he killed himself. George Wren was fobbed off with smooth assurances that Foster's concerns amounted to nothing and Lashley went on his merry way.'

'Are you suggesting Strake had a hand in Kenneth Foster's death?'

'I'm suggesting Strake was Lashley's fixer. And the problem with Kenneth Foster was fixed. Except that his son, Oliver, wouldn't leave it alone and dug and dug until he worked out what was going on. Then he wound up dead too. Like Strake himself, within a year of the takeover. By then, I suppose, he'd outlived his usefulness.'

'Francis Wren killed Strake, Fay. I know that for a fact. Strake was blackmailing him. It doesn't matter what with. It was nothing to do with what you've uncovered.'

'Really?'

'Fraud's one thing. Murder's quite another. I can't imagine Lashley resorting to that.'

'Can't you? Well, I bow to your superior knowledge where Strake's death is concerned, but Kenneth and Oliver Foster both posed a threat to Lashley. And they both died before they could bring him down.'

'Maybe so, but—'

'All this has set me wondering about Muriel Lashley's death, too.'

'Oh, come on.'

'It freed Lashley to make a very advantageous marriage to Jacqueline Hudson, didn't it? You could see that as part of his master plan if you were so inclined.'

'Are you so inclined?'

'Maybe Muriel became suspicious about how her first husband and their son had died. Maybe she was asking too many questions.'

Or maybe she was planning to have Fred Thompson ask some questions on her behalf. There was more to support Fay's theory than she knew. But still I couldn't credit what she was saying. 'If you're right, why on earth would Lashley hire you – or anyone – to write a history of the company, knowing what might come out?'

'Perhaps vanity got the better of him. Perhaps he thought I'd ignore the gap in their records.'

'Then why send me to find out what had happened when you didn't ignore it? And why not destroy the records, rather than have his unreliable son hide them – a son he was trusting with some pretty devastating information, if your speculations are correct? It doesn't make any sense.'

'No. It doesn't, does it? Yet it's what he seems to have done.'

'I can't believe it.'

'I think you may have to.'

'But why? Why would he do that?'

Fay shook her head. 'I don't know. I can't imagine. I'd like to ask him, naturally.' She leant forward, fixing me with her gaze. 'Wouldn't you?'

I stood up then, opened the window and leant out, breathing in the cool spring air. I felt stifled by the sense that I'd been a part, however unwitting, of Lashley's machinations. I wasn't sure yet what they amounted to – whether they really could have encompassed murder. But I was going to have to find out. I was going to have to force the truth into the open – the whole truth and nothing but the truth.

I felt Fay's hand on my shoulder. 'What will you do, Jonathan?' she asked.

I looked round at her. 'I'll see him.'

'When?'

'As soon as possible.'

'I've undertaken to present my findings to the police on Monday. I won't be doing any speculating for them. But I suppose they might do some of their own.'

'That's up to them.'

'Will you be telling anyone else what I've told you? About the fraud, I mean. I imagine you'll want to keep the rest to yourself, at least for the time being.'

'I'll put Pete Newlove in the picture.' Seeing her raise her eyebrows, I added, 'He's earned it.'

'What about Vivien?'

'I need to speak to her stepfather before I say anything to her.'

'Are you sure *he*'ll speak to *you*?'

'Yes.' I nodded. 'I don't intend to give him any choice in the matter.'

FORTY-TWO

The Villa Orchis had changed little in the twenty-six years since I'd last been there, though perhaps the pergola was even more heavily draped in wisteria. It was Monday afternoon when I arrived. The light was mellow, the air fragrant. It wasn't hard to understand why Greville Lashley should want to spend his declining years in such a place, nor why, at his age, he would be reluctant to leave it for any reason. But he'd have to be iller than I guessed he was to miss his son's funeral, unless, as Fay Whitworth's speculations had implied, there were other reasons why he didn't want to return to his homeland.

I'd done a lot of thinking since setting off from St Austell. None of it had clinched the issue in my mind. A fraudster? Evidently, Lashley was that. And, in a way, given the uncanny dexterity he'd always shown as a businessman, that wasn't so surprising. But a murderer? I couldn't bring myself to believe it. If not, though, how was I to account for all the unnatural deaths that had smoothed his path and now seemed, in the light of what Fay had discovered, so obviously suspicious? More to the point, perhaps, how was *he* to account for them?

There was a sense of time turning full circle as I walked along the drive. A slim, glossy-haired young man was washing a car in front of the garage. He didn't have Paolo's cocksure bearing and the car was an unremarkable Lexus rather than a white-wall-tyred Alfa

384

Romeo cabriolet, but the echoes of the past were audible enough. And memories compressed themselves in the moment.

'*Buon giorno,*' I called, to get the young man's attention.

He broke off from his sponging and looked at me without smiling. '*Buon giorno. Desidera?*'

'I'm here to see Signor Lashley.'

'You have . . . *un appuntamento?*'

'No. But—'

'Phone to make one. OK?' He resumed sponging the car, as if he'd said all there was to be said.

'I'll do that.' I moved away, dismissing him from my thoughts. I covered a short distance back down the drive, then diverted across the lawn, striding towards the French windows of the study that I could see were half open.

'*Eh, signor,*' the young man shouted after me. '*Fermatevi!*'

I didn't stop, of course. And before I was overhauled, a figure stepped out of the French windows to greet me. 'It's all right, Toni,' he called. 'He's a friend.'

A ravaged handsomeness clung to Greville Lashley, even at ninety-two. He still wore his hair, white now where once it had been black, just a little too long and carried himself with the same jauntiness I'd always associated with him, albeit stiffened by age. The lines on his face were deeply incised and his eyes had lost some of their clarity, but his expression was authentically Lashleyan: wry, perceptive, genial, calculating. He steadied himself with a silver-topped cane as he stood in the doorway and smiled as if genuinely pleased to see me.

'It's been a long time, Jonathan.'

'The annual conference three years ago,' I corrected him. 'Not so very long really.'

'I meant since you've been here. To the Villa Orchis.'

'Ah. Then you're right, of course.'

'Come inside. We can talk there.'

He headed back the way he'd come and I followed, moving from the glaring brilliance of the afternoon light into the wood-panelled subfusc of the study, where so little had been altered since the days of Francis Wren that it was easy to imagine him watching us from the shadows.

Lashley sat down at the desk, where a sheaf of papers with IK letterheading on them lay on the blotter, and waved for me to draw up a chair. He took a drink from a glass of water as I did so, a cough growling deep in his throat. He was breathing heavily. Simply walking to the French windows and back had taken a lot out of him. Physically, that is. Mentally, he was without question as razor-sharp as ever.

'Old age is a confounded bore,' he said, smiling wanly. 'My doctor can't decide whether my heart or my lungs will give out first. At this rate, it could be a tie. Or a dead heat.' He chuckled drily at his own joke. I didn't join in.

'Jacqueline said you weren't well enough to travel.'

'But I expect you think I am.'

'Adam was your son, for all his faults. I'd have thought—'

'I despaired of the boy years ago. At my stage in life, I can't waste my dwindling energy on a display of affection I don't feel or an observance of conventions I don't respect.' There was an angry edge to his voice. He didn't like having to justify himself. He never had.

'You're a hard man, Greville.'

'I've never pretended otherwise.'

'Then you won't mind my pointing out that you may have had other reasons for declining to travel to Cornwall.'

'Might I?'

'I think you know what I mean. It's why I'm here.'

He nodded. 'Of course.'

'You don't seem surprised to see me.'

'Presley Beaumont passed on the news that the police had asked Doctor Whitworth to examine the files they found in Adam's car. When I phoned the White Hart yesterday and was told you'd checked out, I assumed she'd informed you of her findings . . . and that you were heading in this direction. It was what I expected of you, actually. It was what I'd hoped you'd do. So, welcome. Do you want something to drink, by the way? Elena isn't here at the moment, so if it's to be tea or coffee you'll have to make it yourself, but there's whisky in the cabinet.' He flapped a hand towards it. 'Go ahead.'

'I'm fine as I am.'

'Really? I think I'd like a tot. Would you mind?'

I went to the cabinet. There was a three-quarters-full bottle of Highland Park waiting. I poured Lashley a glass, then poured one for myself as well.

'I'm glad you're joining me,' he said as I delivered it to him.

I sat down again. Lashley raised his glass, as if silently proposing a toast, and took a sip. I looked at him, waiting, as I knew he knew I was waiting, for him to tell me what I'd travelled from Cornwall to hear: the truth.

'You're probably wondering why I hired Doctor Whitworth to write a history of our company, knowing she was bound to discover a gaping hole in Wren's records; and why, after she'd discovered it, I sent you to search for the missing files, knowing there was no one better qualified, one way or another, to find them, and knowing also what the missing files contained.'

'I am wondering, yes.'

'Well, we'll come to that by and by. Suffice to say for the moment that this outcome was what I both expected and desired. Not poor Adam's death, of course. I never foresaw that. I simply had no inkling how . . . self-destructive . . . he'd become. I suppose some would blame me for the follies of my son, but I'm not inclined to. You knew him. His problems were of his own making. Or else they were flaws he was born with. I was sorry for him. But I was also disappointed by him. Many times. There you have it, I'm afraid.

'So, to the nub of the matter. We'd better begin at the beginning. Francis Wren didn't leave the company in 1949 because he was bored with the china clay business, though bored he may have been. He left because George Wren discovered he and Kenneth Foster were lovers. He discovered that because I told him. The information was supplied to me by Gordon Strake in exchange for the settlement of his gambling debts. George was a staunch Methodist and a widower of long standing. He disapproved strongly of all forms of sexual licence. As for homosexuality ... need I say more. This was sixty years ago, remember. It was a different world. Francis was sent packing ... to what ended up as a comfortable exile in this very house. Ken Foster, as the husband of George's beloved only daughter and father-to-be of his first grandchild, was allowed to remain, on the strict understanding that he curb his homosexual tendencies.

'As a result of the upheaval, I became George's trusted right-hand man. I had big ideas even then. I reckoned – and I was right – that Wren's was ripe for expansion. But George was as commercially conservative as he was morally censorious. He'd have none of it. Every well-reasoned proposal I made was rejected. I was given a seat on the board, but only a miserly number of shares, so I could never force any of my plans through. That wasn't a situation I was prepared to tolerate indefinitely. I had some discreet discussions with Percy Faull about going to work for CCC, but he made a more interesting and, in the long run, more rewarding proposal: that I set about bringing Wren's to its knees, so that its capacity to rival CCC, if properly managed, would be nullified and it would become, in time, easy prey to a takeover on modest terms. I was to be rewarded with something I couldn't realistically aspire to otherwise: Faull's post as chairman and managing director of CCC when he retired. I accepted. We shook on the deal. And he honoured it. We both did.

'I knew from the outset that Ken would be a problem. He had a keen eye for detail. Fortunately, and unsurprisingly, he hadn't abided by his father-in-law's injunction. There'd been other ... dalliances ... over the years. Strake had continued to act as my informant. A man with his taste for gambling was frequently in need of a supplement to his salary. I supplied it. He was useful to me in a host of ways.'

'Such as dealing with the Trudgeons.'

'Yes. Such as that. Anyway, the time came when I had to make it clear to Ken that I had chapter and verse on his liaisons and that he'd be wise to stop querying what I was doing. Muriel and I were already ... close ... by then. I think he was aware of that. And I think he was painfully conscious that I had a hold over him he was powerless to break free of. I'm sure that's why he killed himself: because he couldn't see a way out.

'So, I married Muriel, Adam was born and my . . . strategy . . . proceeded satisfactorily. Very satisfactorily. Until Oliver started delving into the matter, in search of the truth about his father. At some point, he salvaged Ken's briefcase from the lake at Relurgis Pit. That can't have been easy. You have to admire his perseverance. He must have found the pig's egg he gave you inside. It was a love token from Francis that Ken had hung on to. One small piece of the jigsaw puzzle Oliver began to assemble. I imagine he collected a few more pieces during his visit here in 1967. Then, when I unveiled the takeover plan the following year, after George had died, Oliver turned his attention to our files. He can't have known what he was looking for, but I knew what he'd eventually uncover, sharp-brained lad that he was. I tried to frighten him off by setting Strake on him. It didn't work. But I wasn't unduly worried. The takeover was essentially a done deal. It only required board approval. I could deal with Oliver at my leisure once it was signed and sealed.

'Then, during the afternoon of the day before the board meeting, Oliver phoned me at the office. He was in a call-box – in Newquay, as I subsequently learnt from Strake. He'd been giving Strake the runaround all day. Oliver told me quite bluntly that he knew what I'd done and, if I wanted to prevent the information reaching the other board members, I should meet him at Relurgis Pit at eight thirty that evening. He hung up before I had a chance to reason with him.

'I didn't have much option but to go. By then Strake had reported that Oliver had lost him, thanks to your intervention. I intended to do my best to talk the lad round. Failing that, I had to hope Francis, Harriet and Muriel simply wouldn't believe him. In the event, though, when I got to Relurgis, he was nowhere to be seen. But he'd been there. I knew that because his camera was hanging from the rail on the jetty, where I couldn't fail to notice it.

'It was beginning to get dark. I waited ten minutes or so, but I knew he wasn't going to show himself. I wondered if he was watching me, from some vantage point in the undergrowth round the lake. I expect he was. Eventually, I took the camera and left.'

'You didn't see him?'

'No.'

'But he'd summoned you there to hear his accusation. Why didn't he go through with it?'

'One can only conjecture. I never expected him to take his own life. I was as shocked as anyone else when I heard the news. He must have decided on that course of action some time before. I think he'd painted himself into a corner, actually. To expose me, he had to expose his father. And he couldn't bear to inflict the truth about Ken's sexuality – not to mention his affair with Francis – on his mother and his sister. But he wanted me to know he'd seen through me. He wanted me to understand that very clearly.'

I looked hard at Lashley. Was this really what had happened? I couldn't believe Oliver would have let him off so lightly, however reluctant he might have been to have his father's relationship with Francis revealed. There was another course events might have followed that evening at Relurgis Pit. And it still ended with Oliver drowned.

'I didn't kill Oliver, Jonathan,' he said quietly. 'I would never have done such a thing.'

'I'm no longer sure what you would or wouldn't have done.'

'A reaction on your part that Oliver no doubt intended to induce. He wanted you to be suspicious. Hence the pantomime with the camera. I had the film developed, you see. There was nothing on it.'

'What do you mean?'

'It was blank.'

'*Blank?*'

'Yes. He'd never wound the film on to the spool.'

I grappled with my memory. Had I tried to wind the film on after taking the last picture and so confirmed there actually was a film on the spool? I might have. I might not have. I couldn't be certain. It was just too long ago. But such a deception would have been typical of Oliver, of course. As Lashley well knew.

'I don't suppose for an instant it was an oversight on Oliver's part,' he went on. 'It was the message he'd chosen to send me in the way he'd chosen to send it. "What did you think you were going to find? What were you afraid of?" A posthumous taunt, if you like. And maybe also a diversionary tactic. The missing camera; the question of what was on the rest of the film before the photographs you thought you were taking at Goss Moor; the meaning of the monogram on the pig's egg: those little mysteries kept you interested, as they were designed to.'

The tale Lashley was telling fitted the way Oliver's mind had worked. I was beginning to believe it, partly, I suppose, because the alternative was so terrible.

'Meanwhile, I ignored the danger that was right under my nose. The files. And his notes on them.' Lashley sighed. 'When I came across the first of his ... mischievous marginalia – purely by chance, I might add – I realized he probably hoped you'd be the person reading them. And drawing the appropriate conclusions. You had to be looking for a pattern, of course. Without some initial level of suspicion, and the determination to see it through, you wouldn't make much headway. But he'd laid a trail for you to follow if you'd had a mind to. It seemed he did want the truth to come out. He just didn't want to be around to see it happen.

'I did my best to put you off the scent by having Strake tell you Oliver had hired him to give the impression he was being tailed. It sounded suitably crackpot. But you weren't the only one I had to worry about. Francis asked a lot of questions and I had the feeling an answer I didn't want to hear was going to form in his mind eventually. When Vivien came out here the following summer, I became seriously concerned, particularly when I established that you'd joined her. I detailed Strake to dig up something – anything – that would give me a hold over Francis. I was no longer confident his homosexual past – or present, come to that – would suffice to silence him if the need arose. Italian society was inconveniently relaxed about such matters. Strake came up with the goods, but was so pleased with what he'd found he decided to blackmail Francis on his own account. Well, you know what came of that. Francis *was* silenced, more conclusively than I'd intended. And so was Strake.

391

No bad thing that, from my point of view. He'd have turned on me sooner or later. He was ever one to bite the hand that fed him.'

'Unlike me.'

Lashley frowned curiously at me. 'Well, that's true, since you mention it.'

'Was I his replacement, Greville?'

'What do you mean?'

'I remember you congratulating me on my handling of the situation after Francis died. Later, you went to great lengths to recruit me into the company. I became your troubleshooter. You dubbed me that yourself. I was more scrupulous than Strake, of course, but also more reliable. As I demonstrated, presumably to your satisfaction, at the time of Muriel's kidnapping.'

'Your help was invaluable. No question about it.'

'But there is a question, Greville. A very troubling one. Was Muriel getting suspicious about your path to the top – too suspicious for you to tolerate any longer?'

His frown deepened. 'What exactly are you suggesting, Jonathan?'

'That the kidnapping might not have been all it appeared. That you might have . . . arranged it.'

He looked away, into the sunlight flooding through the French windows. 'You think I paid the Camorra to kidnap Muriel and later kill her?'

'Well? Did you?'

He sighed. 'How would I know how to contact such people?'

'Maybe you used Paolo Verdelli. Whose own elimination, once he'd served his purpose, was the one part of the deal he didn't know about.'

'In effect, then, I sabotaged the handover and ensured Muriel wouldn't be released alive?'

'Yes. Freeing you to marry into the Hudson family and thereby acquire a position of ascendancy in the international china clay business.'

'That would make me . . . some kind of monster, surely. A ruthless murderer . . . without moral compunction.'

392

'You tell me what it would make you.'

'You're actually asking the wrong question, Jonathan.' He turned back to face me. 'Why would I hire Doctor Whitworth to write a company history, with all these skeletons rattling in the cupboard?'

'I don't know. Why would you?'

'Did Doctor Whitworth suggest a reason?'

'She thought vanity might have addled your judgement.'

'Really?' He smiled. 'Well, vanity is part of it, certainly. But it's a finely judged part. Doctor Whitworth is a high-minded academic. No one can buy her silence. She'll make her findings known. I think we can rely on that. I *am* relying on it.'

'You *want* all this to be known?'

'Certainly. That's why I sent you to find the missing records. So that she could complete her task. When I realized the scale of Oliver's interference with the files, some time after they'd been transferred to CCC's offices, I removed them for safekeeping – to the basement at Nanstrassoe House. When we sold Nanstrassoe, I moved them to Wavecrest. I took Adam into my confidence at that time about my deal with Percy Faull. It only increased his respect for me. He realized I was more devious than he could ever be. He wanted to destroy the records, of course. But I insisted we keep them.'

'Why?'

'I told Adam I wanted to be able to consult them from time to time. Not that I ever did. But he wouldn't disobey me. He wouldn't dare to. That was the measure of his weakness. The records were safe with him.'

'Did he know you'd left a memo about the Trudgeon contract under the shelving unit in the Wren's cage at CCC?'

'Certainly not. I placed it there in case you needed a helping hand when you started your search.'

'You were determined I should succeed?'

'I never seriously doubted you would. It was a foregone conclusion. I'm sorry the exercise almost got you killed. I had no idea Adam possessed a gun – or was desperate enough to use it. I suppose that was partly my fault. I convinced him that if the truth ever came out I'd forfeit my majority shareholding in IK, effectively disinheriting him. He had expensive habits. He couldn't bear to think he might have to . . . economize.'

'You could simply have told me the truth.'

'But then we wouldn't have Doctor Whitworth on hand to broadcast it to the world, would we?'

'Why do you want her to do that? It'll ruin you.'

'Don't you think I deserve to be ruined?'

I stared at him, unable to assimilate the reality of what he was saying. I'd known him most of my life. I'd admired him. I'd trusted him. Now, when he was old and frail and our professional association was nearly at an end, he'd chosen to reveal the truth I'd unwittingly served. I should have been angrier than I was, but sheer disbelief still held me back. 'Are you trying to clear your conscience, Greville? Is that what this is all about – absolution before you meet your maker?'

He took a sip of whisky and studied the amber depths of it for a moment, then said, 'I can understand why you might think so. Old age inevitably focuses one's thoughts on the possibilities of the hereafter. Of course, I might also be reluctant to die without giving everyone a chance to appreciate how very clever I've been. That would count as vanity, though not quite of the kind Doctor Whitworth has in mind.'

'Is your *vanity* served by all the damage you've done?'

'What damage?'

'Ken Foster. Francis. Oliver. Muriel. And your own son. You pretty effectively screwed him up. Not to mention Vivien. You wrecked her whole life.'

'Did I?' He frowned. 'I'm afraid I don't subscribe to your concept of cause and effect. I obliged Ken and Francis to confront the consequences of their actions. They did so in their own way. Oliver too chose his own path. If anyone "screwed up" Adam's life, it was Adam himself. As for Vivien, the tragedies of the family she married into are what brought her to her present sorry pass. I'm not responsible for them.'

394

'And Muriel? What have you got to say about her?'

'I say I knew her better than anyone. I was married to her for twenty-two years. She had an uncompromising side to her character. It wasn't always an asset.'

'You had her killed, for God's sake. And I'm not sure you hadn't already killed her son sixteen years earlier.'

'I can't stop you thinking that. But, really, where's the evidence? The post mortem turned up nothing to suggest Oliver was murdered. As for Muriel, isn't it more likely – far more likely – that Verdelli was responsible for her kidnapping, with no prompting from me? It's what the police concluded at the time. I rather think it's what they'd conclude now too, whatever you told them.'

'So you're just going to stand or fall on what's provable, are you?'

'We all have to. It's the way of the world. It's the law.'

'What law have you been obeying all these years, Greville? Dog eat dog? Devil take the hindmost? King of the dunghill?'

'I've done what I've done and plenty of people besides me, including you, have benefited as a result. I've made money and so have those who've worked with me and for me. I've looked necessity in the face and I haven't flinched.'

'Well, bully for you.'

'Would you top up my whisky, Jonathan?' He slid the nearly empty tumbler towards me. 'There's something important I have to explain to you. Something more important than anything I've yet said.'

I considered telling him to fetch his own drink. But I felt in need of another myself. And I didn't want to risk being made to feel sorry for him by watching him struggle across the room. I collected the whisky bottle from the cabinet and refilled both our glasses. 'Well?' I demanded.

'*Slàinte*,' he said, raising his glass. 'Here's to you.'

'What?'

'To you, Jonathan. The new chairman of Intercontinental Kaolins.'

'What the hell are you talking about?'

'The future. Yours and the company's. I'm passing ownership of my majority shareholding over to you. The transfer document's with my lawyer. He assures me it's legally watertight.'

'You can't be serious.'

'But I am. I've chosen you as my successor. Frankly, I can't think of anyone better qualified. Certainly not Presley Beaumont or any of my spineless fellow directors. No, no. You're the one, Jonathan. This hasn't been about my conscience, you see. It's been about yours. I wanted you to understand what you'll be taking on. I wanted you to be able to make a clean break with the past and a fresh start in your own name. The company's yours. To take in whatever direction you judge best. I know you have reservations about our activities in Brazil. Now you'll be free to act on them. Our share price will take a knock when Doctor Whitworth publicizes her findings, of course. But you'll turn it round. I know you will.'

'What makes you think I'd consider taking over from you for one moment?'

'The staff. They'll need someone to steer them through this. Your colleagues, Jonathan. Men and women with families to support and pensions to look forward to. You'll do it for them. I've been planning this for some time. I decided from the outset that you deserved to know the whole story. Then there couldn't be any nasty surprises for you after you'd taken the reins. I engaged Doctor Whitworth to write the company's history so that, when the truth came out, Adam would blame me – his foolish old father – rather than you. He'd certainly have been looking for someone to blame when he discovered he wasn't going to get control of the company. As it is, he'll never know that now. As for Jacqueline and Michelle, they're generously provided for. I doubt they'll contest the arrangement. And Vivien? Well, if you think she needs help, you'll be able to provide it, won't you?'

I stared at him, appalled by the blatancy of his proposal. 'I'm not going to do it.'

He smiled. 'Yes, you are. You just don't know it yet. I struck up an acquaintance with Countess Covelli in the last few years before she died, you know. A shrewd woman. I miss her. She asked me once, after Adam had been here, making an oaf of himself as usual, whether I wouldn't have preferred you as a son. I admitted to her that I would. So, what I'm doing is natural enough in its way. From now on, you're the boss.'

FORTY-THREE

I had to get out of the villa. I needed time and space to think in. I headed down to Marina Piccola, where a stiffish breeze was getting up and a high surf was running. I walked out on to the rocks and let myself be buffeted by the wind and the spray of the breaking waves. I stood there, assailed by the contradictions and compromises of a lifetime that Lashley had held in the palm of his hand and blown away with a single puff of his failing breath. So much for the truth. Knowing, it seemed, was worse than not knowing.

I found a bar and downed a few beers. They didn't help. I felt hollowed out and overwhelmed. I was going to be a wealthy man, apparently, wealthy and powerful. I could give it all away, of course. I could frustrate Lashley's last act of manipulation. But the best way to ensure he answered for what he'd done was to accept the authority he was determined to confer on me. He knew that, of course. He was expert at baiting a trap.

It was growing dark when I returned to the villa. Elena was there, cooking a meal for me on Lashley's instructions. She'd become a virtual replica of her late mother. She was, I guessed, about the same age Patrizia had been when I first visited Capri back in the long ago summer of 1969.

'It is good to see you again, Jonathan,' she said, hugging me. 'But

Signor Lashley said you are here only for one night. He is going to England with you tomorrow.'

'He said that?'

'*Si*. Is it not right?'

'No, no. It's right. Of course. That's the plan.'

It was a calculated gesture on Lashley's part. 'From now on,' he'd said, 'you're the boss.' And this, he knew, was the least I'd require of him. He was surrendering himself to my judgement by agreeing to what I hadn't yet demanded.

I didn't see him that evening. He stayed in his room. He was tired, Elena said. 'He is tired often, Jonathan. He is very old.' She took him some broth, then left. She'd made up my usual room. There was to be no escape from the past. I was relieved I'd only be there one night. Whatever the consequences of Lashley's revelations were to be, I wanted to face them without delay.

I slept poorly and was up early in the morning. Lashley still hadn't shown himself by the time Elena arrived. She cooked me an omelette before taking him up a cup of his favourite Assam tea.

The telephone rang just after she left the kitchen. I hadn't switched my mobile on since arriving, or even checked it for messages, fearing there'd be several I wasn't ready to respond to. I had an instinct the call was from someone who'd already left such a message. I was tempted to ignore it. But for some reason the answering machine didn't cut in and the telephone went on ringing. Eventually, I picked it up.

'Hello?'

'Jonathan.' It was Vivien, instantly recognizable in her soft, sorrowful announcement of my name. She wasn't one of those I'd expected to hear from, though she was the one I was most dreading having to relate Lashley's confession to.

'Vivien. This is a surprise.' It was more than that. She wasn't supposed to know I'd come to Capri. Though it was clear from the

399

tone of her voice that she did. 'How did you . . . track me down?'

'I went to see you at the White Hart on Sunday. But you'd gone. Without even saying goodbye.'

'I'm not going to be gone long. In fact—'

'Pete Newlove told me everything.'

'What?'

'He had to, considering the state I was in. It's better this way, believe me – better that I should know. Has Greville . . . admitted it's true?'

'Yes.' There it was: so much encompassed in a simple affirmation. 'He has.'

'I want to see him.'

'You soon will. He's agreed to come back with me to Cornwall.'

'It can be sooner than that. I'm in Naples. At the ferry dock.'

'You are?'

'I couldn't sit in St Austell and wait. I have to hear it – all of it – from his own lips. The ferry leaves in ten minutes. Will you meet me . . . at Marina Grande?'

'Of course. Yes. I'll be there.'

'Thank you.' Her gratitude seemed to extend beyond the simple thing I'd agreed to do. 'I realized something on the flight out, Jonathan. I realized you're the only person I've loved who hasn't died or betrayed me.'

'That can't be true.'

'But it is. I'll see you soon.' And with that she rang off.

As I put the telephone down and turned round, I saw Elena standing in the doorway leading from the hall. I knew at once that something was wrong.

'Signor Lashley, Jonathan,' she said. 'I cannot wake him. I think . . . I think he is dead.'

From the peaceful expression on his face it would have been easy to believe he'd slipped away, naturally, in his sleep. But the empty pill bottles on the bedside cabinet told a different story. He'd planned this, as he'd planned so much else. It came to me, as I looked down at him, that the transfer document he'd referred to, lodged with his lawyer, was in fact his will. He'd said all he had to say. I'd heard his final testament.

Almost at once, I noticed an envelope propped against the bedside lamp, with my name written on it in Lashley's hand. I tore it open, expecting to find a note inside.

There was no note. But there was a message for me, nonetheless.

It was a photograph of Oliver. I'd never seen it before. Yet I remembered it very well. It was one of those I'd taken at Goss Moor the last evening of his life. He was dressed in his blue jeans and green sweater, with his knapsack hoisted on his shoulder and the slanting sunlight falling as a splash of gold on his blond, tousled hair.

There'd been a film in the camera after all. This was the proof that Lashley had lied to me about that. I sensed it was his private confession to me that he'd lied about what had happened at Relurgis Pit as well. He'd been unable to face me with the worst of the truth: the part he'd played in Oliver's death and, later, in Muriel's.

I searched the cabinet for the rest of the photographs. They weren't there. He'd probably destroyed them long since. Perhaps it didn't matter. What would they have shown me that I didn't already know or suspect? Oliver would have had no illusions about the risks he was running by confronting Lashley. Now the last of *my* illusions had been stripped away.

Elena phoned Lashley's doctor, who said he'd be there as soon as possible. As it was, I had to leave before he arrived. Meeting Vivien off the ferry seemed more important now than ever. I borrowed the Lexus and, as I sped down the steep, zigzagging road towards Marina Grande, I glanced ahead of me, out to sea. A vessel was approaching across the bay from Naples. It was the ferry, with Vivien aboard. They were so much faster than when she and I had first come to the island, more than forty years before. But no matter. I'd be there in time to meet her at the dock, as promised. And then . . .

401

*

The future. Uncharted territory. Old ends and new beginnings. The story of part – or all – of the rest of my life.

The Wren family in April 2010

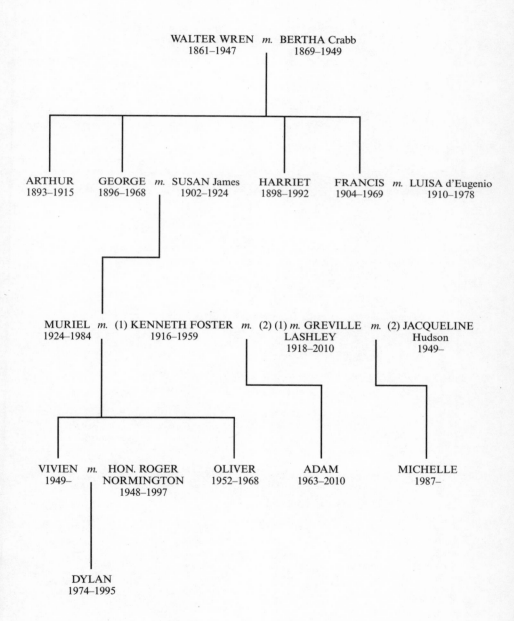

AUTHOR'S NOTE

I am very grateful to Roger Preston, Derek Giles and Ivor Bowditch for sharing with me their extensive knowledge and experience of the china clay industry. This is, of course, a work of fiction and no resemblance is intended, nor should any be inferred, between the companies they worked for and those I have invented for story-telling purposes.

I am also very grateful to Ben Aldington of Westover Sports Cars, Poole, for introducing me to the delights of the Lotus Evora, Adam Lashley's transport of choice.

Robert Goddard was born in Hampshire and read History at Cambridge. His first novel, *Past Caring*, was an instant bestseller. Since then his books have captivated readers worldwide with their edge-of-the-seat pace and their labyrinthine plotting. The first Harry Barnett novel, *Into the Blue*, was winner of the first WHSmith Thumping Good Read Award and was dramatized for TV, starring John Thaw. His thriller, *Long Time Coming*, won an Edgar in the Mystery Writers of America awards.